The MacAllister men were... *[text obscured by barcode]*
But their footloose days were numbered
and all because of The Baby Bet!

ANGELS AND ELVES

Sexy single Forrest MacAllister was the family
baby bet champion—but his wagers always
involved *other* people. Until he met beautiful
Jillian Jones-Jenkins...and he decided to turn his
matchmaking/baby betting skills on himself!

FRIENDS, LOVERS...AND BABIES!

Dangerously attractive—and aloof—
ex-cop Ryan MacAllister was not the marrying kind,
he was sure. But after a night of passion with his
good friend Deedee Hamilton, was his bachelor—
and childless—status about to change?

THE FATHER OF HER CHILD

Ted Sharpe may have been only an honorary
MacAllister, but he shared the baby-bet skills with
the best of the crew. And he's sworn that love and
fatherhood were not in the cards for him. Of course,
that was before his beautiful, *pregnant* neighbor,
Hannah Johnson, came into his life....

THE MacALLISTERS

JOAN ELLIOTT PICKART

MacAllister's Wager

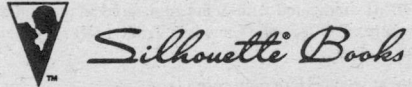

Published by Silhouette Books
America's Publisher of Contemporary Romance

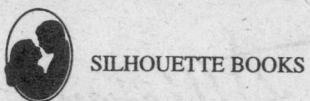 **SILHOUETTE BOOKS**

ISBN 0-373-18503-0

by Request

MacALLISTER'S WAGER

Copyright © 2002 by Harlequin Books S.A.

The publisher acknowledges the copyright holder of the individual works as follows:

ANGELS AND ELVES
Copyright © 1995 by Joan Elliott Pickart

FRIENDS, LOVERS...AND BABIES!
Copyright © 1996 by Joan Elliott Pickart

THE FATHER OF HER CHILD
Copyright © 1996 by Joan Elliott Pickart

Visit Silhouette at www.eHarlequin.com

Printed in U.S.A.

CONTENTS

Dear Reader,

I was so excited when my editor, Ann Leslie Tuttle, told me that the first three books in the MacAllister family series were to be reissued in one volume. It was like curling up with a photograph album and reliving special memories of people who have become very dear to me.

I've written many books about the lives and loves of the MacAllisters and their close friends over the years, and each story is close to my heart. I've enjoyed, as I hope you have, watching the changes take place within this loving family as time went by, and now I am writing the stories of the next generation of MacAllisters.

For those of you who met the MacAllisters years ago, I hope you enjoy your trip down memory lane. For those who are just getting to know this family, *MacAllister's Wager* will give you the opportunity to see how it all began.

I want to thank all of you for your continued loyalty and support. You are wonderful!

Warmest regards,

Joan Elliott Pickart

ANGELS AND ELVES

For my then-agent, Robin Kaigh,
and for
my now-agent, Laurie Feigenbaum.
Thank you, friends.

Prologue

Forrest MacAllister stopped in the doorway to the living room and looked at the woman stretched out on the sofa with pillows propped behind her back to allow her to sit up. She was deeply engrossed in the novel she was reading, and was unaware of Forrest's presence.

Andrea, he mused. His baby sister was a beautiful woman. Her auburn curls were in fetching disarray, and her dark brown eyes were clear and sparkling. The best part, though, was the pure joy, the happiness-to-the-maximum that he could actually feel emanating from her.

She also had, he decided, the largest, roundest stomach he'd ever seen. Twins definitely took up a lot of space in a pregnant lady. Yep, his baby sister was *definitely* awaiting the arrival of her own babies. Big time.

"So what's new, kid?" he asked, breaking the serene silence in the room.

Andrea's head snapped up and a smile instantly appeared on her face.

"Forrest! Oh, my gosh, you're really home. Give me a million hugs. I didn't hear you come into the house."

"John let me in as he was leaving," Forrest said, crossing the room. "Your husband is looking like a proper and prosperous Yuppie." He leaned over and hugged her, then straightened again to meet her gaze. "This is very efficient. I can hug three people at once."

Andrea laughed. "Aren't I awful? I'm impersonating a beached whale. And now I'm confined to either bed, sofa or chair, so these little darlings don't arrive too soon."

"You look fantastic."

"Fat. The word is *fat.* Sit, sit. I want to look at you until I'm cross-eyed. Oh, Forrest, I'm so glad you're back from Japan in time to be here when the babies are born. A year is much too long for you to be away. We all missed you terribly."

"I missed you, too, but it was quite an experience, and one I'll always remember. Japan is beautiful, Andrea, it really is. And it was a tremendous challenge to design a house that would blend in, yet have all the features the client wanted."

"Your letters were super, even if you still can't spell worth a darn," she said.

Forrest chuckled. "Spelling is a hopeless endeavor for me." He yawned. "I have jet lag so bad I don't even know what day it is. I came straight here from the airport, but Mom and Dad are going to have to settle for a phone call until after I get some sleep."

"And our brothers. You'd better call them, too. Michael and Ryan are so glad you're coming home for good."

"That's enough travel for me for a while. Listen, I really do need to get some sleep. I just wanted to stop by and make sure you were doing all right. You're staying put like the doctor said, aren't you?"

"Oh, yes. I'm grumpy and bored, and my darling John has the patience of a saint. But I'm following orders so that the twins have every chance to be healthy.

"Forrest, before you go I'd like to talk to you about something. It won't take long."

"Fire away."

"Well, you know that my favorite author is Jillian Jones-Jenkins, and that I met her several years ago at Deedee Hamilton's store, Books and Books. We've all become good friends since then."

Forrest nodded. "Jillian writes those gooey romance novels you read."

"Don't start. It's extremely bad form to hassle expectant mothers. Anyway, Jillian is arriving home tomorrow from a lengthy autographing tour and is doing a signing at Deedee's store as a special favor. Forrest, please, would you go to the store, buy Jillian's new book, and have her autograph it for me?" Andrea begged.

"Why? Deedee will be right there. Can't she do it? As far as that goes, Jillian could bring you a copy. Since you're friends, and you can't go out, surely she'll come visit you."

"Well—" Andrea smiled brightly "—there's a little more to it than that."

"Uh-oh. Not good," Forrest said. "You have that look in your eyes that says you're up to something. Ever since we were kids, that gleam got *me* in trouble."

"Forrest, Forrest, this is me, Andrea, your adorable, sweet little sister. I'm simply asking you to do me a teeny-tiny favor."

"Spare me," he said, rolling his eyes heavenward. "I've fallen for your innocent routine so many times, it's a crime."

"Keep an open mind," she said. "You're not going back to work for a bit. Right?"

"Right," he said, eyeing her warily. "I'm planning to take a couple of weeks off. I usually worked seven days a week in Japan."

"Perfect. You see, Deedee and I are very worried about Jillian. She's been on this exhausting tour and she was tired even before she left. Why was she tired? I'm glad you asked."

"I didn't."

"Hush. Jillian seems to have forgotten how to relax, have fun, have a proper balance of work and play in her life. She's gotten so caught up in deadlines and her writing schedule, that we hardly see her. We can't pry her out of the office in her house."

"And?"

"Remember when the four of us were kids and Mom would periodically say it was time for her Angels and Elves to get busy?"

"Yeah, I remember. We'd mow the lawn for an elderly couple, run errands for a shut-in, you'd baby-sit for free for a new mother, stuff like that. Every few months we did Angels and Elves assignments."

"Exactly. Forrest, Deedee and I are asking you to make Jillian Jones-Jenkins your Angels and Elves assignment. Take her out, have fun, get her to relax and enjoy life again. Hopefully she'll realize how narrow her existence has become."

"Oh, man," Forrest said, frowning, "are you kidding? That's nuts, Andrea. I don't even know this woman. You expect *me* to convince her to get her priorities back in order? That's the dumbest Angels and Elves assignment I've ever heard."

"It is not. It's custom-made for you. You have some free time right now. You're handsome, charming, intelligent, all that jazz. And you know how to show a woman a good time. Heaven knows, you've got women chasing after you like bees to honey."

"Flattery will get you nothing."

"Don't say no. At least promise me you'll think about it."

"Andrea..."

"Please?"

"Okay, okay," he said, raising both hands. "I'll think about it."

"Good."

"For about five seconds. Then I'll say no."

"Darn it, Forrest, don't be so difficult. Look, go to

Books and Books tomorrow and buy Jillian's new novel for me. You can meet her at the same time.''

"*Then* I'll say no. Andrea, has it ever occurred to you that Jillian might not appreciate the sneaky little program you and Deedee are putting together here?''

"It's for her own good. Deedee and I really are concerned about her. She won't know you're on an Angels and Elves assignment. This is a very humanitarian mission I'm asking you to undertake, Forrest.''

He got to his feet.

"I'll go buy the book,'' he said, "and meet Jillian. Beyond that? I'm not promising anything. I'm thirty-two years old. A person would think that I'd have learned by now that your schemes always spell trouble for me in big, bold letters. I shouldn't be going anywhere near Deedee Hamilton's store.''

"But you will, and you're wonderful, and I adore you, and I'm so glad you're home.''

"Yeah, yeah,'' he said, laughing, "and you've been able to wrap me around your little finger since the day you were born.'' He leaned over and kissed her on the forehead. "Bye for now, brat. Take good care of the dynamic duo you're toting around in there.''

"Bye, Forrest. And thank you.''

Andrea waited until she heard the front door click shut behind Forrest, then snatched up the receiver of the telephone that had been placed on the coffee table within her reach. She pushed buttons in rapid succession.

"Deedee? Forrest was just here. He wouldn't give me a definite yes, but I talked him out of a definite no. Here's the setup. Forrest will come to your store tomorrow to buy Jillian's new book for me and..."

One

Best wishes, Jillian Jones-Jenkins.

Jillian stared at the words she had just written with the appropriate flourish on the title page of the book in front of her.

The flowing handwriting was nothing more than a series of fancy squiggles that had no meaning. She was so thoroughly exhausted that she was beyond being able to recognize even her own name.

She blinked and shook her head slightly, striving to concentrate. She managed to produce a weak but passable smile.

"There you are." She handed the thick, hardcover book to the beaming woman standing on the opposite side of the lace-cloth covered table. "I sincerely hope you enjoy *Midnight Embrace*."

"Oh, I know I will," the woman said, clutching

the treasure to her breasts. "I've loved all your books, Miss Jones-Jenkins. I read them over and over. They're such wonderful stories. So romantic, so touching, so filled with love." She sighed. "Oh, dear, I do go on and on, but I want you to know how much pleasure you've brought into my life with your work."

"That's very kind of you," Jillian said. "I hope I never disappoint you."

The woman moved away and another stepped forward, presenting a book to be autographed. Jillian opened it to the title page, then hesitated, her gaze sweeping over the expanse of the bright, cheerful, well-stocked bookstore.

The man was still there.

He was watching her, she was certain of it.

Jillian, stop it, she admonished herself in the next instant. Tired was tired, but this was a step beyond. If anyone looked at her crooked, or said the slightest cross word, she'd probably burst into hysterical tears like a toddler in need of a nap.

Therefore, she decided, it went without saying that she was overreacting to the presence of the man. He was the only male in the store, and each time she looked in his direction, he was watching her. She was the constant target of his scrutiny, his gaze never seeming to wander from her.

She wrote the name recited by the woman in front of her, then signed her own by rote with the usual flair. Her smile was beginning to feel pasted to her face like a plastic mask.

The man, she mused, as she vaguely heard herself

thanking the woman for her loyal support, was extremely handsome. He was about six feet tall, had thick, dark auburn hair, was well tanned, and had just-rugged-enough features. His eyes were brown as best she could tell, but he'd stayed too far away from where she was seated at the table to be certain.

"You want me to write, 'Merry Christmas, Margaret'?" Jillian asked the next patron. "But this is only February."

"I know, dear." The woman smiled. "I'm shopping early for the holidays in December. That way I feel Christmassy all year long."

"Oh, I see," Jillian said, with a mental shrug.

Whatever floats your boat…dear, she tacked on in her mind. Now where was she in her mental inventory of the tall, handsome stranger skulking in the aisles?

Oh, yes…he was in his early thirties. His nice build was shown to advantage in expensive charcoal-gray slacks and a black V-neck sweater over a white dress shirt worn open at the neck. It was appropriate apparel for Ventura, California, at this time of year.

"I hope Margaret likes the book when she reads it next Christmas," she said.

"Oh, I'm sure she will," the woman said. "Of course, *I'll* read it now. I wouldn't dream of waiting that long for one of your stories."

Jillian laughed. "Happy February to you, and Merry Christmas to Margaret."

"Oh, aren't you a sweet girl?" the woman said. "It was so delightful to meet you, dear." She hurried away.

Delightful? Jillian thought. No, delightful would be

a long bubble bath, with soft music playing on the stereo. Then she would slip between crisp sheets on her bed, burrow into the pillow, snuggle beneath the blankets, and sleep, sleep, sleep. Now *that* scenario was delightful.

Deedee Hamilton, the attractive woman in her early thirties who owned Books and Books, stepped closer to the table.

"Let's keep the line moving, please, ladies," she said pleasantly. "It's getting late, and we don't want to detain Miss Jones-Jenkins past regular store hours. She has just returned from an exhausting ten-city book-signing tour, and was good enough to come here before she went home and collapsed. So, let's hurry right along, shall we? Next?"

Bless you, Deedee, you're a wonderful friend, Jillian thought, accepting the book the next woman handed her. Jillian Jones-Jenkins was tired to the point of being numb. Jillian Jones-Jenkins was— Good grief, she was thinking of herself in the abstract, as though she were a character in one of her books. She desperately needed to crawl into bed and not reappear for at least twenty-four hours.

Ten minutes later, Deedee once again came to the table.

"I'm going to close the store now," she announced to the remaining customers. "I'll unlock the door and let each of you out after you've had your book autographed. If any of you are making other purchases as well, please step up to the register."

Ah-ha, Jillian thought, it was truth time. The man—the Handsome Hunk, aka H.H.—was going to have to put up or shut up. His skulking-in-the-aisles routine had just been called to a halt by Deedee.

Jillian inwardly sobered, although her forced smile remained in place.

She should not be taking the presence of the loitering man so lightly. She had writer friends who had been bothered and actually frightened by mentally off-balance men convinced that a woman who wrote love scenes was automatically available to participate in real sexual encounters. Because she was exhausted to the point of being giddy, she hadn't given the man serious enough attention. There was a reason for his having been in the store for such a long time, wandering around, and *watching her.* She was going on red alert as of that very moment.

She glanced up, only to realize that the man had moved again. A visual sweep of the store found him in the cookbook section, his nose in an open cookbook. *Oh, dear heaven, it was upside down!*

A shiver coursed through Jillian, and her smile slid off her chin, despite her efforts to keep it firmly in place. She handed the book she had just signed to the smiling woman, who grasped it eagerly. Only one more customer waited to have a book autographed.

One more, Jillian thought, then the man was going to have to do something. But what? *Oh, Lord, what was he going to do?*

This was it, Forrest MacAllister thought. Time had run out. He had to do it *now.*

He glanced at the cookbook he was holding, then did a quick double take as he realized that he was holding it upside down. Slamming it shut, he shoved it back onto the shelf.

Get it together, MacAllister, he told himself firmly. The situation was as good as it was going to get. The witnesses were pared down to the minimum. He had to do what he'd come here to do—have Andrea's copy of Jillian's novel autographed.

Jillian Jones-Jenkins was certainly attractive. The spokeswoman for the store, who was probably Deedee Hamilton, had confirmed what Andrea had told him yesterday—Miss Jones-Jenkins had just returned from an exhausting book-signing tour. Well, if that was what the lovely author looked like totally exhausted, she'd be unbelievable when fully rested.

Yes, Forrest decided, she was stunning, tired or not. Her wavy, dark brown hair fell gently to just above her shoulders. She had delicate features, sensual lips, and big, gorgeous, gray eyes framed by long black lashes. Those eyes were fantastic.

At one point during his vigil she'd stood, apparently to relax stiff muscles, and he'd had a delightful view of a slender, yet ultrafeminine figure shown to perfection in a dusty rose suit with a straight skirt, thigh-length jacket, and pale pink silky blouse. She was fairly tall, maybe five-six or -seven, and was, he guessed, about thirty years old.

All in all, Forrest mentally rambled on, she was a lovely representative of the female species.

He sighed.

What Jillian Jones-Jenkins did, or did not, look like had nothing whatsoever to do with why he was there, or the fact that he couldn't stall any longer.

Then there was the nagging problem that Andrea, nutsy little sister that she was, wanted him to take on Jillian Jones-Jenkins as an Angels and Elves assignment. Andrea definitely had too much time on her hands. Her idea was crazy, totally bizarre.

He'd get the book signed by Miss She-needed-to-lighten-up-and-have-some-fun Jillian, deliver it to his sister, and tell her in no uncertain terms that her request was hereby rejected and his answer was an irrevocable no.

"Thank you so much," Jillian said, handing over the signed book. "I hope you enjoy it."

"I'm sure I will," the woman said. "Thank you, Miss Jones-Jenkins. I can't begin to tell you how exciting it was to meet you."

"Good night, and come again," Deedee said. She unlocked the door and the woman said goodbye with an added promise to shop there often. "Christy," Deedee said to the teenager behind the cash register, "off you go. You did splendidly under the gun. That was really quite a crowd we had in here."

Gun? Jillian thought, swallowing a near-hysterical bubble of laughter. Deedee could have gone all week without saying the word *gun*. Oh, Lord, the man with the gun, who read cookbooks upside down, was starting toward her. He was stalking. Yes, perfect word. He had a smooth, athletic gait that was like a panther *stalking* his prey.

And *she* was the prey.

And *he* had a gun.

No, no. Wait. She had to calm down. The man didn't have a gun. Well, not that she knew of, any-

way. Her exhausted brain had simply transferred Deedee's innocently spoken word into a sinister plot. No,
there was *not* a gun. Was there?

He was getting closer, she thought, feeling another
shiver whisper down her spine. His eyes really were
brown. Beautiful eyes. In fact, he was an all-around
beautiful man. What a shame that he was a sex maniac, who was about to kidnap her and...

Jillian jumped to her feet and grabbed the only
weapon available to her—the pen she'd been using to
autograph the books.

"Stay back!" she yelled, thrusting the pen toward
him. "You come one step closer, you fiend, and
I'll...I'll ink you to death!"

Forrest stopped dead in his tracks, his eyes widening in shock.

"Pardon me?" he said.

"Jillian?" Deedee called out. She finished locking
the door after an exiting Christy, then went to Jillian's
side. "What's wrong?"

"This...this villain has been skulking in the aisles
for over two hours."

"Villain?" Forrest repeated, raising his eyebrows.
"Skulking?"

"Don't you move." Jillian whipped the pen back
and forth. "Deedee, call the police. Quickly. Go to
the telephone and—"

"Hey, now wait a minute," Forrest said.

"Jillian," Deedee said, "sweetie, you're so tired
you're not thinking clearly. I'm certain that Mr.—?"
She raised her eyebrows questioningly as she looked
at him.

"MacAllister," he answered quickly. "Forrest MacAllister, but feel free to call me Forrest."

"Right," Jillian said, with a very unladylike snort of disgust. "You probably made up that name the very second Deedee asked you, you miscreant."

"Miscreant?" Forrest said. He looked at Deedee with a frown. "Does she always talk like this? 'Villain? Skulking? Miscreant?'"

Deedee shrugged. "She writes historical novels. The jargon of the era sort of...well, sticks to her at times, especially when she's exhausted or stressed."

"Oh," he said, nodding. "Fascinating."

"Deedee!" Jillian shrieked. "Would you please call the police?"

"Calm down, Jillian," Deedee said gently. "Let's listen to Mr. MacAllister, Forrest's, explanation of why he was 'skulking,' shall we?"

"Would you stop being so condescending?" Jillian said, through clenched teeth. "You're treating me as though I'm a four-year-old throwing a tantrum."

"Then quit acting like one," Forrest said, glowering at her.

"Well!" Jillian said indignantly. "You're not only a cad, you're a rude cad to boot."

"Cad?" He rolled his eyes heavenward. "I don't believe this. A rude cad." He burst into laughter, then grinned at Jillian. "You're really something." She was enchanting, absolutely delightful, as well as being extremely beautiful. "I've always had a fondness for the old-fashioned. You, however, take that premise beyond the scope of my imagination. You're an intriguing woman, Miss Jones-Jenkins." His smile faded, and he looked directly into her eyes. "Yes, very intriguing."

Jillian opened her mouth to retort, then snapped it shut as she realized she had no idea what to say. A tingling sensation danced along her spine and across her breasts before settling low within her. The warm, brown pools of Forrest MacAllister's eyes seemed to be holding her immobile, unable to think clearly, hardly able to breathe.

Dear heaven, she thought hazily, what was this man doing to her?

Not a thing, she mentally answered herself in the next instant. He was just a man, nothing fancy. He put his pants on one leg at time, just like any other man.

Actually, it wasn't a good idea to be focusing on the subject of Mr. MacAllister's pants, Jillian admonished herself.

But, good gracious, he was gorgeous. There was a blatant masculinity about him, an earthy aura that shouted the fact that he was male. Dear heaven, was he ever male. And those eyes, those pinning-her-in-place brown eyes were—

Jillian, stop, stop, stop! she scolded herself. She was overreacting to everything because she was exhausted. She'd had enough of this nonsense.

She tore her gaze from Forrest's, and dropped the pen onto the table.

"Oh, perdition," she said, throwing up her hands. "This is ridiculous. Just what exactly is it that you want, Mr. MacAllister?"

You, Forrest thought. Jillian's big gray eyes were

incredible. He felt as though he were being pulled into their fathomless depths, into a sensual fog that caused heat to rocket through his body and coil low and tight within him.

She was a spell weaver. Miss Jillian Jones-Jenkins talked like she had stepped out of the past and into his present. She was rattling him, throwing him off kilter. Well, hell—and perdition, too, for crying out loud.

"Hello?" Deedee said. "Has a truce been called? Is anyone still awake here?"

"I'm not a miscreant," Forrest said, shaking his head. "Okay? Are we clear on that one? I'm here for a purpose."

"Do tell," Jillian said, crossing her arms over her breasts.

"I'm attempting to do that, madam," he said, glaring at her. "I bought one of your books when I first came in. It's behind the counter and has my name on it."

"So, why were you skulking?" Jillian asked, leaning toward him slightly. "Answer me that."

"Because the book is for my sister, Andrea," he said, his voice rising. "Andrea MacAllister Stewart? Your friend? You know, the one who's expecting twins and has been instructed by her doctor to stay in bed because they don't want the babies to be born too early. She's very disappointed that she couldn't come here today."

"Of course," Deedee said, beaming, "Forrest MacAllister. Andrea has spoken of you so often, and was very excited that you were coming home from

Japan. And, my, my, here you are. Isn't this a marvelous surprise, Jillian? We're finally meeting Andrea's brother, Forrest.''

"Mmm." Jillian lifted her chin a notch. "Being Andrea's brother does not explain Mr. MacAllister's lengthy stretch of skulking."

"Well, hell, what do you expect?" he said, volume now on high. "Do you think I was going to stand in line with a bunch of giggling, fawning women to have a sappy romance novel autographed? Not in this lifetime, sweetheart."

"Uh-oh," Deedee muttered.

Uh-oh, Forrest thought, *that* had not been a brilliant thing to say.

Fury was building in Jillian like a tempestuous storm, gaining force, soon ready to explode. Eyes that had been radiating gray, pussy willow softness, were now silver daggers prepared to strike him dead. The flush on her cheeks was caused by anger, and her breasts, those full, lush breasts, rapidly rose and fell in an enticing rhythm.

She was absolutely sensational.

"You…you…" Jillian sputtered.

"Wait, whoa, halt," Forrest said. He quickly raised both hands in a gesture of peace. "That didn't sound right. What I meant to say is…" *Think, MacAllister!* He was a breath away from being murdered! "A man, any man, is out of his league in a large group of women. It's overwhelming, you know what I mean?" He produced his most dazzling smile. "I was nervous, shaking in my shorts."

"Like hell," Jillian said, narrowing her eyes.

Forrest's smile disappeared. "I don't think they said that back in the old-fashioned days. Anyway, I'm sure your book is great, really wonderful. I like romance. Hell, I love romance. I'm a very romantic guy. Really. You can ask any woman I've ever— Cancel that."

"Mr. MacAllister," Jillian said.

"Forrest. Call me Forrest. Look, I'm in awe of anyone who can write a book and get it published. All I can do in the writing arena is make out checks to pay my bills. I'd appreciate it if you'd autograph the copy of your book I bought for Andrea. Having your newest novel to read will help take her mind off her worries about the babies.

"Listen, I'll read the book myself, cover to cover. I'm sorry if I insulted you. I stressed out because of all those women, that's all. Would you please sign the book for Andrea?"

Oh, perdition, Jillian thought, Forrest MacAllister didn't play fair. There had been an endearing, little-boy quality about him as he spilled forth his sermonette.

Also evident was a genuine sincerity in his voice, and she knew without doubt that he loved his sister, Andrea, very deeply.

Ever since she and Andrea had become friends, Jillian had been aware that the MacAllisters were a close-knit, devoted-to-each-other family. When she was growing up she used to daydream, to fantasize, about how wonderful it would be to have brothers and sisters, and parents who—

"Jillian?" Forrest said.

"Yes, of course," she said, smiling. "I'll be happy to autograph Andrea's book."

"Praise the Lord," Deedee said, looking heavenward. She hurried to retrieve the book from behind the counter, then shoved it into Jillian's hands. "Write."

Jillian sat down behind the table and did as instructed. A few minutes later, she held out the book to Forrest.

"There you are," she said. "I hope Andrea enjoys it. Please tell her that I'll come visit her very soon."

"Thank you," he said, taking the novel from her hand. "Thank you very much."

Again their eyes met, and again neither moved, nor hardly breathed. Currents of crackling sensuality seemed to weave back and forth between them, drawing them close even while they stayed exactly where they were. Their hearts raced, and heat pulsed within as their startling passion heightened.

"Well, I..." Deedee started.

"What!" Jillian and Forrest both jerked in surprise at the sound of Deedee's voice and the spell was broken.

Placing one hand over her heart, Deedee said, "All I was going to say is that we're finished here, and you can head for home and collapse, Jillian. I wish I could drive you, but I'm due at a Women in Business meeting."

"I'll call a taxi," Jillian said, getting to her feet. "Don't give it another thought, Deedee."

"I'd be happy to take you home, Miss..." Forrest paused. "Jillian."

"Oh, no, a taxi will be fine, Mr. MacAllister. Thank you," she said, not looking at him.

"Forrest. Please accept my offer of a ride. It will help make up for my frightening you while I was 'skulking.' At least I now know that I can 'skulk' in case the need for it ever arises. I'll drive you home. Right? Right. That's settled. Let's go."

"Good idea," Deedee said. "There's nothing to worry about, Jillian. We know Andrea, Forrest is Andrea's brother, and that's good enough for me. It's fine with you, too, but you're too tired to realize it."

"But—" Jillian began, but no one paid any attention to her.

"Jillian came here right from the airport," Deedee informed Forrest. "Her luggage is in the back room. I'll let you out the front door so you can get your car. Drive down the alley to the rear entrance and we'll load you up."

"But—" Jillian tried again.

"Got it," Forrest said, starting toward the front door.

Deedee was right behind him.

"Fine," Jillian said, throwing up her hands. "Whatever."

Once the rear door of the store was locked behind Jillian and Forrest, Deedee hurried to the telephone and called Andrea.

"It was touch and go, Andrea," Deedee said breathlessly, "but I did it. Forrest is, as we speak, driving Jillian home. Goodness, your brother is a dreamboat. Anyway, so far, so good...well, providing Jillian doesn't murder him before they get to her house. Now then, tomorrow I'll..."

TWO

Forrest's car was a late-model silver BMW sedan with a plush, gray interior. Jillian settled onto the seat with a weary sigh of pleasure, inhaling the heavenly aroma of rich leather in the process.

Sleep, she thought. It was a twenty-minute drive to her house, and then she could sleep, sleep, sleep. And during said drive, she would not pay one iota of attention to Mr. Forrest MacAllister.

The man was a menace. His blatant masculinity had a disturbing effect on her, making her acutely aware of her own femininity. She had felt it—desire—heated and pulsing deep and low within her. Oh, yes, that had been desire; very *unwelcome* desire.

Big macho deal, she thought, leaning her head back and closing her eyes. It didn't mean a thing. It had all been a product of her bone-weary fatigue. Forrest was driving her home, she would bid him adieu, and that would be that. She'd never see him again.

Never? Never again gaze into those incredible chocolate-brown eyes? Never again imagine what it might be like to sink her fingers into the thick depths of his auburn hair? Never again see his sensual lips, his rugged, handsome face, the wide, solid width of his shoulders? Never again hear the rich timbre of his laughter? Never again...

Oh, Jillian, please. Just shut up. Think about sleep, and shut up.

She blanked her mind and drifted off into a light slumber.

Beautiful, Forrest thought, glancing over at her. He quickly redirected his attention to the heavy rush-hour traffic. He was certain Jillian was asleep. Her breathing was slow and steady, her delicate features relaxed and lovely.

It would be nice to think that she was so comfortable in his presence, and trusted him enough, that she could allow herself to doze off. Nice, but not true. She was exhausted, and would probably have fallen asleep even if he was the miscreant Jack the Ripper.

Perdition, he thought, chuckling softly. He really got a kick out of her bygone-era vocabulary. Jillian Jones-Jenkins was a fascinating woman. Unique. Intelligent. Talented. Compelling. Gorgeous.

But Jillian as one of his Angels and Elves assignments?

Forrest frowned and narrowed his eyes in concentration. He had to think this through in a logical manner.

Getting Jillian to take a fresh look at the structure of her existence, to achieve a healthier balance of work and play, was very important to Andrea and Deedee. That made sense. A concern for another person's well-being was one of the basic ingredients of friendship.

Andrea, due to her extremely pregnant condition, should be spared any kind of stress or upset. Jillian's work habits were causing Andrea stress and upset. If he agreed to take Jillian on as an Angels and Elves assignment, he would be able to remove said stress and upset from Andrea's life.

He certainly hadn't planned to grant Andrea her ridiculous request. No, sir, this was to have been a rare moment in history when his little sister wouldn't get her own way when dealing with big brother Forrest.

But, well, having twins was serious business, and making certain they didn't arrive too early was imperative. He still thought Andrea's idea was ridiculous, and he was absolutely *not* going to be *manipulated* into agreeing to do it.

What he *was* going to do, was ask Jillian to go out on a social basis, and nudge her to reexamine her priorities, because *he* had decided it would be beneficial to Andrea's state of mind. He was being a loyal and loving brother, a true-blue MacAllister.

There, now. He had it all figured out and under control. Andrea might think she'd pushed his buttons again, and that she'd manipulated him into taking this Angels and Elves assignment, but he knew better.

Ah, yes, there were times when a man had to put the needs of others first.

He glanced at Jillian.

Times when he just had to do what he had to do.

Darkness had fallen by the time Forrest reached the address Jillian had given him. He found himself in an affluent neighborhood of large, Spanish-style homes on the edge of Ventura.

As he drove slowly along the circular driveway, motion-sensing security lights came alive, illuminating the entire front of the house.

Forrest glanced over at Jillian to see if the sudden brightness had awakened her, but she slept on. She still didn't stir when he stopped the car and turned off the ignition.

He stared at her for a long moment, resisting the urge to lean across the seat and kiss her inviting and *very* enticing, slightly parted lips. By sheer force of will, he switched his attention to the exterior of the house.

Constructed of white stucco with a red-tile roof, it was one story with tall, narrow windows and an intricately carved, dark wood front door. Low, deep-green shrubbery edged the structure, its vivid color a perfect finishing touch.

Forrest nodded in approval, then turned to look at Jillian again. He tentatively raised one hand, then placed it gently on her shoulder, increasing the pressure of his fingers enough to give her a small shake.

"Jillian?" he said. "You're home. Wake up so you

can go to sleep.'' He frowned; that sounded stupid. ''Jillian, yo, Jillian, rise and shine.''

''Nay, I say,'' she mumbled, settling deeper into the seat. ''Leave me be.''

Forrest grinned, once again enthralled by Jillian's other-era vocabulary.

''Mayhap, Lady Jillian,'' he said, ''it would behoove you to awaken and sally forth to yon hacienda to sleep in your own private chamber.'' Not bad, MacAllister. He was really getting the hang of this nutsy stuff. ''Lady Jillian?''

She slowly lifted her lashes, then a puzzled expression settled over her features.

''What? Where?'' She started, then suddenly straightened. ''Oh, I...'' She looked at Forrest. ''I fell asleep. That was extremely rude of me, to say the least. I'm sorry.''

''Don't give it another thought. I'm a laid-back taxi driver, and you are one very exhausted passenger.''

''I won't argue with you about that,'' she said, opening the car door. ''All I can think about is getting into my bed.''

Interesting thought, Forrest mused, as he got out of the car. *More* than interesting.

Jillian went to the front door, yawning as she inserted the key in the lock. Forrest pulled the luggage from the car, managing to tote the four pieces in one trip, and followed Jillian inside to set the suitcases in the entry hall.

He swept his gaze over as much of the interior of the house as he could see. Jillian had decorated with a Southwestern flair in muted tones of salmon, pale turquoise and creamy white, creating a soothing, cool atmosphere.

"Nice," he said, nodding. "Your home is very nice."

"Thank you. I'd give you a tour, but I'm so tired I'd probably get lost." Jillian yawned again. "I'm a total wreck."

"Would you like me to carry forth your luggage to your chamber, Lady Jillian?"

Jillian giggled, then blinked as she realized she'd made the ridiculous sound.

"No, knave," she said, with a flip of one hand. "Leave it be." She smiled. "Thank you for the ride home, Forrest. It was a pleasure meeting you, and I apologize for my odd behavior at the bookstore. When I'm this exhausted, I'm not myself."

"Well, Miss Whoever-you-are," he said, smiling, "I was wondering if you'd have dinner with me tomorrow night?"

"Dinner? Oh, sure. Fine. Bye." She turned and started to walk away.

"Jillian?"

She stopped and looked at Forrest over one shoulder. "Hmm?"

"Don't you think you should lock the door behind me when I leave?"

"Oh. Yes. Of course I should. Perdition, where is my mind?"

"Already in your bed asleep." He went to the door and Jillian shuffled forward to grip the doorknob. "Seven-thirty."

"It is?" she said, appearing confused. "No, it's not

that late, is it? Well, maybe it is.'' She shrugged. ''Who cares?''

''No, no, I'll pick you up at seven-thirty tomorrow night for dinner.'' He paused. ''Are you going to remember having this conversation?''

''Of course. No problem.''

Forrest took one step back into the house and dropped a quick kiss on her lips.

''Good,'' he said. ''I'll see you then.'' Excellent. His Angels and Elves assignment was officially launched. ''Sleep well, Jillian.''

Jillian closed the door slowly, then locked it. The fingertips of one hand floated up to touch her lips. They still tingled from Forrest's kiss.

''Merciful saints,'' she mumbled. ''Oh, Jillian, go to bed.''

Ten minutes later, she slipped between the cool sheets on her king-size bed, and was asleep the instant her head met the soft pillow.

At 1:00 a.m., Forrest closed the book he'd been reading since he'd arrived back at his apartment, and stared at the cover.

'''*Midnight Embrace*,''' he read aloud, '' 'by Jillian Jones-Jenkins.'''

It was an extremely well-written novel. He hadn't expected to enjoy it, but he *had* said he would read it.

To his surprise, he'd become completely engrossed in the intricate plot, found himself cheering on the hero and heroine, and eagerly turning the pages to discover how their dilemma would be solved.

He'd razzed Andrea for years about the sappy romance novels she read. Well, he'd have to eat crow. Big-time crow, because he intended to ask Andrea if she'd loan him Jillian's other novels so he could read them.

Jillian, he thought, turning the book over to look at the photograph on the back. Lord, she was beautiful. The black-and-white photo didn't do justice to her incredible gray eyes, her silky, dark brown hair, or her peaches-and-cream complexion.

His gaze moved to Jillian's lips.

Oh, yes, those kissable-looking lips were very kissable, indeed. He'd never done anything quite so impulsive and pushy as kissing a woman he'd just met. He hadn't thought about doing it, he'd just suddenly kissed her. And it had been a quick little kiss. No big deal.

Wrong. The moment his lips had touched Jillian's, an explosion of sensations had rocketed through him. He'd wanted to haul her into his arms and deepen the kiss, savor more of her sweet taste, feel her respond to him, woman to man. Heat had thrummed through his body with a nearly staggering intensity.

Miss Jillian Jones-Jenkins had certainly had an impact on him, both physically and mentally. She was endearing and enchanting, with her fatigue-induced old-fashioned vocabulary.

There was a fiery temper there, too, evidenced by her threat to ink him to death with her mighty pen and her volatile reaction to his derogatory remark about romance novels.

Forrest chuckled, placed the book on the table next

to him, and got to his feet. He stared down at the glossy photograph.

"Good night, Lady Jillian," he said. "I am definitely, *most definitely,* looking forward to our dinner date."

Well, one thing was beginning to become clear— his Angels and Elves assignment wasn't going to be a study in misery. Spending time with Jillian Jones-Jenkins, helping her get her life back on track with a better balance of labor and leisure, wouldn't be hard to do. Not at all.

He yawned.

"Perdition," he said aloud, "I need some sleep."

Early the next afternoon, Jillian stirred, opened one eye and wondered foggily what hotel she was in. In the next moment, she opened both eyes, smiled, then stretched like a lazy kitten as she realized she was at home.

"Dee-lightful," she said.

But an instant later she frowned, as she became fully awake.

She'd dreamed about Forrest MacAllister. It had been one of those jumbled dreams that made absolutely no sense, and had no real plot, per se; but Forrest had been there, no doubt about it.

He'd been dressed as a member of the English *ton* in the late 1800s, complete with ruffled shirt and frilly cuffs, and thigh-hugging trousers tucked into shining leather boots that came to midcalf. His rich auburn hair had been caught in a queue with a black velvet ribbon.

Jillian narrowed her eyes, concentrating on details of the dream.

She had been decked out in a gorgeous ballgown of green velvet with bows drawing up both front halves of the skirt to reveal a paler-green satin underskirt. The bodice had been cut low to expose just the tops of her breasts, and her hair had been arranged in an elaborate, upswept creation threaded through with narrow green ribbons.

She and Forrest, she realized, had appeared like characters who had stepped from the pages of one of her books. They were the hero and heroine in all their splendor.

That much was clear, but from then on the dream had been a bit wacky. They had been dancing at a crowded ball, swirling gracefully around the floor. In the next moment, though, they'd been waltzing in Deedee's store, and then later in Jillian's own living room.

"Heavens," she said, throwing back the blankets, "what nonsense."

Leaving the bed, she started across the room, only to stop after going a few feet. She placed the fingertips of one hand on her lips, the sudden remembrance of Forrest's quick but unforgettable kiss causing a shiver to skitter along her spine.

Now wait a minute. That kiss had *not* been in the dream. It had taken place in her very own entry hall. That cocky Forrest MacAllister had actually kissed her.

With a cluck of disgust she went into the bathroom,

and minutes later was standing under the warm spray of the shower, vigorously shampooing her hair.

In all fairness she had to admit it had been a sensational, albeit short, kiss. And it wasn't as though Forrest had hauled her into his arms and kissed the living daylights out of her—which would have been extremely rude.

No, it had been a rather...polite...yes, polite kiss. A tad pushy, considering they'd only just met, but definitely memorable.

As Jillian dried herself with a huge, fluffy towel, she was aware of a sense of something nagging at her. What was she forgetting? What was vying for attention that she couldn't remember? She had been so exhausted the previous night, there was no telling what she didn't recall in the light of a new day.

With a shrug of dismissal, she left the bathroom and dressed in jeans faded in spots to white, a baggy red sweatshirt that boasted the slogan Writers Always Have the Last Word, and red-and-white polka-dot socks.

After a cup of Earl Grey tea and a bowl of granola and yogurt, she called her secretary, Lorraine, to announce her arrival home.

Ever-efficient Lorraine reported that the necessary bills had been paid during Jillian's absence, the newspaper delivery would resume today, the housekeeper had been instructed to stock the refrigerator yesterday per the usual procedure, and everything was under control.

"You're a gift from the heavens," Jillian said.

"I know," Lorraine said. "I'm fantastic. I have

your fan mail here, but fear not, I won't darken your doorway for two weeks. You're officially on vacation as of dawn today. What are you going to do this time?''

''I don't know yet,'' she said, frowning slightly. ''The tour was so hectic I didn't have a spare second to think about it.''

''Well, darn,'' the secretary said. ''I look forward to hearing about The Project. That's in capital letters, you understand. Let's see. Over the years, you've used your two-week hiatus to go on a cruise, take knitting lessons, volunteer to read stories to children in the hospital, and on the list goes. My favorite was when you wallpapered the bathroom.''

Jillian laughed. ''Which had to be redone by a professional.''

''True. Goodness, Jillian, it's hard to believe you haven't settled on The Project. This is day one, you know, and you're wasting time even as we speak.''

''I realize that. I'm thinking, I'm thinking. I'll talk to you later, Lorraine. Oh, how are your husband and your grandchildren?''

''My darling hubby is still a couch potato, and the grandkids are brilliant and incredibly cute. Bye for now, boss.''

Jillian replaced the receiver slowly, then stared at it for a long moment.

Lorraine was right. She'd always decided on The Project well before her coveted two weeks began. Her publisher had her latest book in production, the grueling promotional tour was gratefully over, and she would have her self-indulgent fourteen days before starting a new novel, as per her usual routine.

"Think, Jillian," she told herself.

She thought about The Project while she toted her luggage to her room and unpacked, then stored the suitcases in the back of one of the guest-room closets. She thought while washing and drying clothes, and making a pile to go to the cleaners'. She thought while she sorted through the stack of receipts she'd accumulated during the tour, and made a list of thank-you notes to be written to the bookstore owners who had hosted her autograph parties across the country. She thought while she put the paperwork in her large, sunny office and firmly closed the door, vowing not to open it for fourteen days.

She thought while she ate a peanut-butter and banana sandwich, then watched a talk show on television.

As dusk began to darken the living room, she closed the drapes, turned on several lamps, lit a crackling fire in the hearth, and thought.

She slouched rather ungracefully onto the sofa facing the fireplace, stretching her legs straight out in front of her and wiggling her red-and-white-polka-dot-clad toes. While the wobbling pattern of the socks made her slightly dizzy, it did not transmit a genius-level idea for The Project.

"Food," she said, getting to her feet again. "I'll feed my brain."

A few minutes later, she replaced the receiver of the telephone, having requested a Super Duper Pizza

Supreme Deluxe Extraordinaire to be delivered to the house.

Returning to the living room, she began to pace back and forth in front of the fireplace.

"Skydiving?" she muttered. "Oh, good grief, no, I'd probably break myself. Gourmet cooking lessons?" She shook her head. "I'd become fat as a pig. Learn to speak Russian? Japanese? French?" She frowned. "Who would I talk to in Russian? Oh, darn it, I've already wasted one of my precious fourteen days."

She plopped back onto the sofa with a dejected sigh, and stared gloomily into the nearly-hypnotizing flames of the fire. When the telephone rang, she jerked in surprise as she was startled out of her semitrance. She snatched up the receiver of the telephone on the end table.

"Hello?"

"Jillian? Hi, it's Deedee. I've been trying to call you all day, but it was so busy at the store, I didn't have a chance. There's something important that I need to talk to you about. I'd rather do this in person, but... Do you have time to chat?"

"Sure. What's on your mind?"

"First of all, I want to thank you for doing the autographing yesterday. I know how tired you were, and I appreciate your tacking me onto the end of that grueling tour."

"No problem. I always enjoy doing book-signings at Books and Books. Your customers are such sweethearts. Now, what's this 'something important' you wanted to talk to me about?"

"Oh, well, you see—" Deedee paused. "Since you're speaking to me at the moment, I assume Forrest MacAllister carried out his mission of delivering you safely home. Did you manage to get there without threatening to murder him, or inking him to death?"

"I slept all the way home."

"Oh, you're such a dud. That is one sexy hunk of man on the hoof, Jillian Jones-Jenkins. He's nice, too. You know how highly Andrea speaks of him. You *slept* all the way home? I'm beginning to think you're hopeless."

"Me? Look who's talking. You're cruel to the male populace."

"I am not. I'm dating three different men at the moment. It's just that if any of them get too serious, I shoo them out the door."

"You're a coldhearted wench, Deedee. Is this topic the 'something important'?"

"No. Well, yes, sort of. What I mean is—"

"Deedee!"

"Okay, I'm getting it together now." She cleared her throat. "Jillian, I want you to keep an open mind while I'm explaining my 'something important.' Have you settled on The Project for your time off from work yet?"

"No, much to my frustration. I've already wasted an entire day. Why?"

"Well, you see, Andrea is very concerned about Forrest. He worked extremely hard while he was in Japan, with very little time off. He claims he's not going back to work for a few weeks, but Andrea says he'll never do it. He'll end up in the office slaving away.

"She was getting stressed, really having a fit, as we were talking about Forrest. She's so-o-o-o worried about him, Jillian. To calm her down, I suggested we try to think of a way to get him to relax, enjoy his time off, concentrate on something other than work. So, between us we came up with a plan."

"That's all very nice," Jillian said. "However, I'm totally confused as to how this 'something important,' that has turned out to be Forrest's work habits, has anything to do with me."

"Because you're the solution, the answer. Are you ready? Forrest MacAllister will be The Project you'll take on during your vacation."

"What!" Jillian shrieked.

"Jillian, please, just listen. You know Andrea isn't supposed to get stressed right now, but she's doing exactly that over her concerns about Forrest. Andrea needs you, Jillian. You're the only one who can divert Forrest's attention, get him to balance his life better with work and play. I told Andrea I'd talk to you because she gets uptight just discussing her work-weary brother." Deedee sighed. "It's so sad."

"You two are Looney Tunes," Jillian said. "I can't take on Forrest as The Project. He's a person, a human being, a man, for crying out loud. He doesn't qualify for The Project."

"Sure, he does. Whose project is it? Yours. You can do whatever you want to. You just said you hadn't picked anything, and here it is, right before your very eyes. You'd be doing it for your dear friend

Andrea, for those adorable twins she's going to have. How can you say no to someone in need like she is? Like Forrest is, for that matter?''

''Deedee, Forrest MacAllister is not the type of man who is lacking in female company.''

''Indeed not. But the tricky part is, he doesn't take enough time off to enjoy what's out there. You've got to be brave, courageous and bold. Step right up, invite him out, help him get his life in order. This is a terrific project for you, Jillian. Think how good you'll feel about what you've done for Andrea, and for Forrest.''

''No, I'll think about where to get professional help for you and Andrea. You two are not playing with full decks. Deedee, this is crazy.''

''It is not! Listen, when the MacAllisters were kids, their mother periodically had them do Angels and Elves assignments. You know, nice things for people—like mowing their lawn, or washing their windows, or whatever. Isn't that the sweetest thing?''

''Too sweet for words,'' Jillian said, rolling her eyes heavenward.

''So, that's what we're asking you to do here. Forrest MacAllister will be The Project aka your Angels and Elves assignment.''

''Deedee...''

''Jillian, don't say no. Just promise me you'll think about it. When you really give this some thought, you'll realize it's perfect. You'll have The Project, Forrest will get his priorities in order, and Andrea will relax and stay calm.''

''Deedee, I really don't want—'' The doorbell

rang, causing Jillian to stop speaking. "Someone is at the door. It must be the pizza I ordered."

"Good. Hang up. Just promise me you'll think about what I proposed."

"Yes, fine, all right, I'll think about it. I've got to go, Deedee. Bye." Jillian dropped the receiver into place and shot to her feet. "Pizza. Brain food." She marched across the living room toward the entry hall. "Andrea and Deedee need some help for *their* brains."

Before opening the door, she grabbed a twenty-dollar bill from the credenza in the entry hall. It was her "cash stash" for the frequent delivery of meals that held more appeal than cooking her own. Flipping on the porch light, even though the motion-sensitive lights would have been activated, she opened the door.

"Hi. That was quick. I only called you a few minutes—" She stopped speaking. Her mouth remained opened as her eyes widened.

Standing before her in the bright light, dressed in a dark gray suit, pale blue shirt, and gray paisley-print tie, looking like he'd just stepped out of the pages of *Gentlemen's Quarterly* magazine, was Forrest MacAllister.

"Andrea?" Deedee said. "We've been momentarily saved by a pizza. Jillian was not going for The Project idea, no way, no how. Then the pizza she ordered was delivered and she had to answer the door. I got her to promise to think about Forrest being The Project.

"Now we wait and see what happens, and keep each other posted if we hear anything. I swear, when we decided that Jillian and Forrest would be perfect for each other, I had no idea that Cupids had to work so hard. This is exhausting. But victory shall be ours! Won't it?"

Three

Forrest MacAllister, Jillian mentally repeated incredulously, was standing in her doorway. Forrest, who had been smiling, but who was now frowning and appearing rather confused as his gaze swept over her attire.

Jillian blinked, cleared her throat, and was unable to hide an expression every bit as confused as his.

"Forrest?" she said. "I thought you were the pizza."

"No," he said slowly, "I'm not a pizza. I'm a man. The one you have a dinner date with."

"I do?"

He nodded. "You do. May I come in?"

"Yes, I think you'd better," she said, stepping back.

Gracious but he was gorgeous. She had a funny

little flutter in the pit of her stomach that she couldn't chalk up to hunger. He smelled wonderful, too. His after-shave had a woodsy, very masculine aroma.

As she closed the door, Forrest turned to look at her.

Cute as a button, he thought. Jillian's sweatshirt was baggy, her jeans as old as dirt, and the socks were weird. But she was femininity in spades, causing his heart to increase its tempo.

"I think we've had a communication problem, or something," Jillian said.

"Actually, I was afraid this might happen," he said. "I tried to call you today to confirm our date, but you have an unlisted number."

He could have asked Andrea or Deedee for Jillian's number, he knew, but he wasn't ready to tell either of them that he was taking her out. The cackling glee he would no doubt have been subjected to was something a guy had to gear up for.

"When you agreed to go out with me," he went on, "I wondered if you'd remember."

Jillian splayed one hand on her chest. "*I* agreed to a dinner date for tonight?"

"Yes, ma'am, you did. We were standing right here in your entry hall last night when we made the plans for me to pick you up at seven-thirty."

"Oh, Forrest, I'm so sorry. I don't remember. I *knew* there was something niggling at me, but I couldn't figure out what it was. This is embarrassing, and I sincerely apologize."

"Hey," he said, smiling, "don't worry about it. You were so exhausted that I wasn't certain at the time that you were really tuned in to what we were saying. How about a rain check?''

''Well, I—'' she started, then gasped as the doorbell rang again. ''Pizza.''

She spun around and opened the door. A few minutes later she closed it, and stood holding an enormous, square flat box.

''Mmm,'' she said, inhaling deeply. ''Doesn't that smell delicious?''

''That has got to be the biggest pizza box I've ever seen.''

''Isn't it great? It's a Super Duper Pizza Supreme Deluxe Extraordinaire.''

Forrest laughed. ''That's quite a title.''

''Forrest, listen. I feel so badly about not remembering our date. Why don't you stay and share this pizza with me? There's enough here for a regiment of marines. You could take off your jacket and tie, be more comfortable, and we'll have a pizza party.''

''Sold.''

''Good,'' she said, matching his smile. ''I'm glad.''

She really was *very* glad that Forrest had agreed to stay, Jillian mused, as she walked past him into the living room. She hadn't realized that the evening ahead had been looming before her as a series of long, exasperating hours spent attempting to come up with a brilliant idea for The Project.

Oh, dear…The Project, now also known as an Angels and Elves assignment, or mission, or whatever. Forrest MacAllister as The Project? Zero in on his problem of working far too much, get him to relax, have fun? That was nuts, it really was. Wasn't it?

She'd promised Deedee that she'd think about the absurd idea, and she'd keep her word. Later.

But now? Forrest was there. She felt suddenly lighthearted and cheerful. Her gloomy mood had completely disappeared. Forrest had been so understanding about her forgetting their date, and he was now going to take part in an impromptu pizza party, despite the fact that he was dressed to the nines.

She was certainly going to erase from her memory bank her first impression of him as being a skulking miscreant. Forrest MacAllister was a very nice man.

Forrest MacAllister was also so drop-dead gorgeous, he was enough to make a woman weep.

"I'll get a tablecloth and spread it on the floor in front of the fireplace," Jillian said. "That will be more fun than eating in the kitchen. I'll be right back."

Forrest pulled off his tie as he watched Jillian leave the room.

A pizza picnic, he thought. Jillian Jones-Jenkins was really something. When he'd first seen her at Books and Books, she'd appeared every bit the professional career woman. Who would have guessed that she was the type to wear polka-dot socks and eat pizza while sitting on the floor?

An intriguing woman was Lady Jillian, with many layers to be discovered, like unwrapping a Christmas present. He'd been looking forward to taking her to a classy restaurant, but the evening ahead definitely held much more appeal. Definitely.

Forrest put his tie in his pocket, removed his jacket and set it on a chair, then slipped off his shoes. He rolled the cuffs of his shirt up a bit, and undid the two top buttons.

He was ready for a pizza picnic, *and* for whatever other delights the evening produced.

Jillian returned with a blue-plaid vinyl tablecloth, which Forrest helped spread out on the floor in front of the fire. She brought in glasses of soda and some napkins, then placed the pizza box in the center of the cloth.

Sitting Indian-style next to each other, their backs against the sofa, they peered into the box when Jillian lifted the lid.

"Holy smoke," Forrest said, laughing. "I hope there isn't going to be a test later on what all that stuff is on that creation."

"It's an exquisite work of art," Jillian said. "Dig in, Forrest."

They ate two slices each, with appreciative "mmms," then slowed a bit on the third.

How strange, Jillian thought, as she took a sip of soda. There was a comfortable, rather peaceful feeling settling over her as she sat on the floor next to Forrest. It felt *right* somehow to have him there, sharing her pizza party.

Yet, at the same time, she was acutely aware of Forrest's masculinity and how it caused her to silently rejoice in her own femininity. Frissons of heat coursed deep within her, awakening her slumbering womanliness. The remembrance of Forrest's quick kiss of the night before was becoming more vivid with each passing moment.

How was it possible, she wondered, to be experiencing such opposite emotions at the same time?

"Jillian," Forrest said, bringing her from her confused thoughts, "I read *Midnight Embrace* last night, and I wanted to tell you that I really enjoyed it."

"Thank you," she said, then took another nibble of pizza.

"I obviously had the wrong impression of what romance novels actually are. When I gave the book to Andrea today, I apologized for having hassled her for years about her choice of reading material."

"That's nice. I hope you aren't missing having anchovies on this pizza. I can't abide those yucky little fish."

"What? Oh, no. I don't like them, either. Anyway, your novel was great. I stayed up late to finish it, because I wanted to find out how the hero and heroine were going to solve their problems. It seemed hopeless there for a while, but you really did a fantastic job of putting the pieces of the puzzle together."

"Thank you. Do you have enough soda?"

"Yes, I'm fine. Do you do your own research? You sure covered the details of clothes, furnishings, food, social graces, the whole nine yards of that era. Do you hire someone to gather that information for you?"

"No, I do my own research. I have an extensive library that encompasses different times in history. Oh-h-h, I'm stuffed. Four slices of pizza is definitely my limit."

"I've had plenty, too. It was delicious, and I thank you for inviting me to share it with you. Was *Mid-*

night Embrace your choice, or does your editor decide on the title?''

''I titled it *Midnight Embrace.* Sometimes they change what I've chosen for reasons that make absolutely no sense to me.''

''Does that bother you?''

''Nope, not anymore. I don't care if the readers remember the title. I want my story, my characters, to stay in their minds. I'll go put the rest of this pizza in the refrigerator.''

''Okay.'' He looked at her thoughtfully. ''I'll fold up the tablecloth.''

As Jillian busied herself returning things to the kitchen, Forrest tended to the cloth.

Interesting, he mused. He was getting the distinct impression that Jillian didn't want to talk about her work. He'd assumed that someone with her level of talent would enjoy discussing writing with anyone who showed a flicker of interest. But not Jillian Jones-Jenkins.

He'd dated women who were so involved in their careers they couldn't be bothered to chat about the weather, or anything else, for that matter. Jillian's attitude had caught him off guard, but it was very refreshing.

The confusing part was that Andrea and Deedee were concerned that Jillian was *too* focused on her work. If that was true, then why didn't she want to discuss it? Maybe writers had eccentric superstitions or something, that dictated that they save their mental energies for the actual creative process, and not waste any by talking about their craft. Yes? No? He really didn't know.

Jillian came back into the room, scooped up the tablecloth, then headed for the kitchen again.

Forrest was fascinated by the fact that she was a writer, she mused. Most people she met for the first time found her career intriguing. She usually enjoyed answering all their questions—even while on vacation—as it was easy to talk about something she loved so dearly.

Tonight, however, she needed to direct the conversation to center on Forrest. If, and that was a very big if, she decided to make Forrest The Project, she had to know more about him, what made him tick, determine why he worked harder than was necessary.

Jillian returned to the living room and sat down next to Forrest again. At the same moment, they both shifted slightly to be able to look directly at each other. Their eyes met, and neither spoke.

Lord, Forrest thought, Jillian's eyes were incredible. He'd never seen eyes that gray, eyes that reminded him of a London fog, of a soft, fuzzy kitten. Would they change color when she was consumed with desire, when passion reigned? He wanted to know. He wanted to make love with Jillian Jones-Jenkins.

Jillian tore her gaze from Forrest's and picked an imaginary thread from her sweatshirt.

How much time had passed since she'd looked directly into Forrest's chocolate-brown eyes? She honestly didn't know. She'd been pinned in place, with the sudden rapid tempo of her heartbeat echoing in her ears.

Forrest MacAllister was dangerous because he was exciting, evoking undeniable desire within her, and causing her mind to travel down a road that she had no intention of taking.

''So,'' she said, a tad too loudly. She looked at Forrest's chin. ''Andrea has told me that you're a family of architects. She said your father started the firm years ago on a shoestring and a dream, with your mother as his secretary. Now you're all involved in the company.''

''Yep, we're MacAllister Architects, Incorporated. Our folks are retired now, and are having a fabulous time traveling here, there and everywhere. My brother Ryan isn't an architect. He's a police officer, a very dedicated cop.''

''I don't remember who is the oldest brother.''

''Michael. He's married and has a son. Great kid. Michael likes the challenge of taking on remodeling projects. He's done a lot of plans for restoration work, and is beginning to have more jobs than he can handle. Ryan is next in line as far as age. He got married about three months ago. Andrea is the baby of the family.''

''Did you hire someone to take Andrea's place now that she's been ordered to stay in bed?''

Forrest nodded. ''Andrea hired a sharp gal. You see, not only is Andrea an architect, she also has a bachelor's degree in landscape architecture. Most people don't realize that landscaping can be that complicated, so as to require a college degree.

''Because of Andrea, we're a full-service firm. In other words, we can design a home *and* the landscaping to enhance it, if the client wishes. We're really proud of Andrea. And we miss her now that she's concentrating on her family.''

Jillian smiled and met Forrest's gaze again. ''It's very obvious that you're all very close. That's nice, really lovely.''

''It's always been that way.'' He shrugged. ''It can be a pain in the rear, because family members don't hesitate to give their opinion on what you're doing, whether you've asked for it or not. But the majority of the time it's good to know they're all there.''

''It sounds wonderful. I'm an only child, who grew up wishing I had brothers and sisters, and parents who— Well, brothers and sisters.''

Parents who what? Forrest wondered. What had Jillian been about to say?

''I think I have everyone in your family straight now,'' she said.

It was nitty-gritty, fact-finding time. She'd become very adept over the years at phrasing her questions in a manner that provided her with the information she wanted to know. She was about to do her thing, just in case she decided to make Forrest The Project, which she probably wouldn't, but...well, just in case.

''That leaves you,'' she said, smiling. ''You're what? About thirty?''

''Thirty-two.''

''I had my thirtieth birthday a few months ago. From what everyone said, I was expecting a black depression to settle over me.'' She shrugged. ''It didn't happen.''

''Well, I guess some people feel if you're not married by thirty, you're doomed.''

''I was married at twenty, divorced at twenty-two. Now *that* was a doomed relationship.''

''What happened?''

''It's old news,'' she said, waving one hand breezily in the air. ''It's not worth talking about. We're discussing you. You're the only one in your family who isn't married.'' She laughed. ''If you *are* married, I'm going to be very peeved that you had the nerve to eat my pizza.''

Forrest raised one hand in the air and placed the other over his heart.

''I am not,'' he said, with a mock-serious expression on his face, ''nor have I ever been, married, ma'am.''

''Yes, I know. I was only kidding. Andrea mentioned that you weren't married. But—'' she leaned slightly toward him ''—why not?''

''I haven't found the right woman.'' Heaven knew, he'd been looking, but wherever she was hiding, she was doing a hell of a good job of it. ''It's as simple as that.''

Bingo, Jillian thought. Men had no imagination whatsoever. They should hold a mass meeting and come up with fresh material. She'd heard that line countless times. It was the pat answer—a cliché due to overuse—and easily understood by single women across the country: *Forrest was not interested in marriage.*

Yep, she thought, the "I haven't found the right woman" guys were varying degrees of playboys. No serious commitments for that bunch. No, sir.

"I imagine," she said, adopting a casual tone of voice, "that your house and the landscaping must look like something out of a magazine, considering what you, Andrea and Michael do for a living."

"I don't have a house," he said. He'd once believed that he would. Oh, yeah, a big, sprawling place that would echo with children's laughter. There would be a huge backyard to play in, with plenty of room for kids and a dog. Maybe a cat, too. "I live in a high-rise apartment."

Ah-ha, Jillian thought. Apartment, not a house. *Forrest wanted no part of mowing the lawn, fixing drippy faucets, lugging trash cans to the curb and back. There wasn't a domestic bone in his body.*

She looked at her socks, wiggling her toes and watching the polka dots dance a jig.

"I was thinking about Andrea and John," she said. "Twins. Your entire family must be excited. Twins are so cute."

Forrest laughed. "Twins are an overwhelming thought." Double the joy, as well as the work. "Two of everything, that's what Andrea and John are getting into. Whew."

"That's for sure," she said, nodding. "I'm reading you loud and clear." *Forrest MacAllister wasn't crazy about babies, or the idea of being a father.*

Well done, Jillian, she mentally praised herself. She'd collected the data and computed it. Forrest was an upwardly mobile, swinging single, entertaining absolutely no plans for marriage, hearth, home or child.

"Please don't misunderstand what I'm saying here, Jillian," Forrest said. "I *want* to get married, have kids, a home."

Jillian's eyes widened. "You do? But you said...I mean... You do?"

"Yes, I truly do. I guess I'm gun-shy because I've seen so many of my friends end up getting divorced. The basic problem appears to be that in two-career marriages there just isn't enough time to be a real family. The careers always seem to take first place."

"Oh," Jillian said. Could she really be that far off base on the conclusions she'd drawn? She'd never been so completely wrong before. Maybe Forrest MacAllister wasn't run-of-the-mill after all. "Well, there is a little thing known as compromise, Forrest."

He frowned. "They don't work that often. Oh, it starts out fine, but more and more of the people I know run into trouble. Hey, I'm not a chauvinist who feels a woman belongs in the home being a wife and mother, and shouldn't have a career. I'm just coming to the conclusion that the life-style a two-career marriage produces isn't what I want.

"I'm destined, I guess, to being a bachelor, and satisfying my paternal instincts by interacting with my nieces and nephews."

"Ah, I see," Jillian said thoughtfully. "So you engage in casual dating, and focus the remainder of your energy on your job."

He shrugged. "I enjoy my work. I get a lot of satisfaction out of the ongoing challenge of it."

"Hmm," Jillian said, staring into space.

No wonder Andrea was worried about Forrest. The man had an attitude problem. He'd obviously done some data gathering of his own and had drawn harsh conclusions from the information. But despite what he believed, two-career marriages *could* be happy, fulfilling, and everything Forrest was wistfully wishing for.

She herself wanted no part of being married. Not ever again! But she sincerely believed that those who did want that life-style could create a marvelous union—two careers included—if they shared, and cared, and compromised. Forrest was burying his hopes and dreams in an overload of work, instead of being determined to have what he wanted.

Not good. This man needed help, had to be shown the errors in his thinking. He was sentencing himself to a lonely life, and that was incredibly sad. He just worked, worked, worked, to fill the void in his existence. *Her* heavy work schedule suited her perfectly. Forrest's did not serve him well.

There was no hope for it; she was hooked. She would take Forrest on, reprogram his poor, malfunctioning brain on the subject of marriage and dual careers.

For starters she'd get him to lighten up on his own work schedule to demonstrate how compromise in that area could be accomplished.

As crazy as it was, Forrest MacAllister was now officially The Project, her Angels and Elves assignment as Deedee called it.

"Jillian?" Forrest said, bringing her back to attention. "Is it all right if I put another log on the fire? It's burning pretty low."

Jillian nodded, then watched absently as he began to tend to the chore. Within moments, her casual observation became red-alert awareness, missing no detail of him performing the task at hand.

He had shifted to hunker down in front of the fireplace, balancing on the balls of his feet as only a person with athletic control of his body was capable of doing.

His shirt strained across his broad shoulders as he reached for a log, and was tucked into slacks that defined a narrow waist. There were powerful muscles in his legs, outlined to perfection beneath his expensive slacks. She also had the enticing view of an extremely nice male tush to scrutinize.

The flush on her cheeks and the heat that was swirling within her was not, she knew, caused by the flames in the hearth.

Forrest MacAllister was throwing her off kilter again by the male magnetism emanating from him. She'd have to be on guard against his blatant sexuality during The Project. She didn't intend to go to bed with the man, for heaven's sake; casual sex was not in her plan.

But since she knew that she was easily unsettled by Forrest's masculine appeal, she was one step ahead of things, in total control of herself.

The Project, aka her Angels and Elves assignment, was officially launched.

"There we go," Forrest said, moving back against the couch.

He sat closer to Jillian this time, his shoulder pressed to hers.

Oh, yes, she mused, the prospect of two weeks with Forrest was certainly better than taking knitting lessons. Much, *much* better.

Four

The next two hours flew by, as Jillian and Forrest chatted, never running out of topics to discuss as one subject flowed into the next.

"Tell me about Japan," Jillian said.

"It was fantastic," he said. "Even though I was working seven days a week, I managed to see at least some of the sights. Japan has such grace and elegance."

"My, what a lovely way to describe it."

"Well, it's true. And the people? They're wonderful. I swear, Jillian, the kids steal your heart in a second. I was invited to a birthday party and the children were dressed in authentic Japanese clothing. Cute? Oh, man, they were like walking, talking dolls.

"I took so many pictures of them, they'll probably

remember me as the tall guy with a camera for a face. I wanted to scoop them all up and bring them home.''

What a wonderful father Forrest would be, Jillian mused. His expressive brown eyes were shining as he spoke of the children he'd seen in Japan. He should have a family of his own, he really should.

''Enough about me,'' he said. ''How long does it take you to write a book?''

''Several months. I hardly come up for air when I'm on a deadline.''

There it was, Forrest thought, the first hint of Jillian's working hard; *too* hard, according to Andrea and Deedee.

''Couldn't you ask for more time from your publisher so you *could* come up for air?''

Jillian shrugged. ''The schedule I'm on suits me just fine.''

Andrea and Deedee were right, Forrest decided. This lady needed to be taken in hand, shown how to interweave work and play into her existence. Nice guy that he was, he was going to teach her how to do exactly that.

She believed in the premise of compromises in a two-career relationship. *Those* compromises were rarely successful, but Jillian could compromise with *herself* and have a better balance.

Forrest was pulled from his thoughts as Jillian urged him to relate more delightful tales of growing up with two brothers and a mischievous little sister. As he concluded yet another story, she laughed so hard she had to wrap her arms around her stomach.

What an enchanting sound, Forrest mused, a wide

smile on his face. Jillian's laughter was like tinkling bells, like wind chimes. Her gray eyes were sparkling with merriment, and her smile was real and beautiful.

"Oh, dear," Jillian said, catching her breath. "I hope I don't get the hiccups from laughing. That happens sometimes. Your parents must have the patience of saints to have raised the four of you."

"Either that, or they went numb at some point," he said, chuckling. "We were a handful, all right." He paused. "Tell me about *your* parents, Jillian."

Her smile faded. "There's not much to tell. My father is a foreign diplomat, an ambassador. He's excellent at what he does, and was kept on through the years when the political administrations changed. We lived in England, Mexico, France, you name it. They're in Italy now."

"That's a remarkable childhood. It sounds very exciting."

"It wasn't," she said quietly. "Being a foreign diplomat is a very social existence. My mother is devoted to my father and his career, and I admire and respect that. But I was left in the care of a nanny, or housekeeper, or whatever, the majority of the time.

"I have vivid memories of my parents coming to the nursery to kiss me good-night, but there were no hugs because they'd didn't want to wrinkle their evening clothes."

"You were lonely," Forrest said, in the form of a statement, not a question.

"Yes. They sent me to the United States for high school. I went to a fancy boarding school in upper New York State, then on to Stanford. When I became a published author, which was my dream, I immediately began to save my money to buy a house so that I could stay put, not have to move from place to place.''

"You have a lovely home.''

"Thank you. I like it, and I'm very contented here. I... Goodness, listen to me. I can't remember when I've talked about my childhood. I certainly sounded sorry for myself. It wasn't all that bad. My folks are wonderful people, and I know they love me. They simply didn't have much time for me.''

Forrest frowned. "I'm sorry.''

"Heavens,'' she said, forcing a smile, "don't be. It's because of being alone so much as a child that I was able to achieve my goal in writing. I used to make up stories by the hour to entertain myself. I developed my imagination to its maximum potential. And, ta-da, I'm an author.''

"A very talented author. Is your father Ambassador Jones, or Ambassador Jenkins?''

"Jones. I took back my maiden name after my divorce, but when I sold my first book, my agent urged me to add my married name of Jenkins. She felt that Jillian Jones-Jenkins had a better ring to it than just Jillian Jones. And that, sir, is the story of my life. Dull.''

"Not even close.'' He looked directly into her eyes. "And your marriage?''

"Was a mistake. Like I said before, that's old news, and not worth discussing.'' She cocked her head slightly to one side. "You know, Forrest, you're a wonderful listener. I'm a very private person, despite my having to be in the limelight at times to further my career. I could count on one hand the number of people I've told about my childhood, yet I dumped it all on you.''

''Shared, not dumped, and I'm honored,'' he said. ''I sincerely am.'' He cradled her cheek with one hand, and moved his head slowly toward hers. ''Very—'' he brushed his lips over hers ''—very—'' his other hand lifted to frame her face ''—honored.''

His lips captured hers, parting them, his tongue delving into her mouth.

Jillian's eyes drifted closed, and her hands floated upward to grip Forrest's shoulders. A tremor swept through her, then heat that swirled low and steady within her.

Her senses were heightened as she savored the taste of Forrest, the feel of his work-roughened hands on the soft skin of her face, his aroma of woodsy after-shave, mesquite smoke from the fire, and soap.

She was awash with consuming desire, her breasts suddenly yearning for a soothing caress. She met Forrest's tongue boldly; dueling, dancing, stroking with a rhythm that matched the heated pulse in the dark center of her femininity.

She couldn't think, she could only feel.

And it was ecstasy.

Jillian, Forrest's mind thundered. The kiss had begun as one of comfort, meant to ease the pain of her lonely childhood. He could picture her in his mind's eye as a little girl, creating characters in stories as playmates because there was no one else to keep her company. His heart ached for her as he envisioned the cold emptiness of her youth. He had willed the memories to fade, had wished to bring her back to the present, with him.

And so, he'd kissed her.

But now? Dear Lord, he was at the edge of his control, flung there the moment his lips had claimed hers. He wanted to make love to her. It was a burning need, an intensity like nothing he'd experienced before.

Jillian Jones-Jenkins.

Her name was a melody, a lilting song that echoed like sweet music in his mind. The mental image of the lonely child had faded into oblivion, replaced by the intriguing, compelling, multilayered woman she was now.

A voice began to sift through his passion-laden haze, coming from a source unknown. It was a message of warning, of caution, telling him to slow down, move carefully, so as not to frighten Jillian away.

Despite her breezy dismissal of her brief marriage, the voice declared, Jillian had been hurt, badly hurt, in the past. Why he knew that, he didn't know. Where the voice was coming from was a mystery.

What *was* crystal clear was that he mustn't do anything to cause her to refuse to see him again. Jillian was his Angels and Elves assignment. In his hazy state he'd completely forgotten that she was more than just an enchanting woman.

Mustering his last ounce of willpower, he broke the kiss, then slowly, reluctantly, dropped his hands from her face.

Jillian opened her eyes, and Forrest stifled a groan

at the smoky hue of her gray eyes that mirrored the desire in his own.

"Jillian?" he said, hearing the desire-induced rasp of his voice.

"Hmm?" she murmured dreamily. A soft smile formed on her lips. "Yes, Forrest?"

"We'd better cool off here, don't you think? I want to make love with you, believe me, I really do, but..."

"You're right," she said, then took a wobbly breath. "Things were happening much too quickly. Thank you, Forrest. Most men wouldn't be so gracious about calling a halt."

"Well, I do want to make love with you. You're a very desirable woman. You're also a beautiful, intelligent, and fascinating woman. Kissing you, Jillian, turned me inside out, and I knew I was losing control. You were responding to me, too, I could feel it."

"Yes," she said quietly, "I was."

"This may sound like a bunch of bull, some old-fashioned garbage, but the truth of the matter is," he went on, "I don't engage in casual sex. I never did, not even before the issue of safe sex came to public attention."

Jillian looked at him intently.

"When I'm with a woman, I have to care for her, about her. I've never been in love, but at least emotions of caring and respect have to be present. That takes it out of the sex arena and into the making-love arena. That means a lot to me, it really does."

He looked directly into her eyes.

"I don't know you well enough to have any idea

as to your stand on sex, Jillian, but I'm very aware of mine. If, when, we make love, it will be exactly that—making love.''

''Oh,'' she said softly. Then, for the life of her, she couldn't think of another thing to say.

She had never before, she realized, met a man like Forrest MacAllister, who had such old-fashioned values and self-imposed code of conduct. The men she'd dated in the past were ready, willing, and able to engage in casual sex on the first date.

She'd discussed it with Deedee once, and they'd agreed that the ''no'' had to come from the woman. But not so with Forrest. What an unusual and delightful man.

As for her response to Forrest's kiss—she'd returned it in total abandon—and the incredibly sensual sensations that had swept through her, she would discuss that with herself...later.

Several minutes passed in comfortable silence, each lost in their own thoughts.

''Forrest,'' Jillian said suddenly, ''do you like boats?''

''Boats? Sure.''

''Well, I have some friends who own a cabin cruiser that I'm welcome to borrow because they're on a trip to Greece. Would you like to go out in it tomorrow?''

''I was going to go look at a house with Michael that he's just contracted to restore, but—''

''That's work, you know. Wouldn't you like to have a carefree day?''

He nodded. "Yes, that sounds great. But what about you? Your strict schedule due to deadlines?"

"I'm on vacation," she said, smiling brightly.

"Good for you." Hallelujah and score one for the Angels and Elves. "You decided to take some time off, and you're doing it."

"Well, it's more complicated than that, but the bottom line is I'm on vacation."

"I'd love to go out on the water tomorrow, Jillian. We'll have to bundle up good because it'll be cold, but it sounds like fun."

"I'll pack a picnic lunch." She laughed. "Correct that. I've got a snazzy hamper someone gave me for Christmas a few years ago. We can stop at a deli on the way to the marina and fill it to the brim."

"What time shall I pick you up in the morning?"

"Make it ten o'clock. When I'm on vacation, I indulge myself in sleeping in late."

"I'll be here at ten o'clock on the dot." He glanced at his watch, then rolled to his feet in a smooth motion. "It's getting late. I'm going to head home and read another one of your novels. I borrowed all of them from Andrea."

Jillian got to her feet. "You did?"

"Yep," he said, pushing his feet into his shoes, "I did." He sat down on the edge of the sofa to tie his laces. "I've heard that an author reveals something of herself in everything she writes."

"*I* don't."

He stood again, then crossed the room to pick up his jacket.

"Are you positive of that?" he said, looking at her.

"Of course. I'm the one writing the books, remember? They're drawn totally from my imagination."

"Maybe, maybe not."

"Well, I'm not going to debate the subject. I'll walk you to the door."

Forrest rolled down his cuffs, buttoned them, then shrugged into his jacket. At the front door, he encircled Jillian with his arms and kissed her deeply before she could speak further.

"Good night," he said, then released her. "I'll be here at ten in the morning."

Jillian nodded, not even attempting to answer. She was convinced that there was not one breath of air left in her body after that kiss.

Forrest opened the door and left the house, closing the door behind him with a quiet click. Jillian stood statue-still, allowing herself the luxury of reliving the kisses shared with Forrest—every sensual detail.

When heated desire began to pulse within her once again, she spun around and marched back into the living room. As she flopped down onto the sofa, she told herself that Forrest was no longer in the house and, therefore, she should automatically stop thinking about him.

Fat chance, she thought, mentally throwing up her hands in defeat. Forrest was not easily dismissed from a woman's mind. And her body? Good grief, it was going absolutely nuts.

"Perdition, Jillian," she said aloud. "What is your problem?"

Forget it, she decided in the next instant. She had postponed the internal discussion with herself regard-

ing her startling responses to Forrest's kiss and touch.
Now she was going beyond postponing. She was *canceling* the inner dialogue. Forrest was The Project,
nothing more.

Yes, all right, she knew she had been swept away
to an unknown place when Forrest had kissed her.
But since she was fully aware of her unsettling reactions to him, she was in fine shape.

"You're splendidly in control, Ms. Jones-Jenkins,"
she said, with a decisive nod. "You may carry on
with The Project."

She would read a book until she was sleepy enough
to go to bed, she mused, getting to her feet. As per
her vacation routine, it would be a novel far removed
from the kind she wrote. She'd read a thriller, scare
the socks off herself, and have a wonderful time.

What a satisfying feeling it was to know she was
in complete charge of her own life.

Five

The next day was clear but crisp, typical weather for February.

Jillian dressed in jeans, tennis shoes, and a fisherman's-knit sweater, then took a flannel-lined windbreaker from the closet. She set the jacket next to the empty picnic hamper, along with a canvas tote bag that would serve as her purse for the outing. She'd called the marina manager earlier and arranged to have gas put in the boat. She was ready to go. *At nine o'clock,* she thought, rolling her eyes heavenward.

She always slept late during her vacation, the lazy mornings being one of her indulgences. But today? Her eyes had popped open at 7:00 a.m., and she'd known instantly that there was no chance of her drifting back into blissful sleep.

She glanced at her watch.

Nine-oh-two. This was ridiculous. At this rate, it would seem as though a week had passed before Forrest arrived. She'd write a newsy letter to her parents about the high points of the book-signing tour. Excellent idea.

The letter was written, sealed, stamped, and outside in the mailbox to be picked up by the postman by nine forty-five.

With a snort of self-disgust, she wandered around the living room, straightening throw pillows that didn't need straightening, picking up and setting back in place a variety of knickknacks, watering plants that had already been tended to by the housekeeper.

Oh, bother, she fumed, she was acting like an adolescent waiting for the captain of the high-school football team to pick her up for a date. What in the blue blazes was the matter with her? Her behavior was absurd.

At the sound of a car approaching, Jillian started quickly toward one of the front windows, then stopped dead in her tracks. She forced herself to sit down in an easy chair, and began to examine her fingernails as though they were the most fascinating ten little things she'd ever seen.

When Forrest rang the doorbell, she decided, she would count to sixty before she went to answer the summons. Very good.

Forrest got out of his car and stood quietly for a moment, his gaze sweeping over Jillian's house.

It really was attractive, he mused. It was similar to the one Andrea had designed for her and John, and was a popular style in that area of California. He liked it, and he liked the way Jillian had decorated the interior.

Jillian. He'd read another of her books after returning to his apartment the night before, and had thoroughly enjoyed it.

The hero had been the captain of a sailing ship. The heroine had managed to stow away on the vessel to escape marrying a lecherous older man her heartless father had promised her to.

After a rocky beginning to their relationship, they had slowly fallen in love and shared many adventures, including an escape from the evil clutches of the vengeful would-be husband.

In the end, the hero had given up his life on the high seas to settle down on land and run a shipping company. The happy couple had selected a house, set a date for the wedding, and were discussing how many children they wanted as the story drew to a close.

Ah, fantasy, Forrest thought wistfully. Jillian's novel had produced for the hero and heroine all the things *he* wanted for himself—love, a wife, children, a home.

But in the era Jillian had written about, the heroine didn't have a demanding career outside the home. In present times, what he wanted simply wasn't his to have. Two-career marriages did *not* meet his standards of how a family should function. Damn.

He pushed aside his bleak thoughts and headed for the front door, eager to begin the outing with Jillian.

And eager to have her open the door so he could be the recipient of one of her sunshine smiles.

At the door, he pressed the bell, hearing it chime inside the house.

"Twenty-eight, twenty-nine," Jillian said, "and thirty."

She jumped to her feet.

A person just didn't realize how long sixty seconds were until she started counting them off. *Thirty* seconds were certainly enough of a delay.

She started toward the entry hall, ignoring the fact that she was practically running. When she flung the door open, the smile that lit up her face was genuine.

Forrest MacAllister, her mind hummed. And she was very, *very* glad to see him.

"Hi," she said, stepping back. "Come in." Sinful. Forrest in faded jeans, a dark blue sweater, and a white windbreaker was so ruggedly handsome it was sinful. "How are you this morning?" She closed the door behind him.

"I'm ready to sail the high seas," he said, matching her smile. How was it possible that each time he saw Jillian she appeared even more lovely? "I wish I had one of those shirts with the billowing sleeves like Roman wears."

"Roman?" Jillian repeated, obviously confused. "*My* Roman?"

"Yes, the hero in *Rapture in the Wind*. I read it last night. Great book, really great."

"Well, thank you, sir," she said, dipping her head slightly. "I'm glad you enjoyed it. We'd better be on our way. We have to stop at a deli and fill up the picnic hamper.''

"Sure, let's go." He paused, no hint of a smile remaining. "I came in here talking a blue streak, and didn't greet you the way I intended."

"You didn't?"

He took one step to close the distance between them, then framed her face in his hands. A shiver coursed through Jillian as she looked directly into the warm brown depths of his eyes.

"No, Jillian, I didn't."

Forrest's mouth melted over hers, his tongue slipping between her parted lips.

Jillian placed her hands around his waist, then moved them up his back, savoring the feel of the taut muscles beneath her palms. She met his questing tongue with her own, the now familiar heat of desire beginning to pulse through her. He tasted like minty toothpaste, smelled like soap and fresh air, felt like heaven itself.

The kiss deepened and their hearts beat with wild tempos.

Forrest finally lifted his head and drew a ragged breath.

"Good morning, Jillian," he said, his voice gritty with passion.

"Good morning, Forrest," she whispered.

Slowly, reluctantly, they stepped back, dropping their hands to their sides, seeing their desire mirrored in the smoky hues of each other's eyes. The sensual mist that had encased them began to fade into oblivion. They were once again in Jillian's entry hall.

The kiss was over, but not forgotten.

"We're off, fair maiden," Forrest said, pointing one finger in the air. "Mayhap we shall encounter pirates on the seas, but fear not, for I shall protect you against the miscreants."

"Oh, good night," she said, with a burst of laughter. "Who writes your dialogue?"

"I do," he said, grinning. "Pretty good, huh?"

"Stick with architecture, Forrest. Or as we say in the business, 'Don't quit your day job.'"

"Oh."

Two hours later, they were surrounded by water as Forrest steered the twenty-five-foot cabin cruiser with expertise. Jillian sat on a stool next to where he stood, the semienclosed bridge sheltering her from the wind.

The ocean was choppy and appeared more green than blue. The sky that had been bright and clear earlier was now a blue gray, and dotted with darkening clouds.

"We'd better tune in to the Coast Guard weather channel," Forrest said. "We don't want to get caught out here in a storm."

Jillian tended to the radio, adjusting it by following instructions on a card taped to it.

"Even though it's a little choppy," Forrest said, "there's still a peacefulness about being on the water. There's no one else within our view, either."

"And no telephone, no computer," Jillian added, ticking off the items on her fingers. "No galleys, no deadline, no—"

"Got it," he said, laughing. "You're on vacation today."

She nodded decisively. "In spades."

"I respect that. If you put your mind to it, I bet you could have a very healthy balance of work and play in your life. A lot of people don't, you know. They get centered on their careers, and there isn't room for anything else. You've at least got an idea of how it *should* be."

That was debatable, Jillian mused. According to Deedee, Lorraine, some of her other friends, and even her agent, she was a workaholic during the months she was writing a book. Except for occasional outings, she only surfaced during the adventuresome two-week hiatuses that occurred two or three times a year.

Should she explain all that to Forrest? No, it wasn't necessary. For all she knew, he would be long gone before her two weeks were up, not completing his stint of being The Project. She might not even have enough time to shape up *his* attitudes toward balancing work and play.

Jillian glanced quickly at Forrest, then stared unseeing at the churning water.

A strange sense of emptiness had swept over her, she realized, as she'd entertained the prospect of Forrest walking out of her life.

Perdition, Jillian, she admonished herself. Stop being ridiculous. It didn't matter which one of them faded into the sunset first, because at the end of her vacation their time together would be over. Finished. Kaput. That funny feeling in her stomach had been...hunger. Yes, of course, that was it. She was hungry.

"Forrest, there's a cove a few miles up ahead. It might not be quite so windy there, the water calmer, and we could eat lunch without having to chase all the food across the table."

"Sounds good. Let's check it out."

The cove was edged with trees that acted as a wind-break and the water was smoother. Forrest cut the engine, dropped anchor, and they went below. The cabin was small, but every inch had been put to use. The decor was dark wood with kelly green accents.

The table where Jillian placed the containers of food she took from the hamper was bolted to the floor. The minuscule stove and refrigerator had always reminded her of dollhouse furniture, she told Forrest, and she adored the double bed, which was surrounded by built-in drawers on all four sides.

"It's like sleeping in a secret cave," she said, sitting down at the table.

Forrest chuckled as he sat opposite her. "That's your writer's imagination at work. Someone else would probably say the bed was a hole-in-the-wall where the carpenter got tired of making drawers."

"Architecture, Forrest," she said, laughing. "Stick to architecture."

All traces of his smile faded. "I really like your laughter. It's a delightful sound, like wind chimes or tinkling bells."

"I... Thank you. That was a lovely thing to say."

They continued to gaze at each other, losing track of time, feeling the embers of desire within them begin to grow hotter once again, threatening to burst into consuming flames.

"Hungry," Jillian said finally, her voice sounding strange to her own ears.

"Oh, yes," Forrest said, nodding.

She shook her head slightly. "For lunch. I'm hungry for *lunch.*" She tore her gaze from Forrest's and reached for a plate. "We certainly bought a lot of different things. This is going to be a gourmet feast."

Forrest began to fill a plate while commanding himself to cool off, think about food, and *not* about grabbing Jillian up and carrying her to the "bed-in-the-wall" where the carpenter had run out of steam.

They ate without speaking for several minutes, while the boat rocked gently in the secluded cove.

"You know," Forrest said, slicing through the silence, "I've read two of your books so far. You've said that while some authors might reveal portions of themselves in their work, *you* don't. However, I did pick up on a common theme in both novels."

Jillian glanced up at him. "Oh?" She took a bite of crab salad.

"Trust. You put a lot of emphasis on trust. Not only did the heroines trust the heros to protect them from physical harm, but emotions were involved, as well. The heroes and heroines came to trust each other with their love, the essence of themselves. They rendered themselves vulnerable, laying it all on the line, and trusting each other to treat that love as the precious gift that it is. In both books there were conversations concerning the extreme importance of trust."

"Well, goodness," Jillian said, forcing a lightness

into her voice, "I'd better be on the alert for the glaring error of repeating myself from one book to the next. That is a definite no-no. Although in this particular case..." Her voice trailed off.

"In this case?" he prompted.

"The importance of trust in a loving relationship could be justifiably addressed in every one of my books. Without trust, what do two people actually have? Nothing. It's the foundation that love is centered on, a solid base from which it can grow, if nurtured."

She leaned forward, her voice ringing with conviction when she continued speaking.

"If the trust isn't there, the couple is fooling themselves, mistaking lust for love. If it *is* present, then later destroyed, the relationship is over, beyond repair."

"That's a pretty hard stand on the issue."

Jillian moved back again, folding her arms over her breasts. "It's the way I feel, what I believe."

"Interesting, especially when you consider the fact that you claim that nothing of *you,* per se, is in any of your novels."

"Oh." She felt a warm flush on her cheeks. "Well, I..." She frowned.

"Don't stress, Jillian," he said, smiling. "I obviously want to get to know you better, or I wouldn't be here today. What's the harm in garnering some details through your books?" He shrugged. "Makes sense to me."

"It certainly does not. How will you know what might be my opinions and views, and what are imaginary likes and dislikes I gave the characters to make them more believably human?''

''Well...''

''For example—'' she snatched up a breadstick and waggled it at Forrest ''—in the book that's in production at my publisher's now, the heroine has a good-luck charm. It's a little seashell that she always has with her. It might be in her pocket, her reticule, or in a small velvet pouch attached to a ribbon around her neck. She is never without it. When she gives it to the hero as he's about to go dashing off to face the villain, the hero realizes how deeply she loves him.''

''Your point?''

''My point is,'' she continued, her volume rising as she waved the breadstick in the air, ''I have never owned a good-luck charm in my life. You could, in the present state of your tiny mind, assume I personally have a thing for good-luck charms. You would be drawing a conclusion about me that would be totally wrong.''

Forrest snagged her wrist as it went whizzing by, and took a bite of the breadstick. As he chewed, he stared thoughtfully at the ceiling. After taking a sip of soda, he looked at Jillian again, seeing the very-pleased-with-herself expression on her face.

''Nope,'' he said, ''I wouldn't be wrong at all. Why? I'll be happy to explain.''

''Whoopee,'' she said dryly. ''I can hardly wait.''

''You're getting grumpy, Lady Jillian. Are you going to eat the rest of that breadstick?''

She smacked it into his hand.

''Thank you. To continue—I wouldn't focus on the

good-luck charm itself, wouldn't go charging out to buy you a rabbit's foot to make a favorable impression on you. I would look *beyond* the charm.''

''To what?''

''It's to *whom*. You. What message did you convey when the heroine gave the hero her special seashell? Trust. It's there again, Jillian, loud and clear.''

Easy, MacAllister, he told himself. Don't push too hard. But, damn, he'd bet his last dime that Jillian's marriage had been shattered, and that she had been deeply hurt by a betrayal of trust by the man she'd chosen as her life's partner.

What *he* wanted was for her to trust *him* enough to tell him about what had happened. But she wasn't ready for that yet, not even close. Why was her trusting him to that degree so important? Hell, he had no idea.

''End of dissertation,'' he said lightly. ''I'm going to have some of that strawberry cheesecake. It's calling my name. How about you?''

''What? Oh, no, I don't think so. Maybe I'll have some later.''

Perdition *and* damn it, she thought. She felt terribly exposed, as though Forrest had physically pulled away her protective wall to peer into her heart, her mind, her very soul.

How had he managed to do that? She didn't know, but she didn't like it. Not one little bit.

And it was *not* going to happen again.

Six

As Jillian began to pack the empty containers back into the picnic hamper, she looked at Forrest in surprise when he immediately moved to help her.

His mother, Forrest explained cheerfully, had made it clear early on that there was no such thing in the MacAllister household as "women's work." They were a family, pure and simple, and everyone would pitch in no matter what the task entailed.

"Hooray for Mom," Jillian said, smiling.

"She's terrific," he said, nodding. "We all know how to cook, clean, sew on a button, sort and wash clothes, the whole nine yards. By the same token, Andrea can change a tire, check the oil in her car, fix a leaky faucet—you know, male stuff. It's a good program."

"Indeed it is," Jillian said, nodding. "That's the

type of innovative ideas needed in two-career marriages, which you are so stubbornly convinced are a major disaster from the onset.''

''They are. Look, so the guy helps clean the kitchen after dinner. Then what? He disappears into his den with a briefcase full of papers he's brought home. Or maybe it's the wife who has to work through the evening. Where's the quality family time? The kids get shortchanged.''

''It doesn't have to be that way, Forrest. Where is it written that a person has to bring work home night after night?''

Forrest placed a plastic container of a few remaining green grapes in the hamper, then straightened, looking directly at Jillian.

''In the corporate world you have to really scramble if you want to keep up with the competition. Don't you work into the evenings a great deal?''

''Well, yes, but...''

''I rest my case.''

''Well, I'm not resting mine. I work evenings because I'm free to do so. I'm accountable only to myself. As a husband and father, you could decide that once you come home at night, your first priority would be your family.''

''Not if I wanted to provide for them the way I see myself doing in my mind. Nope, it won't work, not in today's economy.''

''Darn it, Forrest, you have a closed mind on the subject. You're putting too much emphasis on work, work, work. You've narrowed your existence down to slaving away over blueprints.''

"That's how it has to be. *Your* main focus is your career, too."

"But I don't want the same things you do. You'd like a family. I'm perfectly content on my own."

"Are you?" he said quietly.

"Yes. Yes, I am. Absolutely. But you? Forrest, you've got to get your act together, your head on straight. You're going to sentence yourself to a lonely existence if you don't stop and consider some alternatives to the way you're thinking. Two-career marriages are flourishing all around you, but you're only paying attention to the ones that aren't. Are you listening to me?"

"At the volume that you're yelling, how could I *not* be listening?"

"I'm not yelling!" She paused, then sighed. "Yes, I am." She sank back onto her chair. "Ignore me."

Forrest leaned across the table and planted a quick kiss on her forehead.

"Impossible," he said. "I'd have to be dead to be able to ignore you while I'm with you. I can't ignore you when I'm *not* with you. I think about you a great deal when we're apart, Jillian."

She looked up at him. "I think about you, too, Forrest," she said, rather dreamily. In the next instant, her eyes widened and she stiffened. "I did *not* say that."

Forrest moved around the table to where Jillian sat and pulled her gently to her feet, wrapping his arms around her. She stared at his chest.

"Look at me," he said gently.

She raised her head slowly, her expression troubled when she met his gaze.

"Jillian, I don't quite understand why you're suddenly so flustered, stressed, upset, whatever it is you are. We were talking about genderless household chores, for Pete's sake."

"But we moved on to the subject of working too hard, how it affects a marriage, and on and on. I just hate knowing you won't ever be totally happy because you'll miss having a family."

"And you're dead set against ever having a family," he said. Jillian had tried marriage, it had failed. She'd been hurt, and he'd bet money that she wasn't about to go down that road again.

"Well, not everyone wants the same things from life, Forrest."

"True, that's true," he agreed, nodding.

But what, he wondered, was a man supposed to do when he met someone who was poles apart from him as far as what they wanted, but there was something new and special of incredible intensity and depth happening between them? He wanted to know what it was, what it meant.

Oh, man, this whole thing was crazy. He wanted to get married and have a family. Jillian didn't. He felt it was impossible for him to have said family because of the economy making it necessary for both parents to have careers. Jillian believed that dual-career marriages could function just fine with the proper compromises.

The wrong attitudes and beliefs were tacked onto the wrong people in this scenario. If he was smart, he'd cash in his chips and exit stage left before he went out of his beleaguered mind. But he'd never claimed to be a genius.

He did not want, nor did he intend, to walk out of Jillian Jones-Jenkins's life. He should, but he wouldn't, just couldn't.

Well, at least there was one thing they agreed on: trust. He knew how she felt about trust between a man and a woman, and her beliefs matched his own.

Forrest suddenly stiffened. "Thunder," he said, his head snapping up. "We'd better see what's happening with the weather. That's thunder rumbling in them there hills, ma'am."

He gave her a fast, hard kiss, released her, and headed for the stairs. Jillian was right behind him.

On the deck of the boat, they came to an abrupt halt as they saw the heavy dark clouds covering the sky, and the trees lining the cove whipped into a frenzy by a rapidly rising wind.

"Holy smoke," Forrest said.

"We'd better get on the radio," Jillian said. "It's ship-to-shore, and we can contact the Coast Guard and ask what we should do."

They ran to the bridge as lightning zigzagged across the sky and thunder continued to rumble in a nearly steady cadence.

Forrest quickly read the instructions on the laminated card taped to the radio, and minutes later was communicating with the man on duty at the Coast Guard station. As they talked, big drops of cold rain began to fall, being flung in all directions by the wind.

"Roger," Forrest finally said. "Thank you, and

over and out." He grabbed Jillian's hand. "Let's get below," he yelled, above the roar of the wind.

Even though the distance from the bridge to the stairway was short, they were thoroughly soaked by the time they got below deck. The boat rocked back and forth, and the picnic hamper began to slide across the table.

"Whoa," Forrest said, snatching up the hamper and setting it on the floor.

Jillian wrapped her hands around her elbows, unable to stop her teeth from chattering. "Oh-h-h, I'm freezing, turning into an icicle."

"You heard the radio transmission," Forrest said. "The Coast Guard wants us to stay put until this blows over. They said we're safer in this cove than on the open water. We've got to get out of these wet clothes before we catch pneumonia. Do you know what the setup is here for light, heat, hot water?"

Jillian nodded, tightening her hold on her arms. "There's an independent generator that services lights, that space heater on the wall, and a small hot-water tank. I doubt that there are any spare clothes on board other than extra bathing suits, but there's a stack of beach towels in the center drawer beneath the bed."

"Okay. Good."

Forrest turned on two lamps mounted on the wall, which cast a soft glow over the area. Opening the drawer Jillian had indicated, he removed four large, brightly colored towels. He crossed the room and gave two of them to her.

"You go ahead and shower," he said. "I'll do a

quick inspection to see if there's anything that needs securing. We're in for a bumpy ride, or float, or whatever.''

Jillian nodded and hurried to enter the small enclosure she referred to as a bathroom, knowing that nautical jargon said it was the head, which she'd always thought was rather silly.

With difficulty, she managed to peel off her wet jeans, then the remainder of her clothing. She sighed with relief when she stepped into the shower stall and felt the welcome spray of warm water cascading over her chilled body.

She'd have to hurry, she knew, as there was not a great deal of hot water provided by the minisize tank.

Minutes later she stepped out of the stall, and vigorously rubbed her hair with the huge, thirsty towel. She dried the rest of herself until her skin was pink.

Now what? she thought suddenly. Her clothes were soaking wet, including her bra and panties. The towel she'd already used was damp, so— Good grief, she had nothing to wear except the second beach towel. Well, so be it. The only other choice was to walk out of there naked as the day she was born.

She finger-combed her hair into a semblance of order, wrapped the towel around herself like a sarong that fell to just above her knees, and tucked the flap of the towel between her breasts. Picking up her wet clothes and the damp towel, she took a deep, steadying breath, plastered a smile on her face, and opened the door.

''It's all yours,'' she said breezily. Her gaze swept

over the room, taking in the beach towels spread on the table and over the backs of the chairs.

"We can put our clothes on these," Forrest said, placing a towel on the last chair. "Hopefully they'll dry out a bit, and the furniture won't be damaged. I turned on the heat and—" He looked up at Jillian and stopped speaking. "Holy smoke," he whispered.

Jillian walked forward and dumped her clothes in the center of the table.

Do *not*, she told herself, look at that man. She'd heard his hoarsely whispered reaction to her apparel, or lack of same. She was acutely aware of the fact that she was naked beneath that towel, and Forrest was not a stupid person. She didn't want to see what message might be radiating from his expression, or from the depths of those incredible brown eyes of his.

She busied herself with her clothes, letting out a whoosh of breath as she heard the water in the shower. Hesitating when she picked up her soggy lace bra and panties, she mentally shrugged, deciding that a virile man like Forrest MacAllister had no doubt seen his share of woman's undies.

Her laundry tended to, she glanced around for a place to sit. There was a small, cushioned seat against one wall that was the top of a storage box. She'd sat on it in the past, and it was as hard as a rock.

No contest. She was declaring first-come-first-served, and claiming the bed. Forrest could plunk himself on the bench.

She took one of the pillows from beneath the spread and placed it against the back wall. Crawling over the bed, she sat straight up, legs extended, facing the room. After checking to be certain her towel was secure, she folded her hands primly in her lap.

In the next moment, she decided she looked like a Victorian maiden on her wedding night. She crossed her ankles, striving for a more nonchalant pose, then stared at her hands, wondering what on earth to do with them.

"A magazine," she said. "Yes. Perfect."

Hearing the water stop running in the shower, she scrambled off the bed, nearly losing the towel in the process, dashed across the room to snatch a magazine out of a holder mounted on the wall, then hightailed it back to the bed.

The towel was straightened, her ankles crossed in a casual mode, and her nose was buried in the magazine she held up in front of her face, when Forrest returned to the main room.

"That shower was heaven itself," he said. "Man, that felt good."

"Mmm," Jillian said, not looking at him.

"These clothes are sure wet, considering we weren't out in the rain that long."

"Mmm."

"The boat isn't rocking too badly. We'll pretend it's a giant-size cradle."

"Mmm."

Forrest crossed the room and wiggled one of Jillian's big toes. "Hey, you."

She gasped in shock, and smacked the magazine onto her lap.

And then she stopped breathing as she stared up at Forrest MacAllister.

He was beautiful, she mused, finally taking a breath. He'd tucked the towel around his waist, allowing it to fall to midcalf. The soft light made his tanned skin appear like polished bronze. The broad, bare expanse of his chest caused her fingers to itch with the urge to tangle in the mass of damp auburn curls, then slide over the taut, perfectly proportioned muscles of his arms.

Masculinity personified, her mind hummed. Gorgeous. Blatantly male. And naked as a jaybird beneath a scrap of terry cloth.

"Jillian?"

"Who?" she said, then blinked. "I mean…what?"

Forrest picked up the other pillow. "Move over."

"Why?"

"Because we're going to be here for a while, toots, and I'm not sitting on that brick of a bench. There are wet clothes on all the chairs, so…please move over and share the bed."

Share the bed, her mind echoed. They were going to share the bed. This bed, the one she was sitting on in the secret cave created by the lazy carpenter, was the one they were going to share.

Jillian, stop it, she ordered herself. She was getting hysterical. She could handle this. She was a mature woman, not a flaky adolescent. *Yes! She was woman!* But, oh, dear heaven, Forrest was the epitome of man.

"Hey!" he said.

"Yes, I'm sharing. I'm moving over right now. Here I go, wiggling right over here." She clutched the towel at the center of her breasts, then readjusted the pillow. "There. Now you have room. Go for it,

MacAllister.'' She grabbed the magazine and placed it in front of her face again, close to her nose.

She was tense from head to toe as she felt Forrest move onto the bed, prop his pillow next to hers, squirm around, then settle into place.

A long, silent minute ticked by.

''Interesting,'' Forrest said finally.

''Hmm?'' she said, her undivided attention directed toward the magazine.

''You have many facets, Lady Jillian. I wouldn't have thought you'd be so engrossed in a *Popular Mechanics* magazine.''

Jillian's eyes widened as she comprehended for the first time what she was holding.

''Well, of course, I'm interested,'' she said, turning a page. ''One never knows when one might need to do something mechanical...and popular.''

''Oh,'' he said, with a burst of laughter.

''It's true,'' she said firmly. ''I own a home, you know. Things need fixing at times.''

''*Popular* things,'' he said, still smiling.

''Whatever,'' she mumbled.

''Tell me something, Jillian.''

''Hmm?'' She turned another page.

''How can you see to read? Those lights I turned on are pretty dim. It's very shadowy back here in your secret cave. You must have remarkable vision.''

Jillian squinted at the magazine. ''Oh.'' She snapped her head around to look at him, and nodded. ''I do. Oh my, yes, I have excellent vision. Superb vision, as a matter of fact. I— Aaak!'' she yelled, in the next instant.

The boat had suddenly seemed to lift nearly out of the water, then tilt to one side. The magazine flew in one direction, Jillian in the other—toward Forrest.

As she sprawled across his lap, his arms shot out, one wrapping around her beneath her breasts, the other under her knees. He scooped her up and planted her firmly on his lap. The boat returned to the gently rocking motion.

"Easy does it, there," Forrest said. "Either some idiot was whizzing past at the end of the cove, or the Coast Guard went by, but we're all right now. Everything is under control."

Except Jillian Jones-Jenkins, she thought frantically. She was perched on Forrest MacAllister's lap, for crying out loud. Her heart was doing the tango, and the heat... Oh, dear heaven, the heat within her was churning and pulsing, low and deep. Everything was under control? That was the most ridiculous thing she'd ever heard.

"Jillian," Forrest said, his voice quiet as he looked directly into her eyes.

And she was lost.

No longer could she resist the urge to sink her fingers into the auburn curls on the muscled wall of Forrest's chest.

And so, she did.

No longer could she keep from inhaling, then savoring, his scent of soap and man.

And so, she did.

No longer could she ignore the fact that only two terry-cloth towels separated her from him, making her acutely aware of the rock-hard feel of his thighs be-

neath the softness of her own. She wanted to rejoice
in the magnificence of his masculinity compared to
her own femininity.

And so, she did.

No longer could she ignore the raspy sound of Forrest's quickened breathing as he continued to gaze
into her eyes, nor the tempting sight of his lips so
very close to hers. She wanted to kiss those lips, taste
them again, meet his tongue with her own.

And so...she did.

She slipped one hand to the back of his head, burying her fingers in his thick hair, and spread her other
hand flat on his chest, feeling the rapid beat of his
heart. She leaned forward and claimed his lips.

A groan rumbled in Forrest's throat as he met her
mouth eagerly, urgently. He moved his arm from under her knees to wrap it around her, his other arm still
firmly beneath her breasts.

His arousal was instantaneous. Heavy, aching,
pressing against Jillian with the declaration of his
want, his burning need. He jerked his head to break
the kiss.

"Jillian," he said, then drew a rough breath. "I
want to make love with you. *Make love, Jillian.* You
can be certain of that. What's happening here is important, very special." Something that was becoming
much, much more than an Angels and Elves assignment.

"Yes," she whispered. "Yes, Forrest, I want to
make love with you, too."

Jillian? her mind nudged. What are you doing?

Think. Forrest is The Project. He'll be gone in less than two weeks. *Jillian!*

But she ignored the niggling little voice, pushed aside the warnings of her mind, and listened only to her heart.

Yes, yes, yes, she wanted to make love with Forrest.

"Yes," she whispered again.

He captured her mouth once more in a searing kiss, and she leaned into it, taking all he gave, giving in return with total abandon. He pulled the end of her towel free, allowing the material to drop into a colorful pool at her hips. He cupped one breast in his hand, stroking the nipple to a taut bud with his thumb. Jillian whimpered with building passion.

Forrest ended the kiss and lifted her from his lap as though she weighed little more than a feather. He leaned forward and laid her on the bed, stretching out beside her in the next moment, resting on one forearm.

His eyes swept over her bare breasts; then, with a visibly shaking hand, he swept back the towel, revealing the rest of her body to his smoldering gaze. He flicked aside his own towel, exposing his arousal.

Their eyes explored eagerly, visually tracing every inch of each other, fanning the flames of desire burning within them.

"Beautiful," Forrest said. "You're so beautiful, Jillian."

"You're magnificent, you truly are."

He looked deep into her eyes, as though searching for, then finding, the answer to an unspoken question.

He dipped his head to draw the soft flesh of one of her breasts deep into his mouth, his tongue laving the nipple in a steady rhythm.

Jillian closed her eyes for a moment to savor the exquisite sensations swirling within her.

Forrest moved to her other breast, paying homage to its sweet bounty. His hand skimmed over the flat plane of her stomach, then lower, and lower still, to the apex of her thighs.

She trembled from the tantalizing foray, one hand gripping the bunching muscles of his biceps.

Then Forrest's lips traveled the path his hand had taken. Jillian could feel the tension building within her, tightening into a heated coil that pulsed in the dark, moist center of her femininity. She tossed her head restlessly, a near sob escaping from her lips.

"Forrest, please," she whispered. "Please."

"Soon, Jillian," he said, hardly recognizing the sound of his own voice. "Soon."

Control, MacAllister, his mind hammered. He was slipping too close to the edge, wanted to seek release in the beckoning haven of Jillian's body—now. *Now.* But he had to regain a modicum of command over himself, because Jillian's pleasure must be assured. That concern was uppermost in his mind, with a fierce intensity he'd never experienced before.

"Forrest," Jillian said, her voice quivering.

He moved over her, resting his weight on both forearms, seeing the smoky-gray hue of desire radiating from Jillian's eyes. Her cheeks were flushed, her lips moist from his kisses, and parted slightly in an enticing invitation.

He kissed her, then raised his head again, wanting, needing, to see her face in the soft glow of the lights as they became one entity.

Slowly, so slowly, he entered her, a moan rumbling from his throat as he sheathed himself in the dark, moist heat.

Ecstasy.

Jillian sighed with pure feminine pleasure, savoring the sensation of Forrest meshing with her, the strength and power of what he was bringing to her. She could feel his muscles trembling from forced restraint where her hands splayed on his glistening back.

Her heart sang with joy at the realization that he was putting her pleasure before his own, telling her by his actions that they were indeed *making love,* that this *was* special.

But *his* pleasure was important to her as well, and she lifted her hips to draw him fully into her.

"Jillian…"

"I want you so much."

He began to move, increasing the cadence with each thrust, and she met him beat for urgent beat. The tension built within them to a sweet pain, taking them closer and closer to what they sought.

Then waves of passion swept through Jillian, seeming to carry her up and away, flinging her far beyond reason and reality to a glorious place.

"Forrest!"

Seconds later he joined her there, shuddering, with a sound that was thoroughly male, bursting from his throat. Spasm after spasm consumed them as though the ecstasy would last for all time.

They hovered in the beyond, then drifted back, Forrest collapsing against her, his last ounce of energy spent. He rolled onto his side, taking her with him.

Their breathing slowed. Their bodies cooled. Their heartbeats quieted to normal tempos. Their minds and hearts held the memories of what had just transpired, and they treasured them.

The boat continued to rock slowly back and forth, and the rain fell steadily, creating a symphony produced by nature.

Forrest drew the edges of the bedspread over them, then settled again, holding Jillian close, his lips resting lightly on her forehead.

Neither spoke as they lay in sated contentment, listening to the music of the rain.

Somnolence crept over them, and they slept.

Several hours later, Jillian stirred and opened her eyes, having no idea in her foggy state as to where she was. She turned her head, and her breath caught as she saw Forrest sleeping peacefully only inches away.

A soft smile touched her lips as she gazed at him. His strength emanated from his body even while he slept, yet there was a vulnerability there, too; an aura of trust that she found endearing.

Forrest MacAllister, her mind hummed.

She frowned as she tore her gaze from him to stare up at the bottom of the drawers built above the bed.

Sleep on, Forrest, she mentally directed him. Before he awakened, she needed time to sort and sift, to think about what had taken place between them.

She had made love with Forrest MacAllister.

There it was—a fact, right out in front of her—and it needed to be addressed.

Was she sorry? Did she regret her actions? Was she furious with herself for allowing her passion to override reason?

Narrowing her eyes, she focused inward, getting in touch with herself to find the answers to the questions.

And the answers were there, clear and precise—no, no, and no.

That's just dandy, Jillian Jones-Jenkins, she thought dryly. She knew where she stood on the issue, but what she didn't know was *why* she felt as she did. She should be calling herself a featherhead, a flibbertigibbet, a ninnyhammer, a...a dope.

She *knew* her time with Forrest was measured in days. There was no room in her life for a man or a relationship when she was writing a novel.

She'd had it all figured out as far as Forrest being The Project, but had now totally complicated things. Emotions had come into play when she'd made love with Forrest. They'd *made love,* not had casual sex, and from that realization came the confusion and muddled mess.

So, why didn't she regret what she had done?

Oh, fiddle, she didn't know.

Forrest would awaken soon, and she'd better have her head on straight. As any man would, under the circumstances, he'd be watching for what her mood, her attitude was, regarding what had transpired.

Well, so be it. She had *no* regrets, was *not* sorry. That was the truth, and was what Forrest deserved to know. That she was confused was *her* problem to deal with.

Having concluded the conversation between herself and herself, Jillian switched her attention to what was going on around her.

It was quite dark in the room, the small lamps on the wall casting circles of light over a few feet, and leaving the remainder of the expanse in deep shadow. The boat was still, and she realized there was no longer any sound of the musical rain.

Peering through the semidarkness, she squinted at the battery-operated clock on the wall, her eyes widening as she saw it was nearly six o'clock. She and Forrest had slept the afternoon away, blissfully sated.

"Forrest," she said, poking his chest with one finger. "Forrest, wake up."

"Mmm. Later," he mumbled.

Jillian laughed softly. Forrest muttered a few more words that she couldn't understand, then finally opened his eyes.

"Hi," she said.

He shook his head slightly, then a slow smile crept onto his lips.

"I was dreaming," he said, his voice husky with sleep.

The sexy sound caused a shiver to course through Jillian.

"I was Roman on my sailing ship, out on the high seas," Forrest went on. "I even had a terrific shirt with billowing sleeves. It was permanent-press, of course, because I really hate ironing."

"How nice," she said, matching his smile. "However, that was then and this is now, and it's six o'clock.''

"You're kidding.'' He sat up. "No, you're not kidding.'' He paused. "The storm has passed through, I guess. I suppose we'd better head for the marina.''

"Yes.''

He shifted around to rest on one forearm as he looked directly into her eyes. No trace of a smile remained on his face.

"Jillian,'' he said quietly, "making love with you was incredibly beautiful and very special. I want you to know that.''

"I feel the same way.''

"No regrets?''

She hesitated for only a moment. "No, Forrest. No regrets.''

He lowered his head and kissed her deeply. The embers of the passion still within them burst instantly into flames. When he lifted his head again, he drew a ragged breath.

"Nay, I say, MacAllister,'' he said, "or the very night shall pass on this vessel.'' He smiled. "That means, toots, that I've got to quit kissing you right now, or we'll be sharing a half-dozen green grapes for breakfast.''

Jillian laughed, the enchanting sound causing the heated desire within Forrest to coil tighter.

She slid off the bed and crossed the room to where their clothes were spread over the table and chairs.

Forrest drank in the sight of her naked body, slender and soft, totally feminine, a perfect counterpart to the hard contours of his own. What he couldn't see in the shadows, his mind vividly supplied.

Lovely, he mused. Jillian was so beautiful. The lovemaking they'd shared had been exquisite. Not only had their bodies meshed, but there had been undefinable emotions entwined, as well.

It had been complex and rare, very different from anything he'd experienced before. There was, indeed, something important happening between them, and nothing would keep him from discovering what it was.

"The clothes are dry," Jillian said, bringing Forrest from his thoughts, "but stiff as a board." She began to dress. "I'm fantasizing about a warm bubble bath and a soft, cozy robe."

Forrest joined her at the table, reaching for his sweater. "I'm fantasizing about two or three hamburgers, a thick milk shake, and a double order of fries."

"Sold. Hamburgers, *then* a bubble bath."

"Your wish is my command. We'll share a meal, then share—"

"Wrong. You'll go home. *I'll* have a bubble bath."

"Perdition!"

Jillian dissolved in laughter and Forrest, infected by the wind-chime sound, laughed with her.

They were hungry, wearing wrinkled, scratchy clothes, and miles from shore and the comforts they yearned for, but their smiles remained firmly in place all the way back to the marina.

"Deedee?" Andrea said. "I hope I'm not calling during your dinner. Guess what? I haven't been able to reach Forrest or Jillian all day. I got their answering machines every time I phoned.

"I realize I shouldn't get carried away with that information, but at least there's a *chance* they might be together. If they are, I wonder how they got along for that many hours.

"Oh, wouldn't it be grim if they spent the day arguing?"

Seven

The next two days, and nights, flew by in a blur of activity. Jillian felt delightfully alive, invigorated, and was engaged in the best vacation she'd ever had.

On Friday she cleaned her closets, discarding clothes she no longer wanted, and making a list of what she needed to buy.

That night, she and Forrest attended a concert featuring a popular country-and-western singer. They both wore jeans, boots, and Western shirts with pearl snaps.

"My goodness," Jillian said, as they stood in her living room, "we look so authentic. We're awesome, Forrest, totally awesome."

Forrest hooked his thumbs in the front pockets of his jeans.

"Ma'am," he said, in a lazy Western drawl, "you

ain't seen nothin' yet. Y'all come on outside with me, little lady.''

To Jillian's laughing delight, Forrest had borrowed his brother Ryan's Jeep for the evening.

''*Now* we're authentic, ma'am,'' Forrest said.

''Drive this thing, cowboy. It's time to do the boot-scootin' boogie.''

After the show, which they thoroughly enjoyed, they went to a Chinese restaurant. Unable to resist the tempting selections, they ordered enough food for four people.

''This is delicious,'' Jillian said, then took a bite of something with a name she couldn't pronounce.

''Yes, ma'am, it surely is,'' Forrest said.

Jillian laughed. ''Forrest, your Western twang just isn't making it in a Chinese restaurant.''

''Oh. Good point.''

''You know,'' she said, thoughtfully, ''this evening's outing is a perfect example of the kind of perks, per se, that a couple could have if they both worked.''

''That's true. Concert tickets, then dinner out afterward, would take a big bite out of a married couple's single-income household budget. But where are the kids?''

''They're at home with a reliable, trustworthy sitter. We, the parents, need some hours alone together.''

''How much time did we spend with our children during the week? We worked in the evenings. Right? We both have careers and we enjoy expensive entertainment like this evening's. Sunday we're taking the kids out to lunch, then to the zoo. That's a family outing. It also costs big bucks. One, or both of us, worked through the evenings.''

''No, we did not,'' Jillian said, leaning toward him. ''We compromised. There's that word that makes you break out in hives. *Compromise*. We went to the concert, then on home where we made ice-cream sundaes in our own kitchen.''

''I see,'' he said, nodding slowly.

''Do you? On Sunday we'll pack a picnic lunch, then go to the zoo. Compromise, Forrest. Two careers, no slaving away with work every night at home, and nice outings as a couple, and others with the kids. If you weren't so stubbornly narrow-minded, you would realize you can have the wife and family you want, without anyone getting the short end of the stick.''

''Well, you've certainly given me food for thought,'' he said, staring into space. ''Michael's wife, Jenny, stays home with their son, Bobby, but now that I think about it, Michael and Jenny go out alone most weekends.''

''Excellent. That's a one-income family compromising. There's no reason why people in a two-career marriage can't do the same thing.''

''How many kids do we have?''

''What?'' she said, frowning.

''How many little munchkins are we taking to the zoo on Sunday?''

''Have an egg roll, Forrest. You need fuel for your brain.''

"Well, you made our family sound real," he said, smiling.

Jillian shrugged. "I'm a writer with a vivid imagination."

Forrest's smile faded. "And you, of course, don't want any part of the scenario you just painted so clearly."

Jillian met his gaze directly. "No. No, I don't."

"So, while I'm getting the hang of this compromise jazz, leaving my briefcase at the office, you're still working evenings."

"Because I can," she said, splaying one hand on her chest. "I don't have the family you do, who needs my attention."

"Jillian, did it ever occur to you that this famous compromise of yours should apply to you, too?"

"Whatever for?"

"For you. Don't you want more in your life besides work, with an occasional outing like the one we're sharing tonight?"

She lifted her chin. "My life is perfectly fine just the way it is, thank you very much."

"That's *your* opinion," he said, glaring at her.

Jillian opened her mouth to retort, then closed it, and shook her head.

"No, I'm not going any further with this discussion," she said, "because we're headed for an argument. Our evening together has been so lovely. Let's not spoil it, Forrest." She smiled. "Have that egg roll."

He picked up one of the treats, matching her smile. "Sold. I *do* intend to think about what you said, though. I've never had the compromise angle so clearly defined before. It has merit. Yep, food—'' he took a bite of the egg roll ''—for thought.''

"Good," she said.

She was making marvelous progress with The Project, she mused. Yes sirree, she was scoring points in her Angels and Elves mission. It was just that... Well, a funny, cold knot had tightened in her stomach as she'd envisioned Forrest with a faceless wife and children. Oh, how ridiculous. *She* needed an egg roll.

"So," she said, "Michael and Jenny have a son. Right?"

"Oh, yeah, Bobby is one cute kid. Did I tell you that I won The Baby Bet when he was born?"

"The what?"

"It was a high-tech bet. There were too many of us involved in it to go for a straight 'Is it a girl or boy?' So we added date of birth and—get this—time of day."

"*Very* high-tech."

"Indeed, and *I* won. I had the right sex, the right day, *and* I hit the time within twenty minutes. You're looking at The Baby Bet pro, here."

Jillian laughed in delight. "Your talents never fail to amaze me, Mr. MacAllister."

"Darlin'," he said, his voice low and rumbly, "to quote myself, you ain't seen nothin' yet."

Sudden and sensual pictures flitted into Jillian's mind of the lovemaking she'd shared with Forrest, and a warm flush crept onto her cheeks. She cleared her throat, then glanced over the table.

"It's fortune-cookie time," she said. "I can read

it, but I can't eat it. I'll explode if I take one more bite." She broke open the crisp cookie and unfolded the narrow strip of paper, reading it quickly. "Oh."

"Oh?" Forrest leaned toward her. "That's a weird fortune. Let me see that." He took the paper from her hand, read it, then looked at her with a serious expression. "'You are about to experience a major change in your life on an emotional, not material plane.'"

The warm flush on Jillian's cheeks intensified, and was accompanied by heat that swirled through her. Desire was radiating from Forrest's dark brown eyes and was, she knew, mirrored in her own.

"Major emotional change," he repeated, a husky quality in his voice.

Jillian tore her gaze from his, aware that her hand was trembling slightly as she reached for the other cookie.

"Read *your* fortune now, Forrest," she said, handing it to him.

He crushed the cookie and pulled the paper free, hooting with laughter as he read the message.

Jillian peered over at the paper and smiled as she read it aloud: "'Your ship cannot come in because it sank.'"

"Wrong," Forrest said. "They don't know who they're dealing with, here. Roman and I would never let our ships sink."

"Of course not," she said. "You'd get your snazzy shirts wet."

"You've got *that* straight."

"You're crazy."

"You're beautiful," he said, then gave her a quick, but toe-curling kiss. "Let's go home, Lady Jillian."

They made exquisite love far into the night in Jillian's bed. She was sleepily aware of Forrest leaving at dawn to go to his apartment to change clothes, and then on to play golf with Michael.

During the day on Saturday, Jillian talked to Deedee on the telephone to arrange lunch the next day, then a shopping spree. Deedee immediately agreed, stating she'd have Books and Books covered the entire afternoon by one of her part-time employees.

"So, what's new?" Deedee said.

"We'll get caught up at lunch."

"Promise? Cross your heart?"

"Well, sure, Deedee. We always chatter like magpies when we get together."

"I'll be counting the hours, Jillian."

"You're acting like a weird biscuit, Mrs. Hamilton. I'll see you tomorrow. Bye."

Deedee replaced the receiver on the telephone.

"A weird biscuit?" she said, to no one. "No-o-o, I'm a stressed-out Cupid."

The remainder of the day, Jillian ran errands. She went to the cleaners, the drugstore, ordered more business cards, and made the other stops on her list.

She hated errands, and usually assigned most of them to her secretary, Lorraine, but found herself in a chipper mood during the entire excursion.

So, okay, she mused, as she finally relaxed in a

bubble bath, she had thought more about the evening ahead with Forrest as she'd dashed here and there, than about what she was actually doing at the time.

But that was understandable, she reasoned. Forrest was a handsome, charming, fun-to-be-with man. It made perfect sense that she was looking forward to dinner and dancing with Mr. MacAllister. It didn't constitute a ''major emotional change,'' for heaven's sake.

And the lovemaking they'd shared? It was beautiful beyond description. The unnamed emotions that rose to the fore each time she was with Forrest were coming from a new and different place inside her.

Should she be attempting to define those emotions? she wondered, absently watching the bubbles pop in fragrant bursts. No, that wasn't necessary. Those emotions were intertwined with the lovemaking itself, were a part of the exquisite intimate act. It should all be wrapped up like a precious gift, a treasure to be cherished, then tucked away in her heart when Forrest was gone.

When Forrest was gone.

Jillian frowned as the words echoed in her mind. She stepped from the tub and began to dry herself with a fluffy, salmon-colored towel.

When Forrest was gone.

Now, Jillian, she admonished herself, shape up. She knew the facts as they stood, knew the level of self-discipline she had to maintain to achieve her career goals. Nothing was allowed to draw her away from her purpose when she was working. Nothing, and no one.

So, when her vacation was over, Forrest Mac-Allister would be gone.

Besides, she mentally rambled on, as she began to dress, she wanted no part of a serious relationship. Never again would she hand over her heart to another person, render herself totally vulnerable, she'd never again be defenseless and helpless as that heart was smashed to smithereens. She'd learned that lesson the hard and hurtful way, and would not make the same mistake again.

Fine, she thought, lifting her chin. At the end of her two-week hiatus, Forrest would be gone. So be it. The bright side of the picture was that she was making marvelous progress with her Angels and Elves mission. That was great. Right? Right.

During the evening, Jillian felt like Cinderella at the ball. The leisurely dinner was delicious, then they moved into a ballroom where a ten-piece band played dreamy music. Forrest was an excellent dancer, and when he took her into his arms, Jillian welcomed the wondrous sensations that consumed her.

She felt safe, protected, fragile and feminine. There was no reason to think; she needed only to feel, savor, allow the desire within her to build to a fever pitch.

Unlike Cinderella, she would not have to dash away at midnight. The entire night ahead was hers, to share with Forrest.

Although Jillian would have thought it impossible, their lovemaking that night was even more magical, more intense than before. She was unable at times to decipher their bodies as two separate entities. They were meshed, completely one, as they soared to their glorious place.

A few minutes after noon on Sunday, Jillian slid onto the chair opposite Deedee in a busy restaurant.

"Good, I'm only a couple of minutes late," Jillian said, smiling. "The traffic is grim."

"It's so good to see you, Jillian," Deedee said, matching her smile. "Let's order. I'm famished."

Jillian glanced at the menu, decided she would have a chef's salad, then observed Deedee while the other woman was engrossed in the list of selections.

Deedee was so pretty, Jillian mused. She was thirty-one, but appeared younger due to her delicate features, and she wore very little makeup. There was a fresh, wholesome aura about her, accentuated by a dusting of freckles across her nose.

No one would know that the perky, smile-always-at-the-ready woman had been tragically widowed eight years before when her husband had been killed flying an air-force jet in a training exercise.

After a year of intense grieving during which Deedee had barely functioned, she'd taken herself in hand, sought counseling, then used her husband's insurance money to create Books and Books.

Jillian had met her five years ago when Lorraine had arranged a book-signing session at the store. Their friendship had grown steadily, and little by little, Deedee had revealed the sad circumstances of her past.

Strange, Jillian thought, taking a sip of water. She had never told Deedee the details of her own marriage and subsequent divorce. She'd simply said, as she had to Forrest, that the marriage had been a terrible mistake and was old news that wasn't worth discussing. Had it hurt Deedee's feelings over the years to realize that Jillian wasn't sharing her innermost secrets?

A waitress appeared, bringing welcome relief from Jillian's suddenly troubled thoughts.

They ordered, then Deedee propped her elbows on the table and folded her hands beneath her chin. Her short hair was a mass of silky, strawberry-blond curls, and her large brown eyes were sparkling with excitement.

Jillian laughed. "Okay, Mrs. Hamilton, tell all. You're about to wiggle right out of that chair."

"I took the plunge."

"You're getting married?" Jillian asked, all innocence.

Deedee wrinkled her freckle-dotted nose. "Good grief, no, I am *not* getting married, Ms. Jones-Jenkins, and you know it."

Jillian shrugged. "Just thought I'd ask. Tell me about your plunge."

"Well, you know how intrigued I am by rare books. I've collected more than two dozen over the years. It's not a lot, but enough to plunge.

"So, even as we speak, a craftsman is making me a special cupboard to hang on the wall behind the counter at the store. It will have wire-threaded glass, and will be kept locked. I'm going to start an advertising campaign to let it be known that Books and Books now buys and sells rare editions. I'm very excited."

''As well you should be. Oh, Deedee, that's marvelous. I know that dealing in rare books has been a dream of yours. Okay, this lunch is on me to celebrate the expanded service of Books and Books.''

''Hear, hear. Speaking of the store, your novels have been selling like hotcakes ever since the book-signing session. You've been so supportive over the years with your willingness to do an autograph party for each of your books as they came out.

''That, plus all the author friends you begged and-or threatened to get to do autographings, enabled me to launch my rare-book dream much sooner than I'd hoped.''

''It was my pleasure,'' Jillian said. ''All my writer friends were very impressed with your store, by the way. They'd all be happy to come again.''

''Thank you so much, Jillian.''

The waitress arrived at that moment with their meals, and they ate in silence for several minutes.

''I've talked enough about me,'' Deedee finally said. ''What have you been up to?''

''Oh,'' Jillian said, breezily, ''a little of this, a little of that.''

''Would you stop it?'' Deedee said. ''You're perfectly aware that I want to know if you made Forrest MacAllister The Project. You said you'd think about it, then went to the door to get a pizza.''

''Well, the pizza turned out to be Forrest.''

''What?''

Jillian explained how she'd made the dinner date with Forrest, but had been so exhausted she'd forgotten she'd done it. And, yes, yes, yes, nosy Deedee,

Forrest was The Project. The man needed an attitude adjustment, and she was making great progress on the subject of his working far too much.

"That brings you up to date," Jillian said.

"Not quite. What about you? You're the other half of the dates between you and Forrest. Do you like him?"

"Yes."

Deedee stared at her for a long moment.

"That's it?" she said finally. "Yes? Come on, Jillian, could I have some details, here?"

"No."

Deedee's eyes widened. "Oh, my gosh, you and Forrest are lovers."

"Did I say that? I certainly did not."

"Your crisp little answers speak volumes. Oh, Jillian, this is wonderful. Just how serious is your relationship with Forrest?"

"Whoa." Jillian leaned toward her. "There is *no* relationship, Deedee. He's The Project, remember?"

"Well, just because it started out like that doesn't mean—"

"Yes, it does," Jillian interrupted. "I don't want any part of a serious relationship. No commitment. Forrest is very aware of that."

"You've talked about it?"

"It's come up in conversation. I'm concentrating on reprogramming his mind about working too hard. That's what you and Andrea wanted me to do."

"Yes, we did. Yes, of course. But, Jillian, I know you. You don't engage in casual sex. Therefore, there are emotions involved...respect, caring, sharing. Correct?''

''Well, I... Yes, okay, correct.''

''Then how can you say you're not in a relationship with him? What button do you push to turn those emotions off at the end of your vacation? My darling friend, you're scaring me to death. Andrea and I were hoping that— Oh, Jillian, I don't want to see you get hurt. I don't want to see Forrest get hurt.''

''It won't happen. Trust me. So, yes, all right, things are sort of intense between us, and there *are* emotions involved, but Forrest and I realize we're poles apart in what we want in life. At the end of my vacation, I'll go back to work, and Forrest will ride off into the sunset. Meaning he'll go back to work, too. *No one is going to get hurt.*''

''Would you ladies care for some dessert?'' the waitress asked, appearing at the table.

''An aspirin,'' Deedee said, pressing one hand against her forehead. ''I have a roaring, stress headache.''

''Oh, good grief,'' Jillian muttered, rolling her eyes heavenward.

Hours later, Jillian stood in front of the full-length mirror in her bedroom, straightening a new bright-red sweater over the waistband of her jeans.

Forrest had suggested an evening at his apartment spent watching movies on the VCR and eating tons of buttery popcorn.

Fun, Jillian mused as she left the bedroom, and lazily perfect, due to the fact that she was exhausted from the afternoon of shopping. Deedee, thank goodness, had not brought up the subject of Forrest or The Project again, and they'd thoroughly enjoyed their spending spree.

Jillian had nodded in approval as she hung each purchase in the closet after staggering in with an armload of boxes and bags.

She and Forrest had agreed with no argument that they'd watch classic mysteries. Forrest was going to rent a stack on the way to pick her up, and all was well.

Just as Jillian came into the entry hall, the doorbell rang, producing an instant smile on her face. She opened the door, and Forrest entered, pushing the door closed with his foot. He took Jillian into his arms and kissed her.

Oh, yes, she thought dreamily, returning his ardor with total abandon. Hello, Forrest MacAllister.

The kiss deepened.

No one is going to get hurt.

The words she'd spoken with such conviction at lunch suddenly slammed against her mind.

Darn that Deedee, Jillian thought. She'd planted that niggling little seed of doubt. No. She wasn't going to fall prey to Deedee's lovable-but-unnecessary concern. She and Forrest were on the same wavelength regarding their relationship and knew it was *not* a relationship.

Forrest lifted his head. "Hello, Jillian. I missed you."

"You what?" she said, her eyes widening.

He released her and crossed his arms over his chest. "I missed you. I thought about you all day."

"Oh, well, that's nice," she said, managing a weak smile.

He'd missed her? Well, that was no big deal. She'd missed him, too, she supposed. When a person was looking forward to an event, they missed not being part of that event when it wasn't time yet for the event to begin. Did that make sense? Oh, heavens, she was scrambling her brain.

"Let's go," she said. "I have a craving for popcorn."

During the drive to his apartment, Forrest told Jillian he'd finished reading another of her novels. Jillian inwardly groaned, knowing there would be no way to keep him from talking at length about the book. She *really* didn't want to think about her work tonight, as it was connected to her vacation, which was connected to The Project. Oh, blast.

"The message is there again in the book," Forrest said. "Truth, trust. The hero courts the heroine, she agrees to marry him, off they go on their wedding trip in his fancy coach.

"But, shame on them, they've been keeping the truth from each other. He has to have an heir under the terms of his grandfather's will, and she needs money to pay back-taxes on the family home where her widowed mother and four siblings live. She figures she can squirrel away bucks from her wifely allowance."

"Yes, I know, Forrest," Jillian said wearily. "I wrote it."

"Time passes," he went on, as though she hadn't spoken, "and, bingo, they fall in love. But due to the wagging tongues of the *ton,* they discover the truth about why each married the other. They feel betrayed and used. Hell, they've *really hurt* the person they now love."

"Not exactly *really hurt,*" Jillian said. "I mean, okay, they were hurt, but not *really hurt,* with the emphasis you're putting on it. You make it sound as though they're bleeding to death."

"They are, in a way," he said, nodding. "They're emotionally bleeding. You, as the writer, made me feel their pain. Those two were in a world of hurt, Jillian."

"Don't say that," she snapped, then sighed. "I'm sorry. I didn't mean to bark at you. I guess I'm a little frazzled because I've been on the go all day. Once I put my feet up, relax, and start watching a movie, I'll be fine."

"And have popcorn," he said, smiling over at her.

"Yes, oodles of popcorn," she agreed absently.

No one is going to get hurt.

Oh, Jillian, please, she begged herself, shut up.

Two hours later, Forrest left the kitchen with another big bowl of popcorn, then stopped in the doorway of the living room.

He looked at Jillian curled up in the corner of his extra-long sofa, her eyes riveted on the television screen. His gaze swept over the room.

Jillian had said she liked his apartment and he had no reason to doubt her sincerity. He'd decorated in earth tones of brown, tan, and oatmeal, with accents of orange and yellow. The furniture was heavy, dark wood, giving the room a definite masculine aura.

There had been countless women in this room during the past, coming in and going out. But this was the first time he was so acutely aware that it felt incredibly *right* to have a woman in his home. Not just any woman—Jillian.

He had, to his own amazement and chagrin, counted down the hours of the seemingly endless day until finally it was time to pick up Jillian.

Since he'd awakened that morning her image had hovered constantly in his mind's eye. It was so vivid he felt he could reach out and gather her into his arms. When she'd opened the door of her house, he'd registered a sense of completeness, a mental sigh of relief that he was once again with Jillian.

MacAllister, he thought, get it together. Jillian was his Angels and Elves assignment, and he wasn't doing particularly well in changing her mind-set about work. He was caught up in the magic spell of the woman, instead of concentrating on the mission at hand.

Well, hell, that was easy to understand. Jillian was fantastic. She was intelligent, fascinating, fun, and had a great sense of humor. And when they made love, it was like nothing he'd experienced before. It was as though they were meshing their hearts, minds and souls, as well as their bodies.

But he *knew* they were looking for different things

from life. Jillian was adamant in her stand that she preferred to live alone, just as she was doing. The problem was, he just knew that she would view the future differently if she could put the ghosts of her past to rest.

Forrest frowned as he continued to stare at Jillian.

One of Jillian's major concerns had come across loud and clear in each of her novels he'd read so far—the importance of trust. That message was Jillian's voice, her beliefs and values. She had trusted him enough to tell him of her lonely childhood. She trusted him with her very essence each time they made love.

But there was a section of herself she protected. She hadn't shared her past pain, or the details of what had destroyed her brief marriage. He needed her to take that final step, he really did.

Before he could completely believe that Jillian wanted a solitary existence, wanted to concentrate almost totally on her work, he had to be convinced that the past wasn't dictating her future.

Why was he so determined that Jillian should trust him enough to reveal her ghosts? Of course, how else could he complete his assignment in the proper Angels and Elves manner if he didn't have all the data he needed? There, that made perfect sense.

"Hooray," Jillian said, clapping her hands. "They solved the mystery. I love it, I love it. The butler did it. Can you believe that, Forrest? The butler actually did it."

Forrest crossed the room and put the fresh batch of popcorn on the coffee table. Sitting down next to Jillian, he pressed the button on the remote control to rewind the movie.

"Let's take a break before we watch the next one," he said. "All right?"

"Sure," she said, reaching for a handful of popcorn. "You're a terrific popcorn popper, Forrest."

"That's good to know. If things get slow at the office, I can moonlight as a popcorn popper." He paused. "What did your husband do for a living?"

Jillian's head snapped up and she frowned as she met his gaze.

"Where did that come from?" she said, a slight edge in her voice.

He shrugged. "I was wondering, that's all."

"Why?"

"Because, Jillian, we are today the sum total of all we have been. You were married, but it didn't work out. It stands to reason that it was a painful time in your life. I've learned so much about you since we met. We've talked for hours. But that section of your life is closed off, kept behind a protective wall."

"I prefer not to discuss it."

"I realize that, but it leaves a piece of the marvelous puzzle that is you, now, missing. I don't know if this makes sense to you, but it's important to me." He continued to look directly into her eyes.

No, it didn't make sense, Jillian thought. Forrest was talking like a man who was in a committed relationship, wanting to know all and everything about the woman he loved. That wasn't remotely close to what they were together. He wanted love, marriage, a family. So what difference did it make if some of the pieces of Jillian—the puzzle, as he put it—were missing?

You're not being fair, Jillian, she admonished herself. She'd gathered her data about Forrest, found out what *she* needed to know before declaring him to be The Project. Who was she to stand in judgment of what details were important to him?

But, dear heaven, he was asking so much of her. She'd buried it all so deep, refused to allow the pain to touch her again. If she dragged it all out into the open, she'd feel stripped bare and vulnerable. She would be trusting Forrest with a raw wound that might never totally heal.

"Jillian?" he said quietly. Trust me. Ah, Jillian, please, trust me. "Will you tell me about it?"

She drew a shuddering breath. "Do you have any idea what you're asking of me?"

"Yes. I'm asking you to trust me."

"That's exactly it. That's the issue…trust."

"And truth, honesty, respect. Do you trust me, Jillian?"

Yes, her mind whispered.

There were no warring voices beating against her, no chilling doubts, no fear. There was simply a warm, peaceful, whispering word: *yes.*

"My husband was more than twenty years older than me," she said, her voice trembling slightly. "He was one of my college professors. Oh, I was so in love, or I believed I was at the time. I've since wondered if I wasn't seeking a father figure because I'd never had a close relationship with mine."

Forrest's heart thundered, and he was hardly breathing.

She was doing it, he mentally cheered. Jillian was trusting him with her innermost secret. She was giving him, at that very moment, a very special gift, and he would cherish it.

"I got pregnant," she said softly. "He…his name was Roger. He whisked me off and married me, moved me into his house, and that was that. It all happened so fast, I hardly had a chance to think. I continued in school, but two months later I lost the baby."

"Ah, Jillian, I'm sorry."

"I was terribly upset, really devastated, because I wanted that baby so very much." Sudden tears filled her eyes, and she blinked them away angrily. "Anyway, Roger shrugged off the miscarriage and refused to address my sorrow. I felt…I felt as alone as I had as a child. There was no one there for me. No one."

"What about your parents?"

"They never knew I was pregnant. I've never told them."

"Dear God, Jillian, why did you do that to yourself?"

"Because I'm the only one I can truly count on to be there for myself," she said, her voice rising. "That's how it is, how it's always been."

"No, I…"

"Yes! Roger continued on with his life as though he'd forgotten he had a wife. I never knew where he was, when he'd be home. Oh, he was attentive and charming when he showed up, but… One day I cut class because I had a bad cold. I came home and there was Roger in bed with a pretty coed. She was that year's model of the adoring student.''

Forrest swore under his breath.

"There was an awful scene," Jillian went on. "The girl was hysterical, said she was pregnant with Roger's child, demanded that I let him go so he could marry her, the woman he really loved.''

"What did the bastard say?" Forrest said, a muscle twitching in his jaw.

"It would almost have been funny if I hadn't been so shattered. He looked rather bemused, then calmly said that it was best if he married the girl because she was, after all, pregnant with his baby. Surely I understood, as he'd done the same for me. I divorced him.''

"Jillian..."

"So, there you have it," she said, lifting her chin. "Why you wanted that ugly puzzle piece, I don't know. I've trusted you with the whole nasty story, Forrest. I was young, naive and gullible. I was also very stupid. But I learned from that experience. Oh, yes, I certainly learned a great deal.''

Forrest moved closer to her and framed her face in his hands. "I'm sorry you went through that nightmare, Jillian. I'd turn back the clock and change history for you if I could, but I can't. All I can do is thank you for trusting me with your pain. I mean that sincerely. Thank you.''

"Well, it should make it clear to you why I don't want any part of marriage ever again. *Not ever.* I'm doing just fine with my life the way it's structured now. *I* don't need to implement any of the compromises I spoke of so that I don't have to work so hard. I like my schedule just as it is. You're the one who is due to make adjustments so you can have the family you want.

"We're doing fine, Forrest, you and I together, because we understand each other, and we realize that we simply want different things in the future. But for now, there's no problem."

Wrong, Forrest thought, capturing her lips with his. There was definitely a problem. Jillian's dragons from the past had to be slain before she could be free to have a future made up of more than just work.

His Angels and Elves assignment was becoming much more complicated than he'd anticipated, but he could handle it. He had to—for Jillian. It had nothing to do with him, really; Jillian deserved to have more in her life than she was allowing herself.

No, of course it didn't have anything to do with him, personally.

He was simply going to see his Angels and Elves assignment through to its proper end.

Eight

Early the next afternoon, Forrest telephoned Jillian to say he had to make an unexpected trip up the coast to San Francisco. The woman who had replaced Andrea at MacAllister Architects was to have made a presentation to a group of investors planning to build a large apartment complex. The woman was sick in bed with the flu, and Forrest was going in her place.

"Oh, I see," Jillian said, acutely aware of the wave of disappointment that swept through her.

Forrest chuckled. "Now don't start in on me about working while I'm supposed to be taking time off. This is a red-alert emergency."

"I understand that, I really do. How long will you be gone?"

"If everything goes as planned, I'll be back Wednesday afternoon. This is Monday, so...yes, I should be able to wind it up by then.'' He paused. ''I'll miss you, Jillian. That sounds too lightweight for how I'm feeling. I will *really* miss you.''

''I'll miss you, too. Listen, why don't I cook dinner for us Wednesday night? Don't expect fancy, because the few things I can make are very basic. I haven't poisoned myself so far, though.''

''That's comforting,'' he said, laughing. ''I accept your invitation to dinner. Take good care of yourself, Lady Jillian, and I'll see you as soon as I possibly can. Bye for now.''

''Goodbye, Forrest,'' she said, then replaced the receiver slowly, staring at it for a long moment before she moved away.

She wandered into the living room, sat down on the sofa, then got up again, too restless to sit still.

She felt rather…empty, she realized. As a writer she was accustomed to keeping her own company. It was emphasized at every writers' conference she'd ever attended that writing was a lonely profession, requiring the person to spend countless hours alone in order to achieve her goals. She had no problem with that. She liked herself, and the comfortable haven of her home.

No, she'd had no difficulty with the isolation of being an author.

Until now.

Until Forrest.

''Perdition.'' She halted her trek and pressed her hands to her cheeks.

What was happening to her? What was Forrest MacAllister doing to her?

She still found it hard to believe that she'd actually told Forrest the grim details of her disastrous marriage. She'd opened her mouth and the story had just spilled out. The unsettling part was that it had felt right, so good, to share it with him, and in the light of this new day she wasn't one bit sorry that she had. Why?

Jillian threw up her hands and continued to pace around the living room.

She didn't want Forrest to go to San Francisco. She wanted him here, with her. She didn't want to be alone, she wanted to be with Forrest. She didn't want to have to wait until Wednesday night to see him, she wanted to see him right now.

Oh, dear heaven, what did it all mean?

Jillian ordered herself to calm down. She needed to gather her data. She was on vacation, and during any other hiatus would be filling her idle hours with The Project. Since Forrest was The Project, it was perfectly reasonable that she would miss him, would feel incomplete because he wasn't there, and would be a tad lonely.

Thank goodness, she'd figured it out. For a moment there she'd panicked, thought perhaps her emotions had run roughshod over her common sense. Thought perhaps she'd done something as foolish as falling in love with Forrest MacAllister.

Well, that wasn't the case. She was under control, doing fine. She'd have to improvise for a couple of days, come up with miniprojects to tide her over until Forrest returned and resumed his role of The Project.

She would read, watch movies, plan the menu for

Wednesday night's dinner, then shop for the necessary groceries. She'd polish her fingernails, write a letter to her parents, go to Deedee's store and spend oodles of money on books, and wash her car.

All of that sounded as thrilling as having a root canal.

She wanted to be with Forrest!

"Jillian," she said, a warning tone in her voice, "knock it off, shape up, get it together. Now!"

Forrest once again found Andrea propped up against pillows on the sofa in her living room, her nose buried in a book. This time, however, his arrival produced a stormy glare from his sister, rather than a sunny smile.

"Having a bad hair day?" Forrest said pleasantly, sitting down in a chair he pulled next to the sofa.

"You've been avoiding me, Forrest MacAllister," Andrea said. "You haven't returned any of the messages I've left on your answering machine."

"I'm a busy man. I have places to go, people to see. I'm out of here in a minute, and on my way to San Francisco. But I came by to tell you not to have the twins while I'm gone because I'd miss out on The Baby Bet, and that would *not* please me. I'm the current champion of The Baby Bet, and I have my title to protect."

"You'd better protect your nose," she said, glowering, "because I feel like punching it. If it wasn't for Deedee, I wouldn't know that you're dating Jillian. You made her your Angels and Elves assignment and didn't even tell me, you rat."

Forrest snapped his fingers. "Slipped my mind."

"Forrest," Andrea said warningly.

"Don't stress, Andrea. It's not good for the munch-kins. I didn't tell you because you'd want details, details, details."

"Of course, silly man, how else am I to know what's happening?" She folded her hands over her enormous stomach. "Now then, tell all."

Forrest got to his feet. "Can't. Have to hit the road." He kissed her on the forehead. "Bye." He spun around and strode from the room.

"Oh, dear," Andrea said to the empty room, "what have Deedee and I done? She's afraid someone is going to end up with a broken heart because of this fiasco." She patted her stomach. "Your mommy should never have played Cupid, little ones. I'm going to feel terrible if Forrest or Jillian get hurt. Oh, dear, dear, dear."

Late that night, Forrest lay in bed in his hotel room in San Francisco, his hands laced beneath his head as he stared at the ceiling.

He'd called Jillian earlier and they'd had a nice chat. She'd sounded chipper, had told him that the day had flown by as she'd filled the hours with one activity after another, including washing her car. She missed him, of course, and hoped his trip would be a huge success. She'd see him Wednesday evening, and had said, "Good night, Forrest."

He had fully expected to drop off to sleep imme-diately after speaking with Jillian, but three hours had gone by and blissful slumber was remaining annoyingly elusive.

Jillian, Jillian, Jillian, he mused. He replayed the sad tale of her marriage, hearing the trembling of her voice, seeing the flickers of sorrow and pain in her expressive gray eyes.

He'd been consumed with rage directed toward the unfeeling Roger, and had registered the urge to track the jerk down and wring his insensitive neck.

It meant a lot to him, it really did, that Jillian had trusted him enough to tell him about her marriage. That trust was a precious gift he intended to cherish as the treasure it was.

So, where did he stand in his Angels and Elves assignment? Well, if by telling him about her past Jillian was able to put the ghosts to rest, then he was doing great.

She would be free to take a fresh look at the structure of her existence and to reevaluate her adamant "No way" regarding marriage and children.

Jillian married? To a man? Having that man's child? Making love with that man to conceive that baby?

"Damn," he said.

He didn't like that idea one iota. The thought of another man touching her, reaching for her in the night... No!

"Cool it, MacAllister," he said to the ceiling.

Okay, he was calm. Fine. The reason the image of some jerk being with Jillian was upsetting him was because *he,* Forrest MacAllister, was presently the one in Jillian's life *and* in her bed. His initial reaction didn't mean he'd gone off the deep end and fallen in love with her.

To fall in love with Jillian would be very, *very* foolish, as there was no guarantee that his Angels and Elves assignment would be a success. She could very well choose to continue her life exactly the way it was.

As for him? Well, he was registering a surge of hope that he just might be able to have the wife and children he yearned for. Jillian's fresh take on the subject was beginning to make sense. Compromise. Maybe, just maybe, his deepest wish could yet come true.

Forrest yawned, and minutes later he drifted off to sleep, dreaming of sailing ships.

Jillian peered into the oven, then closed the door with a loud bang.

"Oh, posh," she said, flinging out her arms. "Why aren't you cooking, chicken? You're just sitting there like a lump." She swept her gaze over the multitude of dials on top of the stove. "Aaak!" she yelled, smacking her hands onto the top of her head. "I didn't turn it on!"

She flipped the appropriate dial with more force than necessary, then burst into laughter.

When it came to cooking, she was a dud. She and Forrest were going to dine fashionably late. No, actually, they were going to dine so late they would be creating a whole new fashion of their own.

Why couldn't she get the hang of this cooking nonsense? It simply called for organization, planning, a sense of order where one thing led to the next. Those were all abilities she possessed whenever she was writing a book, so why didn't that knowledge follow her out of the office and into the kitchen?

"Beats me," she said, with a shrug. "Go for it, chicken," she added, giving the top of the stove a friendly pat.

As she walked toward the kitchen door, she suddenly stopped, a frown replacing her smile. With a sense of dread, she turned slowly to stare at the calendar that hung on the wall next to the telephone.

Time was passing so quickly, she thought, wrapping her hands around her elbows. There was less than a week left of her vacation, less than a week to be with Forrest.

She edged closer to the calendar, her eyes riveted on the numbered squares. A chill swept through her, causing her to tighten her hold on her arms.

In her mental vision, she saw herself in her large office, pouring over the multitude of reference books, making notes, carefully plotting her next novel. It was a familiar picture, as that room was where she spent the vast majority of her life.

And it suddenly appeared very empty, and very, *very* lonely.

"No," she whispered, feeling the ache of threatening tears in her throat, "no, it isn't lonely. It's my world. It's where I belong, where I'm content. Safe." She took a shuddering breath.

On trembling legs she went to the table, sinking onto one of the chairs.

In her mind's eye she saw Forrest—smiling, talking, then looking at her with an intense message of desire radiating from his beautiful brown eyes. Heat swirled within her as she relived the lovemaking they'd shared; her breasts grew heavy, aching for the exquisite touch of Forrest's hands, the sensuality of his mouth savoring her soft flesh.

She saw him in her bed, naked and bronzed; so powerful, his strength tempered with infinite gentleness. She saw him in the shower, in the kitchen making coffee, eating pizza in front of the roaring fire in the hearth. She saw him in the ballroom where they'd danced, then decked out in Western clothes at the concert, and at the helm of the cabin cruiser.

Then she saw him walking away, out of her life, not looking back as he left.

"Oh, Forrest, please, no," she said, tears misting her eyes.

In the next instant, she got to her feet, lifted her chin, and stomped out of the kitchen.

She was being ridiculous, she fumed, heading for her bedroom. She *knew* Forrest was in her life temporarily. He was The Project, for heaven's sake. The Project was always over at the end of her two-week vacation. Just because he had the added title of being an Angels and Elves assignment, didn't mean the time allowed would be extended.

There was less than one week left to be with Forrest.

She knew that.

"So, get a grip, Jillian," she told herself. "You're behaving like an idiot."

Yes, she cared for Forrest, she truly did, and she

would miss him for a while after he was gone. But she wasn't in love with him, for crying out loud. She wouldn't do something as stupid as falling in love with the man. No, absolutely not.

In her room she changed clothes, donning a full-length Indian-print caftan she'd bought during her shopping spree with Deedee. After brushing her hair, she checked her makeup, sprayed on a floral cologne, then sank onto the side of the bed.

Shadows from the past suddenly crept over her, encasing her in a dark cocoon of memories that began to take the form of hideous, near-human entities, each with a name.

Pain. Betrayal. Disillusionment. Vulnerability. Abandonment. Loneliness.

They were all there, taunting her with hollow, cruel voices that grew louder in a maddening cadence. They were spawned by love, by loving, by having placed her heart in the hands of another.

No! She wouldn't do it, not ever again! There was no way on earth that she would allow herself to fall in love with Forrest. He would not be given that kind of power and control.

Her work, her writing, was her focus and the essence of who she was. It required her complete attention and dedication. There wasn't room for anything else. No space for distractions or temptations that would lure her away and destroy the career to which she'd dedicated herself.

The doorbell chimed, and Jillian jerked in surprise at the sudden intrusion into her tangled thoughts. She went to the mirror, scrutinizing herself critically for any signs of turmoil or stress that would cause Forrest to question her.

She appeared perfectly normal, she decided, then hurried from the room.

The bell rang again before Jillian reached the entryway, and she quickened her step even more. When she opened the door, all rational thought fled.

"Forrest," she whispered.

"Jillian."

Forrest closed the door behind him, then swept her into his arms, his mouth capturing hers, parting her lips; his tongue seeking and finding hers in the sweet darkness.

Jillian flung her arms around his neck and molded her body to his, returning in kind the hungry, urgent force of the kiss. Her breasts were crushed to the hard wall of his chest, and she felt and savored the pressure of his arousal, heavy against her.

. This was Forrest, her mind hummed. Forrest was here. She'd missed him terribly, and was so very glad he was back.

Forrest lifted his head to meet her gaze, but didn't release her. He drew a rough breath before he attempted to speak.

"Lord, I missed you," he said, then brushed his lips over hers.

"I missed you, too."

"I swear, Jillian, never before have floor plans, bathroom designs and square footage seemed like such ridiculous subjects to be pitching to a roomful of megabucks boys. All I could think about was getting out of there and coming home to you."

Jillian's heart skipped a beat.

Coming home to you.

Home.

Jillian, don't, she admonished herself. Forrest hadn't meant that the way it sounded. This was *her* home, not his, not theirs. This was where she lived—alone.

"Did you get the job?" she asked.

"Yep. The contract is signed, sealed, and delivered." He stared into space and sniffed the air. "Either you have a new and unusual cologne, or I smell the delicious scent of baking chicken."

Jillian laughed and stepped back, instantly wishing she was still nestled close to him.

"The aroma of that chicken is all you're going to get for a while," she said, smiling. "I'm officially declaring myself a disaster as a cook. I forgot to turn on the oven. We're going to dine—check that fancy jargon—very late. Come in by the fire. I can at least offer you a drink and some cheese and crackers."

"Sold," he said, putting one arm around her shoulders. "I really like that dress you're wearing. I suppose it has a fancier title than 'dress.'"

"Close enough," she said, as they went into the living room. "You're rather spiffy yourself, sir."

He was gorgeous, she mused. Wearing black slacks and a burgundy sweater that was the exact shade of one of the multitude of colors in her caftan, Forrest looked fabulous. *They* looked fabulous, together.

"Wine, cheese, and crackers?" she said, remaining standing as Forrest sat down on the sofa.

"Great. Do you need some help?"

"No, I'm your official hostess this evening."

"Then you're supposed to say, 'Coffee, tea, or me?' That's the rules of hostessdom."

Jillian laughed as she started toward the kitchen.

Forrest watched her go, filling his senses with the sight of her, her aroma of flowers, the way she'd felt in his arms, the remembrance of the honey-sweet taste of her mouth, the sound of her wind-chime laughter.

Just as Jillian returned carrying a tray, the telephone rang. She hesitated a moment, undecided whether to hurry back to the kitchen, or answer the telephone on the end table by the sofa.

"Would you get that, Forrest?" she finally asked.

He picked up the receiver. "Hello, you've reached the Jones-Jenkins residence."

"Oh, good grief." Jillian rolled her eyes heavenward.

She set the tray on a small table, then moved it in front of the sofa. Looking at Forrest, she frowned as she realized he was ramrod stiff and was now sitting on the edge of the cushion.

"Forrest?" she said. "What is it?"

"You're sure, you're really sure?" he said, into the receiver. "She's had a couple of false alarms, Michael. I know she felt it was different this time. That's why I gave you the telephone number here.... The doctor said that...? Oh, Lord, this is it." He lunged to his feet, nearly yanking the base of the telephone from the table. "You and Jenny are going over there now...? I am *not* repeating everything you say like a damn parrot... Of course, I'm coming. Quit bugging me, will you, so I can get moving!'' He slammed the receiver back into place.

''Forrest?'' Jillian said again.

''Stay calm, MacAllister,'' he muttered. ''You'll drive into a tree if you don't get it together.''

''Forrest MacAllister!'' Jillian yelled. ''Would you talk to me?''

''Oh,'' he said, jerking in surprise at her outburst. ''Sorry. It's Andrea. She and John are at the hospital, and the doctor says this is it. That was Michael on the phone. The doc said the babies are only a couple of weeks early, so that's good. That's good. Michael and Jenny are leaving for the hospital now.'' He grabbed Jillian's hand. ''Come on. We've got to get over there.''

''You want me to come with you?''

He frowned. ''Don't you want to?''

''Yes, of course I do, but this is a family event, Forrest. I'm not certain that it would be appropriate for me to intrude. I mean, I'm Andrea's friend, but—''

''Jillian, trust me, it's fine. I imagine Deedee will be there too.''

''Well, if you're sure. Let's see. The safety screen is in front of the fire, and— Oh, the chicken. I've got to turn the oven off.''

''I'm sorry about the dinner,'' he said, as she started toward the kitchen.

''Don't be. It wasn't exactly going to be a gourmet delight, anyway. I need to grab a shawl, then we're off and running.''

She returned in a few minutes and frowned as she looked at Forrest.

"You're so serious," she said. "Are you worried about Andrea?"

"Yeah, I guess I am. You'd think I'd be cool, considering I've been through this routine with Jenny and Michael. Maybe it's one of those things a person can't ever become casual about. I'd probably pass out cold on my face if it was *my* wife, having *my* baby. Oh, man, I'd never hear the end of that from my family. Okay, let's hit the road."

The drive to the hospital was made in silence as Forrest concentrated on the traffic with more intensity than usual, due to the fact that he was driving far above the speed limit.

Jillian welcomed the mental solitude, using the time to attempt to sift and sort through the maze in her mind.

When Forrest had spoken of *his* wife, having *his* baby, she'd had a vision, to her astonishment and dismay, of that woman being her. As he'd said the words, the image had clicked into place as naturally as breathing. Forcing it away, pushing it from her mind, had not been an easy task.

Why had that happened? She *knew* she didn't wish to ever marry again. She *knew* that. She was also very aware that she had made a career choice that allowed no room for a husband and children.

Well, yes, she was acquainted with many successful authors who combined their writing with a family. But her methods for completing a novel were etched in stone, were the way she had to do it to achieve her goals.

If she made the foolish mistake of falling in love with Forrest MacAllister, it was not going to erase her past or the course she had set for her future.

And that was that.

But as she realized she was about to meet Forrest's entire family and be swept up in the excitement of the soon-to-arrive babies, she wished she'd stayed at home with her stupid, half-baked chicken.

Jillian's apprehensions regarding having accompanied Forrest to the hospital were forgotten within moments of entering the waiting room.

When Forrest introduced her to everyone, she was received with such warmth that she felt as though she'd known the boisterous MacAllister clan for a very long time.

The sons had obviously inherited their height and physiques from their father, Robert, who was still nicely built, with no evidence of a middle-age paunch in sight. His hair was thick and gray, and his smile a delightful carbon copy of Forrest's, Michael's and Ryan's. Ryan's wife, Sherry, was a nurse on duty at another hospital across town.

Margaret MacAllister, Forrest's mother, had a twinkle in her brown eyes, and a smile that lit up her entire face. Her hair was graying, but still had hints of rich auburn, and was attractively styled in a cap of soft curls.

She appeared small and delicate next to the tall, broad-shouldered men of her family, but Jillian knew from the enchanting stories Forrest had told her, that Margaret MacAllister was a force to be reckoned with.

Michael's wife, Jenny, was a stunning blonde, who would make heads turn wherever she went. Yet, Jillian realized, Jenny was natural and at ease with her own beauty. Her friendly smile was genuine.

Also present was a smiling Deedee, who waggled her fingers at Jillian from across the room.

Jillian was also introduced to Ted Sharpe, Ryan's partner on the police force. Ted was tall, blond, tanned, and had the bluest eyes Jillian had ever seen. Ryan and Ted, she mentally decided, should pose for police-academy recruiting posters.

Her gaze swept over the group, lingering on the MacAllisters.

This was Forrest's family—a *real* family, the kind she'd fantasized about having during the years she was a lonely child. They'd all gathered together as a supportive unit for Andrea and John. The babies who would soon come into the world would be received into the embrace of these people, and loved unconditionally for all time.

How blessed they all were. But she could sense, feel, that they all knew that.

"Sit, sit," Margaret said, flapping her hands. "Our little darlings aren't going to be born any quicker by us standing around."

Everyone immediately sat down, causing Jillian to smile as she witnessed Margaret in action.

"I'm taking the bets, Forrest," Michael said. "I've got it covered. Two girls, two boys, one of each, girl born first, boy born first, firstborn weighs more, second born weighs more. Take your pick, and give me twenty bucks.''

"Don't rush me, here. As The Baby Bet champion, I intend to give this the serious consideration it deserves.'' Forrest stared at the ceiling. A few minutes later, he took out his wallet and handed Michael the money. ''Boy and a girl. Boy first and weighs more.''

Michael wrote on a piece of paper. ''Got it.''

"Enjoy your champion status while you have it, Forrest,'' Ted said. ''I'm going to clean your clock. Two boys. Second one is heavier.''

"Dream on, Sharpe,'' Forrest said, grinning. ''You are looking at the pro.'' He paused. ''Anyone seen John? How's the daddy-to-be holding up?''

"Nope, haven't seen him,'' Robert said. ''He's in the labor room with Andrea. He plans on being in the delivery room, too. We weren't allowed to do that in my day. Thank goodness.''

Margaret patted her husband's knee. ''You could have handled it, dear.''

"That's not a bet I would have put twenty dollars on,'' Robert said, chuckling. ''Well, I'm glad John is with our little girl. Andrea may be John's wife, but she'll always be my baby daughter, too.''

"Of course she is,'' Margaret said, then kissed him on the cheek. ''That's just the way it is.''

Not for everyone, Jillian thought. No, not for everyone.

"I enjoy your books immensely, Jillian,'' Margaret said. ''I can't even imagine how hard you must work to produce a novel. The image of an author most of us have is a life of glitz and glamour, fame and fortune. I have a feeling it's just honest, hard work."

"Yes," Jillian said, looking at her in surprise, "it is. It takes a great deal of self-discipline and many, many hours of solitude."

"Solitude?" Jenny said, laughing. "I vaguely remember that. When you're chasing a toddler all day, solitude is hard to come by. Our Bobby is a busy boy."

The conversation continued with Michael relating the latest activities of his and Jenny's son, Robert, commenting on the fact that Bobby was brilliant beyond his years, and Forrest saying that Bobby inherited his intelligence from Jenny.

Jillian only half listened, as her own words spoken a few minutes before beat against her mind.

Solitude.

It was a given, an understood element in her life that made it possible for her to continue to produce her books on schedule. She didn't question it, nor resent it. For many years now, it had been a fact, a part of her day-to-day existence.

But on this night, sitting there surrounded by the MacAllisters and their friends, with Forrest's arm around her shoulders, the word *solitude* was taking on new and ominous connotations. It seemed to be growing steadily, as though it was suddenly a living entity, getting bigger and darker like a threatening force.

As it grew it took on a new identity.

Its name was Loneliness.

Jillian shivered.

"Are you cold?" Forrest said. "Would you like me to put your shawl around you?"

"What? Oh, no, I'm fine," she said, managing to smile.

"I'm hungry," Michael said.

"You're always hungry," Jenny said.

"Amen to that," Robert said. "I hope for the sake of your budget that Bobby didn't inherit your appetite."

"He did," Michael said. "I need a raise."

"Forget it," Forrest said. "Ryan, I assume you called Sherry?"

"Yep," Ryan said. "They'll page her when I have something to report. She sure would like to be here, though."

"Well, it just can't be helped," Margaret said. "The whole family is here in spirit, and Andrea and John know that."

Dear heaven, Jillian thought, she was going to cry in a minute if she didn't get herself together. She'd just never been a part of anything like this—not in her entire life. It was so beautiful, so incredibly beautiful.

A nurse entered the room and everyone got quickly to their feet.

"Just an update, folks," the nurse said. "We're on our way to the delivery room. Those little ones are eager to greet the world. Andrea is doing splendidly. John is a bit gray around the edges, but he's hanging right in there. It won't be long now." She hurried out of the room.

"Lord—" Forrest pressed one hand to his stomach "—this stuff is so damn scary."

"Oh, yeah?" Michael said. "Wait until you're the one in the weird green clothes, taking part up close and personal. That, my little brother, is terror in its purest form."

Forrest nodded. "Yes, I bet it is, but I'd be there every step of the way." He tightened his hold on Jillian's shoulders. "Count on it."

Nine

Forrest won The Baby Bet.

When John appeared in the waiting room in his green garb, Jillian instantly cataloged him in her mind as being tall, good-looking, and very proud. The smile that lit up his face erased the fatigue and strain that had been visible when he first entered the room.

"A boy," he said, beaming, "and a girl. Andrea was fantastic. Absolutely fantastic. She was a lot braver than I was, I can tell you that. She's fine. Exhausted but happy."

"Halt!" Michael said. "Who was born first? Your son, or your daughter?"

"Our son," John said, obviously confused by the question. "Why?"

Michael consulted the piece of paper he held in his hand. "Check. Okay, how much did they weigh?"

"Oh, I get it," John said. "You're doing The Baby Bet bit. Let's see, Forrest is the current champion. Right? Well, here goes. John Matthew, to be called Matt to avoid the two Johns mix-ups, weighed five pounds, eight ounces. Andrea Noel, to be called Noel because Christmas is a very special family celebration, and to avoid the two Andreas mix-ups—"

"John!" Michael said.

"Weighed five pounds," he said, then paused and frowned. "Does my memory fail me?"

"Not if you want to live to tell about it," Michael said.

John chuckled. "Four ounces."

"Yes!" Forrest punched one fist in the air. "I'm still The Baby Bet champion. Man, I'm so great at this, it blows my mind. Pay," he added, waggling his fingers as he extended his hand to Michael.

"Damn." Michael slapped the money into Forrest's hand. "Twice in a row. It's a good thing I know this stuff can't be set up ahead of time."

"Now that that's out of the way," Margaret said, "I intend to hug the new daddy. Come here, John. Robert and I are so thrilled."

"You're sure Andrea's fine?" Robert said, as Margaret hugged John.

"She's great," John said. "She'll be taken to her room in a few minutes."

Jenny hugged John. Then Forrest, Michael, Ryan and Ted shook his hand.

"John," Forrest said, "this is Jillian Jones-Jenkins. She came along to keep me calm, cool and collected through this harrowing ordeal."

"Hello, John," Jillian said, smiling, "and congratulations to you and Andrea. A son and a daughter. What a wonderful family you have."

"Thank you," John said. "I don't think I can really express how I'm feeling right now. It's just...well, bigger than I can find words to explain." He cocked his head slightly. "Words. You're Andrea's writer friend. I thought you looked familiar. I've seen your photograph on the back of a whole stack of your books that Andrea has. She's been wanting me to meet you. Hey, I'll be able to tell the twins that a famous writer was here the night they were born."

Jillian laughed. "Well, the 'famous' is stretching it a bit."

"No, it's not," John said. "The thing is, why are you with a dud like Forrest?"

"I was wondering about that myself," Ted said thoughtfully.

"Now, wait just a damn minute," Forrest said.

"Hush, all of you," Margaret said. "Don't get started on your usual nonsense. What I want to know is when we can see the babies?"

"And Andrea," Robert said. "I want to say hello to my girl."

"I'm sorry, Robert," John said, "but you can't see Andrea tonight. Once she's settled in her room, they said I could come in for two seconds to kiss her goodnight, but then she's supposed to sleep. As for the babies, I'll go check." He spun around and left the room.

Ryan slid a quick glance at his mother, then leaned

toward Jillian. "Forrest really *is* a dud, Jillian," he whispered.

"Ryan Robert," Margaret said, "this is not the time or place to discuss the fact that Forrest is a dud."

"You're agreeing with him?" Forrest said. "What kind of a mother are you? I am *not* a dud."

"Of course, you're not," she said, patting him on the cheek.

"Mothers are prejudiced," Robert said.

"Jillian," Forrest said, "the next time you count your blessings, put being an only child at the very top of your list."

Everyone laughed, then stared at the doorway, watching for John's return.

Oh, she adored this family, Jillian mused. There was so much love and warmth weaving back and forth between them. A stranger passing by that room and hearing the banter might draw the conclusion that these people were at odds with each other and someone was close to being decked.

But she knew better as she stood in their midst. They were wonderful. No, being an only child wasn't one of her blessings to be counted.

"Ladies and gentlemen and Forrest," John announced from the doorway, "John Matthew and Andrea Noel are now receiving visitors. Follow me."

As they all went down the hallway, Jillian felt the increased tempo of her heart as she eagerly anticipated her first glimpse of the twins.

She had not, she realized, ever seen a newborn baby up close. When she'd visited friends to take a gift for a new addition, she'd always waited several weeks before going, having decided there was enough confusion in that household early on.

Andrea and John's babies were not even an hour old. What would they look like? Would they be sleeping? Crying? Would they—

Suddenly, there they were.

Behind a large window, a nurse stood close to the glass, a pink blanket-wrapped bundle tucked in the crook of one arm, a blue bundle in the other. A buzz of comments erupted from the group, but Jillian heard only a faint hum of voices far in the distance.

Her gaze was riveted on the babies. They both had skin the shade of a peach at perfection, and caps of silky, auburn hair. Matthew was crying, his tiny fists flailing in the air, emphasizing his displeasure over an unknown something. Noel was sleeping, delicate lashes fanning her cheeks.

Dear heaven, Jillian thought, aware of threatening tears, they were beautiful. They were miracles. Oh, how she wanted to reach out her arms and hold them, cuddle them, feel their little bodies nestled against her breasts.

It had been so many years since she'd allowed herself to think about the baby she'd lost. She'd buried the pain, the sense of emptiness, deep within her, refusing to acknowledge it. Along with Roger's betrayal, she'd refused to address her yearning for the child who had never been born.

But now? There was nowhere to hide from the memories. A baby. Oh, God, she wanted a baby. She wanted to have *Forrest's* baby.

"Jillian?" Forrest said quietly. "Hey, are you all right?"

"What?" She snapped her head up to look at him. "Oh, yes, of course, I'm fine. It's just that... What I mean is..." She tore her gaze from Forrest's and turned to John. "They're wonderful, John, absolutely beautiful."

"Yes," he said, then was unable to speak further as he was overcome with emotion.

Forrest frowned as he stared at Jillian.

What was she thinking? he wondered. What was going on in that complicated, fascinating mind of hers? He sure as hell knew what *he* was thinking. He wanted to marry Jillian Jones-Jenkins *now,* make a commitment with her and to her *now,* create the miracle that would be their child *now.* He wanted it all.

Because he was in love with Jillian Jones-Jenkins.

During the drive back to Jillian's, for reasons he himself didn't understand, Forrest chattered nonstop, relating the tale of how Andrea had met John.

Forrest and Andrea were to have a luncheon meeting with a prospective client, John, who was in need of landscaping for a rental property he had purchased as an investment. He also wished to have an addition built onto the house to increase its value. He was considering hiring MacAllister Architects, since they were equipped to handle both of his needs.

Forrest had drawn up plans for the new room, and Andrea had prepared several proposals for the landscaping. Andrea and Forrest were to arrive at the restaurant in separate vehicles because Andrea had an earlier appointment.

Everything was fine and dandy, Forrest went on, except for the fact that it was raining cats and dogs. He'd met John at the designated time, but there was no sign of Andrea.

"Where was she?" Jillian said, having to force herself to pay attention to the tale.

"Changing a flat tire. Oh, man, you should have seen her when she came into that swanky restaurant." He chuckled and shook his head at the remembered images. "She was soaked to the skin, splattered with mud, and her shoes were squishing with every sloppy step she took. She looked like a drowned rat, a total wreck. Lord, she was a mess. Believe me, if I had known the word at the time, I would have yelled 'Perdition!' at the top of my lungs."

"Oh, my goodness," Jillian said, smiling. "Then what happened?"

"Andrea," Forrest related, "sat down just as calm as you please and made her presentation as though there wasn't a thing wrong with her appearance. She simply ignored the sound of the water from her clothes dripping steadily onto the floor with a maddening cadence. John was not only impressed with Andrea's expertise as a landscape architect, but also with Andrea, herself, and her unbelievable performance. True love, as well as landscaping, was in bloom.

"And they're in the process of living happily ever after," Forrest said. "Yep, just like in one of your books."

He slid a quick glance at Jillian. Lord, how he loved her. He was honest-to-goodness in love! He was, he guessed, talking a blue streak because his mind was a mess, a tangled maze. He was in love for the first time in his life, and he had no idea if he was ecstatic or terrified.

Why? Because he didn't know if Jillian loved *him*. Oh, man, he was heading for a nervous breakdown, no doubt about it.

"Jenny and Michael are happy little lovebirds, too," he blathered on. "As a matter of fact, so are Sherry and Ryan, *and* my parents. Yes, sir, there's a lot of that happy-ending stuff going around in the *real* world, as well as in your novels."

"Your family," Jillian said quietly, "is a lovely exception to the general rule."

"No, I don't believe that, Jillian. The gloom-and-doomers get a charge out of spouting endless statistics about the soaring divorce rate, but there are a multitude of happily married people in this world."

Easy, MacAllister, he mentally warned himself. Be very careful.

"I realize that you had a marriage that caused you a great deal of pain and disillusionment, Jillian, but that's all in the past. If you allow it to determine your attitude in the present, you could miss out on something rare, something special. Know what I mean?"

As Forrest spoke, dark visions from the past flashed before Jillian's eyes, causing a chill to shimmer through her.

Forrest was preaching at her, she thought angrily, about something of which he knew nothing. How easy it was for someone who had never experienced the horror of betrayal, of divorce, to say 'Hey, forget it. That was then, this is now. Go for the gusto in the present.' Well, it wasn't that simple, damn it.

Besides, even if she *had* managed to escape from the painful ghosts, it wouldn't erase the fact that her work was her focus now. She didn't have time for romance, a committed relationship, a husband and family.

But, oh, those babies, those beautiful, precious twins. Such yearning they'd evoked in her, such aching desire to have a child, Forrest's child. A baby fathered by the man she loved with every breath in her body.

Jillian blinked. What? The man she what? Oh, no. No, no, no. She was in love with Forrest MacAllister? How could she have allowed that to happen? She didn't want to be in love. But she was. Oh, yes, she was deeply in love with Forrest.

"Hello?" Forrest said. "Are you awake over there?"

"What? Oh, I was thinking that I might dedicate my next book to the twins, because I feel very honored to have been there tonight when they were born."

Perdition! Forrest fumed. He hadn't even dented Jillian's protective walls with his gushing report of marital bliss and happy endings. Jillian's dragons were mighty tough dudes to slay.

"Gear up, MacAllister," he muttered.

"Pardon me?"

"Nothing. There's your house up ahead. We have

the sad task awaiting us of pronouncing your chicken officially dead.''

Jillian stared at the house as they drove closer, then turned into the driveway.

Her haven, her safe place, suddenly appeared too big, too empty. In a few short days, she would be back in her office working—alone. She'd spend the nights—alone. She'd exist in the world she'd created for herself—alone. Without Forrest. Oh, dear heaven, without Forrest MacAllister.

When they entered the house, a wave of despair and loneliness swept through Jillian with such bone-chilling intensity that she staggered slightly from the impact. She flung herself into Forrest's arms. He instinctively wrapped his arms around her, surprise evident on his face.

''Make love to me, Forrest,'' Jillian said, her voice trembling. ''Please.''

He frowned. ''That's not a request I'm about to deny, but… Jillian, what's wrong? You're obviously upset about something. Let's talk about it. Okay?''

''No. No, I don't want to talk.''

As Forrest opened his mouth to protest further, Jillian stood on tiptoe and captured his lips with her own, her tongue delving into his mouth to seek and find his. She molded her body to his, crushing her breasts to his chest, feeling his arousal surge against her.

She didn't want to talk, her mind hammered. She didn't want to think. She wished only to feel, fill her senses and the essence of herself with Forrest, savoring all that he was.

Forrest had a fleeting image in his mind of noble Roman tapping him on the shoulder, telling him that this damsel was in distress, that a serious discussion was in order.

But as Jillian sank her fingers into his hair and urged his mouth harder onto hers, Forrest mentally told Roman to take a flying leap off the highest mast of his sailing ship.

Jillian wanted him, Forrest thought hazily, and heaven knew he wanted her. He was on fire, burning with a desire for her that was never, ever, fully extinguished. It smoldered, waiting to be fanned into leaping flames of passion that consumed him with need.

He tore his lips from Jillian's, lifted her into his arms, and carried her down the hall to her bedroom. Setting her on her feet next to the bed, he snapped on the small lamp on the nightstand, flung back the bed linens, then drew her into his embrace once more.

His mouth melted over hers, and the kiss was searing, nearly rough in its intensity. Tongues met, dueled, danced, stroked in a sensual rhythm. Forrest raised his head only long enough to take a sharp breath, then slanted his mouth the other way, drinking in Jillian's sweet taste. She trembled in his arms.

When he gathered handfuls of the material of her caftan, she broke the kiss and shook her head, taking a step backward.

Forrest frowned for a moment, then understood her intentions as she quickly removed the caftan herself, dropping it to the floor. As she continued to shed her clothing, he removed his own. Their eager hands then reached for each other, and they tumbled onto the bed.

Hands, lips and tongues explored—caressing, kissing, tasting, discovering what they had known before but was now somehow new and wondrous.

Whispers and whimpers and moans of pleasure, accompanied by the tantalizing pain of need, escaped from their lips, neither knowing which of them had made the passion-laden sounds.

As Forrest drew the soft flesh of one of her breasts deep into his mouth, Jillian gripped his shoulders tightly, closing her eyes to focus inwardly, not wishing to miss one precious sensation, one lick of the heated flames sweeping through her. The steady pull of Forrest's mouth on her breast was matched by a pulsing tempo deep within her.

He left her breast to reclaim her mouth, then moved over her at last, entering her, thrusting fully into her, bringing to her all that he was.

She gasped as he suddenly slid his arms around her back and rolled over, taking her with him. She moved slowly, tentatively upward, her hands sliding through the moist curls on his muscled chest, her knees on either side of his narrow hips.

Their eyes met, mirroring desire in smoky hues, and then the rhythm began. Forrest grasped her waist, nearly encircling it with his large hands, raising his body to meet each pounding motion.

Exquisite tension coiled within them, tighter and hotter, bringing them closer and closer to the final ecstasy. They each held back by sheer force of will; waiting, anticipating.

And then...

"Forrest!"

Jillian threw her head back, calling his name again, then yet again. He lifted his hips one last time and found his own release, a moan rumbling deep in his chest. Each wave of sensation that rocketed through them carried them higher, delivering them to a glorious place where they could only travel together.

A soft sob escaped from Jillian's lips, then she fell forward to be caught tightly against Forrest's chest by his waiting arms. She shifted her legs to the tops of his, and buried her face in the crook of his neck.

Neither spoke. The haze slowly dissipated as their heated bodies cooled and heartbeats quieted.

"Jillian," Forrest finally said, his voice still gritty with passion.

"Hmm?" she said, not moving.

"I love you."

As he felt Jillian stiffen in his arms, Forrest silently cursed, calling himself seven kinds of fool for allowing his emotions to override his good sense.

But in the next moment, he was aware and surprised as his anger shifted in another direction.

Damn it, he thought, he was the other half of this pair, of Jillian Jones-Jenkins and Forrest MacAllister, together. He had wants, needs, emotions. He had dreams and goals. Not everything could, or should, be geared solely to Jillian's mind-set, *her* emotional timetable.

Yes, there were dragons from Jillian's past to slay, but they could fight them together, united as one unbeatable force. There was a time to keep silent, but the moment had come to speak, to declare his love, to be open and honest about the depth of his feelings. Or...or was he making a terrible mistake?

"Jillian?"

"No," she whispered.

Forrest lifted her off him and nestled her close to his side. He placed one finger beneath her chin and lifted her face, forcing her to meet his gaze.

"Listen to me," he said gently.

"Forrest, no, I—"

"Shh," he interrupted. "Please, just hear me out." He paused and moved his hand to her cheek. "I do love you, Jillian. I know without hearing you say the words that my declaration of love frightens you because of what happened to you in the past. I'm not expecting you to say you love me in return. I *do* believe that you care deeply for me, might even love me. But, to admit that your feelings match mine would form a bond, a commitment, take a step toward a future that you're not prepared to make yet.

"Jillian, do something for me tonight, all right? *Don't say anything.* Just think about what I've told you, knowing it's the truth, that it's honest and real. Think about the fact that from the very beginning, we did *not* have sex, we made love. *Made love,* Jillian. Far more beautiful and intimate, special and rare, than anything I, and hopefully you, have ever experienced before. Think about what you felt as you saw the miracles, the babies that were born tonight, knowing that *our* miracle—the child we would create—is within our reality. Just think and feel."

He kissed her on the forehead. "Good night, Lady Jillian."

Forrest left the bed, dressed quickly and walked out of the room, not looking at her again.

Through the mist of tears filling her eyes, Jillian watched him go, then she buried her face in the pillow and wept, the sobs nearly choking her as tears streamed down her face.

Having no idea how much time had passed, she finally rolled onto her back and pressed the heels of her hands to her now throbbing temples. She drew a shuddering breath, then sighed—a very sad-sounding sigh.

All that she'd accomplished with her wailing, she thought dismally, was to produce a roaring headache. She had to think, sort, sift, deal with all that had happened.

I do love you, Jillian.

"Oh-h-h," she moaned, feeling fresh tears threatening to spill over.

Forrest MacAllister loved her, was *in* love with her. He had, in a roundabout way, said he wanted to marry her, make her his wife, his partner in life, and create the miracle that would be their baby.

Forrest MacAllister loved her, and she loved him in kind.

It was glorious.

No, no, no! It was terrible, a disaster, a frightening scenario in which she could not, would not, take part.

She would *not* tell Forrest that she loved him.

She would *not* place her heart in his hands for safekeeping, thus rendering herself totally vulnerable.

She would *not* give up the career she'd worked so hard for, and that was a part of who she was.

The price tag for loving Forrest MacAllister was far too high, and more than she was prepared to pay.

Jillian flopped back over onto her stomach, and gave the pillow a solid whack.

"Perdition, Forrest," she said aloud, "why didn't you just stay being The Project, like you were supposed to? You gummed up the whole program."

And so had she, because she'd fallen deeply in love with him.

But he would never know the truth, never know that when he was gone, her heart was going to shatter into a million pieces.

Andrea sat propped up in the hospital bed, a smile of delight on her face as she looked at the two huge teddy bears sitting at the foot of the bed. One was pink, the other blue, and they were grinning to beat the band.

"The bears are wonderful, Forrest," she said. "They're as big as two-year-old children, so they'll have to be decorations in the nursery until the twins are older."

"At least they won't eat you out of house and home," Forrest said, settling onto the chair next to the bed.

"Since you're here at three in the afternoon," Andrea said, "I assume you're still on vacation from the ever-famous MacAllister Architects, Incorporated."

Forrest nodded.

"Speaking of famous," she went on, "John told

me that Jillian was here at the hospital with you last night.''

''She was here,'' he said quietly.

''You still haven't given me any details of your social life with Jillian, you rotten rat.''

Forrest shrugged. ''You had other things on your mind. Two little other things, as a matter of fact.''

Andrea folded her hands in her lap and studied her brother. Forrest met her gaze for a moment, then directed his attention to the smiling teddy bears.

''Okay, big brother, what's wrong?'' she said.

''Wrong?'' he echoed, raising his eyebrows as he looked at her again. ''Nothing is wrong. What could be wrong? I mean, jeez, I'm the uncle of two new fantastic kids. Miracles. That's great. You're great. You and John are great. Everything is great. I've got such a long list of great, that—''

''Cut,'' she said, slicing one hand through the air. ''This is me, Andrea, remember? I know you very well, sweetheart, and something is most definitely wrong.'' She paused, narrowed her eyes and nodded. ''Jillian Jones-Jenkins.''

''You're dreaming.''

''I'm right on the money. Talk to me.''

''Speaking of money, I'm going to split the bundle I won on The Baby Bet with you. That seems only fair, since you delivered the twins in my predicted order. I'm still The Baby Bet champion, madam.''

''Would you cut it out? What's going on between you and Jillian that is causing you to look as dreary as yesterday's oatmeal? It's worse than that. You're as grim as today's lunch they served me in this place. Forrest?''

"Hey, Andrea, I didn't come here to dump on you. You just had two babies, for crying out loud. Take off your sister hat and put on your new-mother hat. Just forget about me.''

"Not a chance. Talk to me, or I'll sign you up for diaper duty so John and I can go out to dinner when I've escaped from here.''

Forrest opened his mouth, closed it again, and shook his head. He sighed, looked at the ceiling for a long moment, then met Andrea's now troubled gaze.

"I'm in love with Jillian, Andrea," he said, his voice low and not quite steady.

"That *should* be wonderful. You've waited a long time to love, to be in love, fall in love. I know how much you want to have a wife and babies. The fact that you're not turning cartwheels means there's a major glitch in your relationship with Jillian.

"Is it her career, Forrest? She has to be very devoted, able to exercise extremely strict self-discipline. But, as you know because you accepted the Angels and Elves assignment, she works much too hard.''

"No, it's not her writing. There's no problem there at all. I highly respect her talent and what she has accomplished. I've enjoyed reading her books, too. It's a demanding career, but she seems to have a healthy balance in her life of work and leisure. She's on vacation right now, because she decided she needed a break. You and Deedee overreacted to Jillian's schedule.''

"Well, shame on us. That area is apparently in apple-pie order. So? What's wrong?"

"I wouldn't talk about Jillian's private life because it's just that—private—but you don't count."

"Oh, thanks," Andrea said, laughing.

"You know what I mean."

"Of course, I do," she said, her expression serious again.

"Jillian was badly hurt years ago by a crummy marriage to a real jerk. She's closed herself off, built protective walls around herself. I knew that, damn it. I knew she was wary and skittish, that I mustn't rush her or do anything to cause her to build those walls higher and stronger."

Forrest leaned forward, resting his elbows on his knees and making a steeple of his fingers.

"Jillian cares for me, Andrea, I'm certain of that. She might— Well, she might even be in love with me, but is too frightened to tell me, or maybe too scared to even admit it to herself. Hell, I don't know. What I *do* know is that I blew it. Big time. Major league."

"How?"

"I told her that I loved her. I opened my big, stupid mouth and said that I loved her, wanted to create a miracle, a baby, with her. I didn't come right out and ask her to marry me, but I'm sure my intentions were clear."

"You were being honest and open," Andrea said, nodding decisively. "That's important in a relationship. I think your telling her how you felt was excellent."

"I think it was the dumbest thing I've ever done."

"Oh. Well, what did she say?"

"Nothing."

"Nothing? You declared your love to a woman and she said *nothing?*"

"I wouldn't let her," he said, sinking back in the chair. He dragged a restless hand through his hair. "I blathered on like the idiot of the year, and realized an instant later that I'd made a terrible mistake. Jillian isn't ready to hear that stuff yet. She needs more time, and I should have been patient. I told her not to say anything, but to think about it—everything I'd said. Then I hightailed it out of there, coward that I am. I repeat, I blew it. In spades."

"Oh, dear," Andrea said. "A woman left alone to brood can be a dangerous creature. We have very active minds, you know. It's much better to start the communication process immediately when dealing with a major issue."

"I figured I'd stay out of her way for a few days."

"Wrong. You should see her as soon as possible, then sit her down, and gently—*gently*—say it's time to talk things through."

"Bad plan. I'd rather take on diaper duty for the twins."

"Forrest MacAllister, you really *are* a coward."

"You've got that straight. I'm scared to death, Andrea. I love Jillian and want to spend the rest of my life with her. The thought of losing her just rips me up."

"Go to her, Forrest."

He got to his feet. "You're a tough cookie. John sure does have his hands full being married to you."

"The lucky son of a gun," she said, smiling.

"Yes, he is." He leaned over and kissed her on the forehead.

"Will you do it? Will you go talk to Jillian?"

Forrest nodded. "I have to settle down a bit first, but I'll call her and see if I can set it up for tomorrow night. I'll probably have a complete mental collapse before then, though."

"Talk...to...her."

"Yeah, yeah, okay, I will." Forrest walked to the end of the bed and stopped, staring at the huge teddy bears. "I'm big, strong, healthy, and prepared to slay the dragons for my Lady Jillian, but my physical strength means nothing. Love sure is an equalizer, a powerful force that has the capability of stripping a man bare."

"And of bringing him the greatest joy he's ever known," Andrea said softly.

Forrest nodded slowly, then turned and left the room.

"Deedee?" Andrea said into the telephone receiver. "Are you sitting down?"

Ten

The following evening, Jillian stood in the kitchen looking at the clock on the wall. The hands seemed to be moving at a snail's pace, inching closer to seven o'clock and Forrest's scheduled arrival.

She'd dressed in jeans, a magenta-colored sweater and matching socks, with the hope that the bright, cheerful attire would improve her dark, gloomy mood.

It hadn't helped one iota.

With a cluck of self-disgust, she stomped out of the kitchen, smacking the light switch to Off as she passed. In the living room, she sank onto the sofa in front of the fireplace and stared at the leaping flames.

She was a wreck. Forrest had called late yesterday afternoon, said they needed to talk, and was seven o'clock the next evening convenient?

He'd sounded stiff, stilted, like someone making an appointment to sell her life insurance. She'd agreed to the plan, and had been a bundle of nerves ever since.

She couldn't pretend that she didn't know what Forrest wanted to discuss. The man had told her that he was in love with her, for Pete's sake. He'd then proceeded to tell her to think, think, think, about the list of items he'd clicked off. Now the jig was up. This was it. Forrest was coming for answers, responses to what he'd said.

"Oh-h-h, perdition," Jillian said, leaning her head against the back of the sofa.

Snatches of Forrest's words had echoed in her mind through the entire day and on into the evening.

I do love you, Jillian. It's the truth. It's honest and real. When we made love it was far more beautiful, intimate, special and rare, than anything I, and hopefully you, have ever experienced before. Think about the babies, the miracles, knowing our child is within our reality. I do love you, Jillian. I do love you, Jillian. Just think and feel. Think, think, think.

"Oh-h-h," she moaned again, pressing her palms to her aching temples.

She was so muddled, so confused, so incredibly unhappy. It was as though an exhausting tug-of-war was taking place in her mind, yanking her back and forth between fantasy and reality.

The make-believe was glorious. She had no ghosts from the past haunting her, holding her in a fist of fear. She was free to follow the missive from her heart, to tell Forrest that she loved him, wanted to be his wife, and the mother of his children.

In that fantasyland, she didn't have a demanding career that required her full devotion, both emotionally and physically. She wrote books as a hobby. Yes, that was good—a hobby, where she dashed off a paragraph or two when the mood struck.

But reality? Oh, dear heaven, it was totally opposite from that sugarcoated fairy tale. And reality was synonymous with the truth, and the truth was what she would have to convey to Forrest in a very few minutes.

But not the whole truth, she thought glumly. She would not tell Forrest MacAllister that she was in love with him. It would serve no purpose, because the bottom-line fact that they had no future together could not be changed.

The doorbell rang, and Jillian sighed as she got slowly to her feet and started across the living room.

She wished she was anywhere other than on her way to opening the front door. Siberia held appeal, or Afghanistan, or—

"Jillian, shut up," she muttered.

She stopped in the entry hall, took a deep, steadying breath, then opened the door, hoping to heaven that her smile didn't appear as phony as it felt.

"Hello, Forrest," she said, stepping back. "Please come in."

"Jillian," he said, nodding slightly. There was no trace of a smile on his face.

She closed the door and turned to look at him, allowing herself to savor a quick scrutiny of his magnificent physique presented to perfection in jeans and a black turtleneck sweater.

Forrest looked directly into her eyes, placed one hand on her cheek and brushed his lips over hers.

"It's good to see you," he said, dropping his hand to his side.

"Yes, well, it's nice to see you, too. Shall we go in by the fire?"

She hurried past him without waiting for his reply, and Forrest followed slowly behind. Jillian sat down on the sofa and folded her hands in her lap, suddenly wishing she'd mastered knitting so she could busy herself with something other than the tension-filled moment.

Gently, Forrest ordered himself. Andrea had emphasized that he was to discuss the issues at hand gently, talk things through gently. That was going to be a good trick, considering the fact that he was so stressed he felt like a tightly coiled spring that was apt to go rocketing into orbit at the slightest provocation.

He considered settling onto the sofa next to Jillian, then rejected the idea as futile, knowing he was too wired to sit still. Instead, he planted one forearm on the mantel.

Damn, he thought. Jillian looked like a scared kid who had been summoned to the principal's office. Her beautiful gray eyes were wide and wary, her hands clutched tightly in her lap, her magenta-socked feet planted soldier-square on the floor.

The tension in the room was a nearly palpable entity, and for the life of him he didn't know how to defuse it before it exploded into a disaster.

"Hell," he said.

Jillian blinked in surprise. "Hell?"

He shoved his hands into the back pockets of his jeans for lack of a better thing to do with them, and his frown deepened.

"This is really ridiculous," he said. "This is supposed to be a momentous moment, a special occasion in both of our lives, and I feel as though I came to announce that your dog died."

"Well, I—"

"Damn it, Jillian," he said, his volume now on high, "I love you. I want to marry you. Have you got that? Is it loud and clear enough for you?"

He rolled his eyes heavenward.

"That cooked it," he said, shaking his head.

Pulling his hands free of his pockets, he dragged them down his face.

"Okay," he said, crossing his arms loosely over his chest. "I'm in my 'gently' mode. Jillian, do you believe that I love you with all my heart?"

"Yes," she said softly.

"Oh. Well, that's good, great." He paused. "Look, it's so important that you come to grips with your past, deal with it, then put it away. It's the only way you can have the fulfilling present and future that you deserve to have."

"I realize that, but—"

"You do? That's fantastic, terrific." He stepped forward and sat down next to her, shifting on the sofa so he could face her. "That's wonderful, Jillian."

"No, you're misinterpreting what I'm—"

"Jillian, please," he interrupted, raising one hand. "Let me have my say before I botch this up." He covered her hands with his. "I love you, Jillian. There's nothing to be afraid of by admitting that you love me. Maybe that sounds conceited as hell, but you've been the other half of all we've shared, every step of the way. We've grown together, learned so much, put solid bricks into place as the foundation of our relationship."

"But—"

"Shh." He gave her a quick kiss on the lips. "We can have it all, together, if you'll look forward instead of backward. Because *I* trust *you.* I've come to believe that a fulfilling two-career marriage *is* possible. I really listened to what you said about compromises.

"Ah, Jillian, we'll have a home—not just a house, but a home filled with love and the sound of our children's laughter. I won't put in such long hours or bring work home, and your career isn't a stumbling block, so—"

"Halt." She slipped her hands free of his and raised them, palms out. "Whoa. Why isn't my career a stumbling block?" She crossed her arms under her breasts.

Forrest frowned, confusion evident in his expression.

"It's very simple," he said, with a shrug. "I respect what you do more than I can even tell you. That's important, you know, that a husband and wife respect each other's work. I don't feel threatened by your success, or by your ability to support yourself on a financial level.''

''And?''

''And what?''

''Forrest, my novels don't write themselves. It takes me months to complete a book.''

''Oh, that.''

Jillian narrowed her eyes. ''Meaning?''

''Well, holy smoke, what's the problem? It's been obvious to me from the day I met you that you have a healthy balance in your life of work and leisure time.

''You needed a vacation, so you took one. You're a professional, who's organized, intelligent, the whole nine yards. I can't imagine you having any difficulty revamping your writing schedule to include hearth, home, husband and kids.

''I'd do my share, you know, be right in there pitching. I could hold down the fort if you went on an autographing tour, or whatever. Your writing wouldn't get in the way of anything.''

Jillian jumped to her feet, and Forrest jerked in surprise.

''Get in the way?'' she shrieked, her hands curled into fists at her sides.

''What are you getting stressed-out about? All I'm trying to do is show you that I've changed my opinion on two-career marriages, and it's possible for us to have a wonderful life together. We'll iron out the nitty-gritty details and go for it. There's nothing standing in our way, Jillian.''

Emotions slammed against Jillian's mind in a brutal attack, causing a momentary wave of dizziness to sweep over her.

The fears born of past pain were there, as well as the aching chill of knowing she was in love with Forrest but had no room for him in her life.

And anger. Oh, the fury, the rage. Forrest Mac-Allister, she fumed, was dismissing her career as incidental, something that could be worked in around the edges, something *that wouldn't get in the way of anything.*

"Jillian?" Forrest said tentatively. "What's going on, here? You look mad as hell, but I sure don't understand why."

"You don't understand *anything*," she said, none too quietly. "You've had your say, Forrest Mac-Allister, and now I'll have mine, so listen up. Maybe, just maybe, I could have put the past behind me in regard to the pain I suffered in my marriage. But there's no point in dwelling on that 'maybe,' because it's not the major issue here."

"It isn't?"

"It sure as hell isn't, buster."

"Buster? You *are* mad as hell. What did I do? What did I say wrong to set you off?"

"I am a woman," she said, splaying one hand on her breasts, "and I am a writer, a published author. The writer part of my being is intricately entwined with the woman. Without my writing, I wouldn't be complete, whole, the total essence of who I am.

"My work, Mr. MacAllister, my writing, does not get penciled in on the calendar when I'm in the mood.

It's my focus, my purpose, my center, my life. Everything else takes second seat.''

"But—"

"You just happened to meet me when I was starting a two-week vacation—fourteen days, and not one hour more. Those vacations only happen two or three times a year. The remainder of the time, I work.

"I'm in my office eight, ten, even twelve hours a day. I rarely see anyone, or go anywhere. I'm totally immersed in the story I'm writing, in the characters. I laugh with them, cry with them, become them, in order to make them alive and real to the people who read my books. I have no room for anything or anyone else during those months.''

"Holy smoke," Forrest whispered, staring at her with wide eyes. "I thought—"

"I know what you thought," she rushed on. "A vacation would be nice? Oh, what the heck, I'll just take two weeks off. Have a baby? Tend to a house? Hey, no problem. My little hobby of writing books could be juggled into the system someplace. You're so off base, MacAllister, it's a crime.''

Forrest lunged to his feet. "Why didn't you tell me all of this before? You led me to believe—"

"No! You drew your own conclusions. I was following my strict vacation rules for stepping away from my world of writing. I was concentrating on what Andrea and Deedee convinced me to take on as The Project, what they called an Angels and Elves assignment. They felt you were focusing all your energies on work, and needed to be shown how to relax, have fun.''

Oh, dear heaven, no! she thought frantically. She hadn't meant to say that, to bring up the subject of The Project. It would sound so terribly cold and calculating, so unfeeling.

Forrest stiffened, every muscle in his body tightening to the point of actual pain.

"The project?" he repeated, his voice ominously low. "The rules of your vacation call for you to put space between yourself and your writing, to take on a 'project,' and *I* was it for your little hiatus this time?

"Well, guess what. Andrea and Deedee convinced *me* to take *you* on as *my* Angels and Elves assignment because they were worried about how hard you were working."

"They were matchmaking, being Cupids," Jillian said, her eyes widening.

"Bingo. I'd give them a heavy-duty piece of my mind about their scheme, but I believe they did it out of genuine caring. The thing is, in my case what they hoped would happen actually came to be. I fell in love with you. But you? Ah, damn it, Jillian, you—" He stopped speaking and shook his head.

Jillian pressed trembling fingertips to her lips as she watched Forrest stare up at the ceiling for a long moment, struggling to control his emotions. When he looked at her again, she felt instant tears burn her eyes as she saw the anger in his brown eyes change to stark, raw pain.

"It was all a game to you, wasn't it?" he said, his voice flat. "A project, an Angels and Elves deal, something to do to keep from being bored while you took time off from work."

"Forrest—"

"God, what a fool I've been," he went on, self-disgust ringing in his voice. "How did you keep a straight face, not fall on the floor laughing, when I talked about wanting to marry you, have babies with you, spend the rest of my life with you?"

He dragged one hand through his hair.

"Oh, hey, I've got it." He snapped his fingers. "This was all research for your next book. Right? Well, you'll have some sizzling love scenes to put on paper. No, correct that. *Sex* scenes. That's what it was to you—just casual sex."

"Forrest, no," she said, tears filling her eyes. "Please, it wasn't a game, or research, I swear it wasn't." Two tears spilled onto her pale cheeks.

"Tears, Lady Jillian?" There was, a bitter edge in his voice. "Nice touch. You're an actress, as well as a famous author."

He paused.

"No…" he said slowly. "I think this whole number is more complex than it appears. I think you're playing games with yourself, as well."

"What…what do you mean?" she said, dashing the tears away.

"You're hiding, Jillian. You were hurt once, and you're so damn scared of it happening again that you're using your writing as an excuse not to square off against life and the risks people run if they embrace it. You're so terrified of reality that you live your life through make-believe characters."

"That's not true."

"Isn't it? You can control those characters, decide

on everything they'll say, guarantee them a happy ending by having them do exactly what you dictate. You venture out into the real world for a couple of weeks here and there, then hightail it back behind your protective walls, hole up in your office where it's safe.

"You transport yourself back in time to another era as an extra precaution against the 'now' of your existence being able to touch you. You don't allow anyone into that space, that place in history, where you exist. Oh, yes, Jillian, you're hiding."

"No!"

"Think about it. Or don't think about it. Hell, I don't care. I've had enough of this."

He turned and started across the room.

"Forrest, wait."

He hesitated, then stopped, shifting slightly to look back at her.

"No, thanks. You're a helluva writer, Jillian. I really believed that truth, trust and honesty were important to you because they were emphasized in every novel of yours I read. What a joke. *I* was a joke to you, too, and that hurts. That hurts like hell.

"I just hope it doesn't take me too long to put you entirely out of my heart and mind, to forget that I love you. I don't think it will be too tough, because the truth of the matter is, I never really knew you at all. It was all a game of make-believe."

He turned again and strode away. A few moments later, Jillian heard the front door slam. She flinched as the loud noise reverberated through the house.

"Forrest, don't go," she said, nearly choking on a

sob. Tears streamed unchecked and unnoticed down her face and along her neck. "You're wrong. I love you, Forrest MacAllister."

She sank back onto the sofa and buried her face in her hands.

The only sounds in the large room were the crackling flames in the fireplace, and the heartbroken weeping of Jillian Jones-Jenkins.

Eleven

A week later, Jillian shut off the computer and leaned back in her chair, staring at the darkened screen. She glanced at her watch, then got to her feet to roam around her spacious office.

Jillian, she told herself, it's time to gather some data.

She had relived the final encounter with Forrest over and over in her mind, seeing the raw pain in his beautiful brown eyes, hearing his harsh accusations that she was living her life through the characters in her books, even transporting herself back in time, because of her fear of reality and "now."

Her emotions had swung continually back and forth like a pendulum, moving from tear-producing sorrow to rip-roaring anger.

But two facts remained constant: she loved Forrest

MacAllister with every fiber of her being, and she missed him with an aching intensity.

Those items, however, were not the topics on which she was presently data-gathering. No, the subject at hand was her work.

The morning after the disastrous evening with Forrest, she'd headed for her office, knowing she still had several vacation days left, but having no desire to be idle.

She hadn't expected to be able to accomplish a great deal of writing due to her emotional upheaval, but found to her surprise that the outline for her new book fell nicely into place.

The next day she'd returned to the office with the mind-set that she was still off duty, didn't have to be there, and, hence, anything she produced would be viewed as a bonus against her future deadline.

To her amazement, she once again was pleased with her output and the knowledge that she'd been able to set aside her personal turmoil the moment she'd stepped inside the room designated only for writing.

In the week that followed, she'd met her daily quota of pages in half the normal time allotted each day. *Half the time!*

Why? she wondered, continuing to wander back and forth across the room.

She stopped and wrapped her hands around her elbows in a protective gesture, having realized that the truth of the answer to the question was stark and painfully revealing.

She had subconsciously, for a very long time, made

her day-to-day production schedule take up more hours than were necessary.

"Oh, perdition," she whispered.

Forrest's accusations were right on the mark. She had escaped into her office, into the lives of her characters and the place in history where they existed, rather than face her own reality. She'd been hiding like a frightened child.

"Oh, Jillian, what have you done?"

She'd lost the man who loved her, the man she loved. Her fears had caused her to forfeit a wondrous future with Forrest MacAllister. There would be no marriage, no home overflowing with joy and sunshine, no miracle of a baby created with Forrest.

Tears misted her eyes and she left the office to go to the sofa in front of the warming fire in the living room.

It was all so clear to her now. She'd lived the majority of her childhood in a fantasyland born of her imagination and providing an escape from her loneliness.

When she'd ventured out of her protective cocoon to marry Roger, she'd been betrayed, terribly hurt. So, she'd returned to a world comprised mostly of make-believe, where it was safe, risk free, under her command and control.

She was long overdue to grow up, to behave like the mature woman she professed herself to be. She would muster her courage, defeat the haunting ghosts of the past, and fling them into oblivion forever.

Jillian sniffled, then swept an errant tear from her cheek.

She'd be eligible for high scores in newfound mental health. She'd be the woman she was meant to be; whole, embracing life, functioning as a complete person.

But she would not be with the man she loved!

"Oh, perdition," she said, hiccupping along with a sob. "I love him, I want to spend the rest of my life with the man. I want to have his baby—two babies, four, a whole bunch of babies. I want it all, *and it's too late.* I've lost him. He's gone. And it's all my fault."

If she didn't stop talking aloud to herself, her next stop would be a place with bars on the windows where weird people were kept.

Jillian jumped to her feet and narrowed her eyes.

Wait just a darn minute, here. She'd spent more years than she cared to admit being defeated by her worst enemy—herself. Well, this time she wasn't giving up the battle without a fight. If there was any way possible to share with Forrest the future he'd once wished to have with her, she'd find it, by gum.

Oh, yes, she was ready. Well, she would be, once she figured out a genius-level plan.

Jillian Jones-Jenkins was on the march!

Settling back onto the sofa, she squeezed her eyes tightly closed and began to concentrate on The Plan.

She had a vivid imagination, for heaven's sake. It was time to apply that creativeness to real life. The heroine was intent on winning back the hero. Victory would be hers!

In the late afternoon, one week later, Michael appeared next to Forrest's desk at MacAllister Architects, Incorporated.

"Forrest?"

"What?" he said, not looking up.

"See my face?"

Forrest shifted his gaze to Michael. "It's as ugly as it usually is. What else do you want to know?"

"Whether or not you still recognize this kind of thing," Michael said, pointing to his lips. "It's called a smile. Remember smiles?"

Forrest redirected his attention to the file in front of him. "No." He glanced at his watch. "My day is over. I'm outta here."

"No," Michael said quickly. "You can't leave yet."

"Why not?"

"The phone might ring."

"So answer it, or have our secretary answer it. She's really into answering the phone." Forrest got to his feet. "I hope you didn't pass on your nutso gene to Bobby. Poor little kid. That would be a bum rap. You're strange, Michael, very strange."

The telephone on Forrest's desk rang.

"Ah-ha." Michael pointed to the shrilling phone. "It rang. One should not doubt those who are older and wiser than you, Forrest."

"Bull."

"Answer the damn phone!"

Forrest glared at his brother, then snatched up the receiver. "MacAllister Architects, Incorporated."

"Forrest? It's Andrea."

"Hi, Andrea. How are the munchkins?"

"Phase one of The Plan," Michael said under his breath, as he walked away, "is a done deal."

"The babies are super," Andrea said to Forrest. "I wish they'd get together more on their sleeping routine, though. It seems that when Matt goes to sleep, Noel wakes up."

"I'll speak to them about it," Forrest said. "They'll heed the words of their Uncle Forrest."

"How nice. Listen, you wouldn't happen to be leaving the office now, would you? I mean, I just couldn't possibly know the schedule around there these days. Did I, by some slim chance, get lucky?"

"Yeah, I'm just about to leave."

"Well, fancy that. If you don't have plans for tonight, could you do me a teeny-tiny favor?"

"Andrea, I haven't been able to say no to you from the day you were born, and you know it. What do you need?"

"You're such a sweetheart. John has a business dinner to attend, and Deedee suggested that she and I go out for a quick hamburger. You have no idea how wonderful it sounds, especially if that gourmet meal can't be interrupted by Matt or Noel. Would you come over and stay with the twins?"

"Me? Andrea, I don't know the first thing about taking care of babies."

"There won't be anything for you to do. They'll be fed, diapered, and sound asleep. Guaranteed."

"Yeah, sure," he said dryly.

"Hey, these little guys were the means by which you won The Baby Bet, remember? Would they do something rotten to their favorite uncle?"

Forrest sighed. "Oh, man, I've got to be nuts, but I'll do it. You're lucky I'm even speaking to you, or to Deedee, for that matter, considering the fact your stint as Cupids was a disaster. Your double dose of Angels and Elves assignments failed miserably."

"We're so sorry, Forrest. Deedee and I feel just terrible about what happened between you and Jillian, or what didn't happen, or whatever."

"I don't want to talk about it. I'll be at your place within the hour."

"Wonderful. I'll leave the front door unlocked, so just come on in. I'm going to be putting the finishing touches on my makeup. I'm going to be gorgeous."

"To go eat a hamburger?"

"Mothers of twins do not take the gift of time off lightly. A hamburger calls for 'gorgeous.'"

"If you say so."

"I say so. See you soon. Bye, Forrest."

Andrea replaced the receiver and beamed at Deedee. "Phase two of The Plan," Andrea said, "is a mission accomplished."

"Fantastic," Deedee said.

A circle of warmth tiptoed about Deedee's heart and showed itself as a soft smile as she recalled the long talk she'd shared with Jillian as they sat on the floor in front of the roaring fire at Jillian's house.

Jillian had poured out the sad tale of her marriage and her desire to put those ghosts to rest for all time. She'd talked about her career, and with love shining in her eyes, had spoken of Forrest MacAllister.

Her friendship with Jillian, Deedee knew, had

deepened that night, bonded them as sisters.

"The Plan will work, Andrea. It just has to."

The drive to Andrea's was slowgoing due to heavy traffic. Forrest's frustration grew as he was forced to stop at yet another red light, and he drummed his fingers impatiently on the steering wheel.

The light changed and he pressed on the gas pedal.

He'd caught Michael's not-very-subtle reference to his lousy frame of mind. His brother was letting him know by asking him if he remembered what smiles were, that Mr. Forrest MacAllister had not exactly been sunshine itself over the past two weeks.

So, okay, he'd work on his attitude.

It wasn't his family's fault he was a jerk, had lousy taste in women and had misread Jillian Jones-Jenkins from day one.

It wasn't their fault he wasn't sleeping well, had no appetite and was one very miserable man.

It wasn't their fault that he still loved Jillian with every breath in his rapidly depleting body.

No, that wasn't exactly true. He loved the Jillian he'd *believed* her to be, not the one who had eventually shown her true colors. But the image of Jillian, the fantasy, was in his mind's eye every waking hour of the day and night.

Time, he hoped, would ease his pain, his sense of being betrayed, played for a fool, his chilling loneliness. In the interim, he really had to make more of an effort to smile.

He'd start by smiling at the they'd-better-be-sleeping twins. Those babies were really cute. Matt was easygoing, a laid-back little guy, and Noel was on a short fuse. She wanted a dry diaper right now, and something to eat right now, no excuses, thank you very much. Noel definitely took after Andrea.

What would a baby created by Jillian and him have looked like?

"Shut up, MacAllister," he said. "Quit pouring salt in your own wounds."

At last arriving at Andrea and John's, Forrest parked in front and glanced around as he got out of the car. There were no other vehicles in the circular driveway, and he absently deduced that Andrea's car was still in the double garage.

When he came to the front door, he automatically reached out to ring the bell, then halted, remembering Andrea's instructions to enter the house.

"She's getting gorgeous for a hamburger," he muttered. "Women are weird biscuits."

In the entry hall, he stopped, sniffed the air, then frowned.

He'd swear he was savoring the enticing aroma of baking chicken, but that didn't make sense. Why would someone who was about to engage in the thrilling experience of going out for a fast-food hamburger have a chicken cooking in her oven?

No, he wasn't really smelling chicken. He was simply a hungry man ready for his dinner who *wished* there was a chicken turning crispy brown and juicy in the oven.

As Forrest went on into the living room, he pulled off his tie and stuffed it into his jacket pocket. Next he removed the jacket and draped it over the back of a chair.

"Yo, Andrea," he called. "Your nanny is here to watch over sleeping babies. Catch the word *sleeping*, little sister. Are you gorgeous enough for a hamburger yet?" He paused. "Hey, where are you, brat?"

"Hello, Forrest," a soft voice said.

He spun around and his eyes widened in surprise. Opening his mouth to speak, he instantly realized he'd stopped breathing and had to take a gulp of air.

"Jillian?" he finally managed to say, more in the form of a croak.

"Yes, Forrest, it's me...Jillian."

He swallowed heavily and the sound of his racing heart echoed in his ears as he scrutinized Jillian from head to toe, drinking in the sight of her like a thirsty man.

She was wearing jeans, a purple sweatshirt with a pink elephant on the front, and purple socks. She was the most sensational woman he'd ever seen, an absolute vision of beauty. And, oh, God, how he loved her.

He took one step toward her, then stopped, a frown replacing his shocked expression.

Hold it, MacAllister, he ordered himself. Think, idiot. He had no idea why she was there, what she was up to, but he wasn't having any, by damn. He'd do well to remember that Jillian Jones-Jenkins had used him, toyed with him, made a complete fool of him. He was older and painfully wiser, in regard to Miss Jones-Jenkins.

"So what's the deal?" he said, striving for an I-really-don't-give-a-damn tone of voice. "Are you joining Andrea and Deedee for a hamburger and fries?''

''No. Andrea isn't home, Forrest. She was at Deedee's store when she telephoned and asked you to baby-sit the twins. I'm the only one here with the babies. For all practical purposes, you and I are alone.''

Warning bells went off in Forrest's head, and he narrowed his eyes.

Ho-ho, he thought, the light was dawning. There was a conspiracy afoot. First there had been Michael's crazy demand that Forrest not leave the office as scheduled because the phone might ring. It *had* rung, and there was Andrea with her plea to stay with the twins. Now here was Jillian—alone, obviously having intended to see him while no one else was around.

What were they all up to?

What did Jillian want?

He intended to find out.

But this time he was one step ahead of Jillian's games. He now realized that he'd been duped into coming to Andrea's house. Jillian had rallied the troops for heaven only knew what reason, but he would stay on red alert, follow the dictates of his logical mind, *not* his love-torn heart.

''Okay.'' He nodded slowly. ''It's your ball, Miss Jones-Jenkins.''

Oh, thank goodness, Jillian thought, with a rush of relief. Forrest wasn't going to turn around and walk out of the house in a fit of temper. He wasn't smiling—oh, how she yearned to see that gorgeous smile—but he was cooperating. The Plan had to work; it just had to. She loved him so much, so *very* much.

"Could we sit down?" she said.

Forrest swept one arm through the air. "Whatever you say."

He went to a chair, while Jillian sank onto the sofa facing him, grateful that her trembling legs had carried her that far.

"Forrest," she said, wishing her voice was steadier, "I've been coming here to Andrea and John's in the middle of the afternoon for the past week."

He folded his arms across his chest. "Why?"

Jillian gazed at him for a long moment. Forrest's masculinity was again weaving over her and through her, causing the heat of desire to stir within her.

Her breath caught as she saw the well-remembered strength of his beautifully muscled arms. She vividly recalled how she'd felt when she'd been held tightly in his embrace.

And his lips... Oh, dear heaven, it was suddenly so warm in the room. Hot. His hands. How exquisite was the feel of his hands on her breasts, on her entire body.

She'd missed him so much, she wanted to fling herself across the short space separating them and nestle close to his rugged body.

Stop it, Jillian, she admonished herself. She was in the midst of The Plan, and needed all her wits about her.

"Jillian," Forrest said, snapping her back to attention, "I asked you why you've been coming here every day." His frown deepened. "Wait a minute.

Your vacation is long since over. How is it that you have time to be here and do whatever it is you've been doing? There's no room in your life for anything but your writing when you're working on a book, remember? You do remember saying that, don't you?''

She nodded. ''Yes, that's exactly what I said and it was true—then.''

This was it, she thought. This was the final stage of The Plan. What happened now would determine her entire future happiness.

She took a steadying breath, squared her shoulders, then lifted her chin.

''Forrest, I know you feel that I betrayed you, used you, viewed you as nothing more than The Project— an Angels and Elves assignment, as you and Andrea call it—to occupy my time during my vacation.''

Forrest's jaw tightened, but he didn't speak as he looked directly at Jillian.

''You *were* my Angels and Elves assignment, just as I was yours. Andrea and Deedee were trying to bring us together out of a sense of love.''

''I realize that,'' he said, a slight edge in his voice. ''I'm not angry at *them*. The fact remains that you're intelligent and—I thought—also sensitive and caring enough to realize that something special and ex- tremely important was happening between us. I *be- lieve* that you knew it, but didn't give a damn. You kept up your phony charade because you still had time to fill before your vacation was over.''

''No! That's not true. Oh, Forrest, I know how it

seems to you. I can still hear those horrible things I said to you that last time we were together.''

Forrest dragged one hand through his hair, then leaned forward, resting his elbows on his knees and making a steeple of his fingers.

"I remember everything that was said, too," he murmured. "I wish to hell I could forget."

Tears stung Jillian's eyes as she heard the pain in Forrest's voice, saw it etched on his face.

"Oh, Forrest, I didn't mean to hurt you," she said, willing herself not to cry. "I was terrified, so frightened. My past held me like a cold, iron fist, and I didn't know how to break free. I was behaving like a child, running from ghosts that existed only in my mind. Forrest, are you really *hearing* me as you're listening? I'm speaking in the past tense. I've conquered those ghosts, Forrest. I truly have."

"I'm glad…for you," he said, straightening again in the chair. "There was a time when I thought those ghosts were the only thing standing in our way." He shook his head. "What a joke. The dragon I could never slay is your career. It's all you want or need."

"You accused me," she went on, her voice trembling, "of escaping from reality into a fantasy world because I was too much of a coward to run the risks of embracing life, even to the point of transporting myself back in time as an extra layer of protection. You said I was living through my characters because it was safer and I was in control."

"I shouldn't have said all that," he said, sounding suddenly weary. "I was hurt, angry, and I lashed out at you."

"Forrest," she said, tears echoing in her voice, "everything you said was true."

"What?"

"I've learned a great deal about myself since that painful scene we had. What I've discovered is not flattering, nor am I proud of myself. I *was* hiding from life, Forrest. I escaped into my writing where it was safe and I couldn't be hurt again. It all became very clear to me while we've been apart."

"And?" he prompted, feeling the increased tempo of his heartbeat. Easy, MacAllister. Jillian wasn't finished talking yet; he hadn't heard everything she had to say. He mustn't hope too much, set himself up for another painful fall. But, oh, damn, how he loved her. "Go on, Jillian."

"There's something I want to be certain you know and believe. Forrest, I knew that I loved you before we parted. That's one of the reasons I was so frightened. Despite my resolve to never love again, I had fallen deeply, irrevocably in love with you. Oh, God, Forrest, I was so scared."

"Jillian?" He got slowly to his feet.

"No, wait," she said, raising one hand. "Please let me finish. A successful author has to be disciplined, write every day, but I now know that I had stretched out my work to fill the hours so I could remain in my protective cocoon. I *do* have space in my life for more than my work and I *want* more. I want *you*. I love you, Forrest MacAllister. I want to be your wife and the mother of our babies, our miracles."

She swept one arm in the air.

"This plan to get you here, which Deedee, Andrea,

and Michael helped me put together, is to prove to you that I'm speaking the truth, from my heart, my soul. You have just cause to distrust me, but I hope and pray that I'll be able to convince you that I love you more than I can even say.

"I've been coming here at the end of my workday to have Andrea teach me how to tend to babies. I want to be the best mother I possibly can, and Andrea's been so patient. I can't begin to tell you how wonderful it is to hold Noel and Matt, give them baths, rock them to sleep.

"I've finally put to rest the pain of losing my baby so many years ago. I'm looking to the future with the fervent prayer that someday I'll nestle *our* baby—yours and mine, our miracle—to my breast."

Two tears slid down her cheeks.

"I tried to learn to cook, too, but Andrea finally admitted defeat. I was going to have a delicious dinner waiting for you here, but I forgot to turn the oven on again, and the chicken has only just begun to bake." She threw up her hands. "I'm a complete disaster in the kitchen."

"Jillian..."

"I love you, Forrest MacAllister," she said, nearly choking on a sob. "Please forgive me for hurting you, for causing you pain produced by my own cowardice. I love you, Forrest. I do."

"God, you've worked so hard, put yourself through the painful process of dealing with your ghosts. You've torn down your protective walls, rendered yourself vulnerable out of love for me, trust in me. I will never—" Forrest stopped speaking for a moment as his emotions overcame him "—never forget this night and the precious treasures, the gifts you've given me."

No longer fighting against the tears that glistened in his eyes, Forrest smiled.

"Lady Jillian," he said, his voice husky, "if you will grant me the honor of your hand in marriage, I will be the happiest knave in the country, or kingdom, or whatever. Ah, Jillian, marry me. Please.

"No, wait. Before you answer, I want to tell you something. I've grown and changed, too, Jillian. I truly believe that a two-career marriage can be fantastic, rich and deep and real. Compromise. It calls for compromise. Therefore, I'm going on record as saying that I'm a helluva cook and I'll be the chef of this outfit.

"Ah, Jillian, there's nothing we can't handle if we do it together, loving each other for the remainder of our days. Will you marry me? Please, Jillian? Will you be my wife and the mother of my children?"

"Oh, Forrest, yes!"

She flung herself into his arms, and the kiss they shared was long and searing, igniting their passion into hot, consuming flames.

Suddenly Forrest snapped his head up and frowned.

"What's that noise?" he said. "It sounds almost like squeaking kittens."

Jillian laughed. "That's the twins waking up. They'll need a dry diaper and a bottle. Then they'll have to be burped, diapered again, played with a bit, rocked to sleep, and—"

"Got it," he said, matching her smile. "You're the

baby expert. I want you to teach me everything you've learned so far about tending to munchkins. I think, though, for the well-being of our family, I'm going to ban you from the kitchen.''

"Good plan. Oh, Forrest, I love you.''

"I love you too, Lady Jillian.''

They walked out of the room with their arms encircling each other, knowing that in their hearts, minds and souls, they were taking the first steps toward a glorious future—together.

"Deedee?'' Andrea said into the receiver of the telephone. "I found the most beautiful gown today for Jillian and Forrest's wedding. Oh, and guess what? I'm having the cutest outfits made for the twins to wear to the big event. Noel will be an angel, and Matt an elf.

"The guests will probably think I'm crazy dressing the babies that way for a wedding, but everyone that matters will know how appropriate it is. An angel and an elf—perfect.

"You know, I was thinking about the future. Jillian and Forrest definitely want a family. There's no way Forrest could win The Baby Bet *again* when the time comes— Is there?''

*   *   *   *   *

FRIENDS, LOVERS...
AND BABIES!

I would like to thank Yavapai County Deputy Sheriff
Deon Robison and Deputy Sheriff Gary Ferrato
for their information regarding police procedures.

Prologue

A picture-perfect California sunset streaked across the sky as the patrol car moved slowly along the residential street of Ventura. The windows of the vehicle were rolled down, and the officer who was driving inhaled deeply.

"Oh, yeah," he said, glancing over at his partner. "Can you smell that, Ted? Someone is barbecuing."

"Smell it?" Ted Sharpe said. "MacAllister, I'm drooling on my shirtfront. There is nothing finer than food that has been cooked on an outdoor grill."

Ryan MacAllister frowned. "Sherry and I got a barbecue for a wedding present. We've been married seven months, and the thing is still in the box."

"So drag it out, put it together and cook some steaks. This is June, summer is upon us and barbecuing is part of the package."

"That's not the point," Ryan said. "With our weather a guy could cook outside year-round if he wanted to. What I'm saying is, Sherry and I don't eat many meals together because of our work schedules. Her shift at the hospital and mine on the police force rarely match up. We hardly see each other, unless you want to count watching each other sleep."

"Really? I don't remember you complaining about work schedules before you got married."

"It wasn't a problem then," Ryan said. "She was a floor nurse and her shifts matched mine the majority of the time. She had put in for a transfer to the emergency room, but had been waiting so long for an opening that we really didn't think about it."

"And?"

"And," Ryan said, shaking his head, "the transfer came through a couple of weeks after we were married. Ever since then, we've had one helluva time connecting with each other. I was hoping it would straighten out somehow, but it hasn't. It sure as hell hasn't."

"That's rough," Ted Sharpe said, nodding. "I mean, hell, you're still newlyweds. I imagine you'd want to be together every minute you could."

"No joke. Sherry's on duty now and will get off in about a half an hour. She'll spend the evening alone, then go to bed. I'll get home about two hours before she has to get up and report back to the hospital. It's nuts."

"Have you two talked about it?"

"Sure. Sherry could be a floor nurse again, or go into private care. You know, tend to someone in their house on a straight eight-hour day until their family comes home from work. There are a lot of openings for that kind of nurse. Or she could work in a doctor's office.''

''Sounds good.''

''Yeah, but Sherry's not having any of it,'' Ryan said, then sighed wearily. ''She waited a long time for that transfer, and she likes the excitement and challenge of the emergency room. She doesn't want to go back on the floor, and said she'd be bored out of her mind in an office or private home. She's an emergency room nurse, and that's that. End of story.''

Ryan turned the corner and drove slowly down the next residential street. He raised one finger in greeting to a young boy riding a bike.

''Cute kid,'' he said. ''That's another thing, Ted. I want a family. Sherry and I discussed it before we were married and agreed to wait a couple of years but...'' His voice trailed off.

''But?'' Ted said.

''You were at the hospital with me when my sister, Andrea, and her husband, John, became parents of twins. You saw Noel and Matt right after they were born. Well, they're four months old already, and they're really something special.

''Every time I see those babies, I realize I don't want to wait to start a family. I'm thirty-five years old, for Pete's sake. I want to have kids while I'm still young enough to enjoy them. You know, go camping, play ball, all kinds of stuff.''

Ted chuckled. ''You're an old-fashioned dude, MacAllister. Me? I'm very satisfied with the singles scene, thank you very much.'' He paused and his smile faded. ''Ryan, you and Sherry are headed for some heavy-duty problems. I've seen it happen to a lot of cops on shift work. Marriages get blown away. Big time. Don't think it's going to solve itself, because it's not. You'd better tackle it straight on before it's too late.''

''Believe me, Ted,'' Ryan said, nodding, ''I've given a lot of thought to exactly what you're saying. Sherry and I are going to have to sit down and—''

Ryan was interrupted by the squawk of the radio, then the voice of the female dispatcher.

''All available units One-Beaver-Three. There is a four-seventeen in the R room at Valley Hospital. Approach code three.''

Ryan slammed on the brakes, not hearing the numerous officers responding to the dispatcher's message. The color drained from his face and his hands tightened on the steering wheel until his knuckles turned white.

In the next instant he hit a switch, then pressed hard on the accelerator.

''What are you doing?'' Ted said, his eyes widening.

''Code three. Lights and siren,'' Ryan said, a pulse beating wildly in his temple.

''MacAllister, are you crazy? She said One-Beaver-Three. That's not our sector, not even close. We can't go over there. What in the hell are you doing?''

''Damn it, Ted,'' he yelled. ''There's a shooting in progress in the emergency room at Valley. *Sherry is on duty in that R room!*''

"Lord," Ted said, dragging one hand down his face. He shook his head. "Ryan, we can't leave our sector."

"Go to hell, Sharpe," Ryan said, increasing his speed. "I'm driving. It'll fall on me. You're just along for the ride."

Despite the fact that vehicles pulled quickly to the side of the road as Ryan approached, it seemed to him that everything was moving in agonizingly slow motion. The screaming siren matched the horrifying voice beating against his brain.

Shooting in progress...four-seventeen...four-seventeen...shooting in progress...Sherry...Sherry... Sherry...

Ted kept silent, not wanting to do anything to break his partner's concentration as he drove at breakneck speed.

Ryan was going to catch hell for what he was doing, Ted thought, mentally throwing up his hands in defeat. But he would do exactly the same thing. He knew he would. He'd be prepared to pay whatever career consequences came down, just as Ryan was. Hell, MacAllister, drive faster!

Ryan whipped around the corner of the block where Valley Hospital was located, slowed his speed, then hit the brakes as he was blocked by numerous patrol cars with their lights flashing. Two unmarked dark sedans were also there, along with a fire truck. Several vans with television station call letters painted on the sides sat on the fringes.

A group of uniformed police officers kept an ever-growing crowd back from the hospital, and two officers were stringing yellow tape between wooden saw-horses.

Ryan left the patrol car and raced toward the hospital. Before he'd gone twenty feet, a man in a dark suit and tie gripped Ryan's upper arms to halt him. The man staggered slightly from the impact of Ryan plowing into him at full speed.

"MacAllister," the man said, "what in the hell are you doing here?"

Ryan ripped his arms free of the man's hold.

"I'm going in there, Captain," he said, a steely edge to his voice. "Over you, through you, whatever it takes, I'm going in there. My wife, Sherry, is a nurse on duty in that R room."

"Sherry MacAllister," Captain Bolstad said under his breath, then muttered an earthy expletive. He didn't move from in front of Ryan.

"Slow down. Take it easy," the captain said quietly. "It's all over in there. The shooter went berserk, was strung out on drugs. He's dead, Ryan. He turned the weapon on himself after he... Look, let's go to my vehicle where we can have some privacy. This place is crawling with television camera crews."

"Why? Why do you want me to go to your vehicle?" Ryan grabbed the lapels of Captain Bolstad's suit. "Where is Sherry?"

Ted hurried forward and clamped a hand on one of Ryan's biceps.

"Ryan, let him go," Ted said. "Get your hands off of the captain, for God's sake."

Ryan ignored Ted as he tightened his hold on Captain Bolstad's jacket.

"Ryan," the captain said, "Sherry was shot."

"What?" he said, his voice a hoarse whisper. "How bad is it? Where is she? I have to go to her."

"I'll take you to her," Captain Bolstad said, "but...ah, hell, Ryan, I'm sorry. Your wife...Sherry is...Sherry is dead."

Fury and agonizing pain consumed Ryan with such intensity that a red haze blurred his vision. He dropped his hands from the captain's jacket and took a step backward, shaking his head.

"No," he said, "you're lying, you bastard. Sherry is alive. She's my wife and I love her. She wouldn't die and leave me. You're crazy. Tell me where she is, or I'll take you apart."

Captain Bolstad raised both hands. "Okay, Ryan, we'll go inside the hospital. Ted will come with us."

"Come on, buddy," Ted said, his voice strained with emotion. He placed one hand flat on Ryan's back.

"Get away from me," Ryan yelled, then took off at a run toward the hospital.

"Damn," Captain Bolstad said. "Let's go, Ted."

The two men ran after Ryan. The crowd chattered among themselves, speculating as to what was happening. The television crews filmed the drama on the chance there might be a further story unfolding.

Inside the hospital emergency room, the milling police officers, doctors and nurses had become statue still. An eerie silence hung over the area as Captain Bolstad and Ted entered.

Ryan was kneeling on the floor, holding Sherry in his arms, rocking back and forth and whispering her name over and over. The front of Sherry's white uniform was covered in blood, staining Ryan's shirt and pants.

Sherry MacAllister was dead.

Ryan MacAllister wept.

Three days later at ten o'clock in the morning, Sherry was buried beneath a mulberry tree in a nearby cemetery.

At two o'clock that afternoon, Ryan resigned from the police force.

Chapter One

Twenty Months Later

"Happy birthday to you!"

Deedee Hamilton sang the last line of the traditional song at the top of her lungs and terribly off-key.

"Hooray!" she yelled, clapping her hands along with the others who had gathered for the celebration. "You're both officially two years old. Isn't that wonderful?"

The two-year-olds in the limelight did not appear particularly impressed by the festivities. Matt frowned, obviously confused by the adult nonsense he was being subjected to. Noel sucked her thumb and ignored the entire performance.

"We've got a couple of real party animals here," Robert MacAllister, the twins' grandfather, said. "They're so excited, they can hardly hold themselves back."

Andrea, the toddlers' mother, laughed. "They think we're all nuts. Their hats didn't score any points. Let's see if the presents spark some interest. I want to take oodles of pictures of them opening their gifts, then we'll have some cake and ice cream."

A few minutes later, everyone was gathered in the large living room. Once the babies were shown how to tear away the bright wrapping paper, they dove in with enthusiasm, to the delight of their audience.

Deedee sat on the sofa, smiling and laughing along with the others at the antics of the now-happy children. She paused for a moment and glanced around the room.

How fortunate she was, she mused, to have been welcomed into the loving embrace of this wonderful family. They treated her as though she were one of them, including her in all their celebrations throughout the year. The darling twins were being taught to call her Aunt Deedee, a role she did *not* take lightly.

Mentally counting her blessings, she took an inventory of the people attending the babies' birthday party.

Robert and Margaret MacAllister were the senior MacAllisters.

Their oldest son, Michael, and his youngest brother, Forrest, represented MacAllister Architects, Incorporated, a prestigious firm the elder MacAllister had started on a shoestring many years ago. Robert was now retired, and he and Margaret enjoyed their leisure time by traveling, and being devoted grandparents.

Michael was married to Jenny, and had a son, Bobby, who had turned three a few months before. Bobby eyed the gifts wistfully, but seemed to understand that his cousins were the birthday boy and girl.

Andrea, the youngest MacAllister, was married to John, and had her hands full with the busy twins. Her degree in landscape architecture made her an extremely valuable asset to the family firm and she was once again working on a part-time basis, preferring to spend the majority of her day with the babies.

Forrest MacAllister was married to Deedee's dear friend, Jillian Jones-Jenkins, a highly successful author of many historical romance novels.

Deedee smiled as she looked at Jillian.

Jillian had that special, lovely glow about her, Deedee decided, that so many pregnant women had. She'd just started to wear maternity clothes, and Forrest had bought her the cute top she was wearing that said Baby Under Construction, which he'd proclaimed to be perfect for the wife of an architect.

Deedee's smile faded as her gaze fell on Ryan MacAllister. He was the second son, born between Michael and Forrest. She didn't know Ryan as well as the others, but she did know of the tragic loss of his wife more than a year and a half before. She'd met Sherry at the twins' christening, then had attended her funeral when she'd been slain by a berserk gunman at the hospital where she'd worked.

Since then, Ryan seemed to keep Deedee, as well as his family, at arm's length the majority of the time.

The family had been devastated by Sherry's violent death, then stunned when Ryan immediately resigned from the police force.

At the time, Andrea and Jillian had told Deedee that everyone was extremely worried about Ryan. He'd closed himself into the apartment where he'd lived with Sherry, and refused to allow anyone entry. For the entire month following his wife's death, he drank heavily, emerging only to buy food and more liquor.

At their wit's end, Michael, Forrest and Ted Sharpe, Ryan's former police partner, had gone to Ryan's and threatened to break the door down if he didn't let them in.

When Ryan finally opened the door, they discovered a Ryan who was alarmingly thin and haggard, with wild hair and a bushy beard. The apartment was a mess and reeked of alcohol. Ryan was angry at their intrusion and demanded to be left alone.

By brute force, he was thrown in the shower, told to put on fresh clothes, then hauled to a barbershop for a shave and haircut. The trio then took a fuming Ryan to a restaurant, ordered him a big meal and announced he wasn't leaving until he'd consumed the food.

While he was away from his apartment with his self-appointed rescuers, the women of the family had swooped in to clean, polish, wash clothes and stock the refrigerator.

Ted Sharpe had then threatened to stay at Ryan's,

sleeping on the sofa, and not leave until Ryan came up with a plan of action, a concrete decision as to what he was going to do with his life.

More out of desperation to be left alone than desire, Ryan had started his own business, MacAllister Security Systems.

Andrea had recently told Deedee that Ryan's company was growing, and he now had a secretary as well as two installers. What none of the family knew, Andrea had said with a sad-sounding sigh, was whether or not Ryan was pleased with his new endeavor, or if he was even close to finding an inner peace and had come to terms with Sherry's death. The walls he'd erected around himself after Sherry died were solidly in place.

"These gifts are from Uncle Ted," Andrea said to the twins. "He's on duty today, but he wishes you both a happy, happy birthday."

"Happy burffday," Noel said, clapping her hands. She reached eagerly for one of the presents that Andrea held. "Mine."

"Mine," Matt said.

Andrea laughed and gave them the gifts. "They're really getting with the program here. John, are you remembering to take pictures? I want a record of everything for the family album."

"I'm not missing a thing," John said, holding the camera to one eye. "There will be pages and pages in the album titled Twins Turning Two."

The twins tore open the boxes from Ted and each pulled out a stuffed toy. Ted Sharpe had gotten them teddy bears dressed in police uniforms, one a girl teddy bear and one a boy. As the adults exclaimed over the cute toys, Deedee looked quickly at Ryan.

He was separate and apart from the others, having leaned one shoulder against a far wall and crossed his arms loosely over his chest.

As the teddy bears in the police garb appeared, a slight smile formed on his lips. He shifted his stance, and his eyes collided with hers.

Her breath caught as she saw him immediately change his expression to a closed, unreadable one, revealing nothing of what he was feeling.

She returned her attention to the giggling twins.

Ryan was an extremely handsome man, Deedee thought. He was thirty-six or thirty-seven, about six feet tall with thick brown hair and the MacAllister brown eyes. He was well built, with wide shoulders and nicely proportioned muscles. And according to Jillian, he now focused all his energies on MacAllister Security Systems.

But there was a cold aura to Ryan MacAllister, a hands-off, don't-get-too-close attitude emanating from him with such intensity it was a nearly palpable entity. She had seen him conceal his emotions the moment their eyes met. He had perfected the ability to drop solid walls around himself at will.

Ryan MacAllister would certainly turn women's heads when he entered a room, but Deedee had a sneaky suspicion that he wouldn't care about, or even notice, the feminine attention he was receiving. It was as though, Andrea had once told Deedee, the fun-loving, warm, charming Ryan had died with Sherry.

The family was saddened as they realized that the

Ryan who had emerged from the month-long solitude was there to stay—aloof, empty and existing on not only the fringes of the family, but of life, as well.

Deedee shook her head slightly to bring her back to the activities around her.

Concentrating so intently on Ryan had, she realized, caused a gloomy feeling to settle over her, created by painful thoughts from her own past. She'd laid her ghosts to rest many years ago, and she would not allow Ryan's troubles to cause her dark memories to inch forward once again.

She needed to talk to him one-on-one, something she'd never done before. This party was an excellent opportunity to discuss with Ryan what was on her mind, but she now knew she'd have to be on emotional red alert. As coldhearted as it might sound, she'd have to make certain that Ryan's problems remained just that—his.

"On behalf of Noel and Matt," Andrea said, returning Deedee to the moment at hand, "I want to thank all of you for their lovely gifts."

"And the wrapping paper," John said, laughing as Matt shredded another piece. "Our son has a head for business. He's making confetti to sell next New Year's Eve."

"Cake and ice cream time," Andrea said. "Let's tromp back into the dining room, then you can bring your dessert in here where it's more comfortable."

"Great," Forrest said, rubbing his hands together. "We can play with the toys. These guys got some fascinating-looking stuff."

"Remember to share, Forrest," Jillian said, smiling

at him. "There will be none of this 'mine' business from you. Let Noel and Matt have a turn."

"Yes, ma'am," he said, then dropped a quick kiss on her lips. "This is research, darling wife. You know how you have to do all that heavy-duty research for your books? Well, I have an assignment that will be part of my job description as a daddy. I have to be able to assemble and know how to play with a vast variety of toys."

"Ah, I see," Jillian said, nodding. "It's tough work, but a daddy has to do it, I guess. Your self-sacrifice is duly noted."

"One should hope," he said.

"The writing is on the wall, Margaret," Robert MacAllister said. "In the future when we buy a toy for Jillian and Forrest's little one, we'll have to get two—one for the baby, and one for Forrest."

"Now that," Forrest said, pointing one finger in the air, "is a fantastic idea."

Everyone was laughing and talking as they went into the dining room. Ryan, Deedee noted, seemed to be chatting pleasantly with his mother. As each was served, they wandered back into the living room.

Ryan settled onto the padded bench edging the inside of a bay window at one end of the room.

Go for it, Deedee told herself. This was a perfect chance to speak with Ryan. She simply had to remember not to allow his reality to intrude on hers.

She crossed the room and smiled as she stopped in front of him.

"May I join you, Ryan?"

His head snapped up. "What? Oh, sure thing, Deedee. There's plenty of space here."

She sat down, then shifted so she could look directly at him.

"The twins were so cute with their presents," she said. "I'll be eager to see the pictures John took."

Ryan nodded, then took a bite of cake.

Brother, Deedee thought crossly, he apparently doesn't intend to even attempt to make conversation. If he smiled, his face would probably crack due to it being so long since he'd done it.

She sampled her own cake.

Patience, Deedee, she thought. Stay cheerful. She would *not* allow this grumpy, gloomy man to dim her party mood.

"This cake is delicious," she said, then paused. "Ryan, do you mind talking business on a Sunday afternoon?"

He looked at her again and shrugged. "No."

She'd never been this near to him before, Deedee mused. He really was extremely handsome. His features were rugged and masculine, and she could smell just the faintest hint of musky after-shave.

His eyes, though, were disturbing. All the MacAllisters had warm and expressive brown eyes, but Ryan's were…flat—yes, that was the word—with no clue as to what he was thinking or feeling.

"Deedee?" he said, frowning slightly.

"Oh, I'm sorry. I was daydreaming for a minute. What I wanted to talk to you about was—"

"You have freckles," Ryan said suddenly. "I

never noticed that before. They're dancing a jig right across your nose.''

Lord, MacAllister, he thought, where had that come from? What a stupid thing to open his mouth and say. What difference did it make if Deedee Hamilton had freckles on her pert little nose? It was just that it was rather refreshing that she hadn't covered them with that makeup glop women used. She let them do the two-step on her nose for all the world to see.

Deedee blinked. ''Well, yes, I have freckles on my nose. They've been there forever. In all the time you and I have known each other, I guess you've never been this close—'' she laughed ''—to my nose.''

A shaft of unexpected heat rocketed through Ryan's body at the tinkling sound of Deedee's laughter. As though seeing her for the first time, he quickly cataloged her big, brown eyes, her short hair that was a fetching mass of strawberry blond curls and her delicate features.

Deedee Hamilton, he mused, was very pretty. She wasn't beautiful, or sophisticatedly stunning; she was pretty, in a wholesome, fresh-air-and-sunshine way. And he sure did like those cute freckles.

Why was he having this asinine conversation with himself? he wondered in self-disgust. He really didn't give a rip if Deedee had a polka-dotted nose and laughter like windchimes and... *Ah, hell, MacAllister, can it.*

Ryan cleared his throat and set his plate next to him on the cushion.

''You wanted to discuss business?'' he said, looking at Deedee again.

She continued to smile. "Have we thoroughly exhausted the subject of my nose?"

Ryan smiled.

He couldn't help himself really, because Deedee's laughter was infectious and her smile beckoned to be matched by another one. Her brown eyes—the biggest brown eyes he'd ever seen—were sparkling, actually sparkling. The entire package that was Deedee was extremely appealing.

So he smiled.

And Deedee stopped breathing.

Dear heaven, she thought, then told herself to draw some air into her lungs before she passed out on her freckled nose. Ryan MacAllister's smile was a sight to behold. The stern set of his jaw relaxed, and the creases in his forehead smoothed, making him appear younger. His teeth were white and straight, and his lips were shaped so perfectly.

And those MacAllister brown eyes were now warm and inviting, like chocolate sauce a person would gladly drown in.

"You have a wonderful smile, Ryan," she said, hearing the thread of breathlessness in her voice. "You should use it more often. It's perfectly legal for me to express my opinion regarding your smile, since you commented on my freckled nose."

Ryan chuckled and nodded. "Tit for tat. Now we're even."

Oh, not fair, Deedee thought. That throaty chuckle was without a doubt one of the sexiest, most masculine sounds she'd ever heard. Her cheeks felt warm. If she was blushing because she couldn't ignore the purely feminine flutter in the pit of her stomach, she was going to die of embarrassment right there on the spot.

"You're blushing," Ryan said. "Did I miss something here?"

"No," she said quickly. "I'm not blushing. Well, yes, I guess I am, but that doesn't mean I have any legitimate *reason* to blush. Sometimes I just blush, which is very annoying, considering that I'm thirty-three years old, for crying out loud. Oh, good Lord, now I'm babbling." She waved one hand in the air. "Ignore me."

Ryan's smile faded. "That would be difficult to do, Deedee."

Their eyes met, and Deedee could hear the sudden increased tempo of her heart echoing in her ears.

Heat once again swept through Ryan's body, coiling deep and low within him. He told himself to tear his gaze from Deedee's, to stop looking at those remarkable brown eyes of hers, but he couldn't move.

Damn it, he fumed, what kind of spell weaver was she? What was she doing to him? Well, he wasn't interested—not in her, or any woman, for that matter.

"Attention, folks," Forrest yelled. "I need your undivided attention, one and all."

Deedee and Ryan jerked at the sudden intrusive noise of Forrest's booming voice. They snapped their heads around to stare at Forrest standing in the middle of the room.

Bless you, Forrest, Deedee thought. Ryan Mac-Allister was a dangerous man. There was just something, a blatantly masculine and sensual *something*, about him that was compelling, nearly overpowering. She wanted no part of it, whatever it was. No.

"All right, here it is," Forrest said, rubbing his hands together. "The topic is The Baby Bet."

"Oh, good grief," Jillian said, rolling her eyes heavenward.

"You're a tad early," Michael said. "Well, whatever. Okay, I bet that Jillian *is* going to have a baby. I win. Give me some money."

"Cork it, Michael," Forrest said. "This is serious business. I am, as all of you know, The Baby Bet champion. I won when Bobby was born *and* when the twins arrived. It's only fair to warn you that I've since won The Baby Bet with the mailman, a couple I designed a house for, *and* one of Jillian's author friends. Simply put, I can't be beat." He nodded decisively, a smug expression on his face.

"Margaret," Robert MacAllister said, "where did we go wrong raising that one?"

"I have no idea," she said, patting her husband's knee. "He certainly is full of himself, isn't he?"

Forrest glared at his parents. "I'm stating facts here, Mr. and Mrs. MacAllister. I *am* The Baby Bet champion."

"Yes, dear," his mother said. "I do believe the whole world knows that by now."

"I should hope so," Forrest said.

"It's time to unchampion you," Michael said. "Is that a word?"

Jillian laughed. "I don't think so."

"Okay, big shot," John said. "What's the deal?"

"I'm glad you asked," Forrest said. "Now pay attention, people, because this one is going to be complicated.''

''Jillian,'' Andrea said, ''are you going to strangle him, or run him down with your car?''

''Could I have some respect here?'' Forrest hollered.

''No!'' John and Michael yelled in unison.

''No, no, no,'' Noel said merrily.

''Hush, sweetheart,'' Andrea said. ''Your Uncle Forrest is slipping over the edge.''

''What a group,'' Forrest said, shaking his head.

What a *wonderful* group, Deedee thought, laughing softly. Oh, how she adored this family. They were warm, loving, funny and fun.

Ryan slid a quick glance at Deedee.

Her eyes were sparkling again, he mused. She was enjoying the crazy antics of his family to the max. Deedee was a widow. Yeah, he remembered that now. Her husband had been killed many years ago, though he didn't recall the details of how it had happened. She was alone and had adopted, per se, the MacAllisters as her family.

Why would a pretty, vivacious, refreshing woman like Deedee Hamilton still be alone? Ryan wondered. Oh, hell, what difference did it make? It was none of his business. He really didn't care. But then again, it didn't make sense. Why was Deedee still alone?

''If you're done being dumb,'' Forrest said, ''I'll explain the program. Jillian is having an ultrasound on Wednesday. Therefore, The Baby Bet is high-tech. It includes not only the questions of is it a boy or a girl? One? Twins? But also the stand that they won't be able to tell the sex because the munchkin was modest and stayed curled up. Get it?''

"Ah-h-h," Michael said, stroking his chin. "I like this one. It has pizzazz. Whip out your paper and pencil, Forrest. I'm ready."

Forrest took a small pad of paper and a pen from his shirt pocket.

"Go for it, Michael," he said, "and get ready to kiss your twenty bucks goodbye."

"Says you," Michael said. "Okay, here's my prediction. Jillian is having twins. That's a given, because she's getting very fat, very fast."

"*Him* I'll strangle," Jillian said.

"I'll bet," Michael said, staring at the ceiling, "a girl and an unknown. They won't be able to tell the sex of the second one."

"Got it," Forrest said, writing on the pad.

"No, no way. It's just one big boy," John said.

"One girl," Ryan said, "who will take after Jillian, because the world isn't ready for another Forrest."

Forrest looked at him in surprise. "You want in on The Baby Bet?"

"Yeah, why not?" Ryan said. More to the question...why? He hadn't interacted with his family's nonsense since... Well, The Baby Bet was no big deal. It was sort of fun. What the hell, why not? "I don't mind taking your money, Forrest."

"Not a chance. All right, you're in. Dad? What about you?"

"Well, it seems to me," Robert said, "that we should be told the champion's bet. I want to know where your money is going, Forrest, before I decide on mine.''

"Clever man," Forrest said. "No wonder we all turned out so terrific. You're a smart person."

"Spill it," Ryan said. "What's your bet?"

"Ladies and gentleman," Forrest said, "the champion, and the planning-to-remain champion, is hereby placing his twenty dollars on girls." He paused, sweeping his gaze over the group, then grinned at Jillian. "Three of them!"

"What?" Jillian said, jumping to her feet. "Forrest MacAllister, don't you dare say such a thing out loud. With your uncanny knack for winning The Baby Bet..." She sank back onto her chair and pressed her hands to her cheeks. "Oh, my stars."

"Twins run in the family," Margaret said thoughtfully, "so I suppose it's reasonable that there might be... Goodness gracious."

Deedee looked at Ryan with wide eyes.

"Triplets?" she said. "No, that's crazy. You don't think he's right, do you, Ryan?"

Ryan chuckled and shrugged, realizing to his own amazement that he was actually enjoying himself.

"Forrest is the champion," he said, still smiling. "He hasn't been wrong so far."

"Do you realize," Deedee said, "how many diapers a person would change in one given day if they had three babies?"

"Quite a few."

"No, no, no," Jillian said to no one in particular. "I refuse. That's it. Nope. I'm not having triplets, three baby girls at one time. No, no, no."

''No, no, no,'' Noel said, clapping her hands.

''Thank you, Noel,'' Jillian said. ''I appreciate your support.''

''Wednesday night,'' Forrest said, ''we'll all meet at Mario's for pizza at seven o'clock to hear the results of the test, and to announce the winner of The Baby Bet. Me.''

''This time you're going to lose,'' Jillian said. ''Please, Forrest?''

Everyone started talking at once about Forrest's outrageous prediction.

''Well, Deedee,'' Ryan said, ''will you be at Mario's to see how this comes out?''

''I certainly will.'' She paused. ''Are you planning to go?''

Ryan started to automatically reply in the negative, then hesitated.

What the hell, why not?

''Yes,'' he said, looking directly into her eyes. ''Yes, I'll be there.''

Chapter Two

Before Deedee could comment on Ryan having confirmed that he would be joining everyone for pizza, a buzzing noise sounded.

"Excuse me," Ryan said.

He reached for a small black box that was clipped to the side of his belt. Numbers were moving across a half-inch viewing bar near the top of the device. He nodded, pressed a button to erase the numbers, then slid the box back onto his belt.

"That doesn't surprise me," he said, looking at Deedee again. "I've got my guys working overtime today on a system the customer wanted put in five minutes after he decided to get it. I told my men to give me a holler if they had any problems." He got to his feet. "They obviously have a problem. If you'll excuse me, Deedee, I'll go telephone them."

"Yes, of course."

Deedee watched as Ryan walked across the room, indulging herself in a thorough scrutiny of his very nice tush. He also, she mused, moved with the smooth, athletic grace of a man in excellent physical condition, who was comfortable in his body. She'd never noticed that before.

Good buns, she reaffirmed in her mind, then scolded herself in the next instant for being naughty.

Actually, she was glad that Ryan had been removed from her presence at the moment he had been. Now she would simply refuse to discuss with herself the rush of pleasure that had swept through her when he had said he would be joining everyone for pizza on Wednesday night. Her reaction had been ridiculous and unexplainable. She would, therefore, ignore it.

"I have to go," Ryan announced to the group when he reappeared in the room. "There's a snag on a hurry-up job we're doing, and my crew needs an extra pair of hands." He tousled Noel's hair, then Matt's. "Happy birthday. Check your Uncle Forrest's pockets before he leaves to be sure he doesn't have any of your new toys."

Ryan thanked Andrea and John for the great party, hugged his mother, then looked over at Deedee.

"It was nice talking to you, Deedee," he said from the center of the room. "I'll be seeing you."

She smiled and nodded.

I'll be seeing you, too, she thought, on Wednesday night at Mario's. *Oh, Deedee, for Pete's sake, cut it out.*

As soon as Ryan had left the house, Andrea made a beeline for Deedee and plunked down next to her on the window seat.

"Deedee Hamilton," Andrea said, beaming, "what did you do to my brother?"

"Do?" Deedee repeated, obviously confused.

"Yes, 'do.' Ryan was smiling, laughing...was enjoying himself. I know he was. Plus, he took part in The Baby Bet. He was, here, in this very room, sitting next to you, more like the old Ryan than he has been since Sherry died. So I repeat. What did you do?"

"Nothing," she said, laughing. "You're acting as though I cast a spell over him, or sprinkled magic dust on his cake, or something. We were simply chatting. I didn't urge him to participate in The Baby Bet. He just opened his mouth and did it."

"Amazing," Andrea said, shaking her head. "And wonderful, believe me. Everyone noticed that he was more relaxed, easygoing...well, more like he used to be than we've seen him behave in nearly two years. *You* definitely had a hand in that."

"Andrea," Deedee said, narrowing her eyes, "pay attention to what I'm about to say. Don't you dare get into your Cupid mode in regard to me and Ryan. I am *not* interested."

Andrea splayed one hand on her chest. "Would I do that? Play Cupid? Me?"

"Don't pull your all-innocent routine on me. I was your partner in crime in Cupidville when we got Jillian and Forrest together. Remember? I recognize that gleam in your eyes, because we both had it back then when we thought we were hotshot Cupids. We came very close to creating a total disaster, if you'll recall.''

Andrea sighed. ''I know. It almost backfired big time.'' She smiled again. ''But it turned out all right. Do note that our Jillian and Forrest are as happy as two bugs in a rug.''

''Andrea, do *not* try to be a matchmaker between me and Ryan. Promise?''

''Oh…do I have to?''

''Yes, because I know you'd never break a promise.''

''Well, darn.'' Andrea paused. ''Okay, I promise under protest. It's a shame, because you obviously had a marvelous influence on Ryan.''

''You're reading too much into it. He allowed *himself* to have a good time today. It had nothing to do with me. I wouldn't get too excited about it so you won't be disappointed. It may have been an isolated incident that won't happen again.''

''That's true, I suppose. It breaks my heart to continually see how much he's changed, how closed he is, aloof. He built walls around himself when Sherry died. I wish he'd… Oh, I've been through this wish list a thousand times.''

''I know you have, Andrea. You all love him and want him to be happy again. The thing is, you can't heal his wounds for him. He has to do it himself.''

''But what if he doesn't, Deedee? It's been nearly two years already. Well, it was wonderful to see him smile today, hear him laugh. Wouldn't it be something if he showed up for pizza Wednesday night?

No, I'm dreaming. He only joins the family for special occasions. He wouldn't come for The Baby Bet nonsense of Forrest's.''

Deedee started to speak, then decided against it. There was no point in telling Andrea that Ryan had said he *would* be attending the gathering at Mario's. There was every chance that he'd change his mind, and it wouldn't be kind to get Andrea's hopes up.

''Oh, darn,'' Deedee said, her eyes widening.

''What's wrong?''

''I never got a chance to talk to Ryan about the security system for Books and Books. I'd like him to give me an estimate on what it would cost to install a better system than the landlord provides. According to my lease, I can do it at my own expense. I have over two hundred rare books now, in addition to my regular stock. I need to protect them better against theft.''

''Call Ryan tomorrow,'' Andrea said, studying her fingernails. ''Ask him to stop by the store.'' She looked at Deedee and smiled. ''Then invite him out to dinner.''

''Andrea,'' Deedee said, a warning tone to her voice, ''you promised. Erase the word Cupid from your brain.''

''You're no fun.''

''Tough toasties.''

''Deedee, speaking of Wednesday at Mario's for pizza, are you coming?''

''Sure.''

''Good. Oh, my, can you believe what Forrest predicted? Three baby girls? Triplets? My twins keep me hopping, let me tell you. I can't imagine having three. No, Forrest is wrong. He may be The Baby Bet champion, but he's about to be—what did Michael say?—oh, yes, unchampioned.''

''I wouldn't be so certain of that, Andrea. Jillian is getting quite a tummy for only being four months' pregnant. That's why the doctor wants to do the ultrasound. Plus, Forrest has had a perfect score up to now. He has an uncanny knack, it seems, for winning The Baby Bet.''

''Oh, my,'' Andrea said, shaking her head. ''It boggles the mind.''

''I wouldn't miss that pizza party Wednesday for anything,'' Deedee said. ''I want to hear the results of that test.''

''Mmm,'' Andrea said, tapping one fingertip against her chin. ''I wonder if Ryan will be there?''

''Oh, good night,'' Deedee said, rolling her eyes heavenward.

Would Ryan actually come? she mused. *Deedee Hamilton, that is enough.* She was as bad as Andrea. The subject of Ryan's attendance, or nonattendance, at Mario's was a closed and forgotten topic. If he showed up…fine. If not…no big deal. Then again, he *did* say that he planned to be there and…

''Oh-h-h,'' Deedee said with a moan. She was driving herself crazy.

''What's your problem?'' Andrea said, blinking in surprise at Deedee's outburst.

''Problem? Oh. My problem.'' She jumped to her feet. ''I was trying to talk myself out of having another piece of cake, but I lost the battle.'' She sighed dramatically. ''More calories, here I come.''

''You don't have to watch your weight,'' Andrea said, frowning. ''You eat whatever you want to and don't gain an ounce. You're greenly envied by the general female populace.''

''Oh, well, yes, but one never knows when one's metabolism might change. I may turn into a Pillsbury Dough Girl before your very eyes. Too bad. I'm off to get more cake.''

''Pillsbury Dough Girl?'' Andrea said, laughing as Deedee marched away. ''If Forrest is right, I'm afraid it's Jillian who's going to have that dubious honor.''

Ryan jerked upward in bed and drew a deep, ragged breath. His heart was pounding wildly, and beads of sweat dotted his forehead. He shook his head, hoping to dispel the lingering fogginess of sleep *and* the images of the disturbing dream he'd had.

The clock on the nightstand glowed 2:12 a.m. With a groan, he sank back onto the pillow, wishing it was closer to dawn so he could leave the bed and begin the day.

He did *not* want to run the risk of drifting off to sleep again and having the dream pick up where it had left off.

Damn it, he fumed, dragging both hands down his face. *He'd dreamed about Deedee Hamilton.* It had been so real, not one of those mishmash dreams that made no sense.

Oh, it had made sense, all right. Deedee had been standing in front of him in a vivid field of wildflowers, wearing a pink gauze dress. The sky was a brilliant blue, and a dozen beautiful butterflies had been fluttering through the air above her head.

She had lifted her slender hands in an enticingly feminine and graceful motion, as though to touch the elusive butterflies.

And then she'd laughed in delight, the enchanting sound causing desire to course through him like a roaring current rushing out of control.

In the dream, he'd reached for her, wanting her, aching for her, burning. Just as his hand grazed her arm, she twirled away, her laughter lilting through the flower-scented air.

''I'm a butterfly, Ryan,'' she called. ''Catch me if you can.''

He matched her smile. ''And if I do?''

''Then I'll be yours. We'll make love, here, in the beautiful flowers beneath the blue sky. The butterflies will protect us from outsiders. There will be only the two of us, together. Forever, Ryan. Forever, forever, forever.''

Ryan threw back the blankets, left the bed, then strode naked from the bedroom to the kitchen. He turned on the light, squinting against the bright glare. Moving to the sink, he drank a glass of water, then thudded the glass onto the counter.

Gripping the edge of the sink so tightly his knuckles were white, he stared unseeing at his own reflection in the dark window in front of him.

A painful knot twisted in his gut and he welcomed

it, acknowledged it as his due for having had a sensual dream about a woman other than Sherry.

He mentally scrambled for Sherry's image, wanting it front-row center in his mind's eye. *But it wouldn't come. He couldn't see it.* Every corner of his brain held pictures of Deedee.

Deedee smiling. Laughing. Dancing with the butterflies. Beckoning to him.

Promising him forever.

"Damn it," he said.

He made a fist and slammed it on the counter, pain shooting up his arm like a hot arrow.

"Oh, hell," he said, clutching his fist with his other hand. "Man, oh, man, that hurts."

Turning on the faucet, he held the throbbing hand under cold water, swearing a blue streak in self-disgust.

Why? he asked himself. Why in the name of heaven had he dreamed something like that about Deedee Hamilton? He hadn't looked at another woman since Sherry had been killed. To him, their wedding vows were still firmly in place. He was married to Sherry, and he would be until the day he died. *Death was the only forever that was guaranteed.*

But, dear God, he couldn't see Sherry's face!

In one of his drunken rages following her death, he'd destroyed every picture he'd had of her, unable to bear the agony of looking at the woman he loved, knowing he would never hold her, kiss her, make love to her again.

He'd later regretted his rash action, but what was

done was done. He had the image of Sherry in crystal clarity in his mind, and that would hold him in good stead.

And it had.

Until now.

Until this horrifying, guilt-ridden night, when he'd dreamed of another woman, of Deedee. And the damnable blue sky and butterflies.

As his hand began to grow numb from the icy cold water, he smacked off the faucet and reached for the towel slipped through the handle of the refrigerator.

A few minutes later he returned to bed, staring up at a ceiling he couldn't see in the darkness.

Get a grip, MacAllister, he ordered himself. So okay, the dream had shaken him, made him feel like a scum, but it *was* only a dream. But weren't dreams supposedly messages of truth from a person's subconscious? Hell, he didn't know. He was a cop, not a shrink.

Oh, great, terrific, just dandy. He'd just mentally referred to himself as a cop, something he hadn't been for nearly two years. Where had *that* come from?

Easy, MacAllister, you're losing it.

He had to calm down, sort this through, determine what was going on.

Deedee.

He'd known her for years, but today at the twins' birthday party was the first occasion he'd ever really talked to her. In the past he'd done the usual ''Hello. How are you? Goodbye'' routine at family gatherings. Today they'd had an actual conversation, face-to-face.

And Deedee had freckles on her nose.

Ryan muttered an earthy expletive and told himself to forget about the freckles on Deedee Hamilton's nose. Her nose was not the issue. What was important here was what in the hell that woman had done to him in the short time they'd sat together on the window seat. Sat *close* together, very close.

Actually, now that he thought about it, he'd acted rather weird during the entire birthday party. For reasons he couldn't fathom, he'd taken part in The Baby Bet, told Deedee he'd be joining the group for pizza on Wednesday night and had relaxed and enjoyed the twins' party.

Strange, very strange.

Well, that was fine. His unusual behavior had produced a loving and happy smile on his mother's face. It hadn't strained his brain to be a little more sociable for a change. So okay, that settled that part of this confusing maze.

Which brought him right back to Deedee.

Deedee Hamilton had not been the *cause* of his enjoying the celebration, rather she had been a *result* of his unexpected attitude. He let down his guard, and she'd skittered into place right in front of him, complete with the cutest freckled nose and the biggest brown eyes he'd ever seen.

Ryan released a sigh of relief. There, he'd figured it all out. He hadn't been disloyal to Sherry, not really. Now that he had the facts, everything would fall back into place as it should be. He'd see Sherry clearly in his mind's eye, remember the sound of her laughter and the feel of her lips on his.

''Yes,'' he said, decisively.

He rolled onto his stomach, closed his eyes and, moments later, was asleep.

But when Ryan awoke hours later, his fury returned in full force.

The first thought he'd had, the first vision he'd seen in his mind when he woke up, had been of Deedee.

Chapter Three

"Here you are," Deedee said, handing a woman a plastic bag. "I hope you enjoy the books."

"Oh, I will," the woman said, smiling. "My husband has gone to a business conference for three days in Colorado. I plan to light a fire in the hearth, curl up with my cat and a warm afghan and not budge. These books will be the frosting on my 'it's my turn for me' cake."

"That sounds marvelous," Deedee said, returning the woman's smile.

"Don't misunderstand me, dear. I love my husband every bit, if not more, than when I married him thirty-six years ago. But I've learned that if I indulge myself, pamper myself, when he goes away like this, my emotional batteries get recharged. And I'm so very glad to see him when he arrives home."

"You're a wise woman," Deedee said, nodding.

"My dear," she said, laughing, "I truly believe that women in general are far wiser than men. Well, goodbye for now."

"Goodbye."

A frown replaced Deedee's smile as she watched the woman leave the store.

Thirty-six years, she mused. When that woman had spoken of her husband coming home, love had shone in her eyes, on her face. That couple had been married longer than she, herself, had been on this earth. Incredible. What would it be like to literally spend a lifetime with a man, a soul mate? How glorious it must be to have a forever with a special someone.

Deedee shook her head slightly in self-disgust.

Where were these strange thoughts coming from? During the years since her husband, Jim, had been killed, she'd intentionally avoided any serious relationships with men. She'd considered her options carefully, weighed and measured, sifted and sorted, and decided never to remarry.

What she'd shared with Jim, albeit for a short time, had been rare and beautiful. Love like that, she was convinced, didn't happen twice. Rather than settle for less than what she'd had, she had focused on starting her own business with Jim's insurance money.

She was a dedicated career woman, and had been for a long time. Her life-style suited her perfectly, and she was content and fulfilled. She dated regularly, had wonderful friends and even a family in the form of the MacAllister clan.

Her own parents had passed away within months

of each other seven years ago. She'd been widowed for three years then, and the loss of her parents had been devastating. Once again she'd had to reach deep within herself for the strength to cope with her grief.

Why was she dwelling on the past today? Deedee wondered. She really didn't know, but she'd felt a strange chill of loneliness within her as the customer had spoken of the love for her husband of thirty-six years.

Loneliness? That was absurd. Deedee was *not* lonely. She wasn't a single woman by default, but by choice. She had her existence established exactly the way she wanted it. The MacAllisters were even adding more babies to the ever-growing family, babies she could spoil rotten in her role of Aunt Deedee.

No, that hadn't really been loneliness she'd registered, it was merely fatigue. She was exhausted, because she hadn't slept well the night before. It was very unusual for her to toss and turn, but she'd spent a restless night, only dozing, then waking again. No, she hadn't slept well at all because...

Deedee sighed.

Because she'd been thinking about Ryan Mac-Allister.

There, she'd admitted it.

She glanced at the clock on the wall.

It had taken her until 1:16 in the afternoon to square off against the ridiculous truth, but now she'd done it. She'd been consumed through the seemingly endless night by thoughts and images of Ryan.

Like a silly teenager, she'd been unable to keep

herself from replaying in her mind every moment she'd spent with Ryan at the twins' birthday party.

"Dumb," she said under her breath.

She retrieved a dust cloth from beneath the counter and marched across the room to dust books that didn't need dusting.

Because of her asinine performance of the night before, she'd been reluctant to telephone Ryan's office today to make an appointment with him to come to Books and Books and determine the best security system to protect her collection of rare books.

She now realized she'd been harboring the irrational idea that if she came face-to-face with Ryan, he'd instantly know that her mind had been centered on him through the night.

Even worse, she'd somehow telegraph to him the fact that more than once during those hours she'd experienced the heated thrum of desire pulsing low in her body.

"Dumb, dumb, dumb," she said to a cookbook. "He'd never know how infantile I'd been."

Well, now wait a minute.

She stopped, holding the dust cloth in midair and staring into space.

Maybe she was being too hard on herself. It was...healthy—yes, she liked that conclusion—that she had a normal, womanly, although a tad wanton, reaction to an extremely handsome, virile, masculinity-personified man.

As long as she didn't tear her clothes off and leap into Ryan's arms when she saw him again, she decided with a smile, there was no harm done. Her restless night simply reaffirmed that she was alive and kicking. Healthy.

The next encounter with Ryan would prove without a doubt that she was over her momentary female-to-male reaction to him, and everything would be status quo.

She was perfectly fine *now,* as a matter of fact, and would confirm that knowledge by telephoning him at his office as she should have done the moment she arrived at the store that morning.

With a decisive nod and the self-assurance that she'd logically explained and could therefore dismiss her bizarre and sleepless night, Deedee started back across the room, her destination being the telephone.

When she was within four feet of the counter, the door opened, accompanied by the tinkling of the brass bell above it. She turned with a smile to greet the customer, then froze, the smile disappearing into oblivion.

Ryan MacAllister had just entered Books and Books.

Ryan closed the door, but didn't move forward. Their eyes met. Neither spoke.

Ah, damn, Ryan fumed. His grand plan had just gone up in the smoke being created by the heated desire rocketing through him.

After being wired and edgy the entire morning, and *still* unable to dismiss Deedee Hamilton from his mind, he'd decided to confront her in person. The encounter, he was certain, would get him safely back on track. Deedee would once again become the friendly, attractive woman he'd known for several years, with no major role or impact whatsoever on his life.

He had a legitimate excuse to come to Books and Books. Deedee had expressed the wish to discuss business with him, but he'd been called away before they'd talked about what was on her agenda. He was being an efficient executive by following through on her request.

So there he was, standing in her store, fully prepared to breathe a sigh of relief that whatever nonsense had possessed him during the hideous night before was actually long since gone.

Instead...? His blood was pounding in his veins, his heart was beating like a bongo drum and he had a nearly overpowering urge to cross the room, haul Deedee into his arms and kiss her senseless.

Damn it to hell, what was this woman doing to him?

A deep frown settled over Ryan's features as he swept his gaze around the spacious, attractive store.

"Nice place," he said gruffly.

Deedee gave herself a mental shake, ordered her heart to slow its racing pace and plastered what she hoped would appear to be a normal friendly smile on her face.

Suddenly remembering her irrational thought that Ryan would be able to peer into her brain and see how she'd spent the night, she blushed. The warm flush on her cheeks caused her to silently moan in embarrassment.

Oh, Deedee, she begged herself, *please get it together.*

''Hello?'' Ryan said.

''Oh. Thank you for the compliment about the store. I'm very proud of Books and Books.''

She hurried across the room, deciding to put the counter between her and Ryan, hoping to feel less vulnerable and exposed.

''I was just going to call you, Ryan,'' she said, smiling brightly. ''You must have been reading my mind.'' Oh, good grief, what a dumb thing to say. He'd better *not* be reading her mind. ''I appreciate your coming by.''

''You said at the twins' party that you wanted to discuss business,'' he said with no hint of a smile, ''but we didn't have a chance to do so.'' He shrugged. ''So here I am, ready to discuss business.''

Yes, Deedee thought, there he was, gorgeous as all get-out *and* grumpy. There was no evidence of the warm, friendly, relaxed Ryan of yesterday emanating from the man standing before her now. If this was his business demeanor, it was a miracle that he had so many customers. Well, fine. Two could play at this game.

''I wish to have a cost estimate done,'' she said, lifting her chin, ''on an upgraded security system. As you can see, I've had cabinets custom-made with locks and wired glass to protect my rare books. The landlord has installed an alarm system that sets off a siren if exterior doors or windows are forced open.''

''Mmm,'' Ryan said, nodding. He walked slowly across the room to stand opposite her at the counter. ''Let me guess. All the shops on this block have the same system, and they go off at the slightest provocation. For example, if a heavy truck is driven down the street. No one pays any attention to the sirens because of all the false alerts.''

''That's correct.'' She folded her hands primly on top of the counter. ''My rare-book collection has grown considerably over the past few years and is very valuable. I want to protect those books more effectively and efficiently.''

Ryan narrowed his eyes. ''Is there some reason you're talking like a schoolteacher lecturing a classroom full of kids who aren't paying much attention? You sound stuffy as hell.''

''Well, I beg your humble pardon,'' she said, planting her hands on her hips. ''I was merely matching the tone you set when you came through that door. Not stuffy, Mr. MacAllister. Grumpy.''

''Grumpy?'' he repeated, then laughed in spite of himself. ''Now *that* is a great word.'' He shook his head, still smiling. ''Grumpy.''

The rich timbre of Ryan's oh-so-male laughter had the now-familiar effect on Deedee, and she felt the rush of heat swirling within her. While she'd decided her feminine reaction to Ryan's masculinity was healthy, it was becoming extremely unsettling and definitely annoying.

''Yes, well,'' she said, poking her nose in the air, ''you *were* grumpy when you arrived. You were not in a frame of mind befitting a professional businessman.''

''Want a sample of my cop mode?'' he said, grinning. ''I could give you a demonstration of my 'Up against the wall, scum,' that goes far beyond grumpy.''

''No,'' she said, unable to curb her bubbling laughter any longer. ''I'll pass on that one, thank you.''

They continued to look at each other, sharing their smiles and savoring the warmth of the moment. Then slowly, so slowly, their smiles faded as the sensuality simmering beneath the warmth grew stronger, weaving around and through them, changing the comforting warmth into licking flames of heated desire.

Deedee's breasts were heavy, achy, yearning for a soothing caress. Her heart was pounding, and somewhere in her hazy mind she had the irrational thought that surely Ryan could hear its rapid tempo.

Everything seemed magnified, heightened. She was strangely aware of the feel of the soft curls of her hair against her cheeks and neck, of the gentle slope of her hips and buttocks and of the pulsing heat deep within her femininity.

From a source unknown, a little voice began to whisper to her, gaining volume as it insisted on being heeded.

Deedee, wake up. Ryan is dangerous. He's a threat to your peace of mind and the path you've chosen to walk in your life. Wake up.

She tore her gaze from his and took a step backward, wrapping her hands around her elbows in a protective gesture.

Ryan shook his head slightly to dispel the lingering, passion-laden fog that had consumed his sense of reality. He had been thrown off-kilter by Deedee Hamilton yet again. He knew it, and didn't like the fact, not one damn bit. He was, to quote Ms. Hamilton, now definitely grumpy.

"Hell," he said, running a restless hand over the back of his neck. "This is nuts. We're rather old to be experiencing hormone wars and unbridled lust. Enough is enough here."

Lust? Deedee's mind echoed. What an awful, unappealing word to describe the sensations she'd felt. Ryan was frowning again, retreating behind his walls, being grumpy to the max.

Lust? Ryan was right, of course, she mused on. That's all it could be, as there certainly weren't any romantic emotions involved in what kept happening between them. This was a classic case of chemical attraction, or some such thing. But wasn't there a more gentle word than lust?

"Did you hear what I said, Deedee?" Ryan said. "I don't want any part of..." He stopped speaking for a moment, searching his mind for a suitable description, then giving up the futile attempt. "I don't want any part of whatever this is!"

"You don't have to yell about it," she said, glaring at him.

"Sorry," he mumbled.

"Unbridled lust," she said with a cluck of disgust. "You're so eloquent, Mr. MacAllister."

"Well, what would *you* call it?" he said, matching her glower.

"I don't know. But I wouldn't describe it with something as tacky as *lust*."

"This," he said, pointing one long finger at her, "is an asinine conversation."

"Don't point that thing at me, it has a nail in it." She paused. "That was a joke, Ryan. You know, those funny little things people say so that other people will smile? Oh, forget it. You probably used up a year's quota of smiles at the twins' party, and now you're stuck on automatic grumpy, sullen, cold...all of the above."

"That's a lousy thing to say," he protested.

"It's right up there with 'unbridled lust,' mister."

Ryan opened his mouth to retort, then closed it again. When he finally spoke, there was a nondescript expression on his face and his voice had a pleasant tone to it.

"I can't help wondering," he said, "what that customer who's around the corner there is thinking about this chat we're having."

Deedee's eyes widened in horror and her hands flew to her cheeks.

"Oh, no," she whispered. "Don't tell me there's someone in here. I could have sworn I was alone when you arrived. Oh, my word, how embarrassing. Ryan, please say it isn't true."

He leaned toward her. "It isn't true," he said, matching her whisper for whisper.

"You rat," she said with a burst of laughter. "I believed you."

"You bought it, all right," he said, chuckling. "Even the freckles on your nose were blushing." He paused. "Deedee, look, let's start over. I just now came into the store. Okay? I'm here to discuss the possibility of upgrading your security system. As for the other... Well, we'll forget it. It won't happen again. It wasn't important. Agreed?''

Deedee nodded, while telling herself that what Ryan had just said made perfect sense, and was the best solution for moving past what had transpired between them. She was *not* registering a sense of disappointment at his having said, ''It wasn't important.'' No, of course, she wasn't. It was just that... *Oh, Deedee, shut up.*

''Deedee, do you agree?''

''What? Oh, yes, certainly.'' She waved one hand breezily in the air. ''As you said, it wasn't important.'' She cleared her throat. ''Now then, let's talk about protecting me from...'' *You!* ''What I mean is, protecting my rare books and keeping them from being stolen.''

''Right. First I need to look at the system you have now, then go from there. I want to check the electrical box. Where's your back door?''

Before Deedee could reply, a woman in her sixties entered the store.

''Hello,'' Deedee said, smiling. ''May I help you find something, or would you prefer to browse?''

''I'm looking for a book on butterflies,'' the woman said. ''It's for my grandson, who is about to celebrate his tenth birthday. He's fascinated by butterflies.''

''Let me show you what we have in the children's section,'' Deedee said. ''Ryan, the back door is through the storeroom, around the corner there.''

''I'll find it,'' he said.

Ryan watched as Deedee came from behind the

counter, then joined the woman. As the pair walked across the room, he let out a pent-up breath.

Butterflies? he mentally fumed. A woman comes into the store at exactly that moment and wants a book about butterflies?

Damn, the dream he'd had about Deedee the night before was rolling across his mental vision like a movie he had no way to stop.

There was Deedee, dancing with the butterflies. There was Deedee, looking like a vision of loveliness. There was Deedee, beckoning to him.

I'm a butterfly, Ryan. Catch me if you can. Then I'll be yours. We'll make love, here, in the beautiful flowers beneath the blue sky. There will be only the two of us, together. Forever, Ryan. Forever, forever, forever.

Ah, man, he thought, dragging both hands down his face. Deedee Hamilton was driving him crazy. He had to get out of the store and away from that woman.

With heavy steps, he strode to the storeroom, taking a small notebook and a pen from his shirt pocket as he went. He entered the storeroom and closed the door behind him.

Deedee slid a glance in the direction Ryan had gone, then redirected her attention to the woman next to her after he disappeared from view.

"Why don't I leave you to look through the various books on butterflies at your leisure?" Deedee said. "I'll be at the counter if you have any questions."

"That's fine," the woman said pleasantly. "Thank you so much."

Deedee hurried away, willing her trembling legs to

get her to the stool behind the counter. Safely seated, she drew a steadying breath.

Ryan MacAllister, she thought, narrowing her eyes, was a menace. She wanted him out of her store and far away from her. He pushed sensual buttons within her that she didn't even know she possessed.

It wasn't important.

Have you got that yet, Deedee Hamilton? she thought angrily. *She* was in control of her life. *She* decided on the boundaries when she was involved with someone. If a man wanted a serious commitment from her, *she* sent him shuffling off to Buffalo. Men did *not* dictate to her in the areas of emotional and physical responses.

Nice spiel, she thought dryly. Her little mental speech was true, had been for years. Then Ryan MacAllister had come into her life and wreaked havoc with her program.

No, now wait a minute. It was even worse than that, more ridiculous and unexplainable.

Ryan had not *just* come into her life, he'd been there for several years. She'd known him, spoken to him, seen his gorgeous self, watched him interact with his family. He wasn't a complete stranger who appeared on her doorstep and threw her for a loop.

So why, why, why was she suddenly having a sexual response to him?

Oh, good grief, she didn't know. Didn't have a clue. Forget her conclusion that it was healthy. Absurd was closer to the mark. She was a mental mess, and had to formulate a plan for handling this nonsense.

She squinted at the ceiling.

When a person caught a cold, she mused, they had to resign themself to the fact that there was nothing they could do but let it run its course. They could take precautions, such as getting plenty of rest and drinking juice, but the cold was going to diminish, then finally disappear, in its own sweet time.

"Therefore," she said aloud, pointing one finger in the air. She was going to consider her reactions to Ryan as she would the common cold. Her uncharacteristic behavior and responses were simply going to have to be allowed to run their course. She obviously couldn't order them into oblivion any more than she could the sniffles.

Precautions could and would be taken. Oh, my, yes. She'd make sure she wasn't alone with Ryan, and she'd stay on alert and in complete touch with herself. Her sudden *awareness* of Ryan as a man, rather than just another MacAllister, would dim, flicker, then— poof—be gone.

And that, thank you very much, would be that.

Deedee really didn't care diddly why it had all happened in the first place, as long as it vanished.

Goodness, she felt so much better. She was back in control of herself, under her own command.

Everything was fine and dandy.

Chapter Four

The next afternoon, Ryan signed his name to a typed bid for the security system he was recommending to Deedee for Books and Books.

He leaned back in the creaking office chair and laced his fingers behind his head, staring up at the ceiling.

To properly submit a bid from MacAllister Security Systems, he couldn't just drop it in the mail. Although he didn't use terminology to describe the equipment to be used that would be like a foreign language to the average citizen, there were invariably options to consider and more than one type of system available. This created questions that needed to be answered.

It was his policy, therefore, to make an appointment with the prospective client and thoroughly explain the suggested systems, as well as answer any questions that might arise.

It was up to him to take care of that part of the business, as neither his secretary, nor the two installers, had any experience in verbally presenting a bid.

Which meant, he knew, that he had to once again meet with Deedee Hamilton on a one-to-one basis.

Ryan got to his feet and went to the window, looking out over the parking lot that fronted the row of small, single-story offices in the complex. He folded his arms across his chest and frowned, not really seeing what was within his view.

The current situation with Deedee was disturbing and ridiculous. He was an ex-cop who had faced danger, even death, on more than one occasion in the past. He was physically strong, mentally alert and had sharp, quick reflexes, all of which had held him in good stead during his years on the police force.

And at this moment, this point in time, he'd rather walk into a dark alley where he knew some thugs were waiting to jump him than open the door to Books and Books and enter that store.

Yeah, really ridiculous.

He shook his head and returned to the chair, his frown deepening.

How was it possible that a woman, who probably didn't weigh more than a hundred and twenty pounds, could have him shaking in his shorts, wanting to put as much distance as he could between them?

Deedee caused him to act and react beyond his own control. His size, strength and police training weren't worth a damn when he was in close proximity to Deedee. She tied him in knots, took up space in his brain, made his body hot and hard with the physical want of her.

Hell, she even had freckles on her nose that were so damn cute he couldn't help but smile when he saw them, and big, brown eyes like a delicate fawn.

Ryan muttered an earthy expletive, then propped his elbows on the worn arms of the chair and made a steeple of his fingers. He narrowed his eyes and concentrated on the problem at hand.

He didn't know why Deedee Hamilton could turn him inside out. It wasn't as though he'd been knocked for a loop by a woman he'd just met. That would be bad enough, because he had no intention of allowing anyone to take Sherry's place. But Deedee? He'd known her for several years. Why was she getting to him *now?*

He'd managed to escape from Books and Books yesterday without talking to her further. She'd been busy with a customer, so he'd left his card on the counter, along with a hastily written note saying he'd be in touch soon with the bid.

He'd hightailed it out of there so fast that an observer might surmise that a dozen pit bulls were nipping at his heels.

Damn it, he had to get a grip on this mess. Deedee wasn't going to disappear into thin air. She was considered a part of the MacAllister clan, and would be in attendance at family gatherings in the future. He needed to figure out what plan of action would result in him regaining control of his responses to Deedee and return things to normal.

"Yes," he said aloud.

Yes...what? What was the plan?

Okay, MacAllister, try this. When he'd been a kid, his mother had limited how much candy her brood could eat. In a rebellious move, he'd spent the money he'd earned from his paper route on a huge stash of candy that he'd hidden—crummy criminal that he'd been—under his pillow. His mother had discovered the illegal bounty the next day when she'd changed the sheets on his bed.

Wise woman that Margaret MacAllister was, she'd calmly informed him that at ten years old it was time for him to make more of his own decisions. He could, therefore, keep the candy and consume it with no interference whatsoever from her.

Puffed up with his newly authorized independence, he'd proceeded to eat the entire bag of candy in one sitting. Several hours later, he was convinced he was dying, he wouldn't live until morning. To say he'd been sick was putting it mildly.

Now then, Ryan thought, he needed to apply the lesson learned by that scenario to the dilemma with Deedee. Instead of trying to keep out of her way, put distance between them, he should do just the opposite. He'd see her, be with her, as much as possible. He'd overdose on Deedee, just as he'd done years before on candy.

"Excellent," he said. "Brilliant."

After surviving his candy binge, he'd realized he'd do very well with the occasional treat his mother provided. Candy once again took its proper place in his life.

The same principle applied to Deedee Hamilton. By sticking to her like Super Glue he'd be able, in a very short time he was convinced, to view her as the friendly, pleasant woman she was, but who had no particular effect on him.

"MacAllister," he said with a rush of relief, "you're such a genius, you're awesome."

Ryan was jolted from his self-congratulatory reverie by the office door suddenly being opened.

Ted Sharpe entered the room. Ryan's former partner on the police force was tall, blond and tanned. Handsome and nicely built, as well, he never lacked for female company.

"Hey," Ryan said, smiling, "how's it going? What are you doing here in your spiffy cop clothes?"

"I just got off duty," Ted said, sinking onto a wooden chair in front of the desk. "There's a flu bug sweeping through the department and we're short on healthy bodies. I pulled a double shift. I'm headed for home and some much-needed sleep. Man, it was nuts out there. The radio was squawking almost continually. That new restaurant by the park got ripped off, by the way."

"No kidding? They get much?"

"Didn't go near the cash drawer. They took a valuable painting off the wall, then split. The owner had hung it there to impress his fancy patrons. What it did was impress some sleaze, and now they have it. All we can do is hope one of the fences who keeps us informed of business on the streets will come through with some information."

"Sounds like the scum are trying for class. You

know, showing they have culture, good taste. It's always nice to witness people attempting to improve themselves.''

''Cute,'' Ted said, then paused. ''Mel Poley, the guy they hired to take your place when you quit the force, gave thirty days' notice today. He's going over to Denver because he likes to ski. I won't miss him, believe me. As a partner he didn't cut it for me.''

''So you've said many times. He's trigger happy.''

''In spades. Your old spot will be open again, Ryan. I want you as my partner again, man. Captain Bolstad would hire you back in a New York minute.''

''Don't start, Ted,'' Ryan said wearily. ''We've been over this turf a hundred times.''

''I haven't said one word about it for at least six months.''

Ryan glared at him. ''Go for another six.''

''Come on, Ryan, at least think about it, will you? I don't care how many times you've told me you're doing fine sitting behind that desk, I still don't believe it. You liked being a cop, and you're a damn good one. You quit in a knee-jerk reaction to what happened to Sherry, but you quit on life back then, too. Things are different for you now.''

''Finished?'' Ryan said, his jaw tightening slightly.

''Yeah,'' Ted said, ''I suppose.'' He got to his feet. ''I'm outta here, but...damn it, MacAllister, you're so stubborn. If you'd be honest with yourself, really honest, you'd admit you miss being a cop. Not only that, we were good together, great partners. We were so in tune that we practically read each other's minds when we came up against something we had to handle. Perfect partners, that's what we were, and now your old spot is opening up. That's fate. It's time for you to come back where you belong.''

"Goodbye, Ted."

"Hell." Ted started toward the door, then stopped, half turning to look at Ryan again. "How was the party for the twins?"

"Fine, great. Those cop teddy bears you got them were a hit with the dynamic duo."

"I should buy *you* one and tape it to your desk. You'd realize soon enough that you belong in one of those uniforms, too."

"Lighten up, Ted," Ryan said, a warning tone now evident in his voice.

"Yeah, yeah."

"Are you busy tomorrow night?" Ryan asked. "The whole clan is meeting for pizza in connection with The Baby Bet Forrest has going about Jillian."

Ryan related The Baby Bet details, and Ted whooped with laughter.

"Forrest is dead meat," Ted said. "Three girls? Even if twins *do* run in your family, triplets are a whole new ball game, predicting in the big leagues. Ole Forrest is about to lose The Baby Bet for the first time, and you'd better believe I'll be at Mario's to witness it. Are you going?"

Ryan shrugged. "Thought I would."

"Really? That surprises me."

"It surprises *me,* but what the hell, why not? We can watch Forrest eat crow while we have pizza."

"Yep. Well, I'm off to get some sleep. I'll see you tomorrow night. Think about what I said before,

Ryan. You and I could be partners again, just like it used to be. See ya.''

''Yeah,'' Ryan said quietly as Ted left the room. ''See ya.''

Ryan continued to stare at the open doorway. *Just like it used to be,* Ryan's mind echoed. Nothing would ever be like it used to be. When Sherry had been killed, his whole life had fallen apart, lost purpose and meaning.

So, yeah, Ted was right when he'd said Ryan had resigned from the force in a knee-jerk reaction to Sherry's violent death. He'd admitted that to himself many months ago. He hadn't wanted to be a cop anymore after the nightmare that had happened. He hadn't wanted *anything* but to be left alone.

Ryan glanced around the small, sparsely furnished office.

MacAllister Security Systems was doing all right. He was getting new customers all the time and was establishing a reputation for top-of-the-line installations. He never attempted to sell someone more than they needed in order to accomplish what they were after, and he guaranteed his work.

Yes, his fledgling company was prospering.

And as the days passed into weeks, then months, he was becoming more and more bored. The challenge of starting a business from scratch had probably saved his sanity at the time he'd done it. He owed his family and Ted a helluva lot for hauling him out of his alcohol-induced haze and trashed apartment when they did.

But now? There was a flat-line sameness to each

day, nothing that made him eager to get out of bed in the morning and come to the office.

He picked up a pencil and rolled it back and forth between his palms, staring at it absently.

Ted was his best friend, knew him better than his own family did. They'd spent a lot of hours together in that patrol car over the years and had talked about all and everything. Each knew he would risk his life for the other, and that fact took friendship to a depth that ordinary men didn't experience on a daily basis.

Yes, Ted Sharpe knew him very well. Ted Sharpe knew that his buddy, Ryan MacAllister, was stagnating in an office. Ted Sharpe knew that Ryan wanted to be a police officer again so badly he could taste it.

Ryan snapped the pencil in two, then flung the pieces into the metal wastebasket next to the desk.

"Satisfied, Sharpe?" he said aloud to no one. "I admitted it. Okay?"

He sank back in the chair and dragged his hands down his face.

So? he asked himself. Why wasn't he on the telephone to Captain Bolstad? Why wasn't he saying to the man in charge that he wanted to apply for his former position as Ted's partner on the force?

Because he was scared.

Because he broke out in a cold sweat just thinking about it.

He wasn't afraid of the physical danger that went along with putting on the uniform and gun. Facing possible injury or death wasn't what held him in an iron fist, kept him captive in that shabby little office.

It was the fear of caring.

It was the fear of awakening emotions that he had shut down, put into a hibernating sleep.

A good cop—and he was a damn good cop—had to *care* about the people who cried for help, who needed his expertise, who were counting on him to make everything all right. Each time he responded to a call, he put not just his body on the line, but his emotions, as well. That was what it took to be the kind of cop that he and Ted were.

He had cared deeply in the past, not only as a police officer, but as a man. He had loved. *Sherry.* When she had died, he'd felt as though he were slowly bleeding to death, his life's purpose leaving him drop by painful drop.

If he opened those doors again, tore down the protective walls by rejoining the police force, the ramifications would go far beyond when he was just wearing the uniform.

There would be no halfway measures he could take. If he allowed himself to once again be vulnerable as a cop, it would encompass his entire being, the part of him that was simply a man, as well.

No!

He couldn't, wouldn't, do it.

He had no intention of ever again stripping himself bare, having no defenses. *Not ever.*

Deedee Hamilton was, for some unknown reason, triggering physical reactions in him that he'd been certain he'd put into cold storage with his emotions. But he had formulated a plan to defuse Deedee's unsettling impact on him. The basic principle of overkill was going to remedy that nagging nuisance of a situation in short order.

With a decisive nod, Ryan flipped open a file on his desk. He then spent the next ten minutes rummaging through his desk in search of a new pencil.

The next morning, Ryan was at Books and Books ten minutes after Deedee opened the store. She was standing behind the counter, sipping coffee from a ceramic mug, which she set down in order to greet Ryan.

"Good morning," she said, smiling.

There went her heart again, she realized, suddenly beating in a rapid tempo as though she'd just jogged a mile. Well, fine, let it go nuts. She had her reactions to Ryan all figured out. She must remember the theory of the common cold having to run its course. My, my, wouldn't Mr. MacAllister pitch a fit if he knew she'd categorized him along with a germ?

"How are you this morning, Ryan?"

Totally in control, Ms. Cute Freckles on Your Nose, Ryan thought smugly.

"I'm very well, thank you," he said, then placed a dark blue folder on the counter. "I have the bid you wanted for the security system. You can study it, then get back to me with any questions you might have. Or we can go over it together now. Which would you prefer to..." His voice trailed off as his glance fell on the coffee mug. "Where did you get that?"

"Get what?" she said, totally confused.

"That mug."

She picked it up and held it at eye level. "Isn't it

pretty? I bought it at that new gift shop that opened down the block.''

Ryan frowned as he looked at her. ''It has butter-flies on it.'' Just like in the dream, that damnable dream.

''Well, um, yes, I noticed that myself. I think but-terflies are lovely. You know, delicate and beautiful, especially considering they started out as caterpillars. I think that whole process is rather magical.'' She paused, then put the mug back on the counter. ''Ryan, is there a reasonable reason why you're glaring at my coffee mug, or are you just basically strange?''

''What?'' He snapped his head up to meet her eyes again. ''Oh. I wasn't glaring at it, I was studying it because it's attractive. Yes, that's what I was doing. It's a great mug, very nice.''

''Whatever. Would you like some coffee?''

''No, thank you. What do you prefer to do about the bid?''

''I'll look it over now, if you have the time. Why don't you browse through the store while I'm reading this? Then if I have any questions we can tackle them while you're still here.''

''Okay. Sure. I'll just look around.''

Deedee watched as Ryan wandered off, admiring his physique shown to perfection in dark slacks and a pale blue dress shirt open at the neck.

My stars, she mused wistfully, that man truly does have a marvelous tush.

In the next instant she blinked, picked up the file folder and told herself to behave.

* * *

Ryan flipped absently through a book he'd taken from a shelf, not really seeing what he was looking at.

Butterflies on Deedee's coffee mug, he fumed. He'd come across like an idiot when he'd seen those butterflies, but they had blindsided him, caught him totally off-guard.

Lord, that was eerie. He'd dreamed about Deedee being captivated by beautiful butterflies, only to discover that she actually was enchanted by them enough to have bought that mug.

And then there had been that woman who had come into the store and asked for a book about butterflies at the exact same time he was standing there.

Very eerie.

Deedee Hamilton was a witch, a spell weaver, a...

MacAllister, knock it off, he admonished himself. Deedee was *not* a witch. She was a woman. She was an especially pretty woman this morning in a soft pink sweater and navy blue slacks. He liked her hair, the way the curls fluffed around her head and cheeks. And that nose. That nose with the cute-as-a-button freckles got to him every time.

Yeah, he could feel it, the coiled heat low in his body. Deedee had pushed his sexual buttons again, right on cue. So be it. He had a plan of action to put an end to this nonsense. Deedee Hamilton's days of turning him inside out were numbered, by damn.

Fifteen minutes later, Ryan went back to the counter. Deedee had assisted two customers during his wait, but had now closed the file and given it a pat.

"You write a very clear and understandable report, Ryan," she said pleasantly. "I expected this bid to be so full of technical jargon I wouldn't be able to grasp it at all."

He shrugged. "I could have written it that way, but it serves no purpose, because I'd have to turn right around and explain it in layman terms. This is more efficient in the long run."

"How did you know enough about this type of equipment to open a security systems company right after leaving the police force?"

"We study security systems at the police academy, so I knew the basics. Then I borrowed a stack of textbooks from a buddy of mine who teaches this stuff in a trade school. I crammed for several weeks. Once I investigated who the best suppliers were, I was ready to go. Now I'm on mailing lists that provide me with the information on the new systems being produced. It's not all that tough."

"Well, *I'm* impressed. It must be challenging to come into a home or business and decide what is needed."

No, he thought dryly, it was boring as hell, to *him,* anyway. But he wasn't about to divulge *that* news flash to Deedee.

"Challenging." He nodded. "Yep."

"I think I understand what you're recommending. The cabinets with the rare books will be on a silent alarm connected to the police department. The wiring will be dropped behind the walls so it won't be unsightly, and I'll press a button hidden under the counter to activate it when I leave, and turn it off when I arrive.''

''Right. Or you can have a numbered code activator, which is safer, but more expensive. The sheet is there on that one, too. I recommend the code type because you're running the risk of a thief finding the hidden button and—bingo—he's home free. The chances of him getting lucky and hitting your code are about as good as winning the lottery. In other words...zip.''

Deedee nodded, a thoughtful expression on her face. ''I see. I want my rare books protected, Ryan. Dealing in these editions had been a dream of mine for a long time. I can remember having lunch with Jillian the day the first cabinet with the wired glass was being built. I was so excited I could hardly sit still.''

She swept one arm through the air.

''Now? I have four cabinets and over two hundred rare books. If anything happened to them, I'd be devastated. I want the coded system, Ryan. There's no doubt about it in my mind.''

''All right. Just sign those papers accepting the bid, and I'll order the supplies.''

''Will I be able to add to the system in the future as my inventory increases and I have more cabinets built?''

''Good question, and the answer is yes.''

''Wonderful,'' she said, smiling.

''It's a pleasure to see someone enthused about what they're doing with their life,'' Ryan said quietly.

"Your eyes are sparkling and... Well, I'm happy for you that you get such a rush from what you do."

Deedee's smile faded and she cocked her head slightly to one side.

"Don't *you,* Ryan? What I mean is, you *did* say that you found your work challenging."

"Well, let me put it this way. There are jobs, and there are careers. What you have here at Books and Books is a career. MacAllister Security Systems is my job."

"I understand," Deedee said softly, looking directly into his eyes, "and I'm sorry. You should have *more,* you *deserve* more."

Damn it, Ryan fumed, unable to tear his gaze from Deedee's. Why had he said that, revealed something so deep and personal? She was doing it to him again, this spell weaver of a woman, making him act out of character.

He was in worse shape than he'd thought in regard to the effect Deedee Hamilton had on him.

He shifted his eyes to the folder, then pulled a pen from his shirt pocket. He handed the pen to Deedee, while looking at her chin.

"If you'll sign that, I'll get out of your way. After I talk to the supplier and check the job schedule at the office, I'll give you a call and let you know when we can start.

"You can be thinking about whether you want the work done during regular business hours, or after you've closed. There's drilling to do, which is noisy and creates dust, which you might feel is too disruptive to your customers who like to take their time in here.''

''Not only that,'' Deedee said, pointing one finger in the air, ''there's also the fact that if a would-be crook comes in while you're working, he'll be able to see exactly what you're installing. He might not be able to figure out the code, but he could determine a way to cut the wires inside the walls.''

Ryan chuckled. ''It's a thought, but I think you read too many mysteries.''

Darn him, Deedee thought. She really wished he wouldn't make that sexy sound. It created instant desire that swirled within her, thrumming low and hot.

''Well, Deedee,'' Ryan said, ''whatever you want is fine with me.''

Deedee's eyes widened as she had the irrational thought that he'd read her mind.

''What?'' she said.

''If you want the work done after-hours, that's when we'll do it.''

''Oh. Yes.'' She cleared her throat. ''I'll give it serious consideration and let you know.'' She signed the paper. ''There you are.''

Ryan picked up the folder and accepted his pen that she extended toward him.

Do it, MacAllister, he told himself. *Put your plan into action.*

''Listen,'' he said, ''are you still going to Mario's tonight for pizza, and to witness Forrest's defeat as the champion of The Baby Bet?''

''Yes. I'm looking forward to it. It should be a fun evening.''

"Why don't I pick you up and we'll go together? That will be one less vehicle trying to park in Mario's lot, which isn't all that big."

Not a chance, mister, Deedee thought. One of the stipulations she'd made to herself while Ryan was running the course of the common cold was that she mustn't be alone with him. Having him there in the store didn't count, because people kept popping in and out. But allow him to pick her up at her apartment and go with him—alone—to Mario's and back? Not in this lifetime.

Ryan took one of his business cards from his shirt pocket and set it on the counter.

"I know which complex you live in because Andrea pointed it out to me once, but why don't you write your apartment and phone number on the back of that?"

"Oh, well, I don't think—"

He interrupted her, his voice very low, very rumbly and very, *very* mesmerizing.

"Six-thirty, Deedee. That should give us plenty of time. All right?"

"Yes," Deedee heard herself say.

Chapter Five

Deedee flicked a brush through her curls, then her hand stilled as she glared at her reflection in the bathroom mirror.

She was so angry with herself, she was beyond having any kind of rational inner dialogue. She just fussed and fumed, and called herself uncomplimentary names for allowing herself to be in the predicament she was in.

Per the usual routine, one of her part-time employees had arrived at Books and Books at five-thirty to take charge of the store until closing at eight o'clock.

Deedee had driven home, taken a lilac-scented bubble bath, then dressed in jeans, a chocolate brown sweater and tennis shoes.

Her hand had hovered over the padded hanger holding a lovely peach-colored sweater with lace inserts, the action causing her to purse her lips in self-disgust.

She'd joined the MacAllisters for pizza before and knew they came to Mario's in very casual clothes. The peach sweater was meant to be worn to a fancy outing, not to a rustic pizza parlor. The fact that the image of Ryan had flitted into her mental vision as she'd hesitated over the peach creation did nothing to improve her mood.

That the brown sweater she'd chosen to wear was the exact shade of her eyes was coincidence she was hereby ignoring, having dismissed it as unimportant.

Deedee smacked the light switch in the bathroom and marched into the living room, where she plunked down on the sofa.

Oh, that Ryan MacAllister was a slick son of a gun, she thought, narrowing her eyes. He knew, lady-killer that he was, that suddenly speaking in that low, sexy voice made women putty in his hands. He no doubt had practiced aloud until he'd perfected the rich, rumbly sound, then laughed himself silly every time it worked on some unsuspecting woman.

What she couldn't fathom was why he had done it. His entire family was going to go nosy-nuts when she and Ryan showed up together at the restaurant.

Andrea had nearly raced across the room to get to Deedee at the twins' birthday party after Ryan had left, all because Ryan had smiled, for Pete's sake. Simply smiled!

That Ryan had suddenly pushed some kind of emotional button and changed back into who he had been before Sherry's death was a ridiculous thought. The walls around him were solidly in place, and even if he chose—which Deedee didn't believe—to emerge from behind them, it would take time and effort to accomplish that goal.

No, the real Ryan was still closed and aloof. The tricky Ryan, who was due to arrive in ten minutes, was up to no good. He was trying to accomplish something, was using her as a pawn to do it, and she was rip-roaring mad.

Deedee tapped one fingertip against her chin.

She was not one to play games and was always honest with the men she dated. But, by gum, Ryan was playing some kind of game with *her* and he was definitely *not* going to get away with it.

So, yes, she'd succumbed to that diabolical voice he'd whipped on her, but she now saw it for the farce that it was. He was probably overflowing with nauseating smugness as he drove to her apartment at that very moment.

There wasn't time to even begin to attempt to figure out why Ryan had insisted they go to Mario's together. Male minds were such messes it often took hours to decipher the whys and wherefores of what men said and did. That puzzle solving would have to go on hold.

"However," Deedee said, getting to her feet, "I *can* give as good as I get."

Ryan had started this game-playing fiasco, and she intended to finish it. The cocky, arrogant side of Mr. MacAllister that had surfaced in her store was in for a shock when he got to her apartment.

A knock sounded at the door and Deedee spun around.

"You asked for it, bub," she muttered, then crossed the room.

Flinging open the door, she immediately stepped back and swept one arm through the air.

"Come in, Ryan," she said. Jeans and a black sweater. Nice, very nice. Oh, who cared? She was furious with this man, and he was about to get his comeuppance.

She closed the door and turned to face him.

"Good evening, Deedee," Ryan said pleasantly. "Are you ready to—"

"Oh, my, yes," she said. "I certainly am."

She moved forward, slid her arms around his neck, molded her body to his and kissed him.

Ryan stiffened and his eyes widened in shock at Deedee's unexpected actions. But in the next instant, heated desire exploded within him, consuming him. He wrapped his arms around her slender body, parted her lips and returned her kiss in total abandon.

He was lost, swept away by passion's rush as he savored her taste, her flowery aroma, the exquisite feel of her body pressed to his.

Yes! his mind thundered. Oh, yes, he wanted this woman. He wanted to make love with Deedee Hamilton now. *Right now!*

Dear heaven, Deedee thought hazily, *this kiss is ecstasy.*

This kiss should never end.

This kiss was something she'd been waiting for for a very long time without even realizing it.

This kiss had been a terrible mistake!

With every ounce of willpower she could muster, she tore her mouth from Ryan's, then wiggled out of his embrace. She took two steps backwards and wrapped her hands around her elbows as she drew a deep, steadying breath.

Ryan blinked, shook his head slightly, then frowned.

"I assume..." he started, then cleared his throat, "there's a reasonable explanation for your behavior, Ms. Hamilton?"

Damn, he thought, she was beautiful. The sweater she was wearing was the exact color of her incredible brown eyes. He ached for her, wanted her with an intensity he could not remember experiencing before. His plan of overkill had been a good one. It had been well thought out. But she'd blown his program to smithereens.

And he was mad as hell.

"Well?" he said. "What do you have to say for yourself?"

That did it.

Deedee was thoroughly shaken by her total response to Ryan's kiss, by the desire still thrumming low in her body. She felt out of control, vulnerable, and she hated that truth. Mentally scrambling for a safe hold, something to grab on to, she found her anger beneath the smoldering passion.

"*My* behavior?" she said, none too quietly. She splayed one hand on her chest. "Mine? Oh, look who's talking. It doesn't sit too well when the tables are turned, does it, Mr. Macho?"

Ryan narrowed his eyes and matched her volume. "What in the hell are you talking about?"

"Don't play innocent with me, mister. I fell for your oh-so-sexy voice when you were saying what time you'd pick me up tonight. Score one game-playing point for you, MacAllister. What happened when you walked in here was a dose of your own medicine. *My* point."

"Oh," he said quietly.

"Yes, 'oh.' I don't play games, Ryan MacAllister, but you forced me to by your own actions. Why you wanted us to go to Mario's together, I have no idea, nor do I care. I won't be used. Is that clear?" She lifted her chin. "I'd appreciate it if you'd leave my home."

Ryan looked at her for a long moment before he spoke.

"No," he said finally.

"No?" She pointed to the door. "Go."

"No. I want to apologize for what I did to convince you to go with me tonight. You nailed it—it was calculated and finessed. I must be losing my touch from lack of use, because you're the first woman to figure it out."

"I happen to be extremely intelligent," she said with an indignant little sniff.

"Okay. That's easier to take than my having lost my touch."

"Oh-h-h," she said, rolling her eyes heavenward, "you're despicable. Go away."

"Not until you accept my apology." He paused.

"Then I'll accept *your* apology, and we'll have a clean slate again."

"*My* apology? What on earth for?"

"You're yelling again, Deedee."

"Damn straight I am. Why would I apologize to you? You're the one playing games here."

"Which you could have verbally accused me of when I arrived. Your method of addressing the issue was…"

Ryan stopped speaking as memories of the sensuous kiss shared with Deedee slammed against his mind.

"No, forget it," he said. "You don't owe me an apology. That kiss was sensational. I don't care if you did it for revenge or whatever, it was still sensational."

"Yes," Deedee said softly, "it was. It was supposed to be my way of…but then…oh, dear."

Their eyes met, held and neither moved, or hardly breathed. The embers of desire within them still glowed and began to grow hotter, threatening to burst into raging flames.

Ryan jerked his arm up and studied his watch as though it was the most fascinating thing he'd ever seen.

"We'd better hit the road," he said, tapping the watch, "or we'll be conspicuously late getting to Mario's."

"We're going to be conspicuous just arriving together. I think we should go in separate cars."

"We'd still get there at the same time since we're both leaving from here."

"Well," she said, "I'll drive around the block a couple of times at Mario's and wait for you to get inside."

Ryan folded his arms over his chest. "Oh, really? Doesn't that come under the heading of playing games, Ms. Hamilton?"

Deedee sighed. "Yes, I suppose it does. It's just that your family is going to go ballistic when we walk into the restaurant together. You know that's true, Ryan. It will be 'Wow, look at that. Deedee and Ryan are together. Isn't that something? Isn't that super?'

"Then they'll be watching us like hawks, and trying to get each of us alone for all the details. I love your family as though they were my own, but they definitely like to be in on what's happening in everyone's life."

"We'll weather that inquisitive storm. We'll tell them the truth—there's nothing happening between us. Nothing at all."

Right? Ryan asked himself in the next moment. Yes, of course that was right. He'd already figured out that there was a sexual attraction between him and Deedee that was justifiably labeled old-fashioned lust.

The physical want was causing him to think about Deedee a great deal—to have annoying dreams about her and a bunch of butterflies—but his plan of "overdosing on Deedee" would solve all of that.

There weren't any emotions involved in this mess.

But what about that kiss? a nagging little voice in his mind asked him.

The kiss had been...yeah, okay, sensational. But that was understandable, because she was the first woman he'd kissed in nearly two years. He'd reacted to the kiss like a thirsty man in need of water. That made perfect sense.

Why he wasn't consumed with guilt for having broken his vow to stay loyal to Sherry, he didn't know. Forget it. He wasn't using up any more mental energy analyzing one simple kiss.

"I repeat," he said, "there's nothing happening between us, and that's what we tell my family if they push for information."

"I don't suppose you'd care to explain to me why you were so determined to get me to go with you tonight?"

"Not really."

"Fine, whatever," Deedee said. "I'll get my purse, and off we go to Mario's."

There is nothing happening between us, her mind echoed as she hurried into the bedroom for her purse. That was absolutely correct. She didn't care diddly if that answer did, or did not, satisfy the MacAllister clan. Facts were facts, and the truth was the truth. *There was nothing happening between her and Ryan.*

And that kiss?

What about that kiss?

Oh, well, it had been…it had been…sensational, to borrow Ryan's description. But it didn't *mean* anything, other than they kissed sensationally together, or some such idiotic thing.

And that had *not* been disappointment that had caused a cold knot to tighten in her stomach when Ryan had said nothing was happening between them.

It had been hunger. She was starving, and more than ready for some dinner.

"Pizza," she said, whizzing back into the living room. "Let's go."

The drive in Ryan's Jeep to Mario's was made in total silence, the occupants of the vehicle each lost in their own muddled thoughts.

In spite of Ryan's bravado plan to deal with his inquisitive family with short, precise answers to any questions they might have, Deedee could actually feel the waves of sudden tension emanating from him when they entered the restaurant.

She looked up at him quickly and had the irrational thought that she'd heard his walls clank firmly into place. She recognized the closed expression on his face, and his brown eyes appeared flat and unreadable.

How nice, she mused dryly. The MacAllister clan wouldn't get in an excited verbal dither over her arrival with Ryan once they glimpsed his don't-come-near-me demeanor. They'd had plenty of practice at cutting a wide circle around this frowning, aloof Ryan.

The group was seated against the far wall at a long wooden table with benches. Deedee managed a small smile and a wave as she and Ryan wove their way through the tables in their path. The restaurant was nearly full as Mario's had a reputation for producing some of the best pizza in town, and the noise level was high.

"Hello, hello," Andrea said, beaming at the pair as they reached the table.

"'Lo, 'lo," Noel said, banging on the tray of her high chair.

Ryan nodded, but didn't speak.

Coward, Deedee thought crossly. He was in his not-speaking mode now, leaving her to deal with the family, all of whom were looking at them with a great deal of undisguised interest.

"Ryan and I were discussing the recommendations he'd made for my new security system at the store," Deedee said, "so we decided to come on over here together." That wasn't a lie, it was simply the truth stretched a tad.

"Well, it's lovely to see you both," Margaret said. "Do sit down."

Deedee slid gratefully onto the bench, hoping that once she was seated everyone would forget she was there. She landed next to Ted, then Ryan sat next to her, sandwiching her between the two men.

"Hi, Ted," she said, smiling brightly. "How's things in the world of crime?"

Ted matched her smile. "Business is booming...unfortunately. We seem to suddenly be dealing with crooks with culture. A valuable painting was stolen from a restaurant, and last night an antique vase worth a bundle got ripped from a private home. Nothing else was touched. They snatched the vase and split."

"How strange," Deedee said. "You'd think they'd take as much as they could carry."

Ted shrugged. "They seem to know exactly what

they're after, get it and leave. The same thing happened at the restaurant when they took the painting. We figure the guys who did the first job did the second one, too.''

''Do you have any clues as to who might have—'' Deedee started.

''Where are Jillian and Forrest?'' Ryan interrupted gruffly. ''Forrest organized this get-together.''

''They're on their way,'' Robert MacAllister said. ''Forrest phoned and said they needed to make a quick stop, but to go ahead and order. We're getting those pizzas that Jillian introduced us to.''

''Ah, yes,'' Deedee said, smiling. ''Super Duper Pizza Supreme Deluxe Extraordinaire. One very delicious pizza. Did Forrest give any hint as to the results of Jillian's ultrasound?''

''No,'' Robert said, ''not a word. I couldn't tell a thing by his voice on the phone, either.''

''He's not winning The Baby Bet this time,'' Andrea said. ''He's been the champion for so long that he's getting illusions of grandeur. Triplets. Three baby girls. No way.''

''No way,'' Matt said, throwing a cracker onto the floor.

''You tell 'em, Matt,'' Andrea said, smiling at the toddler. ''Right?''

''Right,'' Matt echoed. ''Right, right, right.''

''Deedee,'' Andrea said, ''would you like to go to the ladies' room with me?''

''No, thank you,'' she said pleasantly. No way, to quote Matt. She wasn't about to be cornered by Andrea, who would grill her unmercifully for more details regarding her arriving with Ryan.

"Nice try, Andrea," Jenny said, laughing, "but no cigar."

"Mmm," Andrea said, wrinkling her nose.

"Jillian and Forrest just came in," Robert said. "Forrest is carrying an enormous shopping bag. The stop they had to make was apparently at that department store."

"Curiouser and curiouser," Michael said. He rubbed his hands together. "I can hardly wait for Forrest to be unchampioned. He's so darn cocky about The Baby Bet."

"With just cause," Ted said. "He always wins."

"Not this time," Michael said.

Jillian and Forrest reached the table and everyone stared at them.

"Sit down, sweet wife," Forrest said, then dropped a quick kiss on her lips.

Jillian sat next to Ryan, a rather bemused expression on her face.

"Get on with it, Forrest," Michael said. "They'll be calling our order number for the pizzas any second now. Admit you lost, then shut up."

"You have an attitude, big brother," Forrest said, smiling. "I trust that I have everyone's undivided attention?"

"Indeed you do, son," Margaret said. "I would suggest, however, that you make your announcement regarding the results of the ultrasound right now, before someone strangles you, dear."

"Oh," Forrest said. "Good point." He shifted the

large shopping bag to one arm. "Okay, here we go. The test showed, with no doubt whatsoever..." He reached into the bag and pulled out a pink, stuffed-toy rabbit, which he set on the table.

"A girl," Jenny said. "It's a girl."

Forrest whipped another pink rabbit out of the bag and placed it next to the first.

"*Twin* girls," Margaret said, laughing in delight. "How marvelous."

"Well, now," Robert said, "isn't that wonderful?"

Then to the group's wide-eyed amazement, Forrest took a *third* pink rabbit from the bag!

"Oh, my gosh," Andrea said, her hands flying to her cheeks.

"I don't believe this," Michael said.

"Believe it," Jillian said weakly. "I don't know if I should laugh or cry. I'm numb."

"Still champion of The Baby Bet," Forrest boomed, "is yours truly, ladies and gentlemen. Jillian and I are expecting triplets, three baby girls."

Everyone started talking at once. Margaret got up and came around the table to hug a pale Jillian and a beaming Forrest.

Deedee stared at the pink rabbits.

Three babies, she thought incredulously. Jillian and Forrest were going to have three precious miracles. It was overwhelming and wonderful at the same time. My, my, she was going to be a busy Aunt Deedee.

But not a mother.

She'd play with the triplets, then go home.

Alone.

Tearing her gaze from the toys, her breath caught

as she realized she'd unknowingly wrapped her arms around herself beneath her breasts. It was as though she was attempting to erase the emptiness, the fact there was no baby of her own for *her* to nestle in her arms.

What in heaven's name was the matter with her? she wondered frantically. Her decision years ago to never marry again, to not have a husband and children, had been completely thought through.

The choice to devote herself to Books and Books had resulted in fulfillment, contentment and inner peace. She was happy with the life-style she had, she truly was.

Then why, why, why was she feeling so chillingly alone?

Why had Forrest's proud announcement, and the three grinning pink rabbits, caused a cold shiver to consume her, and threatening tears to create an achy sensation in her throat?

As everyone around the table continued to chatter on in excited voices about Jillian and Forrest's news flash, Deedee felt as though she had floated outside of herself, was hovering above the group like a ghostly observer. She was suddenly separate and apart; she no longer fit there, no longer belonged there, among the joyful family.

She was alone.

"Deedee?" Ryan said quietly. "Are you all right?"

She blinked and shook her head slightly as Ryan's voice brought her back into herself with a jarring thud.

"What?" She turned her head to meet his gaze, seeing the genuine concern on his face and in his eyes—those brown eyes that now radiated warmth and caring. "Yes, of course. I'm fine. I'm just so...so surprised about the triplets. My goodness, Forrest won The Baby Bet again, didn't he? Isn't that something?"

"Yeah," Ryan said, studying her face. "He's still the champion. Three baby girls. Man, Jillian and Forrest are going to be very busy."

"And very blessed," Deedee said softly.

"They're calling our order number for the pizzas," Michael said, getting to his feet. "Come on, Forrest, you can help tote them. You should pay for them, too, since you won all The Baby Bet money again."

Two waitresses appeared with pitchers of soft drinks and a stack of plates. A flurry of activity commenced with everyone preparing for the pizzas to arrive at the table.

Ryan looked at the pink rabbits again and frowned.

He didn't care how "fine" Deedee claimed she was, he thought, it wasn't true. She was white as a sheet, and he was certain she was very close to bursting into tears.

Why?

Hell, he *knew* why. He wasn't an ex-cop for nothing. He recognized clues and evidence when they were right in front of him.

Deedee Hamilton wanted a baby.

Chapter Six

The drive *back* to Deedee's apartment was as silent as the drive *going* to the restaurant.

Deedee stared out the side window. She was drained, emotionally and physically exhausted and was very cognizant of the fact that she was both confused and angry.

The confusion plaguing her now pushed the muddle over her sensual reactions to Ryan to the back burner. Up close, and disturbingly personal, was the strange and frightening chill of emptiness and loneliness that had consumed her as she'd looked at the three pink rabbits.

She'd been unable to shake off the unsettling emotions, and had forced a false facade of cheerfulness through the remaining hours of the family gathering.

At least she could find solace in the fact that no one had been aware of her inner turmoil.

That she'd been hurled into her gloomy state of mind by three pink toy rabbits was ridiculous. Yes, all right, the rabbits represented babies, were symbols of what she would never have. But that was due to *her* choices, *her* decisions regarding her existence, her future, what she wanted from life.

And, thus, came the anger, which was directed solely at herself for her asinine behavior.

What she needed, she decided, was to put an end to this day, get a good night's sleep and greet tomorrow fresh. She'd then be back to normal, doing fine.

Deedee slid a glance at Ryan.

It was still early evening, she mused, and the expected socially acceptable thing to do would be to invite Ryan in for coffee and chitchat.

Under the circumstances, that was *not* a good idea. The dilemma regarding *him* wasn't going to stay tucked away for long, and she certainly didn't have the mental energy to deal with it tonight.

She would thank him politely at her door for the taxi service to Mario's, bid him adieu, then scramble under the blankets of her bed and not emerge for five years. Well, at least not surface until her alarm went off the next morning. Excellent idea.

Ryan pulled into the lot edging Deedee's apartment complex and parked. He turned off the ignition, unsnapped the seat belt, then got out of the Jeep and came around to assist Deedee from the vehicle. They entered the building without having spoken.

Thank you for the ride. Good-night, Deedee mentally practiced as they approached her door.

"Your key?" Ryan said when they stopped.

"Oh, well, I can..." Deedee started.

"Humor me," he said, holding out one hand. "I'm old-fashioned."

Deedee retrieved the key from her purse and dropped it into Ryan's palm. As he turned to insert the key in the lock, she began her rehearsed speech.

"Thank you for the—"

"Do you have any coffee?" he said, opening the door. He stepped back and extended one arm. "After you."

Deedee entered the living room with Ryan right behind her. He closed the door, clicked the lock into place and gave her the key.

"Coffee?" he repeated, raising his eyebrows.

Deedee mentally threw up her hands in defeat. She couldn't tell him to hit the road without being extremely rude. Coffee. Fine. But this was going to be the fastest cup of coffee ever consumed.

"I'll make a pot," she said, snapping on more lights, then placing her purse on a chair. "Sit down, Ryan. I won't be long."

She hurried across the room and into the small kitchen beyond. As she pulled the coffeemaker forward on the counter, she realized that Ryan was standing next to her.

"I'll bring it into the living room," she said, glancing at him.

He leaned back against the counter, folded his arms over his chest and frowned.

"I'm fine right here," he said.

Deedee shrugged and busied herself preparing the coffee.

Ryan watched her with narrowed eyes.

MacAllister, he ordered himself, *keep your mouth shut.* He'd argued with himself during the drive back here, reaching the conclusion that he had no intention of addressing Deedee's reaction to the dumb pink rabbits.

It was none of his business. So what if he'd witnessed her upset, had seen as clearly as a flashing neon sign the message that she yearned to have a baby of her own? It didn't matter one iota to *him.* He had no desire to learn the inner workings of Deedee's mind, or the secret wishes in her heart.

He had intended to say good-night to her at the door, but had suddenly heard himself request a cup of coffee. Well, that was understandable. He'd been raised to be polite, and since it was still so early, it would have appeared rude to just dump Deedee off and split.

So, fine. He'd drink his cup of coffee...fast, talk about something mundane like the weather, or a current best-selling novel, and be out of there.

Good plan. No problem.

"Deedee," he said, "since you want a baby so badly, why don't you get married and have one? Or don't get married and have one, anyway?"

What? his mind thundered.

"What?" she said, holding two mugs in midair.

"Oh, hell," he said, dragging his hands down his face. "I wonder if early dementia runs in my family."

Deedee plunked the mugs onto the counter, planted her hands on her hips and glowered at him.

"I don't recall saying I wanted a baby, Mr. MacAllister, but even if I did, which I don't, it certainly wouldn't be any concern of yours. A baby? Me? That's absurd."

"The hell it is," he said none too quietly. "I was sitting next to you all evening, remember? I saw your reaction to Forrest's rabbits, to the announcement that Jillian is expecting triplets.

"The smile you plastered on your pretty face for the rest of the evening was as phony as a three-dollar bill. Not only that, you were so pale your freckles looked like spots on a dalmatian. Oh, yes, Ms. Hamilton, you definitely want a baby."

"You've got a lot of nerve, mister," she said. "You have no idea what you're talking about, and I really resent your—"

"Ah, Deedee," he interrupted quietly, a gentle tone to his voice. He cradled her face in his large hands. "Talk to me. Trust me."

It was too much, it really was.

If Ryan had continued to shout, Deedee could have held on, matching him holler for holler. But this? The gentle coaxing of his voice, the warmth of his chocolate brown eyes, the comforting feel of his hands on her cheeks, was her undoing.

She was so exhausted, so confused and frightened, and Ryan was a safe haven, a tower of strength, a chance to lean, just for a moment.

She looked directly into the dark pools of his eyes and burst into tears.

"Oh, man," Ryan said, "now I've done it."

He dropped his hands from her face, wrapped his arms around her and nestled her close. Deedee circled his waist with her arms, laid her head on his chest and wept.

And Ryan held her.

He dipped his head and savored her delicate aroma of lilacs, then rested his rugged cheek on her silky curls, allowing them to caress his skin like soft velvet. Her slender body was pressed tightly to his body, her breasts crushed enticingly to the hard wall of his chest.

She trembled as she cried, and fierce emotions of protectiveness and possessiveness consumed him, causing him to clench his jaw.

Nothing, and no one, would ever hurt Deedee Hamilton, he mentally decreed. She was so fragile, like a...yes, a butterfly. He would stand between her and harm's way, keep her sheltered from pain.

She was so sad, was crying as though her heart was breaking. Deedee was meant to smile, to dance in the sunshine with the butterflies. If she wanted a baby, she should have her baby, and a special man to love and cherish her as the precious treasure she was.

Ryan frowned and lifted his head.

A man? his mind echoed. A faceless man who would reach for her in the night, make love to her, plant his seed in the feminine darkness of her body? A man who would watch her growing big with his child, then witness the miracle of that baby being born? A man who would place a pink or blue toy rabbit in front of the MacAllister family as part of The Baby Bet?

Damn it, if any man touched Deedee Hamilton, he'd take him apart!

Ryan shook his head slightly, and his frown deepened.

What in the hell was the matter with him? His mind was charging full-speed ahead down a road that led to Deedee being *his,* the baby she yearned for being *his.*

No!

He was married in his heart and soul to Sherry, always would be. He couldn't, wouldn't, ever love another woman. He'd chosen Sherry as his wife, and he intended to stay true to that vow. No one could ever take her place.

It was the tears, he reasoned. Deedee's sad weeping was unraveling him, shredding him into pieces. That was understandable. Unless a guy was made of stone, he was undone by a crying woman.

Even tough cop Ted was jangled by a weeping woman, even a strange one encountered while in his role as a police officer.

Deedee wasn't a stranger, someone Ryan didn't know. She was Deedee, who had been on the fringes of his life for several years. His emotions had momentarily run away from him, but he was getting himself together now, back under control. If Deedee wanted a baby, she should have one, but *he* certainly wasn't going to have anything to do with the conception.

The Baby Bet might very well be put into operation

again in the future, featuring Deedee Hamilton, but Ryan MacAllister would place his twenty dollars in Forrest's hand and watch it all unfold from the sidelines.

Deedee sniffled, then stiffened in Ryan's arms, bringing him from his tumbling thoughts.

"Oh, dear," Deedee said, then a wobbly little sob escaped from her lips.

She eased away from Ryan, and he released her. He took a pristine white handkerchief from his back pocket and handed it to her. She dabbed at her nose and eyes, refusing to look at him.

"I'm sorry," she said, staring at the middle of his chest. "I'm so embarrassed. I don't cry." She paused. "Well, I obviously just did, but I usually don't. I can't even remember the last time I cried, it's been so long. I'm very tired, you see, and... But that's no excuse, and I do apologize for—"

"Deedee."

"You're very kind, Ryan, and patient, and... I'd appreciate it if you'd go now and allow me to be mortified alone. Try to forget this happened. Okay? Oh, you didn't get your coffee. I owe you a cup of coffee. Good night and—"

"Deedee, look at me."

She shook her head, pressing the handkerchief to her nose.

"Look...at...me."

She sighed, dropped her hands to her sides and lifted her head slowly to meet his gaze.

Oh, hell, Ryan thought, smothering a moan. Her beautiful brown eyes were shimmering with tears, making them shine like starlight. Her nose was pink, her cheeks were blotchy, her lips were trembling slightly. Deedee was not a pretty crier. But Deedee was the most enchanting sight he'd ever seen.

He wanted to scoop her up and hold her close, kiss away the salty tears still streaking her face, then capture her lips with his. He wanted to feel her give way to her passion, just as she'd done during the kiss they shared earlier that evening.

And he wanted to make love to her for the remaining hours of the night—slow, sweet, sensuous love, meshing their bodies, becoming one entity. He'd take her away from reality, carry her to a place where she could dance with the beautiful butterflies.

He wanted... *Damn it, MacAllister, knock it off.*

"Come on," he said, "let's go into the living room, sit down and talk. Just for a few minutes. Okay?"

Before Deedee could reply in the negative, Ryan strode from the kitchen.

"Whatever," she muttered, following him.

Ryan waited until Deedee had sat down on the sofa, then settled next to her, shifting slightly so he could look directly at her.

"Deedee," he said quietly, "I'm very sorry that I upset you the way I did. The fact that you want a baby is none of my business. Well, it *wasn't* any of my business, but now it *is* my business, because I'm the one who made you cry."

Deedee glared at him. "You're babbling."

"Yeah, well, a crying woman is a very traumatic experience for a guy. Being big and strong, able to leap tall buildings in a single bound, isn't worth squat when a woman is crying all over your shirtfront. It's a very helpless feeling.''

''Oh. Really? I guess I never thought about it from the male point of view. Of course, I don't go around crying every other minute, either.''

''Well, forget all that. The subject here is that something very important to you is missing from your life. What I can't understand is why you haven't done something about it. You're an attractive, intelligent woman. A man would be very fortunate to have you for a wife, a life's partner, the mother of his children. Why are you alone, Deedee?''

''Because I choose to be,'' she said, her voice rising a bit. ''I'm having this conversation with you because it seems like the polite thing to do. You *do* have a soggy shirt because of me and my behavior. However, the bottom line is actually what you babbled about. It's really none of your business.''

''You *made* it my business, remember? Why do you choose to be alone?''

''You must have been a good cop, Ryan. The poor suspect would confess just to get you out of his face.''

''Yep,'' he said, smiling. ''So answer the question.''

Deedee sighed and dabbed at her nose again with Ryan's handkerchief.

''I was married to a wonderful man,'' she said wearily. ''Jim and I were perfect together, absolutely perfect. When he was killed flying an air force jet in a training mission, I was devastated. I hardly functioned for an entire year. I went through the motions of living, but I was actually only existing in a cold, empty void.''

''I understand,'' he said, frowning. ''I've been down that road.''

''I know you have. At some point, a person has to make choices, get on with their life. I decided to dedicate myself to starting Books and Books, making it successful. I've done that, and I'm very fulfilled, very pleased with what I've accomplished.''

''But?'' he prompted.

''I don't know what happened tonight,'' she said, throwing up her hands. ''I haven't been pining away for a baby. Keeping in touch with myself is something I pride myself on. What made me react the way I did to Jillian and Forrest's announcement about the triplets? I have no idea. I *am* happy with my life just the way it is, Ryan.''

He settled back against the sofa, folded his arms over his chest and squinted at the ceiling.

''No, you're not,'' he said. ''Your subconscious was delivering a message to you that your conscious mind was not yet aware of as being a true fact.''

''Oh, good Lord,'' Deedee said, ''now I'm dealing with an amateur shrink. Ryan, go home.''

''In a minute.'' He looked at her again. ''You had a *perfect* marriage?''

''Yes.''

''There wasn't the slightest glitch, not even one small problem?''

''No.''

''Bull.''

''Damn it, MacAllister, that's enough. I was there

with Jim. I know how it was. He's been dead for ten years, and every detail of our life together is still crystal clear in my mind. I had perfection, and I won't settle for less. The way I see it, what Jim and I had doesn't happen twice, it just doesn't.

"As for my reaction tonight about the babies? I'm human. I suppose, as a woman, there's a tiny seed of desire hidden somewhere within me to have a child, and the three pink rabbits nudged it. It was a fleeting moment that is over. Yes, it upset me because it has never happened before, but it's finished, kaput, done. Go home."

"I'm going," he said, not moving. "Look, just because you made a decision to devote your life to your career, doesn't mean you can't change your mind."

"Is that so? All right, Mr. MacAllister, I'll take a long, hard look at my life, on one condition."

"Which is?"

"That *you* do the same thing with *your* life."

Ryan opened his mouth, closed it and tried again.

"What?" he said.

"You heard me. Your entire family is concerned about who you've become since Sherry was killed. Can all those people be wrong? You made choices, decisions, just as I did."

"I'm remaining true to the wedding vows I took with Sherry," he said, his voice harsh. "That's the way it is. That's the way it's going to stay."

"Tsk, tsk. One would think one would practice what one preaches. You *can* change your mind regarding your life-style. You owe it to yourself to re-evaluate your life."

"The hell I do!"

"Neither do I. See? We agree. End of story. Good night, Ryan."

"*You're* the one who cried buckets over pink rabbits, not me. *You're* the one who's in trouble here, not me. I'm doing fine, thank you very much."

"Ha! Any man who kisses a woman the way you kissed me isn't doing so almighty fine in his solitude."

"We covered all that. It's basic lust."

"Oh? But what if it isn't, Ryan MacAllister? What if *your* subconscious is rapping you on your thick skull? What if you want a wife—not me, of course—but a special woman you've yet to meet. And what if *you* want a rabbit?"

"You," he said, pointing a finger at her, "are nuts."

"Am I? Fine. We'll each go on living our lives exactly the way we are."

"You can't do that to yourself, Deedee."

"My deal stands. I examine my existence only if you do the same to yours."

Ryan lunged to his feet. "Man, you're a stubborn woman. You're a real pain in the butt, do you know that?"

Deedee stood, then shrugged. "Whatever."

Ryan ran one hand over the back of his neck and shook his head.

"I don't know why I should care one way or another about what you do with your life." He glared at her. "It's because you cried, I suppose. Tears just wipe me out." He paused, then sighed with exasperation. "All right, you win. If I have to do a reality check on my life to get you to do one on yours, so be it."

"You're kidding."

"Nope. Do you stay late at Books and Books on Friday night?"

"No, one of my employees is scheduled to come in to take the evening shift."

"Good. I'll pick you up here at seven, and we'll go to dinner."

"Why?"

"To discuss what we've thought about, and the conclusions we've reached so far. That's how this is going to work."

"Says who?"

"Me, Ms. Hamilton." He gripped her shoulders, hauled her to him and planted a searing kiss on her lips. "Good night, Deedee," he said when he released her.

"But..." Deedee started, pointing one finger in the air.

Before she could speak further, she heard the door close behind an exiting Ryan.

"Well, hell's bells," she said, rolling her eyes heavenward, then went to bed.

Chapter Seven

Ryan was deep in thought while he shaved the next morning, performing the daily ritual by rote.

He replayed the events with Deedee of the night before over and over in his mind, each time becoming more pleased with how things had unfolded.

Yes, sir, he thought smugly, he'd stepped right in and taken charge, had everything headed in the direction *he'd* decided was the proper way to go. He was calling the shots, making the rules.

He now had a legitimate reason to see Deedee on a regular basis, beyond when he'd be installing the new security system at Books and Books. He would do that job himself, of course, rather than assign it to his employees. The work would keep him in close proximity to Deedee.

Then, due to his genius-level plan, he was in a

position to see Deedee regularly so they could work on reevaluating their lives.

Ryan rinsed the razor in the running tap water, then continued to shave.

Deedee was quick on the uptake, he had to admit. She'd nailed him tit for tat, demanded that *he* examine his existence while she was doing hers. That had thrown him for a second, but he'd regrouped fast enough. He'd dish out some malarkey that would satisfy her, prove he was "doing his thing."

In the meantime, he would be accomplishing his goal of "overdosing on Deedee," so he could get her out of his system. He would have the opportunity to allow his sexual attraction to her to run its course, dim, then finally fade out completely.

"Yep," he said to his reflection.

As for Deedee...well, he truly believed that she *did* need to examine her present life-style and be totally honest with herself about what she wanted and needed to be fulfilled and happy.

But why was he pushing her to do that?

So okay, it was time he emerged from his cocoon...a little. Not a lot, just a tad. He fully intended to stay faithful to the vows he'd taken with Sherry, and he wasn't sticking his neck out emotionally in new arenas. He wouldn't render himself vulnerable by again becoming a cop who cared, or by opening emotional doors for a woman to walk through. No way.

He'd loved. He'd lost.

The memories of Sherry would hold him in good

stead for the rest of his life. He didn't need more than that, not now, not ever.

He wasn't the one who had cried about pink rabbits, for Pete's sake.

Man, oh, man, he was slick. He'd maneuvered things around Deedee last night like a master chess player.

"You're awesome, MacAllister," he said. "Ow! Damn it, I cut myself."

As Deedee drove to Books and Books, she drummed her fingertips on the steering wheel in time to a peppy tune playing on the car radio.

She felt marvelous, her solid night's sleep having replenished both her physical and emotional energies. It was a new day, the sun was shining and she was in an upbeat frame of mind. It was really amazing what a little rest could do for a person.

Her agreeing to reevaluate her life only if Ryan did the same had been brilliant, absolutely brilliant. Where the entire MacAllister family had failed in their attempts to convince Ryan that he needed to move forward with his life, she was going to succeed.

She was totally confident that Ryan, a basically intelligent man, would come to see that existing behind his solid walls deprived him of a full and rich existence. He'd start to live again, embracing life the way it should be.

As for her? Well, no problem. Her crying jag over the pink rabbits had been a momentary lapse of purpose, a thoroughly feminine and explainable event. It was over, wouldn't happen again and all was well.

Ryan believed she wanted a baby, possibly a husband, but she knew better. She'd have to fake her reports to him on the subject matter to keep *him* on *his* examining track. She wouldn't be lying exactly, she'd be using whatever strategy was necessary to help Ryan. Very good.

"Next up on the agenda," she said aloud.

Her sexual attraction to Ryan had been placed on the back burner, but had to be addressed. It was there, front-row center again.

Oh, dear heaven, when he kissed her she melted, when he touched her she dissolved. The man was potent, dangerous, hazardous to her mental health.

But now she knew that.

She had facts that would enable her to maintain control of her very unsettling passion when she was with Ryan. She'd panicked at first from her reactions to him, but she was under control now, doing fine. What continually happened between her and Ryan was a chemical thing, was...lust—nothing more.

Oh, boy, would Ryan be fuming if he realized she was in charge of the present scenario. She would get him to make needed changes in his life, and he'd never know what hit him.

Men might be physically stronger than women, but engage in mental shenanigans? They didn't stand a chance.

"Oh, yes," Deedee said cheerfully, "it's a beautiful day."

* * *

Friday evening, Deedee stood in front of her closet, thoughtfully tapping one fingertip against her chin. She was wrapped in a towel, having just finished showering and washing her hair.

What should she wear for her date with Ryan? He'd simply said they'd go out to dinner, giving no clue as to what type of restaurant he had in mind.

Actually, this wasn't a date, as in *date*. This was a meeting, scheduled so they could discuss the progress made reevaluating their individual lives.

So what did a person wear to a meeting date? Another question to ponder was what in the heck was she going to discuss?

Ryan would pitch a holy fit if she said her plans for the future were centered on increasing her inventory of rare books. Not good, not good at all. He'd want to hear an admission that she yearned for a husband and a pink rabbit. Well, forget *that*.

"I'll wing it," she said aloud. "But what should I wear?"

If they went the fast-food route, it called for jeans and a sport top. A family restaurant meant slacks and a sweater. If they were going to "dine," then a fancy dress was in order.

"Well, darn," she said, frowning, "how can I dress so I'll be prepared for anything?"

Okay, she'd split the difference. She'd wear the peach-colored sweater with the lacy inserts, winter-white slacks, and medium heels.

The last time she wore the peach sweater on a date, she'd added a full-length black skirt and had been dressed to the nines. The outfit she'd just mentally assembled would be halfway between super-fancy and very laid-back.

Forty-five minutes later, her hair dried and brushed into soft curls and makeup applied, she looked smashing, if she did say so herself. All she needed was a couple of spritzes of cologne, and she'd be ready to go.

The flowery cologne applied, she turned off the bedroom light and went into the living room, humming softly.

A few minutes later, a knock sounded at the door and she went to answer it, the smile on her face genuine. When she opened the door, the smile slid right off her chin as she stared at Ryan.

Merciful saints, her mind thundered, Ryan MacAllister was absolutely gorgeous.

He was wearing a charcoal gray suit with a navy blue shirt and gray tie. A navy silk handkerchief peeked above his jacket pocket. The rich colors did marvelous things, sinful things, for his tan, and his shoulders looked a block wide.

"Hello, Deedee," Ryan said, not smiling. "May I come in?"

Deedee blinked. "What? Oh. Come in? Of course you may come in. Hello, Ryan, come in."

"You're babbling," he said dryly, moving past her. "Do you have a problem?"

She closed the door and turned to face him, willing her smile back into place.

"No," she said brightly, "I don't have a problem. Nope, not me."

He sure as hell did, Ryan thought with a flash of

anger. Deedee looked sensational, exquisite, fantastic, and heat had rocketed through his body the moment she'd opened the door.

That sweater she was wearing was a teaser, by damn. A sweater was supposed to be a sweater, not a peekaboo thing with lace whatevers that gave enticing glimpses of the tantalizing woman beneath. Oh, man, this could very well turn into an extremely long evening.

"Are you ready to go?" he said gruffly.

Deedee frowned. "You don't sound very thrilled about the idea. You look about as pleased as a person might if he was leaving for the dentist's office to have a root canal done."

Ryan started to retort, then changed his mind, taking a deep breath instead. He let it out slowly, ran one hand down his tie and squared his shoulders.

"There," he said, smiling. "That's better. I had a hectic day, lots of tedious details to tend to. I didn't have time to 'chill out,' as the kids say, before I came over here. I'm perfectly fine now." *Bull!* "So if you'll get your purse, we'll be on our way."

"Right," she said, eyeing him warily.

The restaurant was a step above "family outing" and a step below "waiters in tuxedos."

She'd dressed appropriately, Deedee decided when they'd been seated.

They ordered from menus offering a wide variety, then Ryan selected, tasted and approved the wine.

"Now then," he said, "we discussed the weather during the drive over here, as well as the royal family of England. Let's get to the nitty-gritty, shall we?''

''Certainly.''

Several long seconds ticked by as they looked at each other expectantly.

''Well?'' Ryan finally said. ''What's your report, Deedee? How far have you gotten in reevaluating your life?''

''Me? Oh, I think you should go first, Ryan. After all, this is your plan, your idea.''

''No, I—''

''I insist.'' She smiled, propped her elbows on the table and folded her hands beneath her chin. ''I'm all ears.''

No, he thought dismally, she was all woman, and he was a dying man. The drive from Deedee's apartment to the restaurant had been pure agony. Her flowery perfume, the lilting sound of her laughter, the very essence of her femininity, had seemed to fill the interior of the vehicle to overflowing. His body had declared war against his common sense.

Oh, man, how he wanted to make love with Deedee Hamilton.

''Ryan?''

''Hmm?'' he said, a rather vague expression on his face.

She leaned slightly toward him. ''Are you with me here? What do you have to report?''

''Your salads,'' the waiter said, suddenly appearing. ''Would you care for ground pepper?''

After the waiter had moved away, Deedee picked up her fork and took a bite of crisp lettuce.

"Did you see the size of that pepper grinder?" Ryan said. "The thing must have been three feet long. I should tell that guy that I'm a cop, and he has twenty-four hours to register it as a lethal weapon."

"Well, my goodness," Deedee said, "that is a very interesting observation."

"I beg your pardon?"

"You want to be a police officer again."

"I didn't say..." he said, much too loudly. He glanced quickly around, then lowered the volume of his voice. "I didn't say I wanted to be a cop again."

"Ryan, Ryan, Ryan," Deedee said, shaking her head, "you amaze me. You're the one who is so big on your subconscious sending messages that your conscious mind might not yet be aware of as being facts. That *does* apply to you, too, you know."

"So?"

"So you didn't say you used to be a cop, you said, 'I should tell that guy that I'm a cop.' Present tense, as in now. Therefore—" she pointed her fork at him "—you're saying that you've discovered you want to rejoin the police force. I think that's wonderful. Everyone says you were a terrific cop. Will you and Ted be able to be partners again?"

Ryan sank back in his chair and stared at Deedee as though she'd just grown an extra nose. She smiled at him pleasantly, then took another bite of salad.

Somehow, he thought, narrowing his eyes, Deedee had gained the upper hand here, was calling the shots. How had she managed to do that? Lord, women were difficult to deal with.

The really rotten part of all this was that she was right. He *did* want to be a cop again. He had no intention of pursuing that desire, but a part of him honestly did want to.

Damn it, what was he going to say? He was a MacAllister, and MacAllisters had been raised to tell the truth. They did *not* tell bold-faced lies.

"Ryan?"

He moved forward again, pushed his salad plate to one side and crossed his arms on the top of the table.

"You're quick, Deedee Hamilton," he said. "You'd be a good cop yourself."

"Thank you, sir."

"Let's get something straight here. Whatever we tell each other is to be held in strict confidence and goes no further than the two of us. Agreed?"

Deedee nodded. "Agreed."

Ryan drummed the fingers of one hand on the tabletop, attempting and failing to discover a way to *not* address the issue of his wanting, or not wanting, to rejoin the police force.

"Hell," he muttered.

"Ryan, you're stalling."

He straightened and folded his arms on his chest.

"You're right," he said, "I *am* stalling. I'm not accustomed to talking about myself, what is, or isn't, on my mind. This isn't that easy to do."

"Ryan," Deedee said gently, "in the past two years you've hardly talked at all. You closed down, shut yourself away behind very solid walls."

"Yeah, I suppose I did."

"It's true, and you know it. Believe me, I understand and can thoroughly relate to it. I did the same for the year following my husband's death. But there comes a time when you have to move forward. I think, I hope, you're beginning to realize that."

"How long were you married, Deedee?"

"About eighteen months." She paused. "Jim was on temporary duty in Germany for six months of that, but I wasn't allowed to go with him because it wasn't a permanent assignment. Later he was overseas again for four months, but I never knew exactly where or why. He was an expert pilot, with top-secret security clearance."

"Whew. The air force really took a chunk out of your time together. Had you known him long before you were married?"

"Three weeks," she said, smiling. "We had a classic case of love at first sight. It actually does happen to people."

"Now wait a minute. You knew him for three weeks, were married approximately eighteen months, and he was away for a total of ten months of that year and a half?"

"Yes," she said, obviously confused by Ryan's verbal tally.

He leaned forward again, resting his arms on the table, a deep frown on his face.

"Deedee, for cripe sake, you're refusing to even consider marrying again because you had the 'perfect' marriage? You and Jim weren't together enough to find out more than that you had great sex. I assume you two were sexually compatible?"

"Yes, we were," she said, feeling a warm flush of embarrassment on her cheeks, "but that's not a topic I care to discuss, thank you. What exactly is your point?"

"My point is, when you and your Jim managed to have the opportunity to live under the same roof, the little stuff probably didn't matter because you were never certain when he'd have to leave again."

"What kind of *little stuff?*" she said, a slight edge to her voice.

"Did he pick up his socks? Squeeze the toothpaste in the middle of the tube? Leave a wet towel on the bathroom floor after his shower? Did he help you with the household chores? Take out the trash? Did he remember your birthday? Anniversary? Was he romantic, thoughtful? Did he listen to you, really listen, when you had something on your mind that was important to you?"

"Ryan, that's enough," Deedee said, her eyes flashing with anger. "I'm not going to sit here and allow you to diminish what I had with my husband. You're picking it apart like...like dissecting a frog, or something."

"I'm spelling it out in realistic terms, instead of looking at it as the *perfect* fairy-tale romance and marriage the way you are. Add ten years since it all took place, and any rough edges there might have been have definitely been smoothed over.

"Based on this...memory, you've sentenced yourself to a life alone? Deedee, come on, wake up here. You're hiding in a fantasy."

"Ryan MacAllister, you have no right to pass judgment on—"

"Excuse me," the waiter said. "Your dinners."

"What?" Ryan said, snapping his head around to look at the man. "Oh, yes, of course. Fine."

Deedee busied herself by moving her salad plate out of the way, smoothing her napkin—which was already smooth—on her lap, then taking a sip of wine. What she did *not* do, was look at Ryan.

How dare he pass such harsh censure on her marriage to Jim? she fumed. Ryan was being cruel and cold. It was as though he wouldn't rest until he'd shattered her beautiful and precious memories into a million pieces.

Not only that, but he was insinuating—no, it was worse than that—he was stating in no uncertain terms that she was *hiding* in a world of fantasy that she'd constructed with rose-colored memories of her marriage.

That wasn't true. It...was...not...true. What she'd shared with Jim *had* been perfect.

It had been very understandable that he hadn't helped with the household chores. His daily routine was so much more exhausting and stressful than her clerical job at the library.

And the time he'd totally forgotten it was her birthday? Well, he'd explained that. He'd had a rookie pilot with the jitters, who had needed some one-on-one man talk and encouragement. She and Jim had celebrated her birthday on another night.

Hadn't they?

Surely they had, but why couldn't she remember what they'd done together to make it special?

Damn Ryan. For two cents she'd punch him smack-dab in the nose. They hadn't even been discussing *her*. She had zeroed in on his slip of the tongue regarding his *being* a police officer, rather than having *been* one. She thought she had control of the direction of the conversation.

But Ryan had somehow, the sneaky beast, turned things around and begun hammering at her about her marriage. How had he managed to do that? It probably stemmed from the training he'd had in interrogation. All that was missing was a bare light bulb hanging above her head.

Oh-h-h, he was infuriating.

Deedee took a nibble of flaky fish, not really tasting it.

Calm down, she told herself. Regroup. Get it together. She *had* agreed to reconsider her life. That her existence was fine and dandy exactly as it was now was not a declaration she could stand on a chair and holler at the top of her lungs.

If she did, Ryan would no doubt declare *his* life to be in order, as well, and cancel the whole exercise. Not good. *His* life was nothing more than a shallow existence.

So okay, she'd have to grin and bear Ryan's scrutiny of her life so she could have equal time to push him to look closely at his.

Brother, whose dumb idea had this been?

Except...

She really did wish she could remember if she and Jim had actually celebrated her neglected birthday.

"Deedee," Ryan said quietly.

She looked up at him. "Yes?"

"I'm sorry if I upset you. I came on pretty strong, I guess. It's just that I truly believe that you should be embracing life, have more than you do. You should be..." He stopped speaking, searching his mind for the words he wanted. "You should be dancing with butterflies."

Deedee blinked, then drew what she realized was a trembling breath. A warmth suffused her, swept through her like rich brandy, then tiptoed around her heart with a gentle caress.

"That," she said, her voice unsteady, "was one of the most beautiful things anyone has ever said to me."

"Yeah, well," he said, shifting in his chair a bit as he was hit with a wave of embarrassment, "I don't usually say gushy things like that." But that dream was still haunting him, damn it. "But you need to take a hard look at your marriage, as well as your present existence. Do you understand what I mean?"

Deedee nodded. "I think so."

"Good, that's very good. You have a lot of things to sift and sort through before we get together again."

"Yes, I certainly do." She paused. "Ryan, we *were* discussing your wanting to rejoin the police force."

"True. You pointed out that my saying I *am* a cop,

rather than I *was* a cop was a message from my subconscious. I need some time to think about that.''

"Oh, well, that makes sense. You have your assignment, so to speak, just as I do. You need to concentrate on that topic until we meet again. Right?"

"Right. Now, we've covered the serious business for tonight, so we can relax and enjoy the rest of the evening." He smiled. "Would you care for some more wine, ma'am?"

Chapter Eight

The brain, Deedee mused an hour later, was a strange blob of gray matter. From the moment Ryan had declared they should now relax and enjoy the evening, she'd begun to do exactly that.

There was, she supposed, the possibility that she'd grabbed hold of his statement like a lifeline, only too happy to escape from the overload of thoughts that were tumbling in a tangled maze in her mind.

She did *not* want to examine her marriage to Jim, or her present and future existence, under a mental microscope. She was going to spend the remainder of the evening in the *now,* savoring each moment, one tick at a time.

Ryan was charming, witty and attentive, and the conversation flowed easily from one interesting topic to the next as they finished their dinners. They topped off the delicious meal with coffee and small snifters of rich brandy.

"More coffee?" the waiter said, appearing at their table.

Ryan looked at Deedee questioningly.

"No, thank you," she said, smiling. "I'll pop a seam if I have anything more. Everything was excellent, very delicious."

"May I have the check, please?" Ryan said.

"Certainly, sir," the man said. "There's a combo playing in the Malibu Ballroom down the hall if you'd care to dance this evening. I'll bring you the check." He hurried away.

"Well, how do you vote?" Ryan said. "Would you like to go dancing, Deedee?"

"Oh, my, it's been so long since I've danced." She paused. "Let's see, it must be a dozen or fifteen years. Do you suppose it's something that you don't forget, like riding a bike? Well, if I trample your toes, we'll know the answer to that one."

"Twelve or fifteen years?" Ryan repeated. "Didn't you and your husband ever go dancing?"

Deedee refolded her napkin in a precise square, giving the task her full attention.

"No," she said, smoothing the corners of the linen. "No, we didn't." She looked at Ryan again. "Did you and Sherry go dancing often?"

Ryan frowned. "No. Now that I think about it, I realize that I never danced with Sherry." He smiled. "I have a feeling it may be *your* toes that are at risk here. Are you game?"

Deedee matched his smile. "Sure. If we both hobble home, we'll have no one to blame but ourselves."

The waiter returned with a leather folder, which he placed by Ryan. While Ryan settled the bill, Deedee's mind wandered.

She'd never danced with Jim, she thought, and Ryan had never danced with Sherry. Therefore, Deedee Hamilton dancing with Ryan MacAllister was an event, a memory in the making, that was exclusively theirs with no ghosts from the past hovering around. She liked that.

You should be dancing with butterflies.

Ryan's words echoed in her mind, and the warmth she'd felt tiptoeing around her heart when he'd said them returned with greater intensity.

Dancing with butterflies.

Oh, what a beautiful image that created. She could see herself on a sunny summer day, the sky a brilliant blue, and she was wearing a pretty dress. She was…yes, in a field of gorgeous, fragrant wildflowers, and a multitude of delicate, vibrantly colored butterflies were fluttering around her. Ryan was there, and they were smiling.

They were happy and carefree.

They were together.

"All set?" Ryan said.

Deedee jerked at the sudden sound of his voice, instantly aware of the flush of embarrassment on her cheeks for having indulged in such a whimsical and ridiculous daydream.

"You're blushing," Ryan said.

"It's the brandy," she said, pushing back her chair.

''Brandy does that to me—makes my cheeks pink. Strange, isn't it? Happens every time.''

''Mmm, I see,'' he said, raising one eyebrow. ''Is that a fact?''

''Yep.'' She smiled brightly.

The Malibu Ballroom was fairly crowded, but Ryan managed to find a free table among those edging the dance floor. Crystal chandeliers had been dimmed to create a romantic glow of soft light. The five-piece band started playing a waltz just as they arrived.

Deedee set her purse on the chair by the minuscule table, and Ryan flipped a plastic sign in a holder to Reserved. They maneuvered their way onto the dance floor, and he drew her into his arms.

As they began to move with the lovely, lilting music, Deedee allowed her lashes to drift slowly down, savoring the moment.

Heavenly, she thought dreamily. Being held fast in Ryan's arms was wonderful. They danced marvelously together, as though they'd been partners on many dance floors in the past.

But, no, there was no past, not tonight. There was no future, not tonight. There was only now, just tonight.

Deedee sighed in contentment and nestled closer to Ryan's powerful body.

Ryan drew a quick, sharp breath as Deedee wiggled against him.

Control, MacAllister, he ordered himself. Dancing had not been one of his brightest ideas. His body was going crazy with Deedee molded to him, the heat within him causing him to ache with the want of her.

Man, she felt sensational, Ryan thought. She fit so perfectly into his arms, against his body, as though she'd been custom-made just for him.

He inhaled her flowery aroma, then dipped his head so her silky curls could whisper against his face. He was going up in flames, but he'd die with a smile.

Deedee felt so delicate, so fragile, so incredibly feminine.

He was dancing with a butterfly.

The waltz ended and the band immediately began to play another slow song. An invisible hand somewhere lowered the glow of the chandeliers another notch. Ryan's hold on Deedee tightened a fraction more.

He attempted to center his mind on the discussion that had taken place with Deedee during dinner, to determine his progress toward getting her to reevaluate her life. He gave up the effort as a lost cause.

He couldn't think, he could only feel.

The hell with it, he decided. He was giving his rational mind the rest of the night off. For the remaining hours he was with Deedee, he wouldn't dwell on the past, or on his loyalty to Sherry. The future, too, would be a taboo subject.

For once in his life, on this night, he was going to simply *be*. He was a man in the company of a lovely and desirable woman. Events would be allowed to unfold with no resistance, no guilt, no ghosts. One stolen night. So be it.

"I guess we remembered how to dance," Deedee said softly.

"Yes, we did," he said, "and we fit together very nicely. You feel good in my arms, Deedee."

"It's nice being here."

They swayed to the dreamy music. The other people on the dance floor seemed to fade into oblivion. There was only the two of them in an otherworld place, where nothing could intrude.

Heated desire swirled within Deedee, pulsing low in her body, and she welcomed it, rejoiced in it. She was so vitally alive. She was woman. This night was special, rare, magical, and hers.

She could feel Ryan's arousal pressing against her, knew he wanted her just as she desired him. The knowledge wasn't frightening, it was wondrous.

"Deedee," Ryan said, his voice low and gritty, "can you feel what you're doing to me?"

"Yes," she whispered.

"I think we should... Hell, I *can't* think, I'm beyond thinking. All I know is that I want you, want to make love with you. I ache for you. It's not fair to dump a decision of this magnitude on you, but I have to. It's up to you, Deedee. You're going to have to decide how this night will end."

Deedee tilted her head back to meet his gaze, knowing the raw desire she saw in his expressive brown eyes was evident in her own.

"This night," she said, "is ours. It's a magical night, Ryan, stolen out of time. We're Cinderella and the prince at the ball. One night. Just one. Ours." She drew a trembling breath. "Let's go home...together."

* * *

During the drive to Deedee's apartment, she mused rather hazily that if she truly wished at some subconscious level to change her mind about making love with Ryan, the reality of a ride across town in a Jeep would jar her sense of reasoning.

But the fleeting thought was there, then gone. She focused on the moment, adamantly refusing to address anything else.

This was their magical night, hers and Ryan's. Nothing mattered beyond the two of them, and what they were going to share.

Deedee had left a small lamp on in the living room, and the soft glow of light greeted them as they entered the apartment.

When Ryan shut the door, he snapped the lock into place, then quickly shifted in front of Deedee. Startled by his sudden movement, she stepped backward, thudding against the door.

Ryan planted his hands on either side of her head, lowered his own head and kissed her deeply. His tongue plummeted into her mouth and she met it eagerly, dueling, stroking. He kept his body tantalizingly inches away from her.

Deedee curled her hands into fists at her sides, resisting the urge to reach for Ryan and pull him near, to feel his magnificent body pressed to hers.

He lifted his head to draw a ragged breath, then slanted his mouth in the other direction, capturing her lips once again. A quivering whimper of need escaped from Deedee's throat.

The heat grew low within her. It matched the maddening rhythm of Ryan's tongue moving seductively against hers. She was on fire, melting, moist, aching for release and fulfillment.

It was heaven and it was hell, in the same breathless moment.

Unable to restrain herself a second longer, she raised her hands to splay them on the hard wall of Ryan's chest, then lifted them an instant later to encircle his back, silently pleading with him to come closer.

He complied, molding his body to hers, his arousal full and heavy against her. The kiss deepened even more. It was hungry, urgent, fanning the flames of passion even higher and hotter.

Ryan finally tore his mouth from Deedee's, his breathing rough.

''Deedee,'' he said, his voice sounding strange to his own ears, ''I want you. Now. Are you sure, really sure, about this? Have you thought—''

She quieted his words by placing two fingertips on his lips. ''I refuse to think about anything other than what I'm feeling, wanting, needing,'' she said. ''We mustn't think, Ryan, either of us. This is our stolen night. There are no yesterdays, no tomorrows, just the now. Make love with me, Ryan, please.''

With a groan that rumbled from low in his chest, he kissed her once more, then swung her up into his arms and carried her into the bedroom. The lamp from the living room cast a nearly ethereal rosy glow over the small room.

He set her on her feet, and she flipped back the spread and blankets on the bed to reveal the sheets.

Ryan stared at the bed, his heart thundering so violently it echoed in his ears.

The pattern on the sheets and pillowcases was a multitude of pastel-colored butterflies.

Yes, his mind hammered. Yes. Perfect. There they were, the butterflies from his dream. *This,* what was happening with Deedee, was all a dream. Real but not real. A step apart from the world as he knew it.

Making love was often called the ancient dance of man and woman together. He was about to dance among the butterflies...with Deedee.

He looked at her again, then framed her face in his hands. He kissed her softly, tenderly, the whispery caress causing her to tremble. Their eyes met and held. Messages of raging desire were sent and received.

Ryan stepped back and they removed their clothes, allowing the garments to fall to the floor in unheeded disarray.

Then they stood naked before the other, each visually tracing every glorious inch of the one within their view.

Ryan was like a wondrous statue, Deedee mused dreamily. He'd been chiseled from the finest marble by a master craftsman, then bronzed to a warm, rich tone. Each section of his magnificent physique was perfectly proportioned to the next, his muscles ropy, his body powerful.

Brown curls, a shade darker than the sun-lightened hair on his head, covered his broad chest, then narrowed at his belly. A smattering of hair covered his strong legs.

His arousal was a bold declaration of all he would bring to the dark haven of her femininity.

Oh, Ryan.

Ryan drank in the sight of Deedee—her small, firm breasts, the gentle slope of her hips, the nest of strawberry blond curls at the apex of her thighs. She was beautiful, like a delicate china doll, with skin that appeared like ivory velvet.

Deedee.

He lifted a hand, palm up, extending it toward her, not caring that she could see how it trembled. She raised her hand and placed it in his.

It was such a simple gesture, two hands nestled together, one large and callused, the other small and soft.

Two hands. Joined.

It was a symbolic affirmation of the journey they were about to take that would result in the joining of their bodies, meshing them into one entity.

They looked at their hands, but neither spoke, couldn't speak, as emotions flooded through them, unnamed, unknown, but making words impossible.

Ryan tightened his hold, and Deedee stepped forward into his waiting embrace. He kissed her as his hands roamed over her silken skin, cupping her buttocks, lifting, pressing her to the cradle of his hips.

She leaned against him, suddenly weak from the heated flames whipping through her. Ryan raised his head and picked her up, placing her gently among the butterflies in the center of the bed.

Deedee's arms floated upward, welcoming him.

He stretched out next to her, bracing himself on

one forearm, his other hand splayed on her flat stomach.

"You're so lovely, Deedee Hamilton," he said hoarsely, looking directly into her smoky brown eyes. "You're beautiful."

"You're beautiful, too, Ryan MacAllister," she whispered. "You truly are."

He kissed her, then moved his lips to one of her breasts, drawing the sweet bounty into his mouth, laving the nipple into a taut button with his tongue. He shifted to the other breast, paying homage there, as well.

Deedee purred in pure womanly pleasure, then the sensuous sound became a near sob of heightening need as Ryan's hand skimmed lower to find the moist curls that shielded her femininity.

Ryan's hand stilled and he lifted his head to look at her.

"Deedee," he said, his voice gritty with passion, "listen to me for a minute. Are you protected, prepared for this?"

"What?" she said, struggling to focus on what he was saying.

"Birth control."

"Oh. Yes. Yes, I'm protected. I haven't been with anyone in such a long time, but I'm on the pill because my body doesn't regulate things too well on its own. It's all right, Ryan."

He dropped a quick kiss on her lips.

"Thank goodness," he said. "If I had to stop now, I'd probably blow a circuit. I want you so much."

"I want you, too, Ryan. I truly do. Now. Please, Ryan, you're driving me out of my mind."

"I don't want to hurt you. You're so small and delicate."

"I won't break. Ryan, please just shut up and—"

"Do it," he said, chuckling. "Your wish is my pleasurable command."

He kissed her once more, then shifted over her and entered her.

"Oh-h-h, yes," she said with a soft sigh. "Yes."

He began to move, slowly at first, then increasing the tempo. Deedee lifted her hips to bring him deeper within her, matching his rhythm.

It was ecstasy.

It was wild, pounding, glorious.

Deedee clung tightly to Ryan's shoulders, feeling the taut, bunching muscles beneath her hands. The heat within her began to swirl and coil low in her body, building to a wondrous tension that seemed to lift her up and away. She savored each thundering thrust that Ryan made, meeting them beat for beat.

Higher...

Reaching...reaching...

Incredible, Ryan's mind hummed. So good, so good. Deedee was tight and hot around him, drawing him deeper within her, giving him as much as he was giving her. They were fantastic together. Oh...man.

On and on...

Higher and higher...

Then...

"Ryan!"

Deedee was flung into oblivion, and Ryan joined

her there an instant later, a moan of pleasure from the exquisite release rumbling in his chest.

"Dancing," he gasped, "with butterflies."

They hovered there for a tick of time.

They hovered there for an eternity.

His last ounce of energy spent, Ryan collapsed against Deedee, his breathing labored.

"Too heavy," he mumbled, then rolled off her, keeping her close to his side.

Their breathing quieted, and heartbeats returned to normal. Ryan reached down for the blankets, covered them, then sank back onto the pillow with a sigh of sated contentment.

"Oh, my," Deedee said, nestling her head on his chest. "Oh, Ryan."

"I know. You're right. Unbelievable."

"Yes. Mmm, I'm so sleepy."

He kissed her on the forehead.

"Then sleep, little butterfly."

"Butterfly?"

"Never mind," he said.

Deedee drifted off into blissful slumber, and a few minutes later Ryan closed his eyes and slept.

Hours later, Deedee stirred and slowly opened her eyes. She glanced at the clock, saw that it was 3:14 a.m., then turned her head to look at Ryan. She frowned at the empty expanse of bed next to her.

Maybe he was getting a drink of water, she mused sleepily.

She fluffed the pillow, wiggled into a more comfortable position, then closed her eyes again, allowing thoughts to float in at will.

Ryan. Their lovemaking had been so beautiful. She couldn't remember having ever experienced such ecstasy, such fulfillment.

It was as though she and Ryan had been created just for each other, were *meant* to mesh their bodies, be one, like two perfectly matched pieces of a magical puzzle.

This night had been glorious.

This night? her mind echoed as she opened her eyes again. It was closer to the ever-famous "morning after." Was she sorry, filled with remorse, regret, over what she had done?

No, oh, no. She would cherish the memories, treasure them like precious gifts. The stolen night was hers to keep in her heart, mind and soul.

With morning came reality. Well, so be it. She once again had a past and a future, as well as the now of the present.

The past. Jim. Her darling Jim. Her beloved, who had, indeed, forgotten her birthday, which she now remembered they never did celebrate. She'd cried tears of disappointment and hurt in solitude.

Jim. She had taken second place, always, after the airplanes. His greatest joy came from flying through the heavens, pushing the envelope, taking daring chances and declaring himself to have "the right stuff." Being her husband, lover, friend, had never come first with Jim Hamilton.

She'd loved him so much. She'd forgiven him so much.

And it was time to face the truth.

Her marriage to Jim had not been perfect.

She'd buried the hurt and unhappiness so deeply within her, she'd truly forgotten there had been bad times along with the good. Jim's death had shattered her, caused her to cringe in emotional fear of ever loving again.

Ryan had been right when he'd said she was hiding in a fantasy.

Deedee drew a shuddering breath.

She'd hung on to the past like a lifeline for ten years. *Ten years.* She used it as a shield to keep men at bay, to avoid the risk of loving again.

But on this night, this beautiful night with Ryan MacAllister, the shield had crumbled into dust and was gone. It was time, long overdue, to move forward, grow, embrace the future.

"Goodbye, my darling Jim," she whispered. "Rest in peace, my love."

A warmth suffused her. With it came a soothing sense of inner peace that caused a lovely, soft smile to form on her lips.

A moment later the smile was replaced by a frown as she realized that Ryan had been gone far too long to be simply getting a drink of water.

She left the bed and picked up his shirt from the floor, slipping it on to cover her nakedness. Crossing the room, she stopped in the doorway as she saw Ryan sitting on the sofa in the living room. He was wearing his trousers, had his elbows propped on his knees and his head sunk into his hands.

She started toward him, hesitated, then stopped halfway across the room.

"Oh, God, Sherry," Ryan said, his voice ringing with anguish, "what have I done?"

Chapter Nine

Ryan's words seemed to strike against Deedee like physical blows, causing her to instinctively wrap her arms around her middle in a protective gesture. A chill swept through her, and a gasp escaped from her lips.

Hearing the soft sound, Ryan snapped his head around to look at Deedee. He lunged to his feet in the next moment, pain etched on his rugged features.

"Deedee." He extended one hand toward her, then dropped it back heavily to his side. "You heard," he said, his voice flat and low.

Deedee shifted her arms higher to beneath her breasts, lifted her chin and swallowed past the ache of tears in her throat.

"Yes, I heard," she said, praying her voice was steady. "You've totally destroyed our night together,

Ryan. What we shared. You allowed Sherry's ghost to come into *our* private place, *our* world. You had no right to do that, because this night belonged to me, too. I was the other half of what happened here.''

He shook his head. ''You don't understand.''

Deedee marched across the room to stand in front of him. She planted her hands on her hips and looked directly into his eyes.

''Oh, I understand perfectly, Mr. MacAllister,'' she said, her cheeks flushed with hurt and anger. ''You accused me of hiding in a fantasy of having had a perfect marriage.

''Well, you were right. I did the ever-famous re-evaluating of my past, and I admit that I *was* hiding, just as you said. But I'm not hiding any longer, Ryan. I've accepted the truth of my time spent with Jim, the good *and* the bad. *It was not perfect.*''

''Deedee—''

''Shut up and listen. *You're* the one who's hiding now, Ryan. You're scrambling as fast as you can back into the past because you're a coward. You're afraid to hang on to the fact that tonight was incredibly beautiful and rare. So very special. You're afraid, Ryan, actually terrified, that it might come to mean something to you, that you might actually *care*.''

''I broke my vow to Sherry,'' he yelled. ''Where am I supposed to put *that?* What about my personal integrity? How can I look at myself in the mirror when I've been unfaithful to the pledge I made?''

''Sherry is dead!'' Deedee shouted. ''If she loved you as you claim she did, she'd want you to get on with your life, laugh again, love again, for heaven's sake…live again. Damn you, Ryan, you're hiding, and you're intelligent enough to realize that you are.

"Why? Why are you hiding? Have you asked yourself that question, Ryan? Do you know the answer?"

"Damn straight I do, lady," he said, volume still on high. He dragged both hands through his tousled hair. "I don't want any part of loving again, caring again, not about anyone, or anything.

"I'd like to return to the police force, be a cop. How do you like that news flash? Oh, yeah, I want that very much. I'm bored out of my mind running MacAllister Security Systems. But I won't ever wear a uniform again. No way. And I won't ever love another woman other than Sherry. It's not going to happen, Deedee."

"Why not?" she queried.

"Because it's all too risky, damn it. I'm not setting myself up to get sliced in two again. I can't do things half measure, don't you see? If I became a cop, I'd care about the people I came in contact with, all of them. I wouldn't be able to keep myself from doing that. I don't know how. And when I love a woman, I give it everything I have. Everything in my heart and mind. My very soul."

A shudder ripped through him.

"No," he went on, his voice suddenly hushed and raspy with emotion. "I can't do it. I can't run the risk of laying it all on the line, then waiting to have it, the essence of myself, crushed, smashed to smithereens. A man can only bleed to death once, drop by drop. I've done it. I won't do it again. Not ever."

"Oh, Ryan."

Deedee's eyes misted with tears, and she closed the short distance between them, wrapping her arms around him and leaning her head on his bare chest. She could feel his muscles tense and the wild beating of his heart, but continued to cling to him.

He slowly, tentatively, lifted his arms to encircle her. His hold was loose, light, just barely touching her. Deedee increased the pressure of her arms. With a moan, he pulled her tightly against him, as though he'd never again let her go.

"Ah, Deedee."

The anguish in Ryan's voice caused fresh tears to brim in Deedee's eyes. Two tears slid slowly and unnoticed down her cheeks.

"Ryan," she whispered, "don't do this to yourself. Don't hide anymore. You deserve to live life to the fullest, to be happy, to have a million special nights like this one we just shared. I don't mean have a relationship with *me,* but you'd find someone special if you'd only break free of the past."

"Deedee, I didn't intend to spoil what we had tonight," he said quietly. "It was truly beautiful. It really was *our* night. We'll keep it separate and apart from everything else. I can do that. I *will* do that. I swear, I promise, I will."

He paused and shifted his hands to her upper arms, easing her back so he could see her face. She lifted her head to meet his gaze, blinking away the last of her tears. He frowned at her.

"What do you mean," he said, "you didn't mean have a relationship with *you?* It sounds as though you're sending me packing to find some woman I haven't even met yet."

Deedee shrugged. "What difference does it make?" She directed her attention to one of the buttons on his shirt she was wearing, pushing it more firmly through the buttonhole. "You've made it clear that you have no intention of having a real present or future. You're staying in the past…with Sherry."

Ryan dropped his hands from her arms and began to pace around the living room with heavy strides. Deedee sank onto the sofa and watched him trek. He finally stopped, folded his arms over his chest and glowered at her.

"You're right," he said. "I'm staying in the past, being true to my vow to Sherry. But suppose, just suppose, I'd decided to let the past go. Why wouldn't you consider having a serious, committed relationship with me? I mean, hell, what am I? Chopped liver?"

Deedee covered her mouth with one hand and coughed to keep from laughing right out loud.

Male egos, she thought, were strange little creatures. Men in total, egos included, were basically weird specimens. Having a relationship with her, or any woman for that matter, was obviously not an option Ryan planned to explore, even consider for a moment.

He certainly didn't want *her* in his life. But her saying she wouldn't have a relationship with him, even if he was available? He was pitching a male-ego fit. Men, men, men. Poor dears, they were such befuddled messes.

A wave of exhaustion suddenly swept through Deedee, and she sighed with fatigue.

It was no wonder she was tired, she thought. It was nearly four in the morning, and she'd dealt with a multitude of intense emotions since the evening with Ryan had begun so many hours before.

"Ryan, look," she said, then yawned. "I need some more sleep. Let's talk about this tomorrow, shall we? I'm out on my feet."

"But..." He paused. "Yeah, you're right. Enough is enough for now. I think the best thing would be for me to leave."

Deedee got to her feet and shuffled slowly toward the bedroom.

"Whatever," she said. "That might be a little tough to do seeing how I'm wearing your shirt, and I'm too pooped to take it off. You could chance it, I guess, and hope you don't bump into anyone you know." She waved one hand breezily in the air. "'Bye."

"Hey! I need that shirt, Deedee."

"Mmm."

Deedee crawled back into bed, pulled the blankets up to her chin and fell soundly asleep within moments after her head nestled in the soft pillow.

A few minutes later, a muttering Ryan slipped into the bed next to her.

The aroma of freshly brewed coffee brought Deedee slowly awake from a deep, dreamless sleep. She opened one eye to see Ryan sitting on the edge of her side of the bed, holding a mug of coffee in each hand.

''Hello,'' he said, smiling slightly. ''This is room service. I hope you weren't supposed to open Books and Books this morning. It's after nine-thirty.''

''No, today is Saturday and one of my employees is working.'' She stretched, then scooted upward. After arranging the pillows behind her, she reached eagerly for one of the mugs. ''Heavenly. I feel very pampered.'' She took a sip of the hot coffee. ''Oh, good grief, this is so strong it could have walked in here on its own.''

''I like a robust cup of coffee to get me started in the morning.'' His gaze flickered over her. ''You wrinkled my shirt.''

She was sexy as hell in his shirt, Ryan thought, but that was beside the point. The fact that she was surrounded by the butterflies on the pillowcases and sheets and looked pretty as a picture wasn't fair to his libido, either. How could a woman be that beautiful so quickly after awakening?

And there were those damnable cute, polka-dot freckles prancing across her pert nose. No, it wasn't fair at all.

''Well,'' he said, ''leaving in a wrinkled shirt is better than having no shirt at all.''

''True.'' She took another swallow of coffee, wiggled her nose at the bitter taste, then set the mug on the nightstand. ''We need to talk, Ryan.''

''Now?''

Deedee folded her hands in her lap, resisting the urge to reach out and touch Ryan's enticingly bare chest that seemed to be beckoning to her tingling fingertips.

''Yes, now,'' she said.

He nodded. ''Go for it.''

She stared at her hands for a long moment, then met his gaze again.

''I meant what I told you last night,'' she went on quietly. ''I really did take an honest look at my marriage to Jim. I've accepted the fact, *the truth,* that what I shared with him was *not* perfect.''

''You were hiding in the fantasy that it was.''

''Well, yes, in a way,'' she said thoughtfully. ''But not because I was afraid to love again. I had considered all my choices and made the conscious decision to dedicate my physical and emotional energies to making Books and Books a success.

''The men I dated over the years constantly took the stand that my business was an acceptable entity, no problem. I couldn't get through to them that I didn't want a serious commitment with a man.

''They did, however, head south when they thought they were competing with a ghost, when I said I'd had a perfect marriage that I had no intention of attempting to duplicate. I used it as a tool to end relationships as gently as possible.''

''And you came to believe it.''

''Yes. I think that's what happened.''

''But now? You did react very strongly to Forrest's pink rabbits, Deedee.''

She sighed. ''I know I did, and that confuses me. I'm still focused on Books and Books, I know I am. I'm enthused, excited, as dedicated to the store's continued success as I ever was. Maybe the pink rabbit episode was a fluke, a blip on my emotional screen that came from a purely womanly part of me. That could happen to any single woman my age. But it came, then it went. End of story.''

"Maybe not. Maybe it's the beginning of a new story. Your subconscious could have been sending you a heavy-duty message about what you really want in the future.''

Deedee frowned. "I guess I need time to sift through all this." She nodded. "I'm sure I need time.

"Ryan, when I said I wasn't interested in a relationship with you, it wasn't personal. At this point in time, I don't want a relationship with any man.''

"That may change after you sift."

She shrugged. "Who knows?"

"Deedee," Ryan said, looking directly into her eyes, "you accused me of being a coward."

"Oh, Ryan, I apologize for that. I had no right to use such a harsh word.''

"It's all right, because I can understand why you'd see it that way. I admitted that I was staying in the past because it was too risky not to. That could easily be construed as being a coward.

"However, I view it as being a realist. A person who got creamed standing in the middle of a freeway would be pretty stupid to march right back out into that traffic. He'd stay on the side of the road, where it was safe. That's not cowardice. It's common sense.''

"Wrong. I'm not buying your metaphoric scenario. Millions of people have loved and lost, Ryan. That doesn't keep them from loving again once they've worked through their grief.''

"Not interested."

"But you've given up being a police officer, too. Darn it, Ryan, why won't you think about all this? You talk about it with a stubborn set of your jaw and a list of what you won't do. I'm the only one working at this 'reevaluation' you invented."

"That's not true. I..." He stopped speaking and stared up at the ceiling for a long moment before looking at her again. "Yes, it is."

"Mmm," she said, nodding decisively.

"Okay, it's confession time." He took a deep breath and released it slowly, puffing out his cheeks in the process. "I, um, well, I never intended to seriously reevaluate my life. I said I would because I truly believed that *you* needed to examine your existence." And I needed to overdose on Deedee, get her out of my system, obliterate the strange and unsettling sensual impact she has on me.

As far as that part went, Ryan's progress was zip. His desire to make love with her again was so intense that he ached. He wanted her. *Now.*

"You conned me," Deedee said, frowning.

"I should apologize, I guess, but I won't, because you *did* achieve a realistic picture of your marriage. You've dealt with the past, know the truth, and you're free to move forward with your life. There are still some kinks to work out, but so far you're doing great."

"Kinks?"

"Well, yeah. The pink rabbit episode is unfinished business. All my instincts tell me you sincerely wish you had a baby, and probably a husband, too. You'll

GET 2

HOW TO GET YOUR
2 FREE BOOKS AND FREE GIFT!

1. Peel off the MIRA sticker on the front cover. Place it in the space provided at right. This automatically entitles you to receive two free books and an exciting mystery gift.

2. Send back this card and you'll get 2 "The Best of the Best™" novels. These books have a combined cover price of $11.00 or more in the U.S. and $13.00 or more in Canada, but they are yours to keep absolutely FREE!

3. There's <u>no</u> catch. You're under <u>no</u> obligation to buy anything. We charge nothing – ZERO – for your first shipment. And you don't have to make any minimum number of purchases – not even one!

4. We call this line "The Best of the Best" because each month you'll receive the best books by some of today's hottest authors. These authors show up time and time again on all the major bestseller lists and their books sell out as soon as they hit the stores. You'll like the convenience of getting them delivered to your home at our special discount prices . . . and you'll love your *Heart to Heart* subscriber newsletter featuring author news, horoscopes, recipes, book reviews and much more!

SPECIAL FREE GIFT!

We'll send you a fabulous surprise gift, absolutely FREE, simply for accepting our no-risk offer!

5. We hope that after receiving your free books you'll want to remain a subscriber. But the choice is yours – to continue or cancel, anytime at all! So why not take us up on our invitation, with no risk of any kind. You'll be glad you did!

6. And remember...we'll send you a mystery gift ABSOLUTELY FREE just for giving "The Best of the Best" a try.

Visit us online at
www.mirabooks.com

® and TM are trademarks of Harlequin Enterprises Limited.

BOOKS FREE!

The Best of the Best™ — Here's How it Works:

Accepting your 2 free books and gift places you under no obligation to buy anything. You may keep the books and gift and return the shipping statement marked "cancel." If you do not cancel, about a month later we will send you 4 additional novels and bill you just $4.24 each in the U.S., or $4.74 each in Canada, plus 25¢ shipping & handling per book and applicable taxes if any.* That's the complete price and — compared to cover prices of $5.50 or more each in the U.S. and $6.50 or more each in Canada — it's quite a bargain! You may cancel at any time, but if you choose to continue, every month we'll send you 4 more books, which you may either purchase at the discount price or return to us and cancel your subscription.

*Terms and prices subject to change without notice. Sales tax applicable in N.Y. Canadian residents will be charged applicable provincial taxes and GST.

If offer card is missing write to: The Best of the Best, 3010 Walden Ave., P.O. Box 1867, Buffalo, NY 14240-1867

BUSINESS REPLY MAIL

FIRST-CLASS MAIL   PERMIT NO. 717   BUFFALO, NY

POSTAGE WILL BE PAID BY ADDRESSEE

**THE BEST OF THE BEST
3010 WALDEN AVE
PO BOX 1867
BUFFALO NY 14240-9952**

NO POSTAGE
NECESSARY
IF MAILED
IN THE
UNITED STATES

cover that when you sift. Are you angry because I tricked you into taking part in this plan?''

''Oh, my, no,'' she said pleasantly. ''I couldn't legitimately be angry at all, because I was doing the exact same thing to you.''

Ryan narrowed his eyes. ''Oh?''

''Yep. I was perfectly content with my life, but was saddened by your determination to cling to the past, to hide behind the walls you'd built around yourself. Your entire family is deeply concerned about you, Ryan. So I agreed to your little exercise with the condition that you do as much mental homework as you were demanding that I do.''

''*You* conned *me*.''

''Yes, sir, I certainly did,'' she said, appearing extremely pleased with herself. ''You've made a teeny tiny bit of progress, but nothing to shout about. You've admitted you want to rejoin the police force, but you won't actually do it. You've admitted you're staying in the past because it's safe, but you've convinced yourself that's common sense bordering on brilliance.''

She leaned slightly toward him.

''You have an attitude, MacAllister, that definitely needs work.''

''You're pushing me, Deedee,'' he said, a warning tone to his voice. ''I don't like being manipulated, which you did. And I don't like being nagged, which you're doing.''

''Matching up to exactly what you did and are doing to me.''

''Oh.''

"Yes, 'oh.' Well, all the truth cards are on the table, and the question is waiting to be answered."

"Question? Which is?" Ryan asked.

"It's very simple. It's 'now what?' The jig is up, so to speak. Do we cancel the whole thing?"

"No! Damn it, you still have to deal with the pink rabbit."

"And you," Deedee said, poking him in the chest with one fingertip, "have to deal with what you want versus your refusal to go after it."

He snagged her hand with one of his, resting both on his chest.

Oh, blast, Deedee thought. The heat from Ryan's hand was traveling up her arm and across her breasts, causing them to feel heavy, in need of his soothing touch. Heat. It was swirling, thrumming lower in her body, pulsing. She wanted to make love with Ryan *right now*.

She tugged on her hand, but Ryan tightened his hold, refusing to release it.

"Now what?" he repeated. "We continue on with the program."

"Only if we're both honest about it, Ryan. I have to know you're doing your part."

"Yeah, I will, but it's a waste of time, because I'm not going to change my stand."

"We'll see. I study my reaction to Forrest's pink rabbit. You study the possibility of actually moving forward with your life. Agreed?"

He nodded slowly. "Agreed." He paused. "There's another question that needs addressing.

What about us?'' His gaze flickered over the rumpled bed. ''What we shared was fantastic.''

''Yes, but you're beating yourself up because it happened.''

''No, I've regrouped on that, remember? I said I'd keep our night separate and apart from everything else. I think—no, I'm certain—that I can continue to do exactly that.''

Deedee yanked her hand free and folded her arms over her breasts. She glared at Ryan.

''So you can have great sex whenever the mood strikes?'' she said. ''Not in this lifetime, bub. I don't have casual sex, Ryan MacAllister, and if that's where your head is, count me out.

''Last night was special, rare, wonderful. It meant a lot to me. You're not a stranger off the street— you're someone I know and care about. I don't love you, have no intention of falling in love with you, but I *do* care about you.''

''Well, hell, Deedee, if I didn't *care* about you as a person, a woman, a friend, I wouldn't have gone to all the trouble to con you into reevaluating your life.''

''You've got a point there.''

''You bet I do. To echo…I don't love you, have no intention of falling in love with you, but I do *care* about you.''

''You said the word *friend* before.''

He nodded. ''It applies.''

''Friends,'' she said, squinting at the ceiling, ''and lovers. Mmm. It has possibilities.'' She looked at him again. ''Ryan, what if we agreed to be friends and lovers? No commitments to the future, no false declarations of feelings that aren't there.

"The whole evening we spent together was lovely—dinner, dancing, sharing, talking, then...then making love."

"True. Go on."

"Well, we're mature adults. Why can't we set the boundaries as we know them and which match perfectly? Why can't we be friends and lovers? Nothing more."

Ryan thudded his coffee mug onto the nightstand, got to his feet, then began to pace the floor, one hand hooked over the back of his neck.

Damn, this was confusing, he thought. He was supposed to be getting Deedee out of his system, not agreeing to a proposal that would keep her in it.

Friends and lovers. Well, maybe... Hell, why not? There was no duplicity going on, everything was up front and honest.

He and Deedee cared enough about each other to make it more than just casual sex. But neither one of them had any intention of falling in love with the other. If a person made up their mind not to fall in love, then they didn't fall in love. It was a matter of having a firm mind-set, and a grip on reality.

It would be nice to have a social life, something to look forward to after a dull, boring day at MacAllister Security Systems. And heaven knew that he and Deedee were terrific together in bed.

Friends and lovers.

"Mmm," he said, continuing to pace.

Deedee watched him, her mind whirling.

Friends and lovers? she thought. Was that a bizarre thing to have proposed? Well, no, not really. It made sense, was custom-tailored for her and Ryan. She did *not* want to fall in love and get married again. Her focus was, and would remain, on Books and Books.

And Ryan? Even if he managed to keep what they shared separate and apart from the sifting and sorting he needed to do about his life, surely *some* of the time they spent together would influence his thinking on not staying in the past. He wouldn't fall in love with *her,* nor did she wish him to, but he just might become free enough to eventually love someone else.

Love someone else? Make love to another woman, the way he'd made love to her? Perhaps fall in love, marry and have a child with that woman?

Why did those thoughts cause a cold fist to tighten in her stomach? Why did the image in Deedee's mind of Ryan with another woman cause her to feel empty, lonely, filled with a hollow sense of despair?

Enough, Deedee, she ordered herself. She was still bordering on emotional overload from all that had transpired. She would be happy for Ryan if he found love again, embraced it, married and had a family. Of course, she would. In the meantime they'd be...

Friends and lovers.

Yes.

Ryan stopped his trek and looked at her.

"Yes," he said. "It'll work. We'll make it work."

"Oh, well, fine, that's fine." She smiled. "Should we shake hands on it, or something?"

"Or something," he said, starting slowly toward her.

Deedee's eyes widened as she watched him approach, seeing the stark desire suddenly evident in the smoky brown depths of his eyes. A shiver coursed through her, and a sense of tantalizing anticipation. It was quickly followed by the now-familiar heat that thrummed low and hot.

Friends and lovers? her mind echoed. Oh, yes, yes, yes!

Ryan sat down on the edge of the bed and looked directly into Deedee's eyes, seeking and finding an affirmation of what he needed to know.

Deedee wanted him, just as he wanted her. They didn't have to discuss it, he knew, because they made no attempt to hide their desire, their raging passion. They were so open and honest with each other now, with no more hidden agendas. They'd talked, shared, communicated, and everything was aboveboard and real.

There was no need to feel guilty, to be plagued with remorse for not staying true to his vow to Sherry. What he and Deedee had agreed upon was very different. It was unusual, but suited them both to perfection. It involved only the two of them, excluding all and everything else.

Friends and lovers.

Yeah, it was good.

"I think," he said, his voice low and rumbly, "that I'll reclaim my shirt."

He reached forward and slid the first button free, his fingers caressing Deedee's soft, warm skin beneath the material.

"Do you..." she started, her voice unsteady, "want me to go iron it?"

"No-o-o," he said slowly, "that won't be necessary." One hand moved to cup one of her breasts. She trembled. "What's a few wrinkles between friends?" His thumb stroked the nipple of her breast to a taut bud. "Right?"

"Oh-h-h," she said, closing her eyes for a moment to savor the exquisite sensations rushing through her. "Right. That is...that is so right."

He pulled the shirt free of the sheet and blanket, undid the remaining buttons, then brushed the material back to reveal her breasts to his smoldering gaze.

Planting his hands flat on either side of her hips, he leaned forward, drawing the lush flesh of one breast into his mouth, suckling, flicking the nipple with his tongue.

A soft sigh of pure feminine pleasure whispered from Deedee's lips.

He moved to the other breast, drinking of its sweetness, as one hand skimmed over her hip, down the side of her leg, then came to rest at the apex of her thighs.

"Oh, Ryan, please."

In a blur of motion, he shed his trousers, threw the bedclothes to the foot of the bed, then lifted Deedee from the pillows to lay flat on the field of lovely, pastel butterflies. He covered her with his naked body, claiming her mouth in a searing kiss.

He entered her with one deep, powerful thrust, filling her, consuming her and her senses. She welcomed him, eagerly receiving all that he was bringing to her.

And they danced.

Chapter Ten

Ryan finally left Deedee's apartment, complete with wrinkled shirt covered by his suit jacket. Deedee showered, dressed, nibbled on a piece of toast, then began to clean the apartment, per her usual Saturday routine.

Much to her annoyance, she realized she'd vacuumed the living room, bedroom, then had turned right around and thoroughly vacuumed the living room again.

She smacked the off switch on the vacuum cleaner, then slouched onto the sofa with a sigh.

Flapping one hand in front of her face, she frowned. ''Go away, Ryan MacAllister. Get out of my brain. I'm trying to do some housework here.''

Ryan, Ryan, Ryan, her mind echoed. Her body was sore in feminine places, but she felt wonderful. She was still acutely aware of every inch of herself, her skin seeming to tingle, her breasts full and womanly.

Oh, such exquisite lovemaking she'd shared with Ryan. She'd never experienced anything so beautiful, complete, anything that had caused her to soar to a wondrous place where she'd never been before, a place where she could only go with Ryan.

He was so strong, yet tempered that strength with infinite gentleness, putting her pleasure before his own. He'd discovered the mysteries of her body, just as she'd done with his, savoring it all.

"Friends and lovers," she said aloud. "Lovers and friends."

Ryan truly *was* her friend. He listened, really listened, when she talked to him. He was concerned about her future happiness, had manipulated her into examining her life out of a sense of caring. She knew, just somehow knew, that if she telephoned him in the middle of the night and said she needed him, he'd come, no questions asked.

Yes, he was her friend.

But he was also very, very dangerous.

It would be extremely easy to fall in love with Ryan MacAllister.

And *that* was not going to happen.

Her existence was constructed exactly the way she wanted it, with her focus on Books and Books. She didn't *really* yearn for her own pink rabbit. She could satisfy her maternal instincts when the urge arose by visiting the ever-growing number of MacAllister babies.

Now she even had a man in her life, a friend, who

would provide enjoyable social outings where she wouldn't have to be alert for signs that he was becoming too serious about her or might soon be asking more of her than she was willing to give.

That friend was also her lover, and together they achieved glorious sensual heights beyond her wildest imagination.

"Yes, indeed, everything is perfect," she said, getting to her feet.

Her relationship with Ryan, within the boundaries they'd mutually agreed upon, was exactly right for him, too. He was giving of himself, caring, slowly emerging from behind his protective walls. He would hopefully become free of the past, and eager to move forward with his life.

"Perfect," she repeated, grasping the handle of the vacuum.

She started to wrap the cord around the hooks on the machine, then stopped, staring into space.

If everything was perfection personified, she mused, then why did the apartment seem so incredibly empty? Why was she feeling strangely alone and lonely? Why did she miss Ryan MacAllister so darn much, wish he was still there with her?

"Deedee," she said, "get a grip. You'll see Ryan when you see him. He'll pop up...whenever. Fine."

But, oh, dear heaven, how long would she have to wait before she was able to once again drink in the magnificent sight of Ryan MacAllister?

When Ryan entered his office on Monday morning, he realized that for the first time since he could remember, he was glad to be there. It was not due, however, to a sudden enthusiasm for being the owner of MacAllister Security Systems, and he knew it.

The remainder of Saturday and all day Sunday had dragged by slowly, tediously, causing him to become restless and out of sorts. He'd rejected every idea that came to mind to fill the hours, and the time had hung heavily on his hands.

And it was all Deedee Hamilton's fault!

Ryan sank onto the chair behind his desk and stared moodily at nothing.

Deedee had hovered in his mind's eye the entire weekend. She'd been a haunting, taunting presence, a pest. He'd seen her smile, heard her laughter *and* the womanly purr of pleasure she made when he touched her. He'd actually smelled her delicate, flowery aroma, and vividly recalled the exquisite taste of her velvet-soft skin.

She'd driven him right up the wall, caused him to toss and turn at night as he ached for her, his body hard and hot.

Ryan smacked the top of his desk with the palm of his hand, then swore a blue streak as the pain from the blow shot up his arm.

''Serves you right,'' Andrea said, coming into his office. ''That's what you get for desk abuse.'' She plopped down in the chair opposite the desk. ''A tad grouchy this Monday morning, are we?''

Ryan glared at her. ''Don't you have a kid who needs a diaper changed?''

''Nope. The twins are at day-care this morning, tormenting the other two-year-olds. I'm on my way to MacAllister Architects, Incorporated.''

''Oh, I see. Well, don't let me keep you. Goodbye, Andrea.''

''Tsk, tsk, Ryan. Did you forget this morning to have that muddy junk you call coffee?''

Ryan leaned back in his chair and sighed. ''No, I had plenty of my delicious coffee, thank you very much. I'm just exhausted, that's all.'' He managed a small smile. ''Hi, Andrea, how's life? What's new and exciting? How's that? Better?''

''Not much, but I'll take what I can get.''

''You haven't come by here in months, little sister. What's on your mind?''

Andrea shrugged. ''I just thought I'd say hello. I haven't had you all to myself in ages. What do you think about Jillian and Forrest expecting triplets? Isn't that something?''

Ryan chuckled. ''Yeah, it sure is. Man, they are going to be busy beyond belief when those babies arrive. Three of everything. Whew.''

''Three girls, just as Forrest predicted. The way he continually wins The Baby Bet is getting eerie. I swear he can't be beat, and he's so darn smug about it.''

''He should be. He's on a real roll. He deserves to be cocky as hell with his winning record.''

''Yes, I suppose he does.'' Andrea paused. ''So! How's Deedee?''

Ryan raised his eyebrows, an expression of pure innocence on his face. ''Who?''

''Don't get cute with me, Ryan MacAllister. A

friend of mine—well, actually a friend of my friend—saw you and Deedee out dancing. I think that's wonderful, and I wanted to tell you how pleased I am that you two went on an official date.''

"Deedee and I are friends," he said. And lovers. Fantastic lovers. "Read my lips, Andrea. That word is *friends*."

"That's fine," she said, smiling. "John is my best friend. I'm John's best friend. Being friends is an important part of a meaningful relationship."

"Oh, man," Ryan said, rolling his eyes heavenward, "here we go."

"No," Andrea said, suddenly serious, "I'm not planning to pester you for details about your... whatever it is...with Deedee. I just wanted to say to you, privately, how happy I am that you went out socially. It's a start, Ryan, and it's long overdue."

Ryan looked directly at his sister, seeing the gentle love radiating from her brown eyes that were the exact shade of his.

"Yeah, you're right, it's overdue," he said quietly. "Deedee and I had a nice evening, a good time. We've talked, Andrea, and neither of us wants anything more than friendship."

"I understand." She got to her feet. "I'm glad you discussed it, because I'd hate to see either of you hurt. You're very special people. So you'll enjoy social outings together as friends. That's great. I guess that means you're both free to date other people. Right?''

"I haven't thought about it. Why?"

"Oh, another friend of a friend has an attorney

cousin she wants Deedee to meet. I guess this guy is a real hunk of stuff, and has megabucks to boot.''

''Whatever,'' he said, lifting one shoulder in a shrug.

''Then you don't mind if I mention the gorgeous lawyer to Deedee?''

''Andrea, I just said that Deedee and I are only friends. I don't have an exclusive claim on her time. She's free to go out with whomever she pleases. If she wants to date a sleazy lawyer with pumped-up muscles, who throws money around to impress her, that's her choice to make.''

Andrea laughed. ''You're getting crabby again, and I'm late for work. Forrest probably won't even notice what time I arrive. It's hard to see the clock from up on cloud nine. 'Bye, sweetheart.'' She blew him a kiss and hurried out of the room.

''Bye,'' Ryan said absently.

A megabucks yuppie attorney? his mind echoed. No, that didn't sound like the type of guy Deedee would be interested in going out with. She'd turn him down flat. Wouldn't she?

Hell, he didn't care one way or another. Did he? Definitely not. So fine, she'd go out with the smooth-talking lawyer, who would wine and dine her, bring her flowers, kiss her and...

Ryan lunged to his feet.

Kiss her? Touch her? Try to hustle her into bed? He'd tear the creep apart! He'd...

''Oh-h-h,'' he moaned, dragging both hands down his face as he sank back onto his chair. ''Deedee Hamilton, you're driving me crazy.''

"Hey, boss," a man said, poking his head in the office, "the equipment you needed for that deal at the bookstore just arrived."

"Good. Thanks for telling me."

"You still planning on doing that job, instead of having me and Jack do it?"

"Yeah. Why?"

"Because talking to yourself is a definite sign of old age. I just wondered if you could handle the work."

"Go play in traffic."

The man hooted with laughter and disappeared.

Ryan glowered at the empty doorway for a moment, then shifted his gaze to the telephone.

He needed to call Deedee and inform her that he was ready to install her new security system, and ask her if she wanted it done during the day, or after the store closed. Yep, he had to get in touch with her right away.

He picked up the receiver and began to punch in numbers he vaguely realized he knew by heart.

What Ryan MacAllister *wasn't* aware of was that he was smiling.

Deedee combed her hair, freshened her lipstick, then practiced three different smiles in the mirror over the sink. In the next moment, she rolled her eyes in self-disgust and left the small bathroom at Books and Books.

Glancing at the clock, she hurried across the room to lock the front door, flipped the sign to Closed, and dropped the bamboo shade into place. She also lowered a shade behind the large front display window.

An automatic timer had turned on several small spotlights to illuminate the arrangements of books in the window, but the shade kept sidewalk browsers from seeing the interior of the store after closing hours.

Ignoring what felt like a full platoon of butterflies in her stomach, she entered the storage room. After flicking on the light, she stood by the back door, waiting for Ryan's arrival.

She was behaving like an adolescent, she admonished herself. This wasn't the captain of the high school football team for heaven's sake, it was Ryan. Her friend. Her...her lover.

She straightened the waistband of her bright red sweater over her black slacks, drew a steadying breath and ordered herself to shape up.

Why was she so nervous? She'd been a wreck ever since Ryan had telephoned to say he was ready to start the installation of her new security system. They'd agreed he'd work after the store closed; he'd see her then, goodbye.

"Fine," she said aloud.

Her jangled state confused her, it truly did. Everything between her and Ryan was under control, up front, honest and open. The structure of their relationship suited them both to perfection, and a dandy time would be had by all.

There was no just cause for her to feel like a kid going to her first prom. Ryan would be there any second now. It was no big deal.

A sharp knock sounded at the back door.

"Oh," she gasped, her hands flying to her cheeks.

Stop it this instant, Deedee Hamilton, she told herself. She had no idea what her ridiculous problem was, but enough was enough. There, she was fine now. Steady as a rock.

She moved closer to the door.

"Who is it?" she said, knowing and hating the fact that her voice had squeaked.

"Ryan" came a muffled reply.

She plastered a smile on her face, then unlocked and opened the door.

Oh, Ryan, her mind hummed. Hello, Ryan MacAllister.

"Hi," she said. "Come in." He was gorgeous in jeans and a black sweatshirt. Simply...gorgeous.

"Hello, Deedee." He moved passed her to place a large box on the counter, then turned to look at her. "This is all I'll need tonight. You can close the door. I'll be in and out, so set the lock on open. That will save you from having to perch in here to let me in every other minute. You said you'd be doing paperwork at the counter. Have you eaten dinner?"

Good Lord, he fumed, he sounded like a record stuck on full speed ahead. He'd delivered that nonsensical dissertation so fast it was a wonder he hadn't run out of oxygen and passed out on his face.

What was the matter with him? This was Deedee, his friend, who looked sensational in that red sweater. Deedee, his lover, who was causing heat to rocket through his aching body. *MacAllister, cool it.*

"So you're all set to begin work," Deedee said, a tad too loudly.

"Yeah, I am. Right. Did Andrea talk to you about the lawyer?"

What? his mind hammered. Where had that come from? Just because the attorney jerk had been on his mind was no excuse for the subject to come out of his mouth.

"Lawyer?" Deedee said, obviously confused. "Do I need one? I have one who handles the legal documents for the store but... Am I being sued, or something?"

"No, no, nothing like that." Ryan shook his head and frowned. "Andrea has a friend with a cousin, or brother—hell, I don't know—an attorney with big bucks and matching muscles they want you to meet. Go out with. On a date. Get the picture?"

"I see," she said slowly. "A lawyer."

"A rich lawyer, who pumps iron."

"Mmm," she said, placing one fingertip on her chin.

"So? Are you going to go out with the yuppie, who will probably spend the evening flexing his biceps?"

Deedee dropped her hand from her chin and cocked her head slightly to one side. "Why are you yelling?"

"I'm not yelling!" He paused. "Yes, I am. Forget it. Just forget I mentioned the creep."

She laughed. "He's a creep?"

"Yes. No. How should I know? I've never met the guy. If you want to go out with him, then do it."

"Thank you for your permission, Mr. Mac-Allister," she said dryly.

"I didn't mean to sound like you needed my permission to... Hell, erase this whole conversation. Pretend I just came in. Hello, Deedee."

A warm glow started somewhere low and deep within Deedee and spread like liquid heat through her entire body, creating a flush on her cheeks.

Ryan MacAllister, she thought, did *not* want her to go out with the muscle-bound, rich, creepy lawyer. Wasn't that something? Why that knowledge pleased her so much, she had no idea, but it did. It truly did.

"Ryan, I don't want to go out with the attorney in question."

"You don't?" A smile broke across his face. "That's great. I mean, that's...interesting."

"Well, you see, you and I have set boundaries for our relationship. Should I call it a relationship?" She shrugged. "I guess so. Anyway, I'm comfortable with what we have. Why would I go out with someone who might press me for more than I wish to give?"

"Good point."

"Besides, you and I are lovers. I never date a man if I'm sleeping with another one. It goes against my code of conduct. You, of course, are free to do what suits you in regard to other women."

"I don't want anyone but you." He blinked. "That is, I'm on the same wavelength as you. Our relationship—yeah, we'll call it a relationship—is structured just fine for me. I have no desire whatsoever to enter the singles dating scene. I'll leave that meat market to Ted. So that's settled, then. We don't date other people while we're involved with each other. Agreed?"

"Agreed."

"Good. That's good."

He stepped forward, slipped one hand to the nape of her neck, lowered his head and kissed her.

Her bones were melting, Deedee thought as her lashes drifted down. Oh, dear heaven, she was on fire. It had been an eternity since Ryan had kissed her, but now he *was* kissing her, and it was glorious.

Ryan dropped his hand from her neck and gathered Deedee close to his heated body, pausing only to take a rough breath before claiming her lips again. His tongue delved eagerly into the sweet darkness of her mouth to seek and find her tongue. Deedee splayed her hands on his back, urging him nearer yet.

Yes! Ryan's mind thundered. He'd wanted, *needed,* this kiss like a thirsty man yearning for water on a scorching desert. Ah, Deedee, yes!

He filled his senses with her taste, the familiar aroma of flowers, the exquisite feel of her breasts being crushed against his chest. Memories of the lovemaking he'd shared with her flitted through his mind, increasing his passion to a fever pitch.

His hands skimmed down over the feminine roundness of her bottom, nestling her to him, his arousal heavy and aching.

Oh, man, how he wanted her.

He would never get enough of her.

For the remaining days and nights of his life, he would savor the ecstasy that was Deedee in his arms—Deedee purring in pleasure as he kissed and caressed every inch of her lissome body; Deedee calling his name as she was flung into oblivion.

Deedee Hamilton was his.

Forever.

Ryan stiffened, breaking the kiss and dragging air into his lungs.

Forever? his mind echoed. No, damn it, he didn't believe in forever, not anymore. Death was the only forever that was absolute, guaranteed. There would be no forever with Deedee.

"Ryan?"

Deedee opened her eyes and looked at him, the desire radiating from the smoky brown depths causing him to stifle a moan of matching need.

"I, um…" He cleared his throat. "I have to get to work, Deedee." He eased her slowly away from his aroused, aching body, missing the feel of her the instant she was gone.

"Oh, yes, of course." She fiddled with the waistband of her sweater, willing her skittering heart to return to a normal rhythm. She looked up at him again. "I'll leave you to it. I have paperwork to do." She hurried out of the room.

Ryan stood statue still, ordering his body back under his command. He told his hazy brain to shift gears, think about electrical wiring. A tug-of-war began in his mind, yanking him back and forth between the intricacies of the security system he was going to install at Books and Books, and Deedee.

And butterflies.

And a cute, freckled nose.

And femininity personified.

And forever.

''No,'' he said, slamming his hand onto the door-knob.

He started to turn it, then stopped, a deep frown knitting his brows.

There would be no forever with Deedee. That was a given.

But...

When two people had structured a relationship based on the premise of friends and lovers, how long did that arrangement last?

How long would Deedee Hamilton be his?

Chapter Eleven

During the next several weeks, Ryan pushed the haunting, unanswered question to the back of his mind and ignored it. He refused to address the issue of how long Deedee would be his and simply lived each day at a time—each day and each lovemaking night...with Deedee.

Since he was spending his free hours with Deedee, he realized it had been far too long since he'd seen or spoken to Ted. He tracked Ted down, and they agreed to meet at their favorite restaurant for dinner the following evening.

Shortly after six o'clock the next night, Ted slid into the booth in the small café and smiled wearily at Ryan, who sat across from him.

"Howdy, buddy," Ted said. "You are looking at

one tired cop. Man, what I wouldn't give to get my hands on those sleazes who are ripping stuff off.''

''Which ones?'' Ryan said, chuckling. ''Or have you cleaned up the city to the point there's only a couple bad guys left?''

''Yeah, right. That won't happen in *my* lifetime. I'm talking about the Culture Creeps. That's what we've dubbed them.''

''Ah,'' Ryan said, nodding, ''the guys who take a valuable whatever and nothing else.''

''Yep. They've hit two more places. They got an expensive necklace on display in a jewelry store window, and a rare coin from a private home. Can you believe this? Why not clean out the jewelry store? Why leave behind the other coins in the collection? I'm telling you, Ryan, they're driving the whole department nuts. There's no word on the streets. Nothing. Zero. Zip.''

''Sounds like they have discerning tastes.''

''Culture Creeps,'' Ted said, then muttered an earthy expletive.

''Have some of Rosie's chili,'' Ryan said. ''It's good for what ails you.''

A waitress appeared, the pair greeted her by name, then ordered chili, salad and beer. The woman reappeared quickly with the drinks and a basket of crunchy, warm French bread.

''Rosie saw you two from the kitchen,'' the waitress said. ''She's rushing right now, but said she'd be out to collect a hug from each of you. Oh, yeah, and she said she ought to be smacking you upside the head instead, 'cause it's been so long since you've been here. End of message.''

''Tell her we love her,'' Ted said. ''She's been on our minds day and night all these months.''

''Ted Sharpe,'' the woman said, ''you're so full of bull it's a shame. Rosie says you've got the smoothest lines she's heard delivered by any man she's met in her sixty-five years. Oops, your order is up. I'll be right back.''

Steaming bowls of chili were placed on the table, along with crisp salads. The two men ate in silence for several minutes, taking the edge off their appetites.

''Rosie hasn't lost her touch,'' Ted eventually said. ''I'm glad you suggested we meet here, Ryan. It's been too long between bowls of Rosie's chili.''

''Yeah, it has.''

''I was in Books and Books today,'' Ted went on.

''Oh?''

''Last Christmas my folks gave me a kit for carving a miniature rocking chair. Little tiny bugger. I finally got around to trying it, and it was a complicated son of a gun, very intricate. It turned out halfway decent, if I do say so myself.

''Surprisingly, it's very relaxing work, even though it's precise, and you have to be slow and careful. I bought a book at Deedee's store on making all kinds of miniature stuff.''

''There you go,'' Ryan said. ''When you retire from the force, you can be a master miniature maker.''

"Yep. Deedee said you installed a security system for her rare-book collection about a month ago."

Ryan nodded and shoveled in another spoonful of the spicy chili.

"I looked at the books through the windows on the cases. She's got some incredible stuff there."

"Yeah, I know. It's an impressive collection, and it's her pride and joy. She enjoys running Books and Books, but get her started talking about those rare books? Man, her eyes sparkle and her cute freckles dance a jig. She got a call the other day from a guy in Paris who wants to buy one of those books. She was so excited, I thought she'd jump right out of her shoes. Then she..."

As a broad smile broke across Ted's face, Ryan frowned.

"Forget it," he said. "What kind of miniature are you going to carve next?"

"Nice dodge, MacAllister, but it didn't work. Why?" Ted held up a finger. "One. Deedee babbled on about you, like you just did about her." Another finger went up. "Two. I bumped into Andrea and she said you and Deedee have been out to dinner with her and John a couple of times, plus you two went to a movie with Forrest and Jillian, and a concert with Michael and Jenny."

"Eat your chili," Ryan said gruffly.

"Three," Ted said, adding the appropriate finger. "You're different."

"What do you mean I'm 'different'?" Ryan glared at Ted.

"*That* expression I recognize, but in the overall

you're not tight or wired like you've been the past couple of years. Whatever is going on between you and Deedee Hamilton is good for you, and I'm happy to see it.''

"Deedee and I are friends.''

"Okay,'' Ted said, lifting one shoulder in a shrug. "Whatever.''

Ryan leaned back in the booth, his hands flat on the table on either side of the large bowl.

"You don't believe me,'' he said.

"Nope, but that's all right. You'll tell me what you want to tell me when you want to tell me what you want to tell me. I can wait.''

"I just told you. Deedee and I are friends.''

"Right. No problem.'' Ted reached for another slice of bread.

"Damn it, Ted,'' Ryan started, then shook his head.

He picked up his spoon again, stirred the chili left in the bowl, then continued to stir, watching the spoon go around and around.

"Deedee is special,'' he said quietly. "She's intelligent, fun, sensitive and, Lord knows, she's pretty. She's lovely, in a cute, wholesome way. She's open and honest, no games, no phony-up junk. She's just… Hell, she's just Deedee, herself, real.''

"And you're in love with her.''

Ryan's head snapped up. "No.''

"For God's sake, Ryan, have you listened to yourself when you talk about her? Have you kept in touch with yourself when you're making love with her?''

"I never said we were—''

"Give me a break. I wasn't born this morning. Look, I've never been in love, but I sure as hell recognize it in other people when I see it. You and Deedee are making love, and you and Deedee *are* in love. With each other. You're both down for the count."

"Sharpe," Ryan said, a muscle jumping in his jaw, "go to hell."

"Okay," he said pleasantly. "I sure hope Rosie isn't out of her homemade cherry pie. If she is, I'll arrest her for breach of promise. Do you want that last slice of bread?" He slid out of the booth. "I'm going into the kitchen to give Rosie her hug *and* to see if by any chance there's a cherry pie with my name on it just coming out of the oven."

"Mmm," Ryan acknowledged absently as Ted walked away.

Ted was wrong, dead wrong. He, Ryan Robert MacAllister, was *not* in love with Deedee Hamilton. Hell, *he* knew what love felt like because he'd been in love with Sherry. Ted had admitted to never having been in love. So what made Sharpe think he was such an expert on the subject?

Ryan shoved the bowl forward, then scowled as he folded his arms on top of the table.

So okay, he was a far different man now than the one who had fallen in love with Sherry. He was older and bitterly wiser. And, too, Deedee was Deedee, not to be compared with Sherry.

But love was love.

Right?

He'd been in love before, so he'd sure as hell know if he was in love again.

Wouldn't he?

Or was it unique each time, sort of custom-tailored to who the people were when it happened?

Good Lord, was it possible that he *was* in love with Deedee, but hadn't recognized the emotion for what it actually was?

"No," he muttered, "that's not possible."

Was it?

Ted plunked a plate in front of Ryan, then slid back into the booth with his own plate.

"A hug goes a long way with Rosie," Ted said, rubbing his hands together. "Look at the size of these pieces of pie. Dig in, MacAllister."

"You're crazy," Ryan said, still glowering.

"You don't want to eat Rosie's cherry pie hot from the oven? More fool you, dude. I'll gladly have your slice after I finish mine."

Ryan pulled the plate toward him. "You touch it, I'll break your arm. Your crazy zone is in regard to your saying I'm in love with Deedee. I'm not in love with her. She's not in love with me."

"You can deny it from here to next Tuesday, but it won't change the facts as they stand." Ted took a bite of pie. "Mmm. This is heaven on this mess called earth. How come you're free to have dinner with me tonight?"

"Deedee had a Women in Business meeting," Ryan said, then sampled the dessert. "Yeah, great pie. Rosie never fails."

"So," Ted said, "if Deedee were free tonight you'd be with her?"

Ryan shrugged. "We're together most evenings.

Her place, mine, whatever. We eat out, or cook dinner, rent a movie, read, or watch the tube. You know, ordinary spending-the-evening-hours-doing-something stuff.''

''Like the millions of married couples across the country.''

''Would you knock it off, Sharpe? Change the subject, or I'm out of here.''

''Chill, MacAllister. The subject is changed.''

''Good.''

''Of course that won't keep you from thinking about it. You'll have trouble sleeping tonight, buddy, because you're going to be replaying this conversation over and over in your tiny mind. You'll be tossing and turning, tossing and turning. Guaranteed.''

''Sharpe,'' Ryan said, a definite warning tone to his voice.

''Okay, okay, don't get hostile. I'm changing the subject.'' He paused to take another big bite of pie, chewed and swallowed. ''I'm riding solo on duty these days. Poley went on over to the Denver force.''

''Why hasn't Captain Bolstad assigned you a new partner?''

''He's advertised the job, but hasn't clicked with any of the applicants. In fact, the city council increased our budget and Bolstad is looking for three cops. So far, he's got zip.''

''Oh,'' Ryan said, nodding, ''I see.''

Ted didn't speak further as he finished his pie. He pushed the plate to one side, then leaned back in the booth, sighing with contentment.

"Okay," Ryan said, "get on with it before you blow a circuit."

Ted raised his eyebrows. "Get on with what?"

"The spiel about me rejoining the force. You laid the groundwork with your 'Bolstad is looking for three cops' jazz, so go for it."

"Nope, I've given up on you. I'm just wasting my breath trying to get you to come back. I'll just have to wait and see who Bolstad hires and assigns as my partner."

"Yeah, well, I'd probably have to do the refresher course at the academy because it's been so long since I resigned. He'd surely have the positions filled by then, anyway."

"You didn't resign."

"What?"

"Well, you did, but that's not how the captain put the paperwork through. You're on an official leave of absence, which means you wouldn't have to do the refresher course. You can *unleave* yourself and be back in uniform within forty-eight hours."

"He had no right to do that!"

"Captains can do whatever they damn well please. But you're not interested, so he'll hire three guys as soon as he can find them. Want me to change the subject again?"

Ryan stared at him for a long moment, then chuckled and shook his head.

"You're good, Ted, very slick, very tricky. I believe it's called reverse psychology." Ryan's smile faded. "I'm going nuts running MacAllister Security Systems. I'm bored out of my mind.

"I messed around a couple of days ago, making up a contract that would enable my two installers to buy the outfit from me if they wanted it. I haven't said anything to them about it. I haven't said anything to anyone, not even Deedee, but..." His voice trailed off.

Ted watched him intently, hardly breathing.

"I miss it, Ted," Ryan continued quietly. "I really miss being a cop. I guess the caring, the emotional involvement with the people, is part of the package when you're wearing the uniform. Risks. Hell, life is a risk at every turn. I'm running risks caring about Deedee. I said *caring*, not *loving*, but it's still risky, yet I'm doing it. I think that..."

He stared up at the ceiling and drew a shuddering breath, before looking at Ted again.

"It's time, Ted," he said, his voice slightly husky. "I'm so damn tired of hiding out in that dingy office." He nodded. "Yeah, it's time to put on the uniform and go back to where I belong. Don't say anything to Captain Bolstad until I've told Deedee. She deserves to hear it from me before I actually do it. Then I guess you'll have yourself a partner."

Ted smiled. "Welcome home, buddy."

Ryan matched his smile. "Yeah."

Hours later, Ryan punched his pillow, gaining momentary satisfaction from pretending it was Ted Sharpe's nose.

Damn that Sharpe, he fumed, rolling onto his back in the rumpled bed. He couldn't sleep because of Ted's power of suggestion at dinner that the night would consist of tossing and turning. Tossing and turning, and thinking about the issue of being, or not being, in love with Deedee Hamilton.

During the short time he *had* slept, he'd had the dream again, the same dream about Deedee dancing with the butterflies.

"Oh, man," Ryan said, dragging both hands down his face.

He was *not,* he refused to be, in love with Deedee.

Why? a niggling little voice asked him.

Because loving someone was too risky. It set a guy up to be cut off at the knees, to be totally vulnerable to heartache and pain. Too risky.

Oh? Wasn't being a cop risky?

Ryan sighed in frustrated defeat.

Yeah, being a cop was physically and emotionally risky. And he was itching to get back into that uniform, to be what he was meant to be. He was once again prepared to run all the risks that being a police officer entailed.

To use "too risky" as a reason not to love was lame, didn't cut it. The risk of loving was no greater in his mind than the risks of being a cop. No, it wasn't the risk of loving that was causing a knot to twist in his gut.

It was...

Sherry.

Ryan swore and threw back the blankets. He sat up on the edge of the bed, rested his elbows on his knees and cupped his head in his hands.

The darkness in the room was oppressive, seeming to crush him with the weight of unwanted memories.

Sherry.

Since her death, he'd stood firm in his inner pledge to stay true to her, to honor the vows they'd taken until he drew his last breath.

He had told himself that what he'd had with Sherry had been fantastic beyond measure, was a once-in-a-lifetime experience that would make anything else second-best. They'd been so happy together, so connected. They'd had it all.

A chill swept through Ryan, and he straightened, bracing his hands on his knees as he stared into the darkness. The chill was followed by sweat that dotted his brow and trickled down his chest.

It's truth time, MacAllister, the little voice insisted.

The truth, his mind hammered. The truth. Oh, God, he'd buried it so deeply within him, couldn't face it along with the violence of Sherry's death. He'd left it there, the truth, hidden beneath his anguish, refusing to allow it to surface.

But now?

There was nowhere to run, nowhere to hide from the truth.

"Oh, Sherry," Ryan said aloud, his voice raspy with emotion.

They hadn't been happy together.

Her requested transfer to the emergency room had come through a few weeks after they'd been married, and everything had fallen apart before they'd hardly begun.

They rarely saw each other, and argued more often than not when they managed to spend time together. Sherry had refused to give up her coveted position.

The more stubborn she got, the more demanding he became, telling her she *had* to leave the emergency room for a place with hours that matched his schedule more closely.

The last time he'd seen her before she was killed, they'd argued bitterly about the subject. He'd slammed out the door in a rage.

And he hadn't even kissed her goodbye.

Their marriage had been as good as over. Finished. They weren't going to make it together, and deep in his gut he'd known that, then buried the knowledge when she died.

There it was—the truth.

Ryan sat statue still, waiting for the pain to assault him, to rip him to emotional shreds. But instead, a strange sense of peace began to fill him with its warmth, moving slowly through him with a gentle, healing touch.

The heavy darkness in the room seemed suddenly lighter, brighter, allowing him to clearly see images flitting before him.

Deedee.

Dancing with the butterflies.

Deedee.

And he loved her.

Ryan sank back against the pillow, so exhausted he hardly had the strength to lift his legs onto the bed. He took a deep breath and let it out slowly, a groan of fatigue escaping from his lips.

Sleep, blessed sleep, began to creep over him like a comforting blanket.

He was in love with Deedee Hamilton, he thought

hazily. He really, truly was. She was there, so clearly in his mind's eye, smiling at him, her dark eyes sparkling. Yeah, there was her cute nose with the adorable freckles, and her lips that were like sweet nectar.

Oh, man, how he loved her.

Ryan drifted off to sleep, not realizing that he was smiling.

The next afternoon, Deedee gave up her attempt to concentrate on the magazine she held. She set it back on the end table and shifted yet again in the less-than-comfortable chair.

She stared at the clock on the wall, willing the hands to move faster.

Ten more minutes. They'd said it would take an hour, and there were still ten long, agonizing minutes left to endure.

Then they would tell her.

Then she would know if she was pregnant.

She sighed wearily and leaned her head against the wall, closing her eyes. Images of Ryan immediately formed in crystal clarity in her mental vision—magnificent Ryan MacAllister.

The past weeks had been so fantastic. Little by little Ryan had lowered his guard, removed the walls around him to reveal, like slowly opening a tantalizing Christmas present, the wonder of the man he truly was.

He had a dry, witty sense of humor that had caught her off guard more than once, causing her to dissolve in laughter.

He listened, *really listened,* when she talked, as

though everything she said was of the utmost importance to him.

She'd answered his endless questions about the running of Books and Books, and how she went about dealing in the rare editions, which were her pride and joy. He wanted to understand the inner workings of her business, he'd said, because it was a part of who she was.

Never before in her life had she felt so special, so cherished, by doing nothing more than being herself—open, honest and real.

And the lovemaking they'd shared! It was beyond description in its splendor. So beautiful, intimate...and theirs.

Ryan.

Whenever he appeared, her heart beat with a wild tempo and a smile instantly formed on her lips. The mere sight of him caused her to feel young, happy and vibrantly alive. She continually rejoiced in his very existence, and the fact that he was an intricate part of her life.

And she loved him with every breath in her body.

Deedee opened her eyes and stared into space.

She didn't know exactly when she'd fallen in love with Ryan, and had a sneaky suspicion she'd subconsciously ignored the reality for as long as she could. She'd broken the rules of their relationship, crossed over the boundaries they had set.

Friends and lovers.

Oh, yes, Ryan was her best friend. Ryan was her lover. But Ryan was also the man she loved.

And now she was waiting to learn if she was going to have his baby.

When she gummed up the program, she thought dryly, she didn't mess around. What if she really was pregnant? How did she feel about it?

She didn't even know, because she'd refused to address a maybe, an unknown. She was in limbo, on mental and emotional hold, waiting for that damnable clock to tick off the time until the unknown would become a known.

"Miss Hamilton?"

Deedee jerked in her chair. "Yes?"

"Dr. Mercer will see you now. You can go to his office at the end of the hall."

Deedee got to her feet, praying her trembling legs would carry her down the hallway.

"Come in, come in, Deedee," Dr. Mercer said when she entered the office. "Close the door and have a seat."

She did as instructed, gratefully sinking onto a chair opposite the doctor's desk.

Dr. Mercer looked, she'd decided years before, like Santa Claus out of uniform. He was a roly-poly man, with bushy white hair, a trim beard and the kindest eyes she'd ever seen. She liked and trusted him, but at that moment she wished she were a hundred miles away from him.

"Well, Deedee, we ran the blood test," Dr. Mercer said. "My dear, you are, indeed, pregnant."

Deedee blinked, opened her mouth to speak, then realized she had no air in her lungs because she'd been holding her breath. She gulped in some air and tried again.

"But I'm on the pill," she said, her voice sounding strange to her own ears.

Dr. Mercer shook his head. "I know, but your body has had a mind of its own ever since I've been your physician. You recall how many different varieties of the pill we had to try before finding one that would regulate you properly."

"Yes, but—"

"Your system simply overrode your method of birth control. It happens. I have a four-year-old-grandson who is proof of that fact. You *are* pregnant, Deedee."

"Well, fancy that," she said, attempting a smile that failed to materialize. "My, my, isn't that something? If Forrest knew, he'd be putting The Baby Bet into operation. Forrest is Jillian's husband. They're expecting triplets. Can you imagine having three baby girls at once? They're all girls. Forrest won The Baby Bet about the triplets, but then he always wins The Baby Bet, you see. Everyone puts twenty dollars in the pot and—"

"Deedee," the doctor interrupted, a gentle tone to his voice, "hush."

"Oh, dear heaven," she said, then burst into tears. "I'm…I'm going…to have…a pink rabbit."

Dr. Mercer chuckled and pushed the tissue box on his desk toward her.

"It might be a blue rabbit, you know," he said. "Blow your nose."

Deedee nodded as she dabbed at her nose with a tissue. She took a steadying breath and lifted her chin.

"So!" she said, then threw up her hands, unable to think of another thing to say.

"All right, young lady," Dr. Mercer said. "You've babbled, then cried, which are par for the course. Now let's get serious. What about the father of your baby?"

"I love him."

"That's helpful."

"No, it's not, because he doesn't love me. We agreed to be friends and lovers, nothing more."

"I see. Well, perhaps this baby will change his mind about that agreement."

"No. No, nothing will. He isn't going to want any part of being a father, of having a more serious relationship."

"He played a definite part in your becoming an expectant mother." Dr. Mercer paused. "Deedee, do you want this baby?"

"Oh, yes," she said, a genuine smile lighting up her face. "I refused to get in touch with myself about how I felt about it until I knew for certain if I was pregnant. But I don't need even one second to ponder the question. I want this baby very, very much."

"You'll be a wonderful mother."

"*Single* mother."

"Perhaps. You do plan to tell the father about the baby, don't you?"

"Yes. Ryan and I are based on honesty. I'll tell him, but I'll make it clear that I don't expect anything from him. It's not his fault I have a weird system in my body. I assured him that I was protected. He's free of obligation here.''

''That's all very noble, but what about the fact that you're in love with him?''

''*That* I won't tell him, because it wouldn't serve any purpose. It's not lying exactly, it's just leaving out a detail.''

Dr. Mercer frowned at her. ''Mmm.''

''Trust me, I know what I'm doing.'' She got to her feet. ''Thank you for being so kind, so caring.''

The doctor stood. ''Make an appointment at the front desk for about two weeks from now. Ask MaryAnn to give you the packet of information for mothers-to-be.''

''Yes, all right.''

''Deedee, if you want to talk, I'm here to listen.''

''Thank you, I appreciate that, but I'm fine...emotionally. I don't feel too swift in the mornings, though.''

''Keep soda crackers by your bed and have a couple before you get up. The morning sickness hopefully won't last too long. We'll see how you're doing with that when you come in again.''

Deedee reached across the desk and shook the doctor's hand. He smiled at her warmly, then she turned and left the office.

''If that Ryan fellow isn't in love with that sweet little girl,'' the doctor said to no one, ''then he's seven kinds of a fool.''

Chapter Twelve

Deedee vaguely remembered driving to Books and Books, thanking her employee for covering for her while she was gone, then assisting a customer who wanted a copy of *The Velveteen Rabbit*.

At last alone in the store, she slid onto the stool behind the counter, propped her elbows on the top of the counter and rested her chin on folded hands.

She was in love with Ryan MacAllister, her mind hammered. While sitting in the doctor's office, which certainly wasn't a very romantic place for such a discovery, she'd come face-to-face with the realization that she loved Ryan.

And if that wasn't enough to send her into a tizzy, she'd been told minutes later that she was pregnant with Ryan's baby!

It was too much to deal with all at once, just too,

too much. Her mind was mush, and her emotions were a tangled maze.

She didn't know whether to shout with joy, or weep in despair.

"Calm down, Deedee," she told herself. "Take it one step at a time."

The bad news was that she was in love with a man who didn't love her in return.

The good news was that she was going to have a pink rabbit...or maybe a blue rabbit. There was no reason to have an ultrasound to find out if it was a girl or a boy. She'd simply wait for Forrest to announce that The Baby Bet was being held on her behalf, then listen for where he placed his money.

The bad news was that once she told Ryan she was pregnant, their relationship would be over. There would be no more lovely evenings together, no more exquisitely beautiful lovemaking. Ryan would be so angry that she'd moved beyond the boundaries of their being just friends and lovers.

Oh, dear heaven, how she would miss him.

The good news was that she was going to be a mother, would have a precious miracle, a tiny baby, to love and nurture.

Deedee sighed.

The good with the bad. The bad with the good. That's how it was, the bottom line. She'd learn to live with that. Somehow.

She straightened and placed her hands on her flat stomach.

"We'll be fine, little rabbit," she whispered. "We'll be a team, just the two of us, together."

My goodness, she was tired, felt emotionally and physically drained. She wanted nothing more than to go home, crawl into bed and sleep.

She glanced at the clock.

Forget *that* wish. She was working until she closed the store at eight o'clock. Ryan had telephoned that morning and said he had something important to share with her. They'd agreed he'd come to Books and Books at eight, they'd buy a pizza and go to her apartment.

Had that call from Ryan been just hours earlier? It seemed like an eternity since they'd made those plans, because so much had happened between then and now.

He had something important to share with her? Boy, oh, boy, did *she* have something to share with *him*. The sad part was that her ''something'' would cause him to walk out of her life.

Deedee sniffled and fought against threatening tears.

Get a grip, Deedee Hamilton, she ordered herself. She'd read the material she got at the doctor's office to find out the do's and don'ts for a mother to be. She'd concentrate on her pink rabbit, be happy, feel blessed. She'd stay in an upbeat mood if it killed her.

Until Ryan got there.

Until it was time to say goodbye to the magnificent man she loved.

She took a wobbly breath, then produced a bright smile as a customer entered the store.

It had been a long day, Ryan thought as he parked in front of Books and Books.

He turned off the ignition, but didn't move to leave the Jeep. He was twenty minutes early for his eight o'clock arrival, but had been unable to sit in his apartment a moment longer.

He was in love with Deedee Hamilton, he thought incredulously. He'd actually fallen head over heels in love. He was, to quote Ted, "down for the count." Even more amazing was the realization that he was *ecstatic* about that fact.

The ghosts of truth from the past had been dealt with, brought to the surface from the place within him where he'd buried them so deeply, then been flung far away from his reality of now.

He felt as though a crushing weight had been lifted from his shoulders. No, more than that. It had been removed from his mind, heart, his very soul.

He was free to live.

He was free to love.

And he loved Deedee.

Ryan frowned as he stared at the front of Books and Books.

He'd better come down off his euphoric high and address the issue that would determine his future happiness: *Was Deedee in love with him?*

According to Ted, Deedee was "down for the count," just as Ryan was. Having dismissed Ted as a blithering idiot at the time, he now wished to believe that Ted was right on the money, knew exactly what he was talking about. Ryan was in love with Deedee, and Deedee was in love with Ryan, so said Mr. Sharpe.

He'd buy Ted a dozen of Rosie's cherry pies if his partner had called it the way it was.

"Hi, Deedee," Ryan said to the steering wheel. "I'm rejoining the police force. Oh, and by the way, I'm in love with you. How do you like them apples, kiddo? Want to get married?"

Ryan groaned and rolled his eyes heavenward, then shook his head in self-disgust.

He was a wreck. There had just been too many hours to deal with while waiting to come to Deedee's store. He'd worked himself into a stressed-out, wired, tense mess. Talk about vulnerable. He was about to bare his soul to the woman who held his tomorrows in her hand.

Was Deedee in love with him?

Would she agree to marry him?

How would she feel about being the wife of a cop?

He had a choice. He could drive away from there right now, not run the risk of seeking the answers to his questions. Or he could go after the future he wanted with Deedee, risks and all.

"Go for it, MacAllister," he said, unsnapping the seat belt.

Deedee drew a sharp breath as she saw Ryan get out of the Jeep and start toward the door of Books and Books. She'd been aware of the exact moment he'd pulled into the parking place, and he'd jangled her nerves even worse than they were by sitting out there like a lump.

But now he was crossing the sidewalk to the door, turning the knob, pushing the door open and...

Oh, dear heaven, there he was. Ryan, the man she loved so very, very much. The man who was the father of the baby nestled within her. Her heart was thudding wildly, and an achy sensation in her throat was a warning that tears were once again threatening.

She would *not* cry.

They'd leave the store as quickly as possible, buy a pizza and go to her apartment. There, with class and dignity, being calm, cool and collected, she'd tell Ryan that she was pregnant and was assuming the responsibility for that fact.

Then she'd watch him walk out of her life forever.

Oh, Ryan.

''Hello,'' she said, managing a small smile.

Ryan didn't move from where he stood just inside the door. He stared at Deedee intently, a slight frown on his face.

He was looking at the woman he loved, he thought. He could hardly believe that this had happened to him. He was, by damn, in love. And, oh, man, it felt great.

He crossed the room, framed Deedee's face in his hands and kissed her, mentally cursing the counter that separated them.

The kiss was soft, gentle, reverent. The kiss was, to him, symbolic, an affirmation of his love for Deedee, a commitment to her and that love, a willingness to risk all and everything. The kiss caused his heart to thunder and emotions to momentarily close his throat.

He released her slowly, looking directly into her brown eyes as he straightened his stance.

"Hello, Deedee," he said, his voice raspy.

She tore her gaze from his, telling herself once again that she would *not* cry.

"How...how was your day?" she said, fiddling with the business cards in the plastic holder on the counter.

Fifty years long, he thought dryly.

"Okay," he said. He glanced at the clock. "We'll close the store in ten minutes and be out of here. We could call ahead to Mario's and order the pizza. Then it will be ready to pick up when we get there."

"I've got to finish unpacking a shipment first and marking the books off on the invoice. There should be several special orders in there that people are eager to have. I really need to have them available first thing in the morning."

"I'll do it. I've done it before without screwing it up. Should I put the books on the counter in the storeroom again?"

"Yes, thank you. All right, you go ahead and do that, and I'll start closing out the cash register, drop the shades and... Yes, that's a good plan."

"Are you upset about something?" he said. "You're awfully pale and seem...I don't know...sort of tense."

"No, no, I'm fine. I'm just tired at the end of a busy day. And I'm hungry. Once I have some pizza and put my feet up, I'll be dandy." She smiled at him. "Really, I will. Now shoo, you have a rendezvous with a half-emptied box in the storeroom."

"Yes, ma'am," he said, matching her smile as he executed a crisp salute. "Anything you say, ma'am."

Deedee watched him disappear around the corner.

Anything you say, ma'am, her mind echoed. *I say I love you, Ryan MacAllister. Oh, God, how I love you.*

She shook her head and forced herself to concentrate on entering the figures from the cash register in a ledger book. A few minutes later she dropped the shade behind the front window.

Just as she reached to snap the lock in place on the door, it opened and two men entered, nearly knocking her backward.

"Oh," she gasped. "You startled me. I was just locking up."

"Do it," one of the men said gruffly.

"Pardon me?"

"Lock the door, lady," the other man said. "We have private business to conduct here."

"I don't understand what—" she began.

One of the men pushed her aside, locked the door and dropped the shade on it.

"You've got some nice rare books we intend to take off your hands," he said.

"No!" Deedee yelled.

Ryan stiffened, every muscle in his body tensing to the point of near pain. He'd heard Deedee's shout of "No," heard the anger laced with panic. She was in some kind of trouble out there. She needed him. *Now.*

He started toward the half-opened door of the storeroom, then stopped, suddenly feeling weak in the knees as though he'd suffered a punishing blow to his solar plexus. Voices slammed against his brain.

Four-seventeen...shooting in progress...Sherry...shot...dead...Sherry is dead...four-seventeen...Deedee...Deedee is dead...dead...Deedee!...Deedee!...

Ryan shook his head sharply, then dragged trembling hands down his face.

Easy, MacAllister, he ordered himself. Calm down. That was then, before, old news. This was now, and Deedee needed him. The woman he loved was in some kind of danger. This was part of the risk of loving. Okay. It was okay.

Nothing was going to happen to his Deedee.

"Let's hurry it up, lady," one of the men said to Deedee. He took a gun from the pocket of his jacket and pointed it at her. He grabbed her arm, pulled her across the room and behind the counter. "Unlock that cabinet."

No! Deedee mentally hollered. Dear heaven, no, this wasn't happening. It was a nightmare, she'd wake up and... The silent alarm... The alarm. Oh, damn it, she hadn't activated it for the night yet. It was worthless the way it was.

Ryan. Oh, God, where was Ryan? The man had a gun. If Ryan heard what was going on, he'd come barreling out there and... No, please, no. He had to stay in the storeroom where he'd be safe from that hideous gun.

"Yes, I'll open it," she said, her voice quivering.

"I'll do whatever you say. The keys are in the cash register under the change drawer."

"You're being smart, lady," the man with the gun said. "Just do as you're told and you won't get hurt." He released her arm. "Get the key."

Ryan inched his way along the wall, stopping at the corner. He peered carefully around the edge, his jaw tightening as he saw the gun in one of the men's hands. He ducked back, flattening himself against the bookcase behind him.

There were two of them. One was armed, the other might be. Ten bucks said these were the Culture Creeps Ted had been after for so long. They wanted Deedee's rare books, not the money in the cash register.

Had Deedee set the silent alarm? Probably not. She'd told him she'd gotten into the routine of turning it on just before she left the store, had made a pattern of her closing chores so she wouldn't forget to activate the alarm. No, there was no help coming from the police.

It was up to him. Deedee was his to love and his to protect. So be it. He'd get her safely out of this mess. He had to.

Ryan looked quickly around for something, anything, he could use as a weapon. He heard the ding of the cash register being opened and envisioned Deedee reaching for the key beneath the change tray.

The man with the gun was sideways to him, halfway blocking Deedee from view. The other creep was standing in front of the counter.

If he could take out the man in front of the counter, it would momentarily distract the one with the gun. He'd have to move fast, put all of his physical skills into maximum play.

He could do it. He *would* do it. Because nothing was going to happen to his Deedee.

He carefully lifted a thick, heavy book from the top shelf behind him, then peered around the corner again. Deedee was inserting the key in the lock on the cabinet. Turning the key. Removing it. Reaching up for the handle. Was wrapping her fingers around it and...

Now!

Ryan threw the heavy book like a guided missile toward the man on the outside of the counter. It caught him square in the head and he fell like a stone to the floor.

"What..." the other man said, spinning toward his partner.

At that moment, Deedee whipped open the cabinet door, smashing it against the man's head. He dropped the gun with a moan and instinctively grabbed his head with his hands. Ryan sprang forward and wrapped both arms around the man, flinging him facedown onto the floor, then dropped to one knee, which he planted firmly on the man's back.

"Call the police, Deedee," Ryan said.

"What?"

"The phone," he yelled. "Call the cops."

She did as instructed, her hands shaking so badly she could hardly press the three numbers for emergency service. As she gave the address of the store to the person who answered, Ryan took a roll of strapping tape from behind the counter and bound the hands and feet of the man he held pinned to the floor.

"You son of a—" the man started.

Ryan slapped a piece of the tape across his mouth, then hurried to secure the wrists and ankles of the man who was still groaning on the floor on the other side of the counter.

Sirens could be heard in the far distance as Ryan bolted to his feet and rushed behind the counter, pulling Deedee into his arms.

"Are you all right?" he said. "Please, tell me you're all right. If anything had happened to you I... You were fantastic the way you decked that guy with the cabinet door. Oh, man, are you okay?"

"Yes. No," she said, clinging to him. "I was so scared. I thought it was a dream and I'd wake up, but it was real, and I was terrified, and—"

"Shh," he said, stroking her back. "It's all over. Take it easy."

"And I was so afraid for you," she rambled on as though he hadn't spoken. "He had a gun, and you didn't have a gun, and I didn't want you to come out here because you might be hurt, and I couldn't bear that. And my baby. Oh, dear God, I was so frightened that they would do something that would harm my baby."

Ryan tensed, then gripped her upper arms to move her away from him so he could see her face.

"Your baby?" he repeated, frowning. "What baby?" His eyes darted to her flat stomach, then back to her face. "You're pregnant?"

Before Deedee could reply, the sirens filled the air and flashing blue and white lights were visible beyond the shades.

"This is the police," a voice boomed over a megaphone. "Put your hands up and come out. You've got five seconds. Do it."

Ryan stared at Deedee for another long moment, then turned and strode to the door, unlocking and flinging it open. He stood in the doorway, arms held high.

"It's a done deal," he called. "I'm Ryan MacAllister, cop on leave, but back in uniform tomorrow. Ted Sharpe is my partner. I think we've got your Culture Creeps in here. Come collect the scum."

"Hey, MacAllister," one of the police officers yelled, "glad to hear you're back. Thought you'd practice before you suited up again, huh?"

The store was instantly swarming with police.

Deedee watched the bustle of activity with a rather detached lack of interest, as though she was there, but not really there.

Ryan was going to become a police officer again? she thought hazily. He'd be back in uniform tomorrow? He was going to be Ted's partner?

That was wonderful, it really was. It meant he'd truly reevaluated his life, sifted and sorted, and gotten in touch with himself. He was returning to where he belonged by rejoining the police force, was putting the past behind him and moving forward with his life.

If only, oh, if only his future included her as his wife. If only he was going to actually take part in the raising of their child. What a fortunate baby the little pink rabbit would be to have Ryan MacAllister as a father on a day-to-day basis.

But that wasn't going to happen because she'd broken the rules of their relationship. When she told Ryan she was pregnant, he would…

Deedee blinked and came back to reality from her foggy place.

When she told Ryan she was pregnant?

She *had* told him.

It was becoming clear to her now. She'd zonked that awful man right in the head with the cabinet door, which had been extremely resourceful of her.

But then she'd babbled on and on as a result of being so frightened. She'd lost it. She'd come apart at the seams, and clung to Ryan all the while she was rambling on like an idiot. In the midst of that uncontrollable chatter, she'd told him about the baby!

"Oh, dear heaven," she said, her hands flying to her pale cheeks.

She'd intended to sit him down in her apartment and quietly explain the situation, not babble the news flash in a fit of hysteria.

Oh, dear, what was Ryan thinking, feeling, about what she'd said?

"Are you all right, ma'am?" a police officer said.

"Me?" she said. "No. Well, yes, but…no."

"Mmm," he said, nodding. He turned and looked around for Ryan. "Hey, MacAllister, you'd better take your lady home before she fades out on us here. She can come down to the department anytime tomorrow and make a statement for the record."

Ryan maneuvered through the crowded store to reach Deedee, but didn't look directly at her.

"Yeah, okay," he said to the officer. "I need to lock this place and set the silent alarm. You guys ready to wrap up here?"

"Yeah, we're gone. Those two you nabbed are singing their little hearts out in the patrol car. They're the Culture Creeps, all right. The reason there wasn't any word on the streets is because they have the stuff stashed, hadn't tried to fence any of it yet. We've been after these scum for weeks. You and your lady make a great team."

"That's us," Ryan said, no hint of a smile on his face. "A great team, really in tune with each other."

"Yep," the officer said. "Okay, you guys, let's clear out of here so the hero and heroine can go home." He looked at Ryan again. "Glad you're coming back on the force, Ryan. Ted must be whooping with joy."

Ryan nodded and shook the man's hand.

A few minutes later, the store was emptied of police officers. A heavy silence fell.

"Ryan..." Deedee started.

"Do you have your keys? Let's lock the cabinet, set the alarm and get out of here."

"Yes, all right. I...I don't think I want any pizza, though. Do you?"

He crossed his arms over his chest and looked at her, a muscle jumping in his tightly clenched jaw.

"No, I don't want any pizza," he said, a steely edge to his voice.

Deedee shivered, the sound of his voice and the

anger evident in his expressive eyes causing a chill to sweep through her.

"What I want," he said, "is to talk. I want the truth. Do you think you can handle that for a change, Deedee? Do you think you could actually manage to tell me the truth?"

Chapter Thirteen

Deedee did not even attempt to talk to Ryan during the drive to her apartment. Tension and anger seemed to emanate from him like rolling, crashing waves that slammed against her.

She leaned her head back on the top of the seat, trying desperately to put aside the lingering horror of what had taken place at Books and Books, and concentrate on what was yet to come during the confrontation with Ryan.

Her world was falling apart completely, she thought dismally. She'd hoped so much that she and Ryan would part gently, at least remain friends, although no longer lovers.

Once she'd explained that her pregnancy was indeed an accident, per se, and that she was assuming full responsibility for it, she prayed that Ryan would understand that it had not, in actuality, been her fault. There was no blame to be placed anywhere, nor would she look to him for financial support for the baby, or emotional involvement.

It was to have been a mature, quiet discussion, where facts were stated and accepted as they were.

But now?

Dear heaven, Ryan was furious. He was also no doubt terribly hurt. The stinging words he'd hurled at her regarding telling him the truth for a change indicated that he was convinced she'd lied to him about...

About what?

Deedee opened her eyes and lifted her head, frowning in confusion.

Now that she'd calmed down enough to really analyze Ryan's reaction to the slip of her blithering tongue about the baby, just what exactly had set him off? What on earth was she supposedly guilty of lying about?

Deedee slid a glance at Ryan, seeing his clenched jaw and the tight hold on the steering wheel that was causing his knuckles to turn white.

Her own anger began to bubble within her, growing stronger by the second.

If he used his tiny brain to think, he'd realize they hadn't been together long enough for her to have kept her pregnancy a deep, dark secret for weeks and weeks.

Was that it? Was he accusing her of a lie of omission? Did he believe she'd been aware of her condition and not told him for reasons known only to herself? Well, she would straighten him out on that data, by golly.

Ryan MacAllister could very well owe her an apology before the forthcoming discussion was over. She didn't appreciate being accused of not being truthful, thank you very much.

Deedee folded her arms over her breasts and executed a very unladylike snort of disgust.

Ryan shot a glare at her, then redirected his attention to the traffic.

Deedee narrowed her eyes and pursed her lips.

There was just no other explanation for Ryan's fury. He'd pronounced her guilty of withholding the news of her pregnancy from him before she'd even had a chance to speak, to explain.

The nerve of the man.

She could be just as angry and hurt about the manner in which she'd learned he intended to rejoin the police force. How long had he known that juicy little tidbit, but hadn't bothered to tell her? That was a major event in *his* life, which she had the right to be told.

Ryan MacAllister should look in the mirror to see who was actually guilty of a lie of omission.

When Ryan parked the Jeep, Deedee got out of the vehicle without waiting for him to come around to open her door as he preferred to do. She started off, and he fell in step beside her.

Great, she thought dryly. She didn't have her car. She often left it parked behind Books and Books overnight when she and Ryan had made plans to leave for an event from the store. They would sleep at her place, or his, and he'd drive her to work in the morning. Each had a supply of toilet articles and several changes of clothes at the other's apartment.

But the frame of mind they were now *both* in, could very well mean she'd have to call a taxi in the morning because Ryan would be long gone.

Yes, she should have driven her own car home.

She should have kept her mouth shut about the baby until they were alone.

She should never have fallen in love with Ryan MacAllister, because her heart was going to be smashed to smithereens.

When they entered Deedee's apartment, she turned on every lamp in the living room, waved Ryan toward the sofa, then sat down in a chair opposite.

He slouched onto the middle of the sofa and spread his arms along the top. The closed, unapproachable expression on his face that Deedee hadn't seen in weeks was firmly in place.

"So, Ryan," she said, lifting her chin, "you're rejoining the police force, going to be Ted's partner again. I think that's wonderful. However, I feel I should have heard an announcement of that magnitude directly from you, not while you were yelling it out the door at a bunch of other cops."

Ryan shook his head. "Nice try, Deedee, but it won't work, not this time. You're attempting to get the ball into your court, be the injured party here as far as not being told something of importance. No dice."

"Oh? You don't believe I had the right to know about your career change before the world did?"

"Indeed I do. If you'll recall, I phoned you this morning and said I had something to share with you. I intended to tell you tonight that I was returning to the force. Ted knew, but I specifically asked him not to inform Captain Bolstad, or anyone else, until I'd spoken with you. I told Ted you had the right to know first."

"Oh," she said in a small voice. "Well, um, I see."

"Do you?" He shifted to prop his elbows on his knees, lacing his fingers as he leaned toward her. "Do you see that I had every intention of being up front and *honest* about what I was planning? Do you?"

Deedee frowned. "What is this emphasis on honesty and truth about, Ryan? I didn't plan to tell you the way I did that I was pregnant. I was upset and words were tumbling out of my mouth beyond my control. I was going to tell you about the baby tonight."

"And then our relationship would be over," he said, his voice low and ringing with anger.

"Yes," she said with a sigh, "because you—"

Ryan lunged to his feet and Deedee stopped speaking. Her eyes widened, and she moved as far back in the chair as possible as he crossed the room toward her. He planted his hands on the arms of the chair, trapping her in place.

She looked up at him, and a shiver coursed through her as she saw the raging fury evident in the brown depths of his eyes.

"Our relationship would be over," he said, "because I'd have done my duty." A vein pulsed wildly in his temple. "Stud service."

"What?" she said, totally confused.

"Damn you, Deedee Hamilton!"

He jerked up from the chair and dragged both hands through his thick hair.

"I don't understand what—" she started.

"Knock it off," he yelled. "Oh, you're good, very good. You ought to go on the stage, considering what a terrific actress you are. Me? I should be shipped to the farm for being so damn gullible."

"What are you talking about?" she said, matching his volume.

"It was all there, right in front of me," he went on, beginning to pace the floor with heavy steps. "It goes all the way back to the night at Mario's, and Forrest's pink rabbits. I knew then—damn it, I knew—that you wanted a baby."

He stopped his trek in front of her and pinned her in place with his eyes.

"You set out to get pregnant, to get your *own* pink rabbit. *You used me, Deedee!* You used me to accomplish that goal."

The color drained from Deedee's face as she stared at him.

"Truth? Honesty?" he shouted. "From you? God, what a joke. You reevaluated your life, all right. Did it up royally. You wanted a baby, and I was putty in your hands. So damn eager to get into your bed, time after time. How did you keep from laughing right out loud at how easy I was to manipulate?"

Deedee attempted to speak, to deny Ryan's horrible accusations, but she was so stunned, shocked, by the hateful words he was hurling at her, she couldn't find the words.

"Risk. Run the risk," Ryan said, a bitter edge to his voice. "No way, I decided. Not a chance. But you got to me, little by little, kept chipping away at the walls I'd built to protect myself, until I had no defenses left against you.

"There you'd be, smiling, so glad to see me, smelling like flowers, reminding me of a delicate butterfly. There you'd be, with those cute freckles on your nose. There you'd be, welcoming me into your arms, your bed, your body. Stud Muffin MacAllister, that's me."

"Ryan, stop it," Deedee yelled, then tears filled her eyes.

"Whew. Forget the stage. Go directly to Hollywood, collect two hundred dollars on the way. You can even produce tears at will."

"Ryan..."

"No more. I don't want to hear anymore of your lies. Risks. Oh, I did the risk-taking trip in spades, to the max. Want to know something else, Deedee? I fell in love with you. Funny, huh? Isn't that rich?" He laughed, the sound a harsh, brittle noise. "I loved again. I lost again. Big time.

"But you? Oh, you won. You got exactly what you wanted. A baby. You *are* happy about your nifty pink rabbit, aren't you?"

"Yes, of course I am, but—"

"Yeah, of course you are," he said, his voice suddenly low and flat.

He stared up at the ceiling for a moment, then looked at Deedee again. Two tears slid down her cheeks as she saw the raw pain in his eyes and etched on his face.

"Ryan, please," she said, a sob nearly choking off her words, "let me explain."

"There's nothing you can say that I want to hear. What should I do now, Deedee? Thank you for making me have the guts to rejoin the police force, be willing to run that risk again?

"No, I doubt you give a damn what I do. Well, you can't take that away from me. I'm going to be a cop, dedicate myself to being a cop and focus only on that. *Nothing else.*"

Deedee got to her feet, praying her trembling legs would support her.

"Ryan, you've got to listen to me. *Please.* You're accusing me of such horrible things, and they're not true. *I love you.*"

Tears flowed unchecked down her cheeks and along her neck.

"I thought our relationship would be over, Ryan, when I told you I was pregnant, because I'd broken the rules, gone beyond the boundaries of what we agreed we would have together. Friends and lovers, that's all we were supposed to be, but *I fell in love with you.*"

"Yeah, right," he said. "You just don't quit, do you? You really expect me to believe that you're in love with me? Do you think I'm too dumb to not have come out of the ether yet? I believed you when you said you were on the pill, that you were protected. How many lies do you expect me to swallow?''

''Oh, but I—''

He sliced one hand through the air. ''That's enough. I've had all I can take. I'll make arrangements through an attorney to provide you with money, child support, every month.''

''No!''

''Oh, let it not be said that a MacAllister didn't provide for his kid. You'll get your money.'' He turned and started toward the door. ''Stay away from me, Deedee, just stay the hell out of my way.''

''Ryan, wait. Dear God, you're so wrong about everything.''

He grabbed the doorknob, then looked at her over one shoulder.

''I'll get over you in time,'' he said quietly, a weary quality to his voice. ''I'll forget what you looked like, just as I did with Sherry. I'll even—'' his voice was suddenly choked with emotion ''—even forget about the cute freckles on your nose.''

He opened the door and left the apartment. The door slammed so hard behind him that Deedee flinched as though suffering from a physical blow.

''No,'' she whispered, sobbing uncontrollably. ''Oh, Ryan, no, don't go. Listen to me. Please, please, Ryan. I love you so much.''

But Ryan MacAllister was gone.

And Deedee Hamilton wept.

Chapter Fourteen

Ryan entered his apartment and removed the gun and holster he was wearing. He wandered toward the kitchen as he unbuttoned the uniform shirt, then decided he wasn't hungry and changed his course for the bedroom.

He and Ted had been late getting off their shift of duty, as they'd apprehended a drunk driver and had been caught up in the paperwork of booking the belligerent man into jail.

In the bedroom, Ryan sank onto the edge of the bed with a weary sigh, then removed his shoes. A few minutes later, he was naked beneath the cool sheets, telling himself that this time, *this time, by damn,* he would fall asleep immediately and not awaken for at least eight hours.

During the two weeks since he'd stormed out of

Deedee's apartment, he'd been extremely busy. He'd intentionally kept himself on the run, not wanting to have any empty hours to dwell on Deedee and her deception.

He had completed the paperwork to sell Mac-Allister Security Systems to the two installers, and it was now a done deal. He'd accompanied them on several bid presentations, the only aspect of the business where they had no actual experience.

Having contacted all his suppliers to explain the change of ownership, the installers had been guaranteed the same lines of credit and payment schedules. The men had changed the company's name to Superior Security Systems, and Ryan was now totally out of the picture.

He spent hours at the police target range, sharpening his somewhat rusty marksmanship. He poured over the policy and procedures manuals he still had from his academy days.

Oh, yes, he'd kept very, very busy.

What he hadn't been prepared for was the nights— the long, dark, solitary hours of the night, which he now viewed as his enemy.

Ryan groaned, dragged both hands down his face, then dropped his arms heavily to the bed.

This night, he knew, was going to be no different from the others. That last scene in Deedee's apartment would play over and over in his mental vision, every detail sharp and clear. The memories haunted him, taunted him, caused him to toss and turn, and get only snatches of sleep.

What a fool he'd been, he thought, for the umpteenth time. What a gullible, naive, vulnerable fool. Deedee had played him like a master fiddler, pulling his strings, making him dance to her tune. She was now pregnant, just as she'd set out to be.

Deedee Hamilton was going to have his baby.

She would get her pink rabbit, or blue rabbit.

His son, or his daughter.

His.

No, he ordered himself, he couldn't, wouldn't, think about that baby. He'd wanted a child for as long as he could remember, but not one conceived in deception.

He had to somehow close off his emotions regarding that baby. It was Deedee's, not his, and he would have nothing to do with it beyond providing financial support.

"Ah, hell," he said.

How long would it take for the memories of Deedee to fade? How long was he to suffer the pain of knowing he'd loved and lost again?

He felt split in two, as though he was operating on separate planes. For one half of him being a cop, having Ted as his partner, was good, really great. He looked forward to going on duty, would have gladly done double shifts to keep him in the arena where he was contented and fulfilled.

Except for one strained episode when Ted had asked how Deedee was and Ryan had snapped that the topic of Deedee Hamilton was off-limits, he and Ted were performing as partners as though Ryan had never left the force.

The other half of him was empty, hollow, cold and

suffering pain beyond measure. Ryan, the cop, was doing fine. Ryan, the man, was smashed to smithereens.

Fatigue finally dulled his mind and he drifted into a light slumber. Deedee's voice began to whisper in the darkness, growing steadily louder.

Ryan, please, let me explain. You've got to listen to me. You're accusing me of such horrible things, and they're not true. Not true. Not true. I love you. Dear God, you're wrong about everything. I love you. I love you. I love—

Ryan shot upward to a sitting position, his heart pounding, his body slick with sweat.

Lord, he thought, his hands trembling as he shoved them through his damp hair. That hadn't happened before. He'd never heard Deedee speaking to him as though she were actually there in the room, her voice choked with tears.

You're wrong about everything. I love you. I love you.

''No, damn it,'' he said, his words echoing loudly in the quiet room.

He hadn't listened to her lies, hadn't wanted to hear any more of them. He'd slammed out of her apartment, shutting the door on her and what they'd had together.

And he hadn't even kissed her goodbye.

Sherry? Deedee? God, the ghosts were doing double duty, tormenting him. He'd squared off against the truth of his failed relationship with Sherry, put it to rest. He'd faced the fact that he'd left Sherry in anger and had never seen her alive again.

And now?

History was beginning to repeat itself. He'd left Deedee in anger, too. But she was very much alive, was haunting him with her tear-filled voice, begging him to let her explain, pleading with him to listen to her.

Ryan flung the blankets away, left the bed and began to pace the floor.

Was that what it was going to take to gain inner peace? Was he going to have to listen to Deedee's story, pile more of her lies on the mountain of them that was crushing the very breath out of his body?

Hell, he didn't want any part of that scenario. But he was desperate, couldn't go on like this. He'd try anything to escape from Deedee's clutches.

Okay, okay, he told himself. He had to do it. He'd go to see Deedee, tell her he'd listen to her spiel. Was that too risky? No, it would be fine, because he'd be prepared for the lies. He knew the truth of her devious plan to use him for nothing more than a means to her end goal of having a baby.

He'd listen and that would end it forever, give him closure and inner peace.

"Yeah," he said, returning to the bed. "I'll see her one more time. One *last* time."

And no, by damn, he wouldn't kiss her goodbye!

The next evening, Deedee tugged a T-shirt over her head, smoothed it onto the waistband of her jeans, then reached for the comb on the edge of the bathroom sink. After flicking her curls into place, she frowned at her reflection in the mirror.

Not good, she mused. Not good at all. She looked like she felt—exhausted. She hadn't been sleeping well for the past two weeks, not since that final, horrible scene with Ryan. On top of that, each new day had brought a spell of morning sickness that rendered her drained.

Deedee sighed, left the bathroom and went into the kitchen in search of dinner.

She'd had an appointment that afternoon with Dr. Mercer, who had declared her to be healthy, albeit a tad underweight. He'd given her a prescription to subdue the morning sickness, told her to eat more and to get some sleep, for mercy's sake.

She was approximately six weeks' pregnant, she thought as she opened the refrigerator. Dr. Mercer had established that fact today. That meant she had conceived Ryan's child very early on during the exquisitely beautiful lovemaking they'd shared.

She removed a carton of milk and a covered dish of homemade stew from the refrigerator, then bumped the door closed with her hip. After pouring a glass of milk, she leaned her backside against the counter and stared into space while waiting for the stew to heat in the microwave.

What a strange thought it was to now realize that during all the outings with Ryan, the evenings spent in each other's company, the wondrous nights of making love, their child had already been nestled deep within her.

They had been together—mother, father and baby—without even knowing it. A family. Mama, Papa and a little pink rabbit.

The microwave dinged and Deedee jerked in surprise at the tinny noise. A few minutes later, she was seated at the table, determined to chew and swallow every morsel of the nutritious meal.

A family, her mind echoed. How glorious that would be. She loved Ryan MacAllister so much, could envision being his wife, greeting him at the door with a loving smile when he got off duty, their child held securely in her arms.

"Deedee, just shut up," she ordered aloud, "and eat your dinner."

She was *not* being kind to herself by indulging in such an impossible fantasy. She needed to stay anchored in reality, accept the situation as it truly was.

Marriage to Ryan was not in the offing. He was convinced she'd used him, betrayed him, lied to him from the very beginning of their relationship. She was a woman alone, who was going to be a single mother, and she'd be just fine, thank you very much.

"So there," she said. "Now eat."

After finishing the meal and cleaning the kitchen, she went into the living room and settled onto the sofa with a thick novel. A moment later, a sharp knock sounded at the door.

"Encyclopedia salesman," she muttered, getting to her feet.

She crossed the room and peered through the hole of the safety-device in the door, her heart instantly quickening.

Ryan, her mind hammered. Ryan MacAllister was standing on the other side of that door!

She reached to undo the security chain, then hesitated.

Why? Why was Ryan there? What did he want?

If he thought for one minute that he could march in there and execute a repeat performance of his horribly unjust list of accusations against her, he was very mistaken. Not in this lifetime, mister.

Ryan knocked again. Deedee quickly undid the chain, unsnapped the lock and opened the door. She lifted her chin and looked directly at him, striving for an aloof, rather disinterested expression.

"Yes?" she said coolly.

Oh, dear heaven, she wanted to fling herself into his arms, touch him, kiss him, feel the strength of his magnificent body, inhale the aroma that was uniquely his. She loved this man so very, *very* much.

"Hello, Deedee," Ryan said quietly, no readable expression on his face. Deedee looked so tired, had dark smudges beneath her beautiful eyes. He wanted to scoop her up, hold her tight, ask her how she was feeling, tell her everything was fine now because he was there to take care of her.

MacAllister, he ordered himself, *get it together.*

"May I come in?" he said.

"Why?" Deedee said, raising her chin another notch.

Ryan glanced quickly along the hallway, then looked at her again.

"I'd like to talk to you," he said, "and I'd prefer to do it privately."

"And briefly," she said, stepping back to allow him to enter. "Very briefly."

She closed and locked the door, moved around him and resumed her seat on the sofa. She crossed her legs, folded her arms over her breasts and nodded toward the chair opposite her.

"Sit," she said. "Or stand. Whatever. I don't care. What is it you want to talk to me about, Ryan?" *I love you, Ryan MacAllister, you stubborn, unbending specimen of a man.* "Hmm?"

Ryan sat down in the chair, leaned forward and rested his elbows on his knees, then clasped his hands tightly.

"I, um..." he started, then cleared his throat. "Look, I keep going over and over that last night we had together, what was said and, even more, what wasn't said. I can't seem to put it away, because there are pieces missing."

"Oh?"

"You kept saying I should listen to you, let you explain things. That's why I'm here now—to listen to your explanation."

"So you can accuse me of lying again? No thank you, Ryan. You had your chance to hear the truth of what actually happened. I begged you to allow me to tell you the facts as they were, and you refused.

"Now you've decided you'll listen to me to fill in the blanks of your mental puzzle so that you can put it all away?" Deedee narrowed her eyes. "MacAllister, you can go straight to hell."

Ryan opened his mouth, ready with an angry retort, then shook his head and leaned back. He drummed the fingers of one hand on the arm of the chair for a moment as he reined in his temper.

"All right," he said finally. "Then I'll fill in the blanks with the data I have. You used me, lied to me, wanted nothing more from me than being the other half of what it would take to achieve your goal of having a child."

"That's not true! I was on the pill. I told you that. You even saw the package on the bathroom sink."

"A sink that contains a handy drain those fancy little pills could be washed down."

"Oh, you're despicable, you really are. You listen to me, Ryan MacAllister, and hear every word. My body has a mind of its own that has always proven difficult to regulate. My system overrode the birth control pills, which was not all that surprising to my doctor.

"I did *not* intentionally get pregnant. I did *not* use you as stud service, as you've so eloquently put it. I was torn in two about the baby. Once I knew I was pregnant, I realized I had truly yearned for a child, just as you'd said. The realization that I was pregnant, carrying your baby, was glorious."

She drew a trembling breath, struggling against threatening tears.

"But the other half of me?" she went on. "I was devastated. I knew our relationship would be over because I'd broken the rules, through no fault of my own. I'd gone beyond the boundaries of being just friends and lovers. I was going to lose you, Ryan."

A sob caught in her throat. "And I did. And I love you so much."

She waved one hand sharply through the air.

"Go away," she said, dashing an errant tear from

one cheek. "Leave me alone. I'd like to salvage at least a modicum of my dignity. Go, Ryan. *Now!*"

Ryan's heart thundered so violently he unconsciously splayed one hand on his chest for a moment as he stared at Deedee.

Dear Lord, he thought, she was telling the truth. He had listened, really *heard*, what she'd said, and she was telling the truth!

The woman he loved, loved him in kind. She hadn't lied to him, hadn't used and betrayed him. No! She'd simply loved him, honestly and openly, just as he'd loved her.

And they were going to have a baby, a miracle.

Ah, Deedee!

But, oh, dear God, what had he done? There were tears in her big brown eyes, such pain in her voice and etched on her delicate features. He'd hurt her so badly, caused her such anguish. How could he make it up to her? Would she ever forgive him? Was it too late for him to undo the damage? No!

"Deedee," he said, his voice raspy with emotion, "I don't know what to say to you."

"Then don't say anything. I asked you to leave, Ryan. Now I'm telling you in no uncertain terms. *Go.*"

"No, wait," he said, getting to his feet. "Please, Deedee, listen to me. I believe you, I truly do. I know you didn't lie to me, didn't use me just to father a child.

"I believe that you love me, and I know I love you, I swear I do. I'm asking you—hell, I'm begging

you to forgive me for doubting you. I want to marry
you, raise our child together. I want—''

''*You* want?'' she interrupted. ''What else is on
your list of 'wants,' Ryan? Do you *want* me to push
a magic button and erase all your horrible accusations
from my memory? Do you *want* me to burst into song
because I'm so thrilled that you've come to believe
me, believe *in* me, after all?''

''Deedee...'' Ryan started toward her.

She got to her feet and raised one hand, palm out,
to stop him.

''No, don't come near me,'' she said, then wrapped
her hands around her elbows in a protective gesture.
''Don't come near *me* or *my* baby.'' Tears began to
slip unnoticed down her pale cheeks. ''You say you
believe me...tonight. I fantasized about hearing those
words, but now I realize I have to think beyond them.
What about tomorrow, then the day after that? Would
you mull it some more and decide that, no, by golly,
you were right the first time? Decide I used you, lied,
betrayed you?''

''No! Ah, Deedee, I'm so sorry for what I did, what
I said. Won't you please listen to me?''

''Hear the echo, Ryan? Those were my words two
weeks ago. I begged you to listen to me, to the truth,
and you refused.'' A sob caught in her throat. ''How
can you possibly expect me to believe *you* now? I'd
be waiting for you to change your mind about me
again.''

''I wouldn't, Deedee. I love you.''

''No, I can't do this,'' she said, shaking her head.
''I can't live that way...waiting, wondering. It's too

risky, too cold, too empty. I'd rather be alone. I'm tired, Ryan, exhausted. Leave, just leave.''

Ryan stared at her, aching to go to her, hold her, demand that she listen and believe in him. Their whole future was at stake, and it was being flung away like grains of sand blown into oblivion by a whipping wind.

Deedee *had* to forgive him. She *had* to see that they could have it all, together. She *had* to…

Easy, MacAllister, he thought suddenly. He needed to slow down, regroup. Deedee, his beautiful, fragile butterfly, was wounded, so hurt, by what he'd done. She needed time to learn to believe in him again. He couldn't snap his fingers and set things to rights.

Yes, she needed time, *but not time alone,* to dwell on what he'd done. He had to think of a way to convince her to forgive him, a way to stay near her, front-row center, where she would be unable to begin to forget he existed.

''I'll go,'' he said quietly, ''but this isn't over, isn't finished.''

''Yes, it is,'' she whispered, tears still streaming down her face. ''Yes, it is.''

He started toward the door, then turned abruptly and retraced his steps to stand directly in front of her. He gripped her shoulders, hauled her to him and gave her a fast, hard kiss. When he released her, he looked directly into her tear-filled eyes.

''That kiss was important, Deedee Hamilton. Yes, I'm leaving but, by damn, *I kissed you goodbye.* That means I'll be back. I'm not giving up on us, on what we can have together. I love you, intend to spend the rest of my life with you and a whole bunch of pink and blue rabbits.''

"No," she said, closing her eyes and shaking her head. "No, it's too late for us. Too late. Goodbye, Ryan."

"Good *night,* Deedee."

He kissed her gently on the forehead, then left the apartment, closing the door behind him with a quiet click.

"Too late," Deedee said, sobbing as she covered her face with her hands.

Chapter Fifteen

"Hell, MacAllister," Ted said, "when it comes to screwing things up, you're in the major leagues, buddy."

"I don't need *you* to tell me that," Ryan said. "Believe me, I know it. Big time. What I'm asking for here is some help, some advice, Sharpe."

"Yeah, okay," Ted said. "Well, shut up and let me think."

The pair had just finished a shift of day duty and were still wearing their police uniforms. Because Ted's car was in the shop for routine servicing, Ryan had picked him up that morning. They'd agreed to go to Rosie's for chili after work.

Now sitting in the café with steaming bowls of the delicious chili in front of them, they ate in silence. Ted was deep in thought. Ryan was a study in misery.

His appetite gone, Ryan pushed the half-empty bowl to one side, then stared into space. He slid an occasional glance at Ted, as though hoping to glimpse a light bulb suddenly appearing above his partner's head.

"Pie?" Ted finally asked Ryan.

"No."

"Rosie," Ted hollered, "two slices of cherry pie, please."

"I said I didn't want any."

"Well, *I* want two pieces," Ted said. He leaned back in the booth and crossed his arms over his chest. "Man, oh, man, you really blew it with Deedee."

"Would you cut it out?" Ryan said, glaring at him. "I admit I'm a jerk. Okay? I'm a jerk. Ted, I left Deedee's apartment four nights ago with every intention of formulating a plan to win her back. So far, I've come up with zip, absolutely nothing."

He smacked the table with the palm of one hand.

"Every day that goes by and I don't do something positive toward getting Deedee to forgive me is dangerous. Each day is twenty-four more hours she's had to work toward forgetting me, putting me in some dark, dusty corner of her mind."

Ted nodded. "Yep. You've definitely got to get a plan, buddy."

"For what?" a woman said, placing two plates containing huge slices of hot cherry pie on the table. She was short, plump, with gray hair twisted into a figure-eight at the back of her head, and a warm smile always at the ready. "What do my favorite boys need a plan for?"

"Ryan has major heart trouble, Rosie," Ted said. "He's in love, but he messed it up royally. The lady in question loves him, but she doesn't *like* him. Do you know what I mean? We don't have a clue as to how he can get her to forgive him and take him back."

"Ah, I see," Rosie said. "Eat your pie. Well, it's good to know you're in love again, Ryan. It's bad to know you have troubles with your lady. Does she have just cause to love but not like you?"

"Yeah," Ryan said with a sigh, "she sure does. I accused her of something rotten, wouldn't listen when she tried to tell me the true facts. Then later I listened and believed her, but now she's lost her trust in me, won't hear *me* when I speak."

"I don't blame her," Rosie said.

"Thanks a lot," Ryan said.

"You reap what you sow," she said.

"Amen," Ted said.

"So!" Rosie said. "You have to court her, be romantic, break down her defenses. If she really loves you, you have a chance. Maybe."

"Court her?" Ryan said, raising his eyebrows. "People don't do that sort of stuff anymore."

"*You* do, as of right now. What does she like? You know, what does she have a weakness for?"

Ryan sighed again. "Pink rabbits and butterflies."

"There's your answer," Rosie said, beaming. "Be innovative, exhibit some imagination. Eat your pie. This will require all the energy you can muster."

"Amen," Ted said.

"Shut up, Sharpe," Ryan said. "You're really getting on my nerves."

"Oh, yeah?" Ted said. "You'd better be nice to me, chum. You're going to need all the help you can get with this fiasco. Pink rabbits and butterflies? Geez, whatever happened to flowers and candy? Rosie, bring Ryan the bill. This dinner is on him."

"Would you look at that?" Ted said. "Amazing. Those little baby tennis shoes are no bigger than my thumb. Hey, they've got racing stripes on the sides, the whole bit. Isn't that something?"

Ryan peered at the tiny shoes. "Yeah, you're right. I wonder how they make something that small with details like that?"

"Beats me."

"Good evening, Officers," a matronly woman said. "My clerk informed me that you were in our department. How may I be of service? Did someone in higher management telephone for police assistance? *I* certainly didn't."

In unison, Ryan and Ted glanced down at their uniforms, as though surprised to see them on their bodies. With Rosie's help, they'd formulated the first action to be taken in Ryan's campaign to make amends with Deedee. The two men had left the café and headed for the nearest large department store.

"Oh, we're not cops," Ryan said. "I mean, we are, but we're not on duty. We just haven't taken the time to change clothes since getting off our shift because this is an emergency situation."

"I understand," the woman said, obviously not understanding at all. "You have an emergency that brings you to the baby department?"

"Well, yes," Ryan said. "We started out in the toy section, but they didn't have what I wanted. The lady there suggested we come over here."

"Oh," she said. "Just what is it that you're looking for, sir? I mean, Officer?"

"A small pink rabbit."

"Or a butterfly," Ted interjected.

"No, I think the rabbit would be the best move," Ryan said. "That's the issue at hand, after all. The whole disaster is over the pink rabbit, and how I screwed up so badly. It's really more symbolic than the butterfly at this point."

Ted nodded. "You're right. Okay, we want a little pink rabbit." He looked at the woman. "Do you have one?"

The woman backed up a step and eyed them warily. "Over there." She waved one hand in the air. "There's a display of soft, baby-safe stuffed toys. I'll...I'll leave you to browse. If you have any questions, feel free to ask the clerk on duty." She pressed one hand to her forehead. "I'm going home."

"Thanks," Ryan said as the woman hurried away. He looked at Ted. "What's her problem?"

"I don't know. Cops shake people up sometimes." He paused, then laughed. "Could be, buddy, that she's never had two big guys in uniform show up in her department before, asking for a little pink rabbit due to our being in emergency mode."

"True," Ryan said, grinning. His smile faded as he glanced around. "Look at all this stuff, Ted. Baby paraphernalia. It's really sinking in that I'm going to be a father. It's great, just so fantastic.''

"You're going to be a dead man if you don't mend fences with Deedee, dude. Come on, let's check out those shelves over there.''

"A baby," Ryan said, following Ted. "Man, oh, man, I'm going to have a baby!''

"A baby?" Andrea said, her eyes widening. "You're carrying Ryan's baby?''

Deedee nodded. "I asked you to come to the store because I don't dare cry here, Andrea. This is the fifth day since I sent Ryan away. I've told you the whole story, and there's no denying it's a terrible mess.''

"No joke. Ryan wouldn't listen to you, then you wouldn't listen to him. There is some good old-fashioned listening called for here.''

Deedee sighed. "I was so hurt and exhausted. Ryan had been so hateful, accused me of lying and... Then suddenly he said he *did* believe me. I just couldn't deal with it. If he changed his mind once, what's to say he wouldn't flip the coin over again? I couldn't live like that. No, it's finished, just isn't going to work between Ryan and me." She sniffled. "Oh-h-h, I'm such a wreck.''

"Now calm down," Andrea said. "I know my brother can be a giant-size dolt at times, Deedee, but believe me, if that man says he loves you, then Ryan MacAllister is definitely in love with you. And you're in love with him.''

"Yes, but..." Deedee started, throwing up her hands.

"I'm so happy for you two. I *knew* something wonderful was happening way back at the twins' birthday party." Andrea laughed. "Forrest will be so tickled. He'll be able to put The Baby Bet into operation down the road."

"Andrea, would you quit being so cheerful? Ryan and I aren't even speaking to each other. I'm upset and confused. I'm miserable. Yes, I love him, but my faith and trust in him is shaken so badly. I just don't see a happy ending in the picture."

"Deedee, you're understandably not jumping with joy, but you've got to settle down and think things through. Ryan made a mistake, a *big* mistake. Are you going to compound it by refusing to accept his sincere apology to you for what he did?"

"Well!" Deedee said with an indignant sniff. "Now *I'm* the villain?"

"Oh, sweetie, there aren't good guys and bad guys in this scenario. There are human beings who are fallible." Andrea paused. "Do you remember that movie that came out years ago where the characters said that being in love meant you never had to say you were sorry?"

Deedee nodded.

"At the time, I thought that was so-o-o romantic. But now? I don't agree with it at all. To me, as John's wife, being in love means you *can* say you're sorry. You'll be heard, understood, forgiven, and whatever had caused the upset is put behind you so you can move forward. Think about it, Deedee. Please."

"Move forward," Deedee said quietly. "Let the past stay in the past."

"Yes."

Before Deedee could respond further, the door to Books and Books opened and a man in a khaki messenger's uniform entered, carrying a clipboard and a small package. The box was wrapped in paper with pretty butterflies in pastel shades.

"Ms. Deedee Hamilton?" the man said, glancing at Deedee, then Andrea.

"Yes, I'm Deedee Hamilton."

He put the box on the counter and extended the clipboard toward her.

"Sign on line six please, ma'am."

Deedee did as instructed, then tentatively reached for the pretty package as the messenger left the store.

"Butterflies," Deedee said. "Aren't they lovely? I adore butterflies."

"Someone obviously knows that," Andrea said. "Open it before I pop a seam, due to the fact that I'm basically nosy."

Deedee carefully removed the paper, took the lid off the box, then brushed aside the pale pink tissue inside.

"Oh," she gasped.

She lifted the treasure out of the box. It was a soft pink rabbit, approximately five inches high. It had a smile on its face and a carrot between its paws.

Andrea peered into the box. "No card."

"It's from Ryan," Deedee said, sudden tears filling her eyes. "I know it is."

"Ah," Andrea said, smiling and nodding. "The plot thickens. I'm off to collect Matt and Noel. I'm not needed here any longer with my pearls of womanly wisdom.'' She gave Deedee a quick hug. ''Enjoy your present. *And remember to think.*''

''Yes. Yes, I will. Thank you so much, Andrea. You're a wonderful friend.''

''Bye for now.''

Alone in the store, Deedee brushed the stuffed toy gently against her cheek, then cradled it in both hands as though it were made of the finest crystal.

''Oh, Ryan,'' she whispered.

The stuffed pink rabbit that was delivered to Deedee at the store the next day was twelve inches tall, wore a perky sunbonnet and held a tiny bouquet of silk flowers. The same butterfly wrapping paper covered the box.

Deedee burst into tears and had to tell the next four customers who entered Books and Books that she was suffering from an allergy attack.

The following day, the pink rabbit was three feet tall.

''Oh-h-h,'' Deedee wailed.

''No,'' Ted said. ''No way. Not a chance. MacAllister, get out of my face.''

''Ted,'' Ryan said, ''you've got to do this for me. I'm fighting for my life here. I got Andrea to find out Deedee's work schedule. She's leaving the store at six o'clock tomorrow night. It's perfect.''

''It's ridiculous.''

''Name your price.''

''I'm not doing it, MacAllister!''

"A cherry pie from Rosie's every week for the next year. Fifty-two of Rosie's cherry pies, Sharpe. Count them. *Fifty-two.*"

Ted rolled his eyes heavenward. "Sold. You sure know how to hit a man where he lives. But so help me, MacAllister, if one cop, even one, hears about this, I'll strangle you with my bare hands."

"My lips are sealed."

"Fifty-two of Rosie's cherry pies?"

"Yep."

"Damn."

At five minutes to six the next evening, Deedee picked up her purse, moved from behind the counter and said good-night to Christy, the young woman who had come on duty at Books and Books.

"Have a nice evening," Christy said. "I'll... Aaak!" she suddenly screamed. "Oh, my gosh!"

Deedee spun around to see what had caused Christy's startling outburst.

"Dear heaven," Deedee said, her eyes widening.

Standing before her was a pink rabbit more than six-feet tall!

It had a big smile, bright eyes with long eyelashes, floppy ears and a fluffy round tail.

The rabbit shuffled across the floor to where Deedee stood by the counter.

"Come with me," the rabbit whispered.

A woman entered the store and immediately stood statue still, her mouth open.

"I..." Deedee started, then had to take a breath of much-needed air. "You want me to go with you?"

The rabbit nodded.

"Deedee," Christy said, her voice trembling, "you can't go off with just any rabbit that happens to walk in the door. What if it's a sex maniac rabbit or something? Oh, Lord, I'm hysterical."

"Damn it, Deedee," the rabbit said. "It's me… Ted. Would you just come on?"

"Ted?" she repeated.

"Shh, not so loud. If anyone learns about this, I'll have to leave town. Are you coming?"

Oh, Ryan, Deedee thought, a soft smile forming on her lips. Her wonderful Ryan was behind this crazy stunt. Andrea was right. It was time to forgive, put the mistakes in the past and move forward.

It was time to love Ryan MacAllister with all she was, the very essence of herself—heart, mind, body and soul.

"Yes," she said, "I'll go with you."

Ted bent one furry pink arm, and Deedee slid her hand into the crook of his elbow. They went toward the door, Deedee smiling pleasantly at the woman who still stood with her mouth open like a goldfish.

"Good evening, ma'am," Deedee said. "Goodbye, Christy."

"'Bye," Christy said weakly.

"The feet on this thing are too big," Ted said, shuffling along.

Deedee swallowed a bubble of laughter, her heart nearly bursting with love for Ryan MacAllister.

Outside, people slowed their pace, staring at Deedee and her escort as the strange pair started down the sidewalk.

"I'm going to kill him," Ted muttered. "He caught me in a weak moment. Fifty-two pies doesn't cut it. One hundred and fifty-two isn't enough. It's settled. I'm going to kill him."

"Don't kill him, Ted," Deedee said, smiling. "I love him."

"Oh. Well, in that case, this might be worth it. No, forget it. He's dead." He paused. "Are you two going to live happily ever after with your little pink rabbit?"

"Yes. Oh, yes."

"Amen."

In the next block, Ted stopped in front of a restaurant and opened the door. To the ongoing stares of people passing by, he bowed and swept one arm through the air.

"After you," he said.

"Thank you."

They entered the restaurant and were immediately greeted by a man in a suit and tie. He gave no impression that having a woman accompanied by a human-size pink rabbit arrive in the establishment was anything out of the ordinary.

"Ah, good evening," the man said. "We've been expecting you. Madam, if you'll come with me please?"

"I'm outta here," Ted said.

"Ted." Deedee stood on tiptoe and kissed him on his furry nose. "Thank you."

"Be happy. You both deserve it. I'm gone."

The rabbit shuffled back out the door.

"Madam?" the man said.

Deedee followed him across the crowded room, ignoring the strange looks and whispered speculations of the patrons. The man opened a door on the back wall; Deedee moved ahead of him, then heard the door click closed behind her.

In the center of the small room was a table set for two, with candles burning in crystal holders and champagne chilling in a silver bucket.

And standing by the table, looking magnificent in a charcoal gray suit, was Ryan.

"Hello, Deedee," he said, no hint of a smile on his face. "You came."

"I came," she said softly.

"I love you."

"I know."

"Deedee, right now, standing here, I'm more terrified than I've been in my life, including times when I was scared spitless as a cop. This is it. Nothing, or forever."

"Ryan..."

"I sent the pink rabbits to tell you, to hopefully convince you, that I... Ah, damn, I'm so sorry for the pain I caused you. Deedee, please, *please,* forgive me. Give me, us, another chance. I don't want to lose you, our baby, the life we can have together. Will you forgive me?"

"Only if—" tears misted Deedee's eyes "—you forgive me. You wouldn't listen to me, but I'm just as guilty of not listening to you. I'm so sorry, Ryan. I love you. Oh, God, how I love you. We'll put our mistakes in the past, we truly will. The future is ours. Will you marry me, Ryan MacAllister?"

"Oh, yes. Come here, Deedee Hamilton," he said, opening his arms.

And she went.

With tears of happiness spilling down her flushed cheeks, she rushed into Ryan's embrace, holding him fast as he wrapped his arms around her.

"Ah, my Deedee," he said, his voice choked with emotion. "Deedee."

She tilted her head back to meet his gaze, and neither made any attempt to hide the tears glistening in their eyes.

Ryan lowered his head and kissed her, sealing their commitment to forever, putting the pain of mistakes securely away in the past and dreaming only of their future...together.

Slowly and reluctantly, Ryan raised his head.

"Would you like to order dinner now?" he said, his voice raspy with desire.

"No. No, my love, let's go home."

Ryan nodded, then encircled her shoulders with his arm. "Home. *Our* home. The three of us."

"Yes," Deedee said, smiling. "Mama, Papa and the little pink rabbit."

The wedding was held in Andrea and John's backyard with the MacAllister family in attendance. Spring flowers were woven through a wicker archway where the bride and groom stood before the minister. Vows were exchanged and simple gold wedding bands slipped into place.

"You may kiss your bride," the minister finally said to Ryan.

Just as Ryan leaned toward Deedee, she gasped softly. They both straightened in surprise that was immediately followed by delight.

A delicate butterfly fluttered between them, as though giving its blessing to their union. It glided gracefully upward, hovered a moment, then flew toward the heavens.

"Oh, Ryan," Deedee said, awe and wonder in her voice, "it's as though the butterfly is dancing, just for us."

"Perfect," Ryan said, watching the beautiful butterfly disappear from view.

"Amen," Deedee said.

Then Ryan MacAllister smiled.

And Deedee MacAllister did, too.

*   *   *   *   *

THE FATHER OF HER CHILD

For Ryan Schmidt,
my friend

Chapter One

Ted Sharpe leaned against the wall of the elevator, closed his eyes and drew a weary breath.

He could easily fall asleep standing right here on his feet, he thought. He'd just ride the elevator up and down for ten or twelve hours until he had rejuvenated his tired body.

If anyone poked him and questioned what he was doing there, he'd switch into his tough-cop mode and tell them he was on official elevator-security detail. That ought to impress 'em.

He and his partner, Ryan MacAllister, had pulled a double shift of duty in their patrol car, due to the fact that the Labor Day weekend brought people flocking to Ventura and the surrounding area. It was the last hurrah of summer, and the party goers did it up royally, overindulging in food, drink and reckless driving.

Police officers all along the California coast were kept busy, hauling in the drunken drivers and the brawlers who lost their common sense for the duration of the extra-long holiday weekend.

But now, midmorning on Tuesday, things were back to normal, as though someone had waved a magic wand and restored peace and order. People had returned to work, some a bit worse for wear, the visitors had exited and Ventura was once again as it should be.

Sleep, Ted thought foggily as the elevator bumped to a gentle stop at his floor. His kingdom for a long stretch of blissful, uninterrupted sleep.

The doors swished open and he left the elevator. His feet felt as though they weighed a hundred pounds each. As he plodded along the carpeted hallway, he absently noted that the door to the apartment before his was ajar and two men in white coveralls were coming out, leaving the door open behind them.

The men stopped in their tracks when they saw Ted, a common reaction when suddenly confronting a police officer in full uniform.

In spite of his bone-deep fatigue, Ted cataloged a detailed description of the pair, including the red stitching above the pockets on the upper left of the front of their uniforms. The red thread spelled out the message that they represented Ace Moving and Storage, one of them was Pete, the other was Jake.

"Hi," Pete said. "Nice day, huh?"

Ted stopped his sluggish trek. "Yep. You must be

moving someone in. The previous tenant left a couple of weeks ago.''

"You live in this building?'' Jake said.

Ted nodded. "Next apartment.''

"Good," Pete said, smiling for the first time. "We've had the cops called on us twice in the past year. People watch television one night, see a dumb flick about robberies pulled off by guys posing as moving men, and the next day...bingo...they're reaching for the phone when we show up at the house next door. What a hassle.''

Ted smiled and nodded. "My partner and I went out on a call like that a few years ago. It was a false alarm, just like you're talking about. You guys are covered today. That place has been empty, so there's nothing to rip off. You have to be bringing stuff in, not out.''

"Are we ever," Pete said. "The big pieces don't fit in the elevator. We just hauled a sofa up four very long flights of stairs. We're really earning our pay on this one.''

"Well, enjoy," Ted said, starting away. "Me? I'm hitting the cool sheets. Someone could probably rip off the whole building, brick by brick, and I'd sleep right through it.''

"See ya," Jake said.

"Yep," Ted mumbled.

As he entered his apartment, he gave fleeting thought to the fact that he should have asked ole Pete and Jake about the person, or persons, who were moving in. His previous neighbor had been a mousy little guy, an accountant, who was as quiet as the mouse he looked like.

Since Ted had the last apartment on the floor, he only had one close neighbor to be concerned about, as far as noise sifting through the connecting wall. A tiny, elderly widow lived directly above him on the fifth floor, and he never heard her footsteps.

A man on shift work was very often asleep while others were awake, and neighbors could play a bigger role than normal in his life.

Yeah, he thought, removing his gun and holster. He definitely should have asked the movers about who was taking up residence beyond the mutual wall. Well, too bad. He was so beat, he didn't have the energy to retrace his steps. He'd just wait and be surprised. Pleasantly surprised, he hoped. Yep, he was casting his vote for another mousy accountant.

Ted yawned three times in succession as he stripped off his clothes, then sighed in pleasure as he sank onto the unmade bed, pulling the rumpled sheet and blankets over his naked body.

"Mmm," he said at the sheer ecstasy of the soft pillow cushioning his head.

Within moments, he was asleep, wrapped in a protective cocoon of soothing silence.

Two hours later, Ted shot straight up in bed, his heart beating wildly. He'd been having a rather nondescript, boring dream. He'd been ambling through a huge grocery store, pushing a cart and tossing things in without bothering to see what he was taking from the shelves. The dream no doubt meant that he was hungry.

So what had jolted him awake?

A sound reached him and he shook his head in disbelief, attempting to dispel the lingering fogginess of sleep.

He was now, he knew, wide awake, and the noise was real, not a leftover memory from the dream. He was hearing… Yes, it was a piano being played with a great deal of enthusiasm *and* volume. Someone was pounding out "Yankee Doodle" on a piano!

"No way," Ted said, flinging back the blankets. He left the bed and pulled on the uniform trousers that he had dumped on the floor in a heap. "Not a chance. I need sleep. I'm going to *get* some sleep. Mr. Doodle can take a hike."

Adding nothing more to his limited apparel, he strode from the bedroom with heavy, angry steps. Leaving the apartment, he stopped for a moment to determine the source of the music.

"Mmm," he said, starting down the hallway.

The door to the apartment next to his was open, as it had been earlier. Ted went to the doorway, intent on marching right in and making it clear to the merry music-maker that playing the piano at an ear-splitting level was not remotely close to acceptable. Not when the closest neighbor was a wiped-out cop who had just gotten off a grueling double shift.

Instead, he took one step into the living room and stopped so suddenly that he teetered for a second. His eyes widened, and he had to order himself to close his mouth that had dropped open as he took in the view before him.

The piano was on the far side of the room at an odd angle, as though not yet placed in its designated spot by the movers. The piano player was facing him, although obviously unaware he was there.

The "Yankee Doodle" enthusiast was a woman.

And she was absolutely beautiful.

Because several cartons were stacked next to the piano, Ted could only see the woman's face and shoulders.

Like a cameo, he thought. Lovely.

She had silky black hair that swung in graceful waves around her face and brushed the tops of her shoulders as she moved her head to the beat of the peppy tune. Her eyes were large and very dark, further accentuating her fair skin. Her features were delicate...femininity personified.

And she was smiling.

Man, oh, man, Ted thought as heat rocketed through his body. This woman could wake him up any day of the week if she wanted to. He would wholeheartedly prefer, however, that when she did, she be next to him in bed, wearing nothing more than that pretty smile.

Forget the mousy accountant type. This was a new neighbor a man could *really* appreciate.

No, now wait a minute, he thought in the next instant. His rapidly heating-up body was running roughshod over his mind. Gorgeous or not, the lady had to be made to understand that pounding on a piano was not socially correct apartment-living behavior.

Ted moved farther into the room, stopped, crossed his arms over his bare chest and cleared his throat to gain the woman's attention.

She continued her rousing rendition of "Yankee Doodle."

"Hey," he yelled, "Ms. Doodle. Could I have a minute of your time here?"

Hannah Johnson jerked at the sudden bellowing sound of a man's voice, her hands crashing onto the piano keys. She snapped her head up, then stared at the man standing in the middle of her cluttered living room.

Heavenly days, she thought. *From where had this half-naked, magnificent specimen of a man come?* He was tall, with blond, sun-streaked tousled hair, tanned skin and the bluest eyes she'd ever seen.

His shoulders were wide, his chest broad, his arms nicely muscled. The curly hair on his chest was a shade darker than the hair on his head. His features were rugged, removing him from the pretty-boy arena to a place clearly labeled *male.*

Oh, yes, he was gorgeous.

But if the volume of his voice and the frown on his face were clues to his frame of mind, he was not a happy camper. So, what was Mr. Body Beautiful's problem?

"Hello," she said pleasantly. "You startled me. I'm Hannah Johnson."

"Ted Sharpe," he said gruffly. "I'm your neighbor." He nodded briskly in the direction of his apartment. "I live next door. I also *sleep* over there when I'm not jarred awake by a piano concert."

''Oh, I see,'' Hannah said slowly. ''You're a late sleeper? It *is* past noon, you know.''

''I realize that, but I've only been asleep for two hours. Ms. Doodle, I'm a cop. I just put in a helluva double shift. I need sleep. Are you with me here? *Knock off pounding on that damn piano.*''

Hannah matched his frown. ''There's no call to be rude, Mr. Sharpe. A quiet explanation as to the fact that I was disturbing you would have sufficed.'' She slid her eyes over him from head to toe. ''Do you always greet your neighbors half-naked?''

''I'm half-dressed. You're lucky I stopped long enough to put on my pants before I came over here. A dead-tired man who is blasted out of a sound sleep by a lousy rendition of 'Yankee Doodle' is not in a friendly-neighbor mind-set.''

''Lousy rendition? Lousy! I'll have you know, Mr. Sharpe, that I play the piano extremely well. Thank you very much.''

''No, you play very *loud*.''

''You really are rude. What happened to the motto of 'Policemen are our friends'?''

''It got blown away by 'Yankee Doodle.' I assume we've reached an understanding here? If you're going to play that damn thing, *do it quietly*.''

''Or what? You'll arrest me?''

Ted nodded. ''You've got it, darlin'. I'll slap you with a citation for disturbing the peace, Ms. Doodle.''

''Johnson. It's Hannah Johnson.''

''Whatever.''

''And I'll have *you* arrested for indecent exposure. You can't waltz into my home half-naked.''

"Like I said, I'm half-dressed. And your door was open. You don't have a case."

"My door," she said, "is about to be closed. Behind you. After you leave. Now." She got to her feet and came around the stack of cartons.

Ted's eyes widened as he stared at her.

Ms. Doodle, his mind hammered, *was pregnant!*

"You're pregnant," he said.

"Really? Gosh, I'm glad you pointed that out. I wondered what this funny lump was under my blouse. My, my, I'm going to have a baby. I certainly appreciate your telling me that, Mr. Sharpe."

Ted rolled his eyes heavenward. "You must drive your husband totally nuts. You've got a real temper there, Mrs. Doodle."

"It's *Ms.* Doodle. I mean, *Ms.* Johnson. I'm divorced, Mr. Sharpe. There's no husband to drive totally nuts. I sincerely hope for the sake of Mrs. Sharpe that there *isn't* a Mrs. Sharpe. You are *not* a pleasant man."

"There's no Mrs. Sharpe, and I can be as pleasant as the next guy, once I've had a decent stretch of sleep."

"Fine," she said, starting toward him. "Go tuck yourself back in bed with your teddy bear. If I decide to play the piano, I'll do it more quietly."

"Thank you," Ted said, glaring at her.

Just then, Pete and Jake entered the room carrying boxes, which they set on the floor.

"That's the last of it," Pete said. He took a clipboard from the top of one of the cartons. "If you'll sign this receipt, we'll be on our way." He glanced at Ted. "Let me guess. You got yourself mugged and they ripped off your cop suit."

"Cute," Ted said.

Hannah signed the paper, thanked the men, then followed them to the door.

Pregnant, Ted thought, watching her. *Divorced and pregnant.* Ms. Doodle had a lot to deal with on her own. She sure was feisty, though; gave as good as she got.

Did she have a family who would be showing up to help her unpack, move furniture, set this mess to rights? Hell, what difference did it make? It was really none of his business.

After Pete and Jake disappeared, Hannah stood with one hand on the doorknob.

"Good day, Mr. Sharpe," she said, lifting her chin.

Ted dragged one hand through his already sleep-tousled hair, then started slowly forward, finally stopping in front of Hannah. He looked directly into her eyes, realizing they were so dark he could hardly discern the pupils.

"Look," he said, "I apologize for storming in here and yelling my head off. Exhaustion is no excuse for being…um…"

"Rude," Hannah supplied.

"Yeah, okay, I was rude, and I'm sorry."

Hannah sighed. "Well, I'm not without fault, Mr. Sharpe. I was feeling a bit overwhelmed by this move, the mess, the general confusion of it all. I've found that by playing an upbeat tune on the piano, I can often gather myself together.

"I've been living in a house, and I now realize that

apartment dwelling is going to require some changes in my behavior. I'm sorry that I woke you.''

"Let's start over, shall we?" Ted extended his hand. "Hello, Ms. Doodle, I'm Ted Sharpe, your neighbor. Would you like to borrow a cup of sugar?"

Hannah smiled, then tentatively raised her hand to place it in Ted's.

"Hello, Ted," she said, her smile fading. "Thank you for the offer, but I have sugar somewhere in this disaster area."

Dear heaven, she thought, Ted Sharpe was even better looking up close than from across the room. She'd never seen such blue eyes, and they were framed by long, blond lashes. He had tiny lines by those incredible eyes, created from squinting against the California sun, or maybe from smiling that knock-'em-dead smile of his.

His hand was big and warm, so very warm, and the heat was traveling up her arm and across her breasts. That chest...so broad, tanned and beautifully muscled. The hair there caused her fingertips to tingle with the urge to touch, then weave, through the enticing curls.

Oh, Hannah, she admonished herself. *What on earth is the matter with you? Retrieve your hand. Right now!*

She started to remove her hand from Ted's, only to have him tighten his hold enough to keep it firmly in his.

The beautiful Ms. Doodle, he thought. *Hannah.* It was an old-fashioned name and it suited her perfectly. She really was as lovely as a cameo picture, with her dark, dark eyes and hair, and her skin that would feel, he just somehow knew, like ivory velvet when he caressed it.

When? his mind echoed. *Whoa, Sharpe, hold it right there.* The last thing Ted needed in his life was to get involved with a woman who was going to have a baby in a few months. He kept his social scene uncomplicated; easy come, easy go. And he only dated women who played the game by those rules.

Yes, Hannah Johnson was enchanting.

No, he wasn't going to do more than say hello to her if they happened to pass each other in the hall.

"May I have my hand back now, please?" Hannah said quietly.

"Your what?" Ted blinked. "Oh, your hand." He released it quickly, as though it had suddenly become a hot potato. He glanced around the cluttered room. "When I moved into this building, I had the movers put my furniture in place. Your buddies Pete and Jake shouldn't have left things like this."

"That was our agreement. They gave me two estimates for the move. I took the less expensive one, which means they brought in my belongings and plunked them down."

"Is your family coming over to help you get squared away?"

"I have no family, Mr....Ted, but several of my friends will be here after school to pitch in."

"School?"

"Summer vacation is over and classes started today, but I'm on leave for this school year. I taught music appreciation at an elementary school."

Ted nodded. "I see. I bet those little kids could really belt out 'Yankee Doodle.'"

"They certainly could," she said, laughing.

Oh, hell, Ted thought, that cooked it. Hannah's laughter was like tinkling bells. A coiling heat steadily built low in his body. He had to get out of here and safely back to his own bed.

"Well, it sounds like you're all set," he said, "so I'll go catch some more z's. It was nice meeting you, Ms. Doodle, once we got past the war."

Hannah raised her right hand. "I solemnly swear I won't play the piano for the remainder of the afternoon."

"My tired body will certainly appreciate that. I'll see ya."

Ted left the apartment, strode down the hall to his own and hurried inside.

Hannah stood in her doorway until Ted disappeared, then continued to stand there, staring at the empty hallway.

A swift kick from the baby caused her to jerk in surprise, come out of her somewhat hazy state and step back into the living room. She closed the door, turned to survey the clutter, then allowed herself to execute a long, weary sigh.

"Well, Ms. Doodle," she said aloud, "unpack a box, or two, or three. Oh, ugh."

She started across the room, but changed her direction and went to the piano, gently lowering the cover over the keys. She shifted her gaze to the wall separating her apartment from Ted's.

''Sleep well, Officer Sharpe,'' she said, saluting the wall.

Smiling, she took the lid off the nearest box.

Late that night, Hannah turned off the small lamp on the nightstand next to her bed, then shifted into a more comfortable position beneath the blankets. As she closed her eyes with a weary sigh, her hands floated upward to rest on her stomach.

''Good night, little one,'' she whispered.

As though hearing the softly spoken words, the baby moved, then stilled.

So tired, Hannah thought. Oh, goodness, she was exhausted. Even with the help of four friends from school, getting the apartment into a livable condition had been very hard work. There were still boxes to unpack, but she'd run out of energy and had finally quit for the day.

Her friends had been wonderful, pitching in like troopers and moving the furniture into place. One of the women had discovered the box of linens, then had made up Hannah's bed, stating it would be ready and waiting for Hannah to climb into.

They'd sent out for pizza for dinner, insisting that Hannah take a break and put her feet up. The two men had toted the emptied packing boxes down to the Dumpster, and except for a half-dozen small cartons, her home was in order.

Home.

This was it. This medium-size, two-bedroom apartment was now her home. Oh, how quickly her life had changed, falling apart and shattering hopes and dreams for the future, as well as the trust and belief in the man she'd vowed to love until death parted them.

A man she'd never really known at all.

A man who turned out to be far, far different than who he presented himself to be when they had married over two years ago.

"Go to sleep, Hannah," she told herself.

She'd get an energy-restoring night's sleep and wake up in the morning refreshed in mind and body. Wake up in her new home.

While Hannah's friends had been there, everything had been dandy. They were busy working, laughing, talking. The teachers had shared the tales of woe of the first day back at school.

But finally they'd gone, each hugging her, saying they'd see her soon, that they would keep in constant touch.

And then it had been so quiet.

Exhaustion had swept over Hannah like a heavy cloak, accompanied by the silence that seemed to have an oppressive weight of its own.

She'd taken the lid off a box, stared at the contents as though she'd never seen them before in her life, then thrown up her hands in defeat.

After a warm bath, she'd gone to bed, the soft pillow feeling heavenly as she lowered her head onto it. It was *her* familiar pillow, *her* bed, *her* sheets and blankets.

But how long would it be until this place really felt like *her* home?

''Attitude, Hannah,'' she said to the darkness. ''It's all in the attitude.''

The apartment was cheery, with sunny rooms that were spacious enough to hold the furniture she'd kept. The piano was polished and ready for her to give private lessons to her young students.

She'd shop tomorrow for more food for the cupboards, unpack the last of the boxes, and everything would be shipshape.

She could start to make plans for the baby's nursery that would occupy the now-empty second bedroom. That would be fun, exciting.

Heavens, she even had a gorgeous hunk of man as a neighbor. She could gawk at him if she happened to see him in the elevator or hallway.

Ted Sharpe, she mused, smiling. How many women had a half-naked, drop-dead handsome man show up in their living room the day they moved into their new apartment? No, no, half-*dressed,* to quote Officer Sharpe.

And that was another thing to be grateful for. She had a policeman living right next door in case a band of thieves tried to break in. How lucky could a woman alone get?

A woman alone.

Oh, dear, Hannah thought, she mustn't dwell on *that* while she was so tired. She'd frighten herself to death if she gave further thought to going through the remainder of her pregnancy, the birth of the baby, then raising the child, all alone.

Facts were facts. She *was* alone. She was twenty-five years old, divorced, pregnant and alone. So be it.

She and this baby she loved and wanted with every breath in her body would be *all right*. Whatever came along, she would handle it, one day at a time.

Two tears slid down Hannah's cheeks and she dashed them away angrily. She was overtired, that was all. Overtired and momentarily overwhelmed by everything. She was going to sleep. Right now.

"I'm trying, Gran," she whispered with a wobbly little sob. "I'll be fine tomorrow. Yes, in the morning there will be daffodils and daisies."

Chapter Two

Ted and his partner, Ryan, had the next two days
off, then they would go on a three-week duty shift of
straight days, meaning their working hours would
match those of an average businessman.

While Ryan MacAllister eagerly anticipated the ro-
tation of duty that brought him straight days so he
could spend more time with his family, Ted Sharpe
saw it as a ticket to the busy social life he enjoyed.

The two men led lives that were at opposite ends
of the poles, yet had been close friends for many
years. The endless hours they spent together cruising
the streets of Ventura in their patrol car had resulted
in many intimate conversations on topics they
wouldn't consider sharing with anyone else.

There was also the special bond between them
formed from the knowledge that each would risk his

life for the other if the need arose in the line of duty. Their friendship, therefore, went even deeper than most brothers'.

When Ted left his apartment in the early morning, he glanced at Hannah Johnson's door as he passed it, idly wondering if her teacher friends had shown up as promised to give her a hand straightening out the mess in her apartment.

Ms. Doodle had been good on her word. No further piano playing had disturbed Ted's sleep the previous day, and he'd awakened refreshed.

As he rode down in the elevator, Ted frowned.

Hannah must have been in a helluva rotten marriage, he thought, to get divorced while pregnant, then have to move and settle into a new place. He assumed she had divorced her husband, rather than the man divorcing her.

Either way, Ted decided, the guy must be a real scum to have the situation end up for Hannah as it had. She was young, didn't look more than twenty-four or twenty-five, and had said she had no family. *That was rough, really rough.*

Ted dropped his laundry off at the establishment he always used, knowing it would be ready for him to pick up the next day.

Ryan had razzed him unmercifully about being too lazy to wash his own socks and underwear. But Ted's one attempt at tackling the chore had resulted in an entire wash emerging a strange shade of puce.

After taking his uniforms to the cleaners used by many of the police officers, Ted headed for Ryan's house. Today, they were scheduled to put the last touches on the redwood deck they'd built onto the back of the MacAllister home.

During the drive to Ryan's, Ted's mind floated once again to Hannah Johnson. Did any of her teacher friends include her in their family celebrations? he wondered. Where did she spend Thanksgiving and Christmas? On her birthday, did someone bake her a cake?

An even bigger question, Ted thought dryly, was why he was using his mental energies thinking about such stuff? *Maybe it was because he was on his way to Ryan's.*

The MacAllisters were a large family of warm, loving people, who considered Ted one of the clan. He, himself, was an only child, and his parents lived in a retirement community in Arizona. He managed to see them several times a year, and they had a good time whenever they got together.

His mother was a gem. His father? Well, they did all right during short visits, but that special bond with his dad had been broken ever since...

Ted automatically jerked his thoughts from the direction they were headed. He wouldn't allow his mind to travel down that road.

He was thinking about... *Yes, okay, Ms. Doodle.* She was a safe subject, as it might be weeks before he even saw her again, in the hallway or elevator.

Did Hannah have a family, Ted's thoughts continued, the way he did with the MacAllisters? Were there people who would take on the roles of aunts and uncles for her baby? Were there kids for her child to play with, grow up with?

Ted chuckled. There was *definitely* a slew of kids bouncing around at the MacAllister gatherings.

Michael, the oldest son, and his wife, Jenny, had a son, Bobby. Forrest MacAllister and his wife, Jillian, had triplet girls. *Triplets.* The adorable little girls had celebrated their first birthday a couple of weeks ago. *Man, were they cute. And busy!*

Ryan's sister, Andrea MacAllister, was married to John Stewart, and their twins, Noel and Matt, were always bundles of energy. And Ted's partner, Ryan, and his wife, Deedee, had a son they'd named after Ted. Theodore Ryan MacAllister, called Teddy, would be a year old around Thanksgiving.

Ted would never forget how proud, how touched he'd been, when Deedee and Ryan had announced they were naming their son after him. They had been convinced they were expecting a girl.

But Forrest, The Baby Bet champion of the family, had declared that all pink rabbit toys would have to go on a shelf because Deedee was going to have a boy.

And Forrest had never lost The Baby Bet.

How did he do it? It was getting creepy, the way Forrest always won.

Yeah, those MacAllisters were something special, including Margaret and Robert, the parents of the group. Did Hannah have a family like that who made her feel as though she belonged? Ted wondered.

Hell, he didn't know. And since Ryan's house was just up ahead, he didn't have to think about it any longer, nor wonder why he was dwelling on the subject at all.

* * *

Ryan and Deedee MacAllister lived in a modest, three-bedroom ranch style home on a standard, sub-division-size lot. Robert MacAllister and sons Michael and Forrest, as well as daughter, Andrea, were architects, all of whom would have been delighted to design a made-to-order house for Ryan and Deedee.

Ryan, however, had been adamant about their living on a policeman's salary. Deedee had agreed, and the income from her store, Books and Books, was being invested for Teddy's college education, as well as their emergency-only fund.

Ted parked in the driveway, cut across the lawn to the front door and rang the bell. Deedee answered the summons with a smile.

"Hi, Ted," she said. "Come in."

He entered the house and immediately inhaled the delicious aroma of cinnamon.

"Mmm," he said. "Coffee cake?"

"Your favorite kind. I just took it out of the oven." Deedee laughed. "You're wiggling your nose like a pink rabbit."

"Hey, I'm a blue rabbit," Ted said, following her across the living room. "Do you suppose there's a contest we can enter Forrest in where we'd all make a bundle?"

"That's a thought," she said. "He's never lost The Baby Bet. I can remember when Michael said Forrest should be 'unchampioned,' but it hasn't happened. Forrest is incredible."

"Yep."

The pair entered the sunny kitchen to find Ryan just about to slip Teddy into his high chair.

"Whoa," Ted said. "We have a tradition, you know. Teddy has to be an airplane before he has coffee cake. Right, sport? We always do our airplane bit."

"'Pane," the baby said, holding out his arms toward Ted.

Ted took the baby from Ryan and held him high in the air while making roaring-engine noises. Teddy laughed in delight.

Ryan smiled at them, then poured coffee into three mugs decorated with brightly colored butterflies. Ryan MacAllister was tall, nicely built, very good-looking and a dedicated police officer.

When his first wife, Sherry, had been killed by a berserk gunman in the emergency room of the hospital where she worked, Ryan had quit the force and withdrawn from life for nearly two years.

His love for Deedee had brought him out of his near solitude to once again embrace each new day. He'd rejoined the police force as Ted's partner.

"Zoom," Ted said. "Ready to come in for a landing." He settled Teddy in the high chair. The baby began to pound happily on the plastic tray. "I turned off your engine, sport. What do you need? Fuel? Me, too. It's coffee cake time."

The coffee cake was served and Ted and Ryan discussed the final work to be done on the deck.

"The deck is going to be great," Deedee said. "We can sit out there, barbecue, watch Teddy tear around the yard. Thank you again, Ted, for helping Ryan build it."

"That's about the fiftieth thank-you," Ted said.

"Hey, I enjoyed it. It sure was different making something that size after working on my miniatures."

"I can imagine," Deedee said. "What kind of miniature are you carving now?"

"A tiny baby cradle, complete with rungs. It's tough, but very challenging. When I'm finished with it, the thing is supposed to rock back and forth like the tiny rocking chair I made. The rungs are a killer."

"I'd go nuts handling something that small," Ryan said. "You've said it's very relaxing, but I'd be a blithering idiot."

"Short trip, MacAllister," Ted said. "Great coffee cake, Deedee. Are you going into Books and Books today?"

"No, I'll work tomorrow while Teddy plays with Noel and Matt. Then I'll have the twins the next day so Andrea can put in some hours at MacAllister Architects. The triplets have the sniffles, so Jillian isn't in the baby-sitting trade-off routine this week."

"Three little kids with runny noses," Ted said, shaking his head. "They're probably cranky. What a handful they must be. For Ms. Doodle's sake, I hope she has one, only one, laid-back, easygoing type."

"Who?" Ryan said, placing another slice of coffee cake on his plate.

"Ms. Doodle?" Deedee said. "You've met a mother-to-be whose last name is Doodle?"

Ted chuckled. "No, her name is Johnson. Hannah Johnson. She moved into the apartment next to mine yesterday. I was dead tired and she woke me up playing 'Yankee Doodle' on the piano."

"Uh-oh," Ryan said. "I can picture it clearly in

my mind. You did *not* ask her politely and quietly to please lower the volume of the serenade.''

''No-o-o, I didn't, and I was informed that I was extremely rude. Oh, and she hoped for the sake of Mrs. Sharpe that there *wasn't* a Mrs. Sharpe, because I was *not* a pleasant man.''

Deedee laughed. ''Good for Ms. Doodle. Ms. Is she married?''

''Divorced,'' Ted said. ''She's a music teacher on leave and has teacher friends, but no family.''

''Oh, dear, that's grim,'' Deedee said. ''Divorced, no family and pregnant. That's a lot to handle. When is her baby due?''

Ted shrugged. ''I don't know. She looks like she's hiding a volleyball under her shirt. How many months pregnant is a volleyball?''

''Oh, Lord,'' Ryan said. ''Even *I* know every woman does this number differently. Deedee got to about beachball size with Teddy. Jillian was more like a life raft with the triplets.''

''Amazing,'' Deedee said, shaking her head.

''What is?'' Ryan said.

''That you've managed to stay alive as long as you have without being murdered, Ryan. Those are not flattering descriptions you're dishing out there, mister. Ted, is Hannah nice? Is she pretty?''

''Very nice, very pretty. Yeah, she's lovely.''

Ted averted his eyes from Deedee's, and cut another slice of coffee cake. He lifted it onto his plate, then stared at it.

''Hannah reminds me of a cameo,'' he went on quietly. ''She has dark hair and eyes, and very fair skin, like fine, porcelain china. Put that together with her old-fashioned name and...well, she's like a cameo." He cleared his throat. "Whatever. It's not important."

Deedee and Ryan exchanged quick glances, Ryan raising his eyebrows slightly as he looked at his wife.

"Uh-oh," Teddy said merrily. "Uh-oh, uh-oh."

"Out of the mouths of babes," Ryan said, grinning.

"What?" Ted said, looking over at him.

"Nothing, buddy. Finish stuffing your face, then we'll get to work."

"Okay."

"You're welcome to stay for dinner tonight, Ted," Deedee said. "We're going to officially christen the deck by Ryan barbecuing some steaks. I should have invited you sooner, but with the long hours you guys put in over the holiday, I wasn't certain you'd be doing the deck today."

"I appreciate the invitation," Ted said, "but I..."

"Have a date," Deedee said, laughing. "I swear, Ted Sharpe, your little black book must be bulging at the seams. Is there an unattached woman in Ventura and beyond that you *haven't* taken out?"

Ms. Doodle, Ted thought, then instantly frowned in self-disgust. Where had *that* come from? He had no intention of seeing Hannah Johnson socially. No way.

"There are a few left," he said, smiling. He popped the last bite of coffee cake into his mouth, then drained his mug. "MacAllister, let's do it. That deck is calling our names."

"Uh-oh," Teddy said again, then flung a handful of cake crumbs onto the floor.

"That settles it," Deedee said. "We've got to get a dog, Ryan. I need a furry vacuum cleaner to stand ready by Teddy's high chair."

"Good thought," Ryan said, getting to his feet. "We'll decide what kind of dog we want, then go to the pound or pet store."

"Let me know when you're going," Ted said, "and I'll tag along. I want to have a voice in the choice of my godson's first dog. It's a momentous event."

"It is?" Deedee said. "Well, okay, if you say so, Uncle Ted."

"I say so," he said firmly.

Late that afternoon, Ted parked in his numbered slot at the apartment complex, got out of his Blazer and locked it. As he started toward the building, he heard a car door slam and automatically turned in the direction of the sound.

Hannah was farther down the row of cars, juggling her purse and two large grocery sacks as she made her way slowly to the front of her car.

"Hey," Ted yelled, sprinting toward her. "Hold it right there."

Hannah stopped in surprise as Ted halted directly in front of her. In the next instant, he'd wrapped his arms around the sacks and snatched them from her grasp.

"What—"

"These are heavy," he said, shifting them against

his chest. "You shouldn't be carrying stuff like this." He frowned. "Haven't you read books about dos and don'ts, the rules about being pregnant, what you can and can't do?"

"Of course I have," she said, matching his frown. "Those sacks aren't too heavy for me. The biggest problem was trying to see my feet while I was carrying them."

"Well, you watch your feet. I'll tote the groceries." He started away. "Come on."

Hannah hurried after him. "I can't decide if you're being rude again, or if I should thank you for the help."

Ted chuckled and a funny flutter whispered down Hannah's spine. She slid a glare at him from beneath her lashes.

"When is your baby due?" Ted asked, as they walked along the sidewalk.

"January first."

"A New Year's baby, huh? Well, that settles that mystery. A volleyball means five months' pregnant."

Hannah looked at her stomach, then back at Ted.

"A volleyball?" she said. "I'm as big as a volleyball?"

Ted nodded. "Yep. I was telling my partner, Ryan MacAllister, and his wife, Deedee, about you. You know, the fact that I had a new neighbor who is going to have a baby. Deedee wondered when your baby was due, and I said I hadn't asked, but your stomach looked like a volleyball."

"You were discussing my stomach with strangers?" Hannah said, her voice rising.

"No," he said, an expression of pure innocence on his face, "not strangers. They're like family to me. I'm the godfather of their son, who was named after me."

"You know what I meant."

"It just came up in conversation, that's all. Say, if you need any pregnant advice or whatever, there are a whole slew of MacAllisters who can answer your questions. They're good people, all of them. Not only that, they do babies one at a time, twins, even triplets. Jillian had three pretty little girls all in one pop."

"Goodness, what an overwhelming thought," Hannah said. She paused. "Jillian? Triplet girls? That rings a bell. I remember seeing an article in the paper a year or so ago about a well-known author giving birth to triplets. Jillian Jones-Jenkins. Yes, that's who it was. I've read several of her books. She's an excellent writer."

"That's Jillian. She's married to Forrest MacAllister, my partner's older brother. The triplets were a year old a couple of weeks ago. They're walking now. You should see them. They each pick a different direction and take off. They're not into the buddy system of traveling together."

Hannah laughed as she opened the door to the building, then stepped back to allow Ted to enter.

There was that tinkling-bell laughter, Ted thought, moving past her. And there was his body, going nuts again, with instant heat rocketing through him. Hannah looked so pretty. She was wearing dark slacks and a pink top that made her sort of...glow. *Yeah, glow.*

"You certainly seem fond of babies," Hannah said, bringing Ted from his thoughts.

They crossed the lobby and arrived at the elevators. Hannah pressed the button.

"Babies?" he said. "Yeah, I like the little critters. They're fascinating. It amazes me the way they have opinions, likes and dislikes, from the moment they're born. They're people in small packages."

Hannah laughed again and Ted nearly groaned aloud as the heat within him coiled tighter and lower.

"That's an interesting way to put it," she said. "But I guess you're right."

"Noel and Matt are Andrea and John's twins. Andrea is my partner's sister. From day one, Matt made it clear he wanted to sleep on his back. Noel yelled her head off if she wasn't put in the crib on her stomach. How in the heck do newborn babies know how they like to sleep?" Ted shook his head. "Amazing."

The doors to the elevator swished open and they entered, Hannah pushing the button for the fourth floor.

"Yes, you're definitely right," she said. "Babies are people who know their own minds from the moment they're born. I apparently haven't gotten to that chapter in the book yet." She sighed. "I have so much to learn before my baby is born."

"You'll be a great mother, Ms. Doodle. Your natural maternal instincts will kick in, you'll see. You'll be able to tell what the problem is from the way the munchkin cries. You know...hungry, wet, mad as hell. Trust me here. It's true."

"You're quite an expert, Officer Sharpe. You

sound like a man who would thoroughly enjoy being a father.''

''Me? No, no, I'll pass on that one. I'm a Professional Uncle. That's my official title, in capital letters.''

''Ah, I see,'' she said, nodding. ''I understand.''

No, she didn't, Ted thought. No one knew the truth, not even his best friend, Ryan. And no one ever would.

At Hannah's apartment, she unlocked the door, pushed it open, then turned to face Ted.

''I'll take those sacks now,'' she said. ''Thank you for carrying them up for me.''

''I'll put them on your kitchen counter. Lead the way, ma'am.''

They entered the living room and Hannah closed the door. Ted stopped and swept his gaze over the room.

''Very nice,'' he said. ''You really shaped up this place. No one would know that you moved in just yesterday.''

''My friends were marvelous,'' she said, starting toward the kitchen. ''I only have a few small cartons left to unpack.''

Ted followed her and set the groceries on the counter.

''Your furniture matches,'' he said, smiling. ''Mine are leftovers from when my folks sold their house and retired to a smaller place in Arizona. I have one of these, one of those.'' He shrugged. ''It suits me fine. I must admit, though, your place is very homey.''

Hannah looked up at him quickly. "Homey? Like a home?"

"Yes."

"Oh. Well, that's good, very good. I—" She stopped speaking and shook her head. "Never mind." She took a can of peas out of one of the bags.

Ted removed the can from her hand, placed it on the counter, then gripping her shoulders gently, he turned her to face him.

"What were you going to say, Hannah? You suddenly sounded sort of...I don't know...sad."

"No, no, I..."

"Hannah," he said quietly. "Talk to me."

She took a step backward, forcing him to drop his hands to his sides.

"I just have a lot of adjustments to make, that's all," she said. "Things happened very quickly and at times it seems that I was swept along, totally out of control. Now I'm here, in this apartment, and it doesn't feel like it's mine yet, my home. Does that make sense?"

Ted nodded. "Sure." He paused. "Do you know what you need? A kitten."

"A kitten? What for?"

"To finish making this your home. You've got four months before the baby arrives. In the meantime, you need company, a kitten to greet you when you come in the door. You'll feed it, take care of it, talk to it, share your home with it."

"Well, maybe a kitten *would* make a difference. You know, add a sense of permanence to this place." She paused and frowned. "No, forget it. I could probably find a kitten in the For Free section of the newspaper, but I'd have to buy a litter box, food, that sandy stuff that goes in the box, take the kitten in for shots, all kinds of things. My budget is very tight and I have so much to get to be ready for the baby."

"Okay, try this. I'll ask around the department, see if anyone has kitten equipment stashed in their garage. People get pets, something doesn't work out for whatever reason, and they have doghouses, cat boxes, all kinds of jazz just taking up storage space."

"Well..."

"No harm in asking. Right?"

"Yes, all right. I'd appreciate that, Ted. Thank you. I seem to spend a lot of time thanking you for things."

"I'm just being neighborly."

"You're a very nice man, Ted Sharpe," she said softly.

Their eyes met. Dark, dark eyes looked deeply into eyes as blue as a summer sky. Heartbeats quickened and time lost meaning.

An invisible thread seemed to wrap itself around them, making it impossible to move or breathe. Heat thrummed in their bodies, and desire began to change the color of their eyes to smoky hues.

Hannah forced herself to tear her gaze from Ted's.

"I..." She drew a steadying breath, then turned toward the counter. "I'd better put away these groceries."

Ted blinked, bringing himself back from a hazy, sensual place.

"Hannah, I..." He stopped speaking as he heard the rasp of passion in his voice.

"Thank you again, Ted," Hannah said, not looking at him as she took items from the bag. "Would you mind seeing yourself out? There's ice cream in here somewhere and it's probably getting soupy."

Ted stared at her for a long moment. "I'll be seeing you, Hannah," he said finally, then moved past her.

"Goodbye, Ted."

He hesitated, then kept going without looking at her again.

As she heard the door shut behind him, Hannah closed her eyes and gripped the edge of the counter.

Dear heaven, she thought. *What had come over her?*

Hannah opened her eyes again and continued unpacking the groceries with jerky motions.

She'd felt it, the heated pulse of desire deep within her as she'd been held immobile by Ted's mesmerizing blue eyes.

She was a pregnant woman, for mercy's sake, and she'd been consumed by desire for a man she hardly knew. That was disgusting, wanton, tacky. It probably wasn't even normal!

Well, she was putting the entire incident out of her mind.

And from now on, she was going to avoid any contact with Ted Sharpe. As far as she was concerned, the man did *not* exist.

Ted entered his apartment, slouched onto the sofa, then was on his feet again in the next instant. He began to pace the floor with heavy strides.

Get a grip, Sharpe, he ordered himself. *Calm down.* So, okay, he'd had a sexual reaction to Hannah. No problem. He was a healthy man, for crying out loud.

But Hannah was pregnant!

He'd wanted her, damn it, and the woman was pregnant. Was that sick? Shabby to the max? Hell, he didn't know.

What he *was* certain of was that from this very moment, he was going to cut a wide berth between himself and Ms. Doodle.

He was steering clear of Hannah Johnson!

Chapter Three

Ted did not see Hannah for the remainder of the week. He thought he heard the quiet playing of the piano on one occasion, but by the time he moved close to the wall connecting Hannah's apartment with his, there was no sound of music.

His Wednesday-night date was so-so at best. He took an advertising executive to dinner, but she spent the evening expounding on the various ad campaigns she was working on. She related every minute detail of the wording, the colors used, the length of time and where the ads would run and the psychological impact the ads would have on consumers.

While one of her dissertations would have been interesting, by the sixth one Ted was bored stiff and eager to take the chatty lady home.

His Friday-night date canceled due to a cold and

he realized he was relieved that his evening was free.
He simply wasn't in the mood to do the town. He'd
dated the woman many times and knew she would
expect him to spend the night in her bed. The fact
that he wasn't in the mood for *that*, either, led him
to wonder if he was on the brink of a mid-life crisis.

On Saturday morning, Ted was restless and edgy.
He wandered around his apartment, rejected the idea
of working on the miniature cradle, then vacuumed
for lack of anything better to do, ignoring the fact that
the cleaning service had been there the day before.

When the telephone rang shortly after lunch, Ted
snatched the receiver, more than ready to hear the
voice of another human being.

"Hello?" he said.

"Were you sitting on the phone? It didn't even do
one full ring."

"Just happened to be standing right here, Ryan.
What's doing?"

"There's a deal going on in the mall on Kennedy.
The Friends of Animals are setting up in the parking
lot with all kinds of pets they need to find homes
for."

"Oh, yeah?"

"You make a donation, and you can also pay for
a certificate for shots from a local vet. He's giving a
portion of the fees to the organization. It's a good
outfit. They take care of abandoned animals, and
some people bring them litters of puppies and kittens
that they can't deal with...stuff like that."

"I take it you're going over there to look for
Teddy's dog?"

"Yes."

"I'll meet you there. What time?"

"Half an hour."

"Roger," Ted said, then replaced the receiver. He got to his feet. "Thank you, Officer MacAllister. I'm outta here."

A roped-off area of the mall parking lot was crowded with people walking down rows of boarded pens, wire carrying cases, bird cages and sundry other methods of containing a wide variety of animals.

Ted managed to find Ryan, Deedee and Teddy in the throng.

"Busy place," Ted said.

"That's for sure," Ryan said. "Well, let's browse. Teddy isn't going to be happy in that stroller for too long. He gets tired of looking at people's kneecaps."

"I don't blame him," Ted said. "What kind of dog are you thinking of getting?"

"Something medium-size," Deedee said. "Big enough to hold its own with Teddy, but not so enormous it will knock him over just by wagging its tail. I think it should be fairly young, not set in its ways. Teddy and the dog can grow up together."

"Sounds like a plan," Ted said. "Let's check it out."

They walked slowly down the first row, Teddy chattering happily in his stroller.

"Hey, there we go," Ryan said, smiling. "Rabbits. Want a rabbit, Ted?"

"I won't say in front of my godson what you can do with a rabbit, MacAllister. A dog, we want a *dog*."

Ryan whooped with laughter.

Twenty minutes later, Deedee stopped in front of a wire cage.

"Oh, look at that darling," she said.

"A beagle," Ryan said. He leaned forward to read the card attached to the cage. "Female. Six months old. Good with children. Housebroken. Owners moved out of state. Shots up-to-date."

Ted hunkered down and looked at the dog. The beagle wiggled and whined, her tail wagging with excitement.

"Would you like to hold her?" a woman said. "I'll open the cage, but don't let her run off. She's a busy girl. Her name is Scooter, but she's young enough to learn to answer to another name if you prefer."

"Yes, please open the cage," Deedee said. "She's so cute."

The woman unlatched the door and the dog bounded out. She whizzed passed Ted and went directly to the stroller. Planting her front paws on the stroller tray, she gave Teddy a sloppy kiss on the nose. The baby laughed in delight.

"Sold," Ted said, getting to his feet.

"I'd say so," Ryan said, chuckling. "We have instant rapport here. Deedee?"

"She's perfect, and I think the name Scooter is very appropriate."

The transaction was completed and the next stop was at a table selling collars and leashes. Scooter literally bounced along, causing Teddy to laugh and clap his tiny hands. A bag of food and two dishes were purchased.

''Would you like to come back to the house, Ted?'' Deedee said. ''We've got to take some pictures of Ms. Scooter MacAllister.''

''No, thanks,'' Ted said. ''I...um...I have some shopping to do.'' He ruffled Teddy's hair. ''Enjoy your first dog, sport. She's a beauty.''

Farewells were exchanged and Ted watched as the MacAllister quartet disappeared from view. Once they were out of sight, he spun around and made a beeline for the third row of pets.

Hannah massaged her aching lower back, then sat down on the sofa. She'd given four hours of private piano lessons to four wiggly young students that day, and her back was killing her.

She'd had a sandwich and a bowl of soup as an early dinner and now had to decide how she wished to spend the evening. During the past few months, she'd spent every spare moment sorting through household items, then packing what she wished to move to her new home.

Home, her mind echoed as she swept her gaze over the room. No, she wasn't going to dwell on that theme again tonight. In time, the apartment *would* seem like home. It was just a matter of adjustment and attitude, she kept telling herself.

With a decisive nod, she rested her hands on her stomach, smiled as she felt the baby move beneath her palms, then sighed.

What should she do with the long hours of the evening that loomed before her? Read a book? Work on the bib she was embroidering for the baby? Watch television? Go to the video store and rent a movie? No, she didn't have the energy for that. Forget renting a movie.

"Oh, I know," she said aloud.

She'd reread one of the novels she owned written by Jillian Jones-Jenkins. It would be fun because she sort of knew Jillian now. Well, that was stretching it a tad. She knew Ted, who knew Jillian.

Heavens, Jillian had given birth to triplet girls. She had three babies to tend to all at the same time. What an overwhelming and exhausting thought. Of course, Jillian no doubt could afford to hire help; a nanny, cleaning lady, maybe even a housekeeper who lived in and did the cooking as well as cleaning.

"I'll see my child now," Hannah said, poking her nose in the air. "Do be certain his nappy is dry. I can't abide a wet diaper." She fluttered one hand in the air to dismiss the obedient servant.

Laughing softly at her own silliness, Hannah shook her head, then stared into space.

Ted had said the triplets were very pretty, she mused, and were walking all over the place, each in a different direction. Ted certainly seemed fond of all the MacAllister babies. For a bachelor, he was amazingly involved in the little ones' lives.

What had he said his official title was? Oh, yes, he was a Professional Uncle. In capital letters, if you please. Strange. If he liked children so much, why didn't he get married and have a family of his own?

Hannah thought Ted appeared to be in his early thirties. Surely the swinging singles' life had lost some of its appeal by now. She'd hated that whole scene—not that she'd taken a very active part in it. Ted must still like it, though, or he would have opted out. He was so gorgeous, Hannah was sure he could have his pick of the multitude of available women out there on the loose.

Ted Sharpe. Why on earth was she wasting her mental energy and time sitting here like a lump thinking about Officer Sharpe?

Just then, a knock sounded at the door. Hannah was grateful for the intrusion, realizing she wouldn't have to answer the question she'd just asked herself.

She went to the door and peered through the peephole.

"Ted," she whispered, her eyes widening.

Dear heaven, she'd made him materialize by thinking about him!

Oh, Hannah, stop it, she admonished herself, undoing the safety chain. What a ridiculous thought.

She opened the door.

"Hi," Ted said, smiling. "Here." He pushed a cardboard box at her. It had handles at the top and a series of holes along the sides.

"What," Hannah started to say, taking the box.

Ted lifted a large bag from the floor and moved past her into the living room.

"May I come in?" he said. "Thanks. I'm in." He turned and closed the door, snapping the lock into place. "I hope you weren't busy."

"No, I wasn't, but—"

"Good. Okay, let's unpack this stuff."

"Wait a minute," she said. "Oh," she gasped in

the next instant, as a funny noise came from the box. "What's in this thing?"

Ted beamed at her. "Your kitten."

"My what?" She looked at the box, at Ted, then back at the box. "I don't have a kitten."

"Sure you do. It's in the box. Consider it a house-warming present. See, Teddy is really into throwing food on the floor when he's in his high chair. So, Deedee said they should get a dog to vacuum up the debris."

"Oh, well," Hannah said dryly, "that explains everything."

"Let me finish. I told Deedee and Ryan that a little kid getting his first dog is an important event, and as Teddy's godfather I should be there when they picked it out.

"An organization had a deal going today in the parking lot of a mall and we went over there. Teddy has a beagle puppy named Scooter. Cute dog. Teddy loves it. Anyway, they had all kinds of pets...even rabbits...so I got you a kitten."

"But..."

"Don't worry about a thing." Ted placed the sack on the sofa and began to pull things out. "You're all set. Here's a litter tray, a big box of litter, a scoop, a bunch of food and a ball with a bell inside.

"Oh, and this certificate entitles you to the shots the kitten needs. You go to the vet whose name and address is on here. Okay?"

"I can't allow you to buy me all of this, Ted."

"I already did," he said with a shrug. "When I was growing up, my mom baked a cake whenever new neighbors moved onto the block. She told me it was a way to say welcome. Believe me, Ms. Doodle, you would *not* want me to bake you a cake. So, I substituted a kitten instead.''

''But—''

''Just say, 'Thanks, Ted.'''

Hannah smiled. ''Thank you, Ted. Thank you so much. I shouldn't accept such a generous gift, but I'm going to. Oh, this is wonderful.''

''Open the box.''

Hannah set the carrying carton on the sofa and unlatched the cardboard handles. As she pulled the sides free, a furry, sandy-colored head popped up.

''Oh, how sweet,'' she said, picking up the kitten. She held the tiny bundle to her cheek. ''It's so soft, so small.''

''She's six weeks old. She. It's a girl. Cute, huh? I like her feet. All four feet are white, like she's wearing socks. Great tail, too. It's as long as her body. What are you going to name her?''

''Thank you.''

Ted frowned. ''Weird name.''

''No, no, I just feel as though I should say thank you a hundred times,'' she said, smiling. She cuddled the kitten beneath her chin.

''Your eyes are sparkling,'' Ted said quietly. ''I wouldn't have thought that eyes as dark as yours could sparkle, but they really are. You look…I don't know, Hannah…happy. Yeah, you look happy, and that's nice, really great.''

''I…'' Hannah stopped speaking as she shook her head, her eyes filling with tears. ''Oh, dear, ignore me. I'm a classic case of a pregnant woman who cries at the slightest provocation.

"It's just that I can't remember when anyone has done such a thoughtful thing for me. Not since my gran." Two tears slid down her cheeks. "Oh, drat."

Ted smiled at her warmly, then framed her face in his hands and wiped the tears away with his thumbs in a soft, gentle motion.

A flutter of heat whispered along Hannah's spine.

"If you get weepy over a tiny little kitten," Ted said, "I'd hate to see what would happen if someone gave you a big horse. You'd probably flood the place."

Hannah managed to produce a trembling smile, but in the next instant it faded as she continued to look directly into the blue depths of Ted's eyes. His hands cradling her face stilled, but remained in place as he met her gaze.

A cameo, his mind hummed. So lovely. There Hannah stood, tears glistening in her incredible eyes, a tiny kitten tucked beneath her chin. She looked so young, vulnerable, so beautiful.

He wanted to wrap her up in a cocoon, protect her, take care of her, assure her that she wasn't alone. She had so much to deal with, so much to face, but *she wasn't alone* because *he* was there.

Sharpe, he ordered himself, *get a grip.*

Abruptly, he dropped his hands from her face and cleared his throat.

"So, Ms. Doodle," he said, looking at the paraphernalia spread out on the sofa, "let's get set up here. Where do you want the litter box?"

Damn it, he fumed, the heat low in his body was taking its sweet time to cool down. He ached for Hannah Johnson. He wanted her, wanted to make slow, gentle love to her for hours. What in the hell was this woman doing to him?

No, now wait. Ted cautioned himself. He was over-reacting, panicking for no reason. She pushed his sexual buttons, but that was understandable because she was a lovely, desirable woman. The fact that she was volleyball-size pregnant didn't seem to enter into his sensual attraction to her, and it certainly didn't diminish it in any way.

As for his never-before-experienced emotions of protectiveness, of momentarily seeing himself as the one who would ease her burdens...well, that was understandable, too.

He was a cop who cared, a compassionate man who spent his life in the role of the knight to the rescue. He shielded the good from the bad, took care of those who couldn't fend for themselves.

Therefore, he mentally rambled on, it stood to reason that Hannah's plight would touch a chord, cause his police officer, protector-of-the-people instincts to rise to the fore.

Yes, sir, he had it all figured out.

There wasn't a thing to worry about in regard to his reactions to Hannah Johnson.

"What do you think?" Hannah said.

"What?" he said. "I'm sorry, I was daydreaming for a minute there."

"I said, I thought I'd put the litter box in the corner

of the bathroom so it will be on a tile floor. That will be easier to clean if she tracks any of the litter.''

Ted nodded. ''Good plan.'' He picked up the tray and box. ''Let's do it now, in case Her Highness gets a call of nature.''

They tended to the litter box, then Hannah put a plastic place mat on the floor in the kitchen next to the refrigerator. She filled one bowl with food, another with water and put the kitten in front of it. She then offered Ted a soft drink.

''Sure,'' he said. ''Thanks.''

They settled onto opposite ends of the sofa with their drinks. The kitten finished eating, wandered back into the living room and crawled up on the sofa. She looked at Hannah, then climbed onto Ted's thigh, curled into a ball and went to sleep.

Hannah laughed. ''Well, she definitely prefers men over women.''

''She's missing a bet. I'm certain that your leg is much softer than mine and would make a nicer pillow.'' He ran one fingertip over the sleeping kitten's head. ''Cute. I like her. She does need a name, though, Hannah.''

''Daisy. I'm going to call her Daisy.''

Ted nodded. ''That works for me. It's very... girly.''

''Well, it means more than that to me. It's a symbolic name.''

Ted shifted his gaze from Daisy to Hannah. ''Oh?''

''You see,'' she started, then hesitated, giving Ted the impression she was deciding whether or not to continue to say what had prompted her to name the kitten Daisy.

"I'm listening, Hannah."

"Yes, you are, aren't you?" She cocked her head slightly to one side as she studied him for a long moment. "You really are."

She was so fragile, Ted thought. She moved so tentatively, as though afraid the next step she took might hurt her in some way. Man, the guy she'd been married to must have been a scum from the word go.

"Well, you see," Hannah said, "I was raised by my grandmother, my gran, from the time I was three. My parents were killed in an automobile accident. My gran was a wonderful, warm, loving and wise person. I loved her very, very much."

"Loved? Past tense?"

"She died when I was twenty. I still miss her, and I think of her every day. When I was growing up, she'd tell me that whenever I had a bad day, a gloomy day, with problems or troubles of any kind, I should remember that tomorrow would be sunny and would bring me daffodils and daisies."

"Nice," Ted said. "Very nice."

"I can't begin to tell you how many times I've reached for that. Something upsetting would happen and I'd tell myself, 'Tomorrow will be sunny. I'll have daffodils and daisies.' It sounds silly, I suppose, but it has gotten me through some rough moments."

"Daffodils and daisies," Ted repeated, nodding.

"The kitten was such a wonderful surprise, such a thoughtful gift. She *is* going to help me feel this is my home now. She deserves the name Daisy, the way my gran taught it to me.''

"I think I would have liked your gran."

"And she would have liked you, Ted."

Once again, time stopped as they looked into each other's eyes. Once again, the maddening heat coiled tight and low in Ted's body. Once again, Hannah felt the strange flutter dance along her spine.

Enough, Ted thought. Damn it, enough was enough.

He tore his gaze from Hannah's, then lifted the kitten from his thigh with both hands and set her gently on the sofa next to him. He got to his feet.

"I'd better shove off," he said, starting toward the door.

Hannah pushed herself from the soft cushion and followed him.

"Thank you again, Ted." She stood on tiptoe and kissed him on the cheek.

"Sure," he said, then hurried out the door.

Hannah locked it behind him, slid the safety chain into place and returned to the sofa. She cradled the sleeping kitten in both hands and lifted her to eye level.

"Welcome home, Daisy," she said, smiling.

Chapter Four

On Monday afternoon, dark clouds began to build in the sky and thunder rumbled in the distance. Ted and Ryan were parked in the patrol car in plain view at the side of an elementary school.

The boisterous children were getting out for the day and the street was lined with yellow buses and parents in cars. The silent presence of the police kept traffic at the proper speed.

"Man, those kids have a lot of energy," Ted said. "We should be that good after a day's work."

"Feeling your age today, Sharpe?" Ryan said, chuckling. "I've tried to warn you that the party life would catch up with you, but you weren't having any of my worldly wisdom. Big weekend, huh?"

Ted shot a glare at his partner, then redirected his

attention to the slow-moving, congested traffic in front of the school.

"No, MacAllister," he said. "I did *not* have a big weekend."

"Why not?"

Ted shrugged. "I wasn't in the mood." He paused. "Do you think I'm too young for a mid-life crisis?"

"Beats me. I don't think every guy has one. You know, it's not a given, like women going through the change of life. Then again, there are some experts who say men definitely have a sort of mid-life-change thing, too. Hell, I really don't know."

"You're a lot of help."

"Why the question?"

"It's not that big a deal. It's just that lately I've felt restless, kind of edgy. In the past, I never had trouble filling idle hours. In fact, I didn't seem to have enough time to do everything I wanted to. Now? I'm flat, dulled-out. I decide to do something, then realize I really don't want to. It's weird."

"Not good, buddy," Ryan answered. "It sounds like how I felt toward the end of owning MacAllister Security Systems. I have to give you credit, though, for being in touch with yourself and knowing something is off-kilter. I denied it far longer than I should have."

"Yeah, well, it turned out all right. You're back where you belong, being a cop."

"You're not getting bored on the force, are you?"

"No, no, the job is fine," Ted reassured him. "No problem there. It's my leisure time that's suddenly tripping me up."

"You seemed okay at the mall when we were getting Teddy's dog. Scooter is nuts, by the way. She bounces like a pogo stick when she's excited about something. She goes straight up in the air. Teddy thinks she's great. I've never seen a dog bounce like that."

Ted chuckled as he envisioned the bouncing beagle.

"Anyway, back at the mall," Ryan said, "you were loose, relaxed, your usual self. Or were you faking it?"

"No, I enjoyed myself. Before you called, though, I was pacing the floor."

"And after you went home?"

"I had a good time at Hannah's because of Daisy but—" Ted stopped speaking and inwardly groaned.

Damn, he'd had no intention of revealing the fact that he'd bought a kitten for Hannah. Ryan would razz him to no end, he just knew it. He'd make a simple thing like buying a new neighbor a welcoming gift into a major man-woman event. Oh, hell, Ted didn't need the hassle he was about to get.

"Hannah is your new neighbor, Ms. Doodle," Ryan said. "But who's Daisy?"

"The kitten I bought Hannah at the mall after you left," Ted said. *Gear up, Sharpe. Here it comes.*

"Oh."

A few seconds ticked by, then a few more, but Ryan kept silent.

"Okay, MacAllister," Ted said. "Spit it out before you blow a fuse."

Ryan glanced over at him. "Spit what out?"

"I bought Hannah a kitten. Okay? Fine. What would you expect me to do? Bake her a cake? She was having a problem feeling like the apartment was home. You know what I mean? I figured the kitten would be there, greet her, be company for her, make the place more homey."

"Oh."

"She was really tickled with the kitten. She got tears in her eyes, but said pregnant women are very emotional. A volleyball is five months along, by the way. Her baby is due New Year's Day."

Ryan nodded. "Oh."

"She named the kitten Daisy to represent the daffodils-and-daisies theory her gran taught her. Her grandmother raised her because her parents were killed when she was three. Whenever Hannah was bummed, her gran would say that tomorrow would be sunny and bring her daffodils and daisies. Nice, huh?"

"Yeah."

"So she named the kitten Daisy because she felt the little bugger would make her days sunnier, and make the apartment seem more like a home. I called it exactly right and I was glad, I really was. Hannah just lit up and her eyes sparkled. There. That's it. Don't make a big deal out of it."

"Okay."

Ted drummed the fingers of one hand on his knee. "You're getting on my nerves, MacAllister."

Ryan swallowed a burst of laughter, then stiffened. "Heads up. That joker is going at least thirty-five in a fifteen."

Ryan started the engine, turned on the lights and siren and pulled out into the street in pursuit of the speeding vehicle.

That evening after Teddy was in bed, Ryan related the story of Hannah and Daisy to Deedee. Rain pelted the windows and thunder roared across the heavens.

"Very interesting," Deedee said, tapping one fingertip against her chin. "Ted was defensive about buying the kitten for Hannah?"

"Like a hostile witness on the stand. I really got under his skin because I reacted as though he were talking about the weather. Ready for this? Ted thinks he might be having a mid-life crisis."

"Oh, dear," she said, smiling. "What he's having is an attraction to a lady who is far removed from the type of woman with whom he usually associates. Oh, Ryan, his buying Hannah that kitten is the sweetest thing. And I adore the daffodils-and-daisies story. Hannah sounds like she's absolutely lovely."

"Well, I wouldn't mention any of this to Ted if I were you. He's very touchy about the subject of Hannah Johnson, aka Ms. Doodle."

"You'd better keep me posted on all of this, Ryan MacAllister."

"I will, but if I come home strangled, it's because Officer Theodore Sharpe is a tad hard to live with right now."

"Oh, you poor baby," she said, slipping onto his lap. "Do you need some tender loving care?"

"Yes, ma'am," he said, wrapping his arms around her. "A whole lot of TLC."

Ryan captured Deedee's lips with his. No more words were spoken for a long, long time.

Ted sat in front of the long table that covered one wall of the second bedroom in his apartment. As he slowly and carefully sanded one of the minuscule rungs that would be part of the miniature cradle he was making, he hummed along with the country-western music playing on the stereo in the living room.

On the opposite wall was a glass-fronted cabinet which held about two dozen small pieces of furniture he'd made over the past months.

A bookcase next to it contained tools, brushes, a variety of paints and stains and several stacks of woodworking books and magazines.

Earlier in the evening, he'd begun reading the latest book he'd purchased at Deedee's store, an instruction manual for constructing a dollhouse.

As Ted worked, he smiled, realizing that if he built the house and eventually filled it with handcrafted furniture, it would never leave this room.

Nope, he thought. One furnished dollhouse wouldn't cut it when he considered how many little MacAllister girls there were.

And what about the boys? They'd expect some-thing made especially for them by their uncle Ted, too. No, the dollhouse and furniture would remain right there. He'd give the MacAllister munchkins vis-itation rights.

His smiled faded and he sighed.

Uncle Ted. Ted Sharpe, Professional Uncle Extraordinaire, that's who he was. Not a father, just an uncle. Not an everyday part of those kids' lives, just a drop-in entity. Out of sight, out of mind. And all the MacAllisters assumed that was the way he wanted it.

Damn it, Sharpe, he admonished himself. *Knock it off.* His life was structured just fine the way it was. He had the best of both worlds; the family scene when the mood struck, the singles scene the remainder of the time.

He came and went as he pleased, and had no major responsibilities, no worries or woes. He was sitting pretty, doing great.

Or so he'd believed until the last week or so.

He'd been off the mark, feeling weird, strange, not like himself at all. Restless, edgy, wired, he couldn't get a handle on what was wrong.

It was like…yeah, like people who came home, moved through their house and didn't realize for an hour or more that the television had been ripped off. They were so used to it being there, that it took a while for it to sink in that it was missing.

Missing.

Ted set the sandpaper and cradle rung on the table and stared into space.

Missing. Something was missing from his life, his day-to-day existence. Well, hell, what a lousy conclusion to come to as to why he was out of sorts. His life as it stood had suited him just dandy for many years.

Why would it suddenly seem as if something was missing?

If this was his mid-life crisis, Ted sure as hell hoped it wouldn't last long. He wasn't accustomed to being bummed-out, mentally listless, physically dragging through the days, tossing and turning at night.

Uncle Ted.

No, damn it, not being married, not having children, was *not* the source of his dilemma.

Ted got to his feet and left the room, smacking the light switch off as he passed. Shoving his hands into the back pockets of his faded jeans, he wandered around the living room, a frown on his face. In the background, Vince Gill crooned about loneliness.

Okay, Sharpe, get it together, he told himself. *Analyze the situation.*

He was single. He liked it that way. He had kids who clambered all over him whenever he visited them. That was the end of *that* story.

Women. He had plenty of women to pick from...every age, shape, size, career and IQ imaginable. Plenty of women. Check. No problem.

Career. Set. A-OK. He was doing exactly what he wanted to do. And he was a damn good cop.

Friends. He had great friends, true and loyal friends.

Money. No sweat. He lived well, had a healthy retirement portfolio growing steadily and didn't do without anything he really wished to have.

"So what in the hell is missing?" he said aloud, pulling his hands free and flinging out his arms.

Before the discussion between Ted and Ted could continue, a boom of thunder crashed overhead and in the next moment the lights went out.

''Well, hell,'' Ted said.

He stood statue-still, planting his hands on his hips as he waited for his eyes to adapt to the inky darkness. When he could see well enough to move, he made his way into the kitchen and retrieved a flashlight from the drawer designated for odds and ends.

With the bright beam of light ahead of him, he went to the sofa, slouched onto it and flicked off the flashlight. In the next instant, he turned it back on and lunged to his feet.

Ms. Doodle, he thought. Did Hannah have a flashlight? Candles? Had that extremely loud thunder frightened her?

Could she remember where all her furniture was placed so she could find a flashlight, if she had one, without falling over something?

What if she hurt herself? Or the baby? Or stepped on Daisy and smashed the kitten flat?

Hannah could be in trouble over there! Ted realized. He'd better go find out if she was all right. Yes, it was his duty as a police officer to leap into action in a single bound at the slightest hint of potential disaster or possible danger.

''Sharpe, you're so corny,'' he said, shaking his head in self-disgust. ''Just shut up and go see if Hannah is okay.''

The hallway was pitch-black and Ted's flashlight cast eerie shadows beyond its bright circle of light. The thunder continued to rumble and roar as it rolled across the sky.

At Hannah's apartment, he knocked sharply.

''Hannah?'' he called. ''It's Ted.''

Nothing.

He leaned his ear against the door, silently cursing the noisy thunder. Straightening, he pounded his fist on the door.

"Hannah?"

Nothing.

Ted's heart began to race, as well as his imagination.

Why didn't she answer? Was she hurt, unable to get to the door? He could kick in the door. Or maybe he should make his way down the back stairs to the ground floor, find the manager's apartment and drag the guy up here with the master key.

Yeah, he'd have to use the stairway because the elevator wouldn't be working.

Ted stiffened, beads of sweat dotting his forehead.

The elevator!

Lord, what if Hannah was stuck in the elevator?

Maybe she'd gone out to dinner with some of her teacher friends, saw the ominous clouds building in the sky and headed for home. Then the storm broke before she arrived at the complex, and she hurried inside but was already drenched as she entered the elevator. Halfway to the fourth floor...*blam*...no electricity...!

Hannah could be cold and wet, held captive in a dark cage...terrified!

He had to call the police!

"Damn it," Ted said. "I *am* the police."

Sharpe, slow down, he ordered himself. He wasn't behaving to form at all. He didn't usually go off the deep end, panic, automatically think the worst.

He was an in-control officer of the law who approached each new situation he encountered with a swift and analytical appraisal of what needed to be done.

Ted splayed one hand on his heart, took a deep, steadying breath and let it out slowly.

There. He was fine now calm, cool and collected. Right? Right.

In the next instant Ted began to beat on Hannah's door again with his fist.

"Hannah! Hannah, are you in there? It's Ted. Say something. Anything. Speak to me."

"Ted?" came a muffled reply.

"Oh, thank God." He leaned his forehead against the door.

"Ted?"

He lifted his head. "Yeah, I'm here. Can you get to the door?"

"I'm trying to, but...*ow!*"

"Ow?" he yelled. "Why ow?" What happened? Are you hurt?"

He heard the faint sound of the safety chain rattling, then the lock being unsnapped. The door was opened slowly, no more than three inches. Ted raised the flashlight and saw Hannah's tilted head, giving him a rather lopsided view of her eyes.

"Let me in," he said.

"Lower the flashlight."

"What?"

"Ted, I'd just gotten out of the shower when the lights went out. I'm wrapped in a towel. I made my way to the linen cupboard where I'd put the flashlight, but the batteries were dead.''

''Oh.''

''I have candles in the kitchen drawer, but I've stubbed my toe twice already trying to get there. I'd really appreciate your finding my candles for me, but could you shine the light on the floor, please? I'm not exactly dressed to receive company.''

''Oh. Sure.''

Ted did as instructed with the beam of light as he entered the apartment, deciding absently that Hannah had cute toes as he directed the light on her feet.

She closed the door and locked it.

''I'm so glad you're here,'' she said, her voice trembling slightly. ''Thank you for thinking of me. I'm being childish, I know, but it was so dark and I was bumping into things and...''

''Ah, Hannah,'' he said. ''I was so damn worried about you.''

Before he realized he was moving, Ted wrapped his arms around Hannah and pulled her close, feeling the damp towel and the slope of her stomach. The beam of light was directed toward the ceiling.

Hannah encircled his waist with her arms and leaned her head on his chest, the towel tucked into itself between her breasts.

Ted inhaled her aroma of flowers and soap, savoring it. He was acutely aware of her breasts pressing against his chest and felt a hot surge of heat low in his body.

Hannah's protruding stomach, with her baby was safely nestled inside, was, to his startled amazement, extremely sensuous. She was the epitome of womanliness, of femininity.

Ah, Hannah, his mind hummed. She was safe, nothing had happened to her, she was all right. Ted was holding her fast and wasn't going to let her go. He would protect her from harm. She was so fragile, delicate and vulnerable…and so was her precious baby. And the part of Hannah that was pure woman was sending Ted up in flames of desire.

Hannah closed her eyes, relishing the strength of Ted's powerful body. He was so strong, so masculine, so…so there.

She'd been frightened, afraid she'd fall over a piece of furniture and hurt the baby. Icy fear had clutched her heart, causing unshed tears to sting her eyes and close her throat. She'd been so alone in the dark, so terribly alone.

But now Ted was here.

For this stolen moment out of time, she was going to allow herself the luxury of leaning on him, of gathering inner fortitude from a source other than herself.

During the weeks, months, years ahead, there would be no one there for her to turn to. She'd raise her child to the best of her ability, cope with crises as they came, greet each new day with the daffodils-and-daisies outlook taught to her by her beloved gran.

But now, right now, Hannah was so very tired, both physically and emotionally. The fright she'd experienced in the suddenly dark apartment had drained her.

But Ted was here, holding her in an embrace that was like a cocoon; a comforting warmth like a soft blanket. She was safe. Ted represented a solid shield between her and the reality of her life.

It felt so good, so right…just for a moment.

Hannah sighed and Ted's arms tightened around her slightly. She pressed more firmly against him, filling the essence of herself with his strength that seemed to flow into her, giving her what she so desperately needed to carry on, to stand alone.

But then…slowly, slowly something began to stir deep within her. A tiny whisper of heat, like a glowing ember, was burning brighter, hotter, causing passion to heighten and thrum through her.

Hannah was so incredibly *aware* of her own body and the exquisite feel of it being molded to Ted's. Her breasts were crushed to the hard wall of his chest, yet the pain was sweet, an affirmation of her femininity compared to his rugged masculinity. The baby inside her was not a barrier between her and Ted, it was a precious connection, touching them both, its very existence meshing them into one entity.

Oh, dear heaven, Hannah thought, she was awash with desire, wanting Ted.

Hannah, don't, her mind yelled. This was wrong, terribly wrong. She had to move away from Ted, borrow the flashlight so she could get to the bedroom and put on some clothes. She had to regain her sense of reason, her sense of self. *Now.*

Hannah shifted and tilted her head back to look up at Ted. The shadowy luminescence of the flashlight made it possible for her to see him, not clearly, but enough to be able to meet his gaze.

"Ted, I..." She stopped speaking, hating the thread of desire-induced breathlessness in her voice.

"Hannah."

That was all he said, just her name, spoken in a voice gritty with smoldering passion.

Hannah's breath caught and rational thought fled into oblivion.

Ah, Hannah, Ted's hazy mind echoed.

Then he lowered his head and kissed her.

Chapter Five

The kiss was soft and gentle, tentative at first. But then it deepened, becoming intense and urgent as the licking flames of desire within Hannah and Ted leaped higher, consuming them.

The flashlight slipped from Ted's hand to land with a quiet thud on the carpet. The light created a glowing circle around them. It was as though nothing existed beyond that sphere. They were in a place that was meant only for them, and passions soared.

Ted drank of the taste of Hannah, his tongue delving into her mouth to seek and find her tongue. His arousal was heavy, aching with the want of her as his hands roamed over the damp towel, then up to the velvet softness of her dewy skin. His heart thundered and a groan rumbled deep in his chest.

Hannah returned the kiss in total abandon, filling

her senses with the taste, the aroma, the feel of Ted. She splayed her hands on his back, relishing the taut muscles that bunched and moved beneath her palms.

She felt alive, so incredibly alive, and inwardly rejoiced in her own womanliness that was a counterpart to Ted's wondrous masculinity.

Ted lifted his head to draw a rough breath, then slanted his mouth in the other direction, capturing Hannah's lips once again.

Hannah, his mind hummed. *Hannah.* He wanted her with a raging need far greater than anything he'd experienced before. Emotions of protectiveness and possessiveness slammed against his mind, intertwining with heated desire.

He felt as though he'd been lifted up and away from the world as he knew it, and transported into a hazy mist that belonged to him and to Hannah, with no one else allowed to intrude.

It was magical.

It was theirs.

Again Ted raised his head a fraction of an inch, speaking close to her lips.

"Hannah," he said, his voice raspy, "I want you. Hannah?"

"Yes," she whispered. "Oh, yes. I want you too, Ted. I've never felt so…"

Suddenly, the baby shifted, rolled, then delivered a swift kick. Hannah blinked as she was jarringly returned to reality. She stiffened in Ted's arms.

"Dear heaven," Hannah said. "What am I doing?"

"Kissing me, wanting me," he said. "I want to make love with you, Hannah."

She wiggled out of his arms, clutching the towel with both hands where it was tucked between her breasts.

"No, no," she said, shaking her head. "I can't do this." She took another step backward. "I'm sorry if I led you to believe that I... Oh, my God, I can imagine what you must think of me."

"I think," he said quietly, willing his body back under control, "that you're a very desirable woman who isn't afraid to acknowledge her own sexuality. I think, I know, you want me as much as I want you. There's nothing wrong with that, Hannah. We're adults, free to make our own choices."

"This adult," she said, her voice rising, "is pregnant, in case you didn't notice."

"We wouldn't hurt the baby. I asked Ryan about that when Deedee was pregnant. I just wondered, you know, so I asked him."

"That's not the point. What kind of person leaps into a man's arms when she's pregnant with another man's child? I'm...I'm a wanton woman."

Ted chuckled, then dragged a restless hand through his hair.

"No, you're not," he said, smiling. "Wanton woman? I can't believe you actually said that. Look, you're a normal, healthy woman in touch with herself, with her wants and needs. There's nothing to get upset about."

"Oh, ha! I'm standing here in nothing more than a skimpy towel, pregnant as a volleyball, to quote your eloquent description, flinging myself at a man I hardly know. That, Mr. Sharpe, is disgusting.''

"No. It's delightful, real and right, Ms. Doodle."

"Oh-h-h, there's no talking to you." She leaned down and picked up the flashlight. "I'm going to get dressed. Then I'll find my candles, give you back your flashlight and see you out. I'd appreciate it if you'd forget that this incident took place."

"Can't."

"Why not?"

Ted shrugged. "It's imprinted on my brain with indelible memory ink. Besides, why would I want to forget it? Kissing you was fantastic, Hannah Johnson. I may have to go home and stand under a cold shower for an hour, but it'll be worth it. Oh, yes ma'am, holding you, kissing you, your kissing me, was sensational, really something.''

"Oh, well, fancy that." Hannah smiled, but in the next second frowned. "No, no, no. I don't want to discuss this. *I'm* going to forget it happened."

She moved past him and started toward the bedroom, shining the flashlight ahead of her.

"Hannah."

She stopped, her back to Ted.

"What?" she said, a sharp edge to her voice.

"It won't work, you know. Kisses like the ones we shared can't be dusted off that easily. Give it your best shot if it will make you feel better, but you're wasting your time. You *will* remember, Hannah."

"Shut up, Sharpe."

Hannah marched from the room to the accompaniment of Ted's soft laughter.

He watched the light disappear, then turned, making his way carefully to the kitchen in search of the candles. He found a drawer, opened it and rummaged around in the dark hole. His fingers closed around two taper candles. Further exploring produced two square, wooden holders and a book of matches.

After lighting one of the candles, he returned to the living room, sat down on the sofa, lit the other candle and placed both lighted candles on the coffee table.

Daisy appeared out of nowhere and crawled up onto the sofa.

"Hi, Daisy," Ted said, patting the kitten on the head. "How's life?"

He sank back against the puffy cushions.

Life? he thought. Life was strange, very weird. If someone would have told him that he'd soon be kissing a volleyball-size pregnant woman in a room with no electricity because of a storm, he'd have told that idiot to give it up and ship himself to the farm.

But not only was that insane statement true, it went further than that. Kissing said person had been, without a doubt, dynamite. Man, oh, man, he'd been on fire. He had wanted Hannah so badly he ached.

And the maze of emotions? They'd been tumbling through his mind so fast, he couldn't even decipher all of them. *That* had never happened to him before. *But* he'd never spent time with a woman like Ms. Doodle before, either.

She was very, very different from the women he associated with.

"No joke, fool," he muttered. "She's pregnant. That is definitely different."

Ted frowned and shook his head.

No, that wasn't it...the fact that Hannah was pregnant. There was no ignoring that she was going to have a baby, but it wasn't a turnoff, not by a long shot. It made her seem very feminine, womanly, very appealing. And it caused him to feel extremely masculine and protective, like a knight prepared to slay the dragon.

As for the man who had fathered her child? Forget him, Ted cautioned, he was worthless. The baby is Hannah's, pure and simple.

Hannah...a charming combination of stand-on-her-own-two-feet strength and independence, and needing-protection-vulnerability. She'd looked him square in the eye and told him he was a rude, unpleasant man, then she'd wept at the sight of a furry little kitten.

There was a childlike innocence about her at times, yet when she allowed her sexuality to surface, she was one-hundred-percent woman.

Oh, Ted decided, she was something, all right, Ms. Hannah Johnson. That was firmly established, a given. The question that was driving him nuts was why he, Theodore Sharpe, was attracted to her? She wasn't even remotely close to being his type.

"I'm losing it, Daisy," he said to the kitten. "My mid-life crisis is scrambling my gray matter. Sad, huh? Yeah, I knew you'd agree with me."

The flashlight beam shone across the floor as Hannah returned to the living room. She came to the sofa, turned off the light and extended the flashlight to Ted.

He took it without really looking at it, his gaze riveted on Hannah.

She was wearing a rose-colored, velour robe that fell to the floor in soft folds and had long, full sleeves. It zipped up the front, in one long enticing line that caused Ted's fingertips to tingle at the thought of slowly, so very slowly, inching that zipper downward.

The candlelight cast a glow over her, and once again she looked like a lovely cameo, delicate and beautiful beyond measure.

Oh, man, how he wanted this woman, Ted thought.

"Thank you for coming here, Ted," Hannah said quietly. "I appreciate your concern. It was very... neighborly of you."

Ted patted the sofa cushion next to him.

"Sit down, Hannah," he said. "Please?"

"No."

He frowned. "Hey, I'm not going to seduce you, for Pete's sake. I just want to talk to you for a minute or two."

"Two. Maximum."

She sat down on the far end of the sofa and smoothed the robe over her stomach before turning to look at Ted.

What candlelight did for Ted Sharpe's rugged features and sun-streaked hair, she thought, was sinful. It should be declared against the law and he should arrest himself.

Ted, Hannah thought. She'd lectured herself firmly and at great length while she was in the bedroom. What had happened with Ted, those exquisite kisses shared with Ted, the intense desire she'd felt for Ted, the burning want and need, were now erased from her memory bank.

Well, that was stretching the truth a tad. She *would* forget what had transpired once Ted left the apartment and she was alone. The mere presence of the man was enough to cause the desire still simmering within her to be fanned hotter and hotter.

"Two minutes, remember?" she said.

Ted scooted closer to her, nearly squashing Daisy in the process. The kitten jumped to the floor and dashed away.

"I can hear you from the other end of the sofa, Ted," Hannah said, lifting her chin.

"It's my two minutes. You didn't put any distance restrictions on it."

"Mmm."

He slid one arm across the top of the sofa behind her, being careful not to touch her, then shifted slightly to look directly at her.

"Hannah," he said, "what happened here tonight wasn't wrong. It wasn't something to regret. It was honest and real, and equally shared. There was nothing 'wanton,' to use your quaint word, about it. I really hate knowing you're upset over it."

Hannah sighed. "Yes, all right, I'll admit I was being rather dramatic with my 'wanton woman' spiel. And, yes, I'll take responsibility for my half of it. The thing is, Ted, that nothing like that neither should, nor will, happen again."

"Why not?"

"Because I'm not free to engage in…to allow myself to…you know what I mean."

"You're free. You're divorced. You're a single woman. If you're referring to being pregnant, you're off base. That baby is a part of you, a lovely part."

She smiled slightly. "Cute as a volleyball."

"You're the cutest volleyball I've ever seen."

"Ted, listen to me," she said, her smile gone. "I'm not *emotionally* free."

"You're still in love with and loyal to your ex-husband?"

"No, no, no. You see, he wasn't who I thought he was or who I believed him to be. When I told him I was pregnant, his true colors came to light. I had to choose, he said, between him and the baby because he wanted no part of raising a child. I went to Nevada and obtained a quick and quiet divorce."

Ted muttered a very earthy expletive.

"I'm obviously not capable of seeing a man as he truly is. I buy into the facade, trust far too easily. It's a flaw, a major flaw of mine. That's what I mean when I say I'm not emotionally free. I'm held captive by my inability to tell the good guys from the bad."

"Based on one mistake? Hannah, come on, that's not fair."

"No, not *one*. I dated a boy in high school for two years. He said he loved me, respected me, the whole nine yards. It turned out he was telling his friends that we had sex all the time. It wasn't true. He wasn't who I believed him to be."

"He was a kid."

"He was my choice. The first year of college, I went out with a football player. Guess what? He had a pregnant wife back in Oklahoma. Then a year or so later, I met the man I married. His name is Maxwell. He was ten years older than me, had a thriving insurance company and said he'd postponed marriage until he was financially stable.''

"Maxwell? Anyone with a name like that is definitely a dud. Did he use 'Max'?''

"No. Maxwell, always Maxwell.''

"A dud.''

"He was wonderful...I thought. He was mature and considerate, took me to nice places, treated me like I was so special. He had a house that he said would never be a real home until I married him and lived there.''

"And you did.''

"Yes. I was so happy. Everything was glorious until I discovered I was pregnant. Then the real Maxwell surfaced and I had to face my flaw again. I had made a horrible mistake...trusted and believed in the wrong man...again. I will not *ever* put myself in that position in the future...waiting, waiting, waiting, to find out who a man proves to *really* be.''

"Whew,'' Ted said. "I'm sorry you've had so much heartache, Hannah, I truly am. But you're giving the whole male populace a bum rap. Some of us are the real goods, you know.''

"Oh, yes, of course I know that, but *I* can't decipher one from the next. I just don't know how. I refuse to run the risk of attempting to unravel that puzzle again.''

"Hannah, I'm a nice guy!'' Ted said, nearly yelling.

"Maybe.'' She shrugged. "Maybe not. *I* don't intend to find out.'' She folded her hands on top of her protruding stomach and smiled at him pleasantly. ''Well, there you have it, neat and tidy, the story of my life.''

Ted leaned toward her. ''How can you be so calm? You recited all that like someone reading off their grocery list.''

''Because I'm tired of crying, Ted,'' she said, serious again. ''Entering into a relationship with a man is guaranteed heartbreak for me. I've accepted that. As the psychologists say, 'I own it.' Since I've acknowledged it, I can forgive myself for my glitch.''

She pointed one finger in the air.

''However,'' she went on, ''having faced the situation as it stands, I can no longer make excuses or place the blame on anyone but myself. I must proceed with at least a modicum of maturity and realize that a serious relationship is not territory in which I am equipped to travel. So I won't. Not ever.''

She nodded decisively and patted her stomach.

''My baby and I will do just fine together. We'll be Mommy, Baby and Daisy. How's that?''

''It stinks,'' Ted said, frowning.

''It certainly does not. We'll be The Terrific Trio. That title is in capital letters.'' She paused. ''I took a cash settlement at the time of my divorce, having decided I wished to have no part of monthly child-support payments from a man who wanted nothing to do with the child.

''Maxwell signed papers saying he would make no claim on this baby, nor attempt to see it or interact with it in the future. One of my friends told me that he's already engaged to a nineteen-year-old girl who wants to be an actress.''

''Dandy,'' Ted said, rolling his eyes heavenward.

''So, if I live on a tight budget and give private piano lessons, which I'm doing, I should be all right during this year off from teaching. I'm trying to have my students practice quietly when they're here so they won't disturb you, especially if they're playing 'Yankee Doodle.'''

''Oh, man,'' Ted said, getting to his feet. He started forward, immediately whacking his shin on the edge of the coffee table. ''Ow! Damn it, that hurt.''

He moved around the table and began to pace the floor in front of the table, back and forth, back and forth.

Hannah watched him, feeling as though she were at a tennis match.

''Not good,'' Ted said, continuing his trek. ''This is not good at all. You're too young to have set a program into place for the rest of your life, especially one this drastic, restricting, narrow.''

''Realistic,'' Hannah added.

Ted stopped, planted his hands on his hips and glared at her. ''Try this on for size, Ms. Doodle. Are you going to raise your child with this crummy philosophy? Teach him, or her, not to trust their own judgment when picking their life's partner?''

''Of course not. This isn't a genetic flaw, for crying out loud. It's mine alone and has nothing to do with the baby. I know my personal limitations and will conduct myself accordingly in the future.''

''You're so wrong, it's a crime.''

"So arrest me, Officer Sharpe."

"Don't tempt me. If I thought it might make you come to your senses, I'd toss you in the clink."

"That," Hannah said, laughing, "was funny."

Before Ted could retort, the lights flickered, went out, then came on full force. Hannah blinked against the sudden brightness, then leaned forward and blew out the candles.

Daisy bounded into the room, crawled up the arm of the sofa, perched there and began to methodically wash a paw.

"Let there be light," Hannah said, flinging out her arms. "End of crisis."

"Not even close. *You* are a walking, talking crisis. Hannah, what about the daffodils-and-daisies theory your gran taught you?"

"Oh, how sweet of you to remember my telling you that. Thank you."

"You're welcome. Answer the question."

"It's perfectly clear, Ted. In order to have sunny tomorrows with daffodils and daisies, I must steer clear of what I know to be a danger zone. That is just plain, old-fashioned common sense. I'm implementing Gran's theory extremely well."

"You're an exasperating woman at times, do you know that? My mid-life crisis is tough enough to handle without having to deal with this cockeyed program of yours."

Hannah's eyes widened. "My stars, you're having a mid-life crisis? Aren't you rather young for that?"

"At thirty-four? Yeah, I think I am, but there's no other explanation for the way I've been feeling."

"Such as?"

"Restless, edgy, wired. My leisure time is the pits all of a sudden, and I—" He stopped speaking and sliced one hand through the air. "Cut. You're tricky, Ms. Doodle, very clever, but it didn't work. We're discussing you here, not me."

"Actually, this discussion is finished because I'm exhausted and I'm going to bed." She got to her feet. "I want to thank you again for coming over when the electricity went out. It was very kind and thoughtful of you. I'll buy some batteries for my flashlight so I'll be properly prepared in the future."

"Well, keep my flashlight in the meantime. I have another one." He started toward the door. "I'll get out of here and let you get some sleep."

Hannah followed him to the door. Ted opened it, then turned to look at her.

"And the discussion is *not* finished." He brushed a kiss over her lips. "Good night, Hannah."

"Good night, Ted," she said softly.

He left the apartment and Hannah locked the door behind him. She stood statue-still for a moment, the fingertips of one hand floating upward to rest on her lips.

"Forget it," she said aloud. "Come on, Daisy. It's time for bed."

The next evening, Ted, Deedee and Ryan sat at a round table on the MacAllisters' deck, enjoying dinner.

Teddy was already in bed for the night, having refused to take an afternoon nap. The tired baby had been more than ready to be tucked into his crib shortly after Ted had arrived.

Scooter the beagle was planted firmly across Ryan's feet.

"Why does she do that?" Ryan said, peering under the table. "Every time I sit down, she flops onto my feet. When I move or get up, she's disturbed, then does it all over again."

"Maybe she has a foot fetish," Ted said.

"Only for Ryan's feet," Deedee said, laughing. "She doesn't do it to anyone else."

"Lucky me," Ryan said dryly. "I can't tell you how thrilled I am."

"Have some more pizza, honey," Deedee said. "Just pretend she's not there." She reached for a slice for herself. "Super-Duper Pizza Supreme Deluxe Extraordinaire. Mmm, delicious. I'm so glad Jillian introduced us to this delight from Mario's. It was awfully nice of you to bring it, Ted."

"It's a bribe," he said, taking another slice. "I need the two of you to give me some advice."

"Really?" Ryan said. "We were together the entire day, Sharpe, and you didn't tap into my genius-level brain."

"Because," he said, glaring at Ryan, "you're not a woman."

"He certainly isn't," Deedee said, batting her eyelashes at her husband. "And I can't begin to tell you how pleased I am about that fact."

"Could we get serious here, people?" Ted said.

"I told you he was hard to live with, Deedee," Ryan said. "I may have to shoot him to put him out of his mid-life-crisis misery and save my own sanity."

"Hush, Ryan," she said. "Ted is, even as we speak, contemplating punching you in the nose."

"Oh. Okay, Theodore, you have the floor."

"I don't want to talk about my mid-life crisis," Ted said, frowning. "The subject matter is Hannah."

"Ms. Doodle?" Deedee said.

"Yeah. Now then, listen up."

Ted related the conversation he'd had with Hannah the previous evening, omitting the fact that he'd kissed her. He also failed to mention that he'd spent the night tossing and turning, due to his body aching with desire.

"Goodness," Deedee said when Ted stopped speaking. "Let me sum this up, to be certain I understand it all correctly."

"Whatever," Ted muttered.

"Hannah Johnson," Deedee said, staring into space, "believes she is unable to properly perceive the true nature of a man. Her choices in the past have been wrong, because the men were never who she believed them to be."

Ted nodded. "Yup."

"Therefore," Deedee went on, "she's determined to never again become seriously involved with a man. She's very calm about her conclusion, has moved past the pain of being hurt time and again and now presents the philosophy for her entire future as calmly as she might report on the weather. Right?"

"That's it in a nutshell," Ted said.

"Okay," Ryan said. "But what are we supposed to give you advice about?"

"You're so dense, MacAllister," Ted said. "Read my lips. How do I convince Hannah that she's making a terrible mistake? She's sentencing herself to a life alone for no reason. So, yeah, she picked some duds, including her husband, but there *are* nice guys in this world."

"Like you?" Deedee said.

"No, Deedee, not like me." Ted paused. "I mean, I consider myself a nice guy, but that's beside the point. I'm not attempting to get her to trust and believe in *me*, or have a relationship with *me*. I just think I should convince her to chuck her lousy philosophy, and keep an open mind about men in general, so she doesn't miss out on the happiness she deserves to have."

"Oh-h-h, I see," Deedee said. "That makes sense."

"It does?" Ryan said.

Deedee patted his hand. "Trust me. It does."

"Why do you consider this *your* mission to undertake?" Ryan asked Ted.

"Because I'm a nice guy, remember?" he said, nearly shouting.

"Stay calm, gentlemen," Deedee said. "Ted, I'm very impressed by your noble intentions."

"Oh, brother," Ryan said, rolling his eyes heavenward.

"Hush, Ryan," Deedee said. "Ted, the first order of business is for us to meet Hannah. It's extremely difficult to give you advice about a person we know in name only. Why don't the four of us go out to dinner Saturday night? We'll pick a place that isn't too fancy, but quiet enough to chat easily.''

''What am I supposed to say to her?'' Ted said. '''Hey, Hannah, want to go out to dinner so Deedee...forget about Ryan being any help...can gather data on you, and formulate a plan I can use to straighten out your wacko thinking?' Give me a break.''

''No, idiot,'' Ryan said. ''You say that as her friendly neighbor it has occurred to you that you know some terrific people she might like to meet, so how about going out to dinner with you and them?''

''Ryan MacAllister,'' Deedee said, ''that's marvelous.'' She narrowed her eyes. ''When did you become such a slick operator?''

He grinned at her. ''I have hidden talents.''

''Mmm,'' she said, raising one eyebrow.

''Well,'' Ted said, ''I could try that approach, I guess. I'll let you know how it goes.'' He looked at Ryan. ''Terrific people?''

''Terrific,'' Ryan repeated decisively, then his eyes widened. ''Oh, hell.''

''What's wrong?'' Deedee said.

''Scooter just wet on my shoes!''

Deedee and Ted dissolved in laughter.

After Ted left, Deedee and Ryan remained on the deck, watching the stars appear like sparkling diamonds on black velvet.

''Hannah Johnson,'' Deedee said finally, breaking the comfortable silence.

"I told you Ted was acting weird. Some people get hooked on saving the whales. Sharpe is determined to save Ms. Doodle...from herself."

"Tsk, tsk," Deedee said. "You didn't see the forest for the tree in front of your nose."

"Huh?"

"Honey, remember when I said that Ted was attracted to Hannah? What he doesn't realize yet is that he's on this campaign *for himself*. He wants to change Hannah's philosophy so she'll give *him* a chance to be an important part of her life."

"He does?"

"Yes, my sweet, he most certainly does."

"Well," Hannah said, "I don't know, Ted."

"Hey, Deedee and Ryan are *terrific* people," Ted assured her. "Wouldn't you like to make some new friends?"

"They're the ones who are parents to your godson, Teddy?"

"Yes."

"That would be nice. You know...to talk to the mother of a baby. My teacher friends don't have any children."

"It's settled then. We'll all go out to dinner Saturday night to a casual but quiet restaurant. I'll pick you up at seven o'clock."

Chapter Six

On Saturday evening, Hannah sat at the piano playing *Claire de Lune,* willing the lovely melody to soothe her jangled nerves.

She did *not* want to go to dinner with Ted and his *terrific* friends. Why she had accepted the invitation, she had no idea.

She was going to feel like a bug under a microscope the entire evening, she just knew it.

Ted Sharpe, Mr. Swinging Bachelor of the Decade, was going to parade a pregnant, divorced woman in front of Deedee and Ryan MacAllister, instantly evoking their curiosity about her personal circumstances, *and* bringing to the front of their minds the question of what on earth a man like Ted was doing with the likes of her.

So, yes, all right, Ted's intentions had been admirable. He seemed very sincere about the conclusion he'd drawn that she might like to make new friends. The fact that Deedee and Ryan were parents of a baby held appeal, and she'd agreed to the proposal before thoroughly thinking it through.

She hadn't had one glimpse of Ted since he'd shown up at her door to present the plans for Saturday night.

On two occasions, she'd stood in the hallway fully prepared to march to his apartment and inform him that she'd changed her mind about the dinner date.

Both times, she'd decided she would sound like a childish idiot, and had rushed back into the safe haven of her living room.

Dinner date, her mind echoed. Dinner *date?* No, no, no, this was *not* a date in the usual sense of the word. She didn't have a *date* with Ted, swinging single that he was. That thought was really absurd. She didn't go out with men like him, whether she was pregnant or not.

No, this wasn't a date. It was a...

"Well, drat," she said, increasing the volume of her playing, "I don't know what this thing is, but I don't want to go."

Daisy managed to climb up one of the legs of the piano bench, then sat next to Hannah, giving the impression she'd arrived for the sole purpose of listening to the music.

Hannah smiled at the kitten, then continued to play, her fingers flying over the keys, pounding out *Claire de Lune* louder and louder.

* * *

A grin broke across Ted's face as he stood in front of the bathroom mirror to comb his hair.

Claire de Lune, he thought, was being played on the piano by Ms. Doodle at a volume that was probably being heard by the occupants of the apartment on the other side of her, as well as by those on the floor above and below.

Hannah certainly was an accomplished pianist, and the song was hauntingly beautiful. That, however, was beside the point. What *was* being telegraphed was the fact that Hannah was stressed, nervous about the evening ahead.

Ted nodded at his reflection, a smug expression on his face.

He'd known, just somehow known, that Hannah would get cold feet about the dinner date with him, Deedee and Ryan. He'd very carefully kept out of sight since issuing the invitation so she'd have no opportunity to cancel.

Each time he arrived at the apartment complex, he'd checked to see if her car was in the parking lot. If it was, he used the back stairs, to be certain she couldn't corner him in the elevator. He'd peer down the hall, then hightail it to his own apartment.

To wiggle out of going to dinner, Hannah would be forced to knock on his door, then present whatever lame excuse she'd manufactured. She might have considered doing exactly that, but he'd figured—and had been right—that she wouldn't have the courage to do it.

"You clever son-of-a-gun," he said to his image.

Ted left the bathroom, then shrugged into a gray

sport coat that he wore over black trousers and a pale
blue dress shirt open at the neck.

Without realizing he was doing it, he began to hum
along with the music still reverberating through the
wall. He shot the cuff of his shirt to check his watch,
and realized he was ready to go far too early.

Wandering around the living room, he continued to
hum as he straightened some magazines on the coffee
table, then scooped a pile of junk mail off the sofa
and dumped it in the trash.

In the kitchen, he put three glasses and two coffee
mugs in the dishwasher, then wiped a blob of catsup
off the counter.

As he surveyed the area for anything else needing
his attention, he suddenly frowned.

Why was he spit-shining his apartment? He was
admittedly a bit of a slob, and had never apologized
to anyone for that fact. So, why was he fussing over
a few dirty dishes and scattered mail?

It wasn't as though he was expecting company.
He'd collect and deposit Hannah at her own place.
She'd have no reason to be in *his*. Even if she *was*
going to come in, he'd never worried about appear-
ances when he'd brought other women in here.

Lord, was his mid-life crisis going to change him
into a neatnick? What a disconcerting thought.

"Forget it," he said, starting across the room.

He had a dinner date with a lovely lady and two
of his closest friends. Everyone would have a nice
time. Deedee would get to know Hannah, and therefore be able to give him advice on how to tackle Ms.
Doodle's ridiculous program for her future.

He left one lamp on, turned off another, went to the door and grabbed the knob.

Dinner date? he thought, not opening the door. As in, he had a *date* with Hannah Johnson to go out to dinner? Well, no, not really. Sort of. But not exactly. The evening ahead was set in motion so Deedee could accomplish a fact-finding mission regarding Hannah.

It wasn't a date, per se.

Well, yeah, okay, so he'd found himself looking forward to the event. Hell, he'd been in a better mood today than he'd enjoyed in quite a while.

Fine, that made sense. Hannah was an attractive, nice-to-be-with woman. Why shouldn't he be anticipating the pleasure of her company? Not, of course, that this was officially a date.

"Sharpe," he said aloud, shaking his head in self-disgust, "get out of here before you think yourself to death."

When Ted knocked on Hannah's door, the lilting music within the apartment stopped abruptly. A few moments later, Hannah opened the door.

"Hello, Ted," she said, not smiling. She stepped backward, her hand on the doorknob. "Come in."

Ted didn't move. When a sharp pain radiated across his chest, he realized he was also not breathing and attempted to unobtrusively draw much-needed air into his lungs.

Oh, Lord, his mind hammered, Hannah was a vision of loveliness. She was just so...so beautiful.

His gaze swept over her, missing no detail of her silky dark hair, those incredible big dark eyes, the white velvet texture of her skin. And her lips, those kissable lips, that were beckoning to him.

She was wearing a powder blue maternity dress with a gracefully draping bow tied at the neck and tiny pleats across the bodice. The slope of her stomach beneath the soft material was sensuously feminine. Her medium-heel navy blue pumps accentuated her shapely calves and slender ankles.

Hannah cocked her head slightly to one side, causing her hair to swing in an enticing dark curtain around her face. She looked at him questioningly.

"Ted?" she said. "Is something wrong?"

He blinked. "What? Oh!"

He stepped into the room and Hannah shut the door as he turned to face her, his heart thundering.

Then Hannah smiled.

"Oh, hell," he said, dropping his chin to his chest. He raised his head again and closed the distance between them. Framing her face in his hands, he lowered his head and kissed her.

Hannah's smothered gasp of surprise instantly changed into a purr of pleasure as she parted her lips to receive Ted's tongue. Her hands floated upward to encircle his neck as he wrapped his arms around her. The kiss deepened and passions soared.

It had been an eternity since he'd kissed Hannah, Ted thought hazily. A lifetime. Forever. He *needed* this kiss with an intensity beyond description. It was filling him with a warmth separate and apart from the heated desire coiling in his body.

Hannah, his mind hummed. *Yes.*

Hannah inched her fingertips into Ted's thick hair,

urging his mouth harder onto hers, savoring his taste, aroma, the ecstasy of his tongue dueling with hers.

A part of her knew that kissing Ted was wrong. It was what she had pledged *not* to do ever again. But the other section of herself didn't care. The kiss was heavenly, and she wanted it to go on and on.

Ted lifted his head, drew a ragged breath, then shifted his hands to Hannah's shoulders, easing her away from his throbbing, aching body.

"Hannah," he said, then cleared his throat as he heard the gritty quality of his voice.

"Hmm?" she said dreamily, then ordered herself to pay attention to what Ted was saying. "Yes?"

"Don't go nuts because of that kiss. Okay? You know, don't whip your that-shouldn't-have-happened spiel on me, because it was a perfectly justifiable kiss."

"This ought to be good," she said, smiling. "All right, Ted, I'm all ears. Why was that a perfectly justifiable kiss?"

"Because, Ms. Doodle, it was a hello-Hannah-it's-good-to-see-you kiss. Neat and tidy. Get it?"

"You're so crazy." She laughed. "Okay, I won't go nuts. I'm glad to see you, too, Ted."

He matched her smile. "Well, good, that's great." He nodded. "Some things should be kept simple, uncomplicated. We wrapped that kiss in a nice little package and put a label on it. No problem."

"Whatever you say," she said, still smiling. "I can't always follow your out-of-left-field rationale, but I don't feel like arguing the point. I'll go get my purse and sweater."

"Wait a minute," he said, not releasing her. "First of all, I want to tell you how pretty you look. You're really lovely, Hannah."

"Oh, well, thank you. You look very spiffy yourself, Mr. Sharpe."

"Subject two." His smile faded. "Did you give a concert of *Claire de Lune* to the entire building because you get a rush from playing *Claire de Lune* at sonic-level volume, or was it therapy because you're stressed about the evening ahead?"

Hannah sighed. "I admit I'm nervous. I suddenly didn't know why on earth I'd agreed to this outing. I would have canceled, but you seemed to have disappeared for the past few days."

"I was around," he said. Man, he really was a clever son-of-a-gun. Creeping up the back stairs had been well worth the effort. "Look, there's nothing to be jittery about. You know me, and within ten minutes of meeting Deedee and Ryan, you'll feel as though you've known them for a long time. Trust me."

He grimaced.

"Erase that. Bad choice of words. So, okay, don't dwell on whether or not to trust me. Just keep an open mind and be receptive. Yes? Yes. Let's go."

Ted dropped his hands from her shoulders and glanced around the room.

"Hey, Daisy," he said. "There you are. Listen, kid, stay out of the refrigerator and don't watch any dirty flicks on the cable channels. Got that?"

Hannah laughed in delight at Ted's nonsense, then went to retrieve her purse and sweater.

As they left the apartment, she realized her jangled nerves were now calm, cool and collected, and she had a lovely sense of anticipation about the evening.

"Oh, my goodness," Hannah said. "I can't eat another bite. It was all so delicious, but I've definitely reached my limit."

"Waste not, want not," Ted said. He slid Hannah's plate in front of him and took a bite of the remainder of her cherry pie. "Mmm, not bad."

"When I was pregnant with Teddy," Deedee said, "I never seemed to fill up. I ate like a piggy the entire time. Jillian didn't have much of an appetite when she was carrying the triplets, though."

"She still ended up looking like a life raft," Ryan said.

Deedee rolled her eyes heavenward. "Don't you dare start *that* again. You're lucky you lived through your last crummy descriptions."

"Ah, yes," Hannah said, smiling. "I've been informed that I'm the size of a volleyball."

"You're hopeless, Ted," Deedee said.

"Why? Volleyballs are nice," he said, with a shrug. "I've never met a volleyball I didn't like. There's nothing insulting about being called a volleyball."

"We're ignoring you, Ted," Deedee said. "Hannah, have you started putting the baby's nursery together yet?"

"No, I need to explore the used-furniture stores. I'm hoping to find a crib, changing dresser, high chair, all of those sorts of things at reasonable prices.''

"That's a good idea," Deedee said, nodding.

"Do those places deliver?" Ted said.

"Oh," Hannah said, frowning, "I didn't think about that."

"No problem," Ted said. "My Blazer can carry a lot in the back. We'll load it up and bring it all home."

He glanced up quickly at Hannah, Deedee and Ryan, all of whom were staring at him.

"To *your* home, Hannah," he said. "Your apartment, the place where Daisy allows you to live with her."

"Thank you, Ted," she said quietly. "That's a very generous offer, and I appreciate it. I realize you're busy, so I'll see if I can make a deposit on what I find, then we'll go get it."

"Not good," he said, pushing the now-empty plate to one side. "You might not know what to look for as far as construction, sturdiness, that sort of thing. I'd better tag along when you're shopping."

"I can't ask you to—"

"Take him with you," Ryan said. "It'll keep him off the streets and out of the bars. Listen, Ted, have a measuring tape with you to check the distance between the rungs on the crib. Some of the old ones aren't up to code."

Ted nodded. "Got it."

"Ask about lead-free paint, too," Ryan said. "That's very important."

"Let's leave the baby-furniture experts to their

madness, Hannah,'' Deedee said. ''You and I are off to the powder room.''

''Why do they call it that?'' Ted said. ''I've never seen a woman trek in that direction with a big can of talcum powder.''

Deedee got to her feet. ''You are so strange, Ted Sharpe.''

''Well, I think about stuff like that. Powder room. Lord, that's dumb.''

Hannah laughed, then walked away with Deedee.

As Hannah and Deedee stood in front of the mirror in the powder room freshening their lipstick, Deedee suddenly laughed and shook her head.

''Darn that Ted,'' she said. ''From now on, every time I go into a ladies' room, I'm going to be watching to see if anyone uses powder, even if it's only on their nose.''

''I know what you mean,'' Hannah said, smiling. ''I don't think Ted's mind ever stops.'' She paused, meeting Deedee's gaze in the reflection of the mirror. ''Did you know that Ted bought me a darling kitten the day you got Teddy the puppy? Well, yes, I guess you were there when he found Daisy for me.''

''No, actually, we had already headed for home with our bouncing beagle. Ted told us about Daisy later. He also shared the story of why you named her that. Your gran sounds like she was wonderful, Hannah.''

''Yes. Yes, she was. And Daisy? She's so cute. She has really made my apartment seem more like a home, too. That probably doesn't make sense, but it's true. It was so thoughtful of Ted to get me a kitten."

"Ted Sharpe," Deedee said, nodding, "is a *very* nice man. You should see him with Teddy and the other MacAllister kids. He's a natural as a father. All the little guys absolutely adore him."

Hannah replaced the lipstick in her purse. "I can tell he's very fond of them, but he's made it clear that he's a Professional Uncle. That's in capital letters, I'll have you know. I'd say Ted is a confirmed bachelor."

"Oh, I don't know," Deedee said, snapping her purse closed. "Granted, he has industrial-strength sex appeal and women dissolve at his feet, but even the mighty tumble. He's just liable to go down for the count one of these days. You know, fall in love, get married, have a whole bushel of kids."

Hannah shrugged.

"Hannah Johnson," Deedee said, "that shrug spoke volumes. Don't you view Ted as an available man?"

"Well, yes, I suppose, but I'm not an available woman."

"Why not? Because you're expecting a baby?"

"There's that, plus the fact that I never intend to become seriously involved with a man again. Not ever."

"Oh, that's how you feel now," Deedee said breezily, while watching Hannah's face intently. "But we women are notorious for changing our minds."

"*I* won't. You see, Deedee, I lack the ability to determine whether a man is really who he presents himself to be. I have a track record of being very wrong.''

Deedee smiled brightly. ''But in Ted's case, you have reference letters, of a sort. I guarantee that he's really a good guy.''

''No, he's a good *friend* to you and Ryan, and a super uncle to Teddy and the other MacAllister children. You have no way of really knowing how he treats women on a man-to-woman plane.''

Deedee frowned. ''Oh.''

''And *I* don't intend to find out. Are you ready to go back to the table?''

''Wait, wait,'' Deedee said quickly. ''You *are* going to allow Ted to be your friend, aren't you? Help you shop for baby furniture and what have you?''

''Well,'' Hannah said thoughtfully, ''yes, I guess so. He *is* a good friend. Daisy is proof of that. Yes, I'd like Ted to be my friend.'' She walked toward the door.

''Well,'' Deedee mumbled, ''that's a start.''

The couples chatted comfortably over cups of coffee, then left the restaurant. In the parking lot, Deedee told Hannah she'd call soon so they could get together.

''Wonderful,'' Hannah said. ''I'm eager to meet Teddy.''

''And Scooter,'' Ryan said. ''You just haven't experienced life until you've had Scooter MacAllister bounce straight up in the air and lick your nose. Man, that is one weird dog.''

"Scooter is emotionally attached to Ryan's feet," Deedee said. "It's amazing."

"It's ridiculous," Ryan said.

"Scooter probably needs a dog shrink," Ted said. "You know, some guy to hold her paw and ask her how she got along with her mother."

"Oh, good grief," Hannah said, laughing.

Goodbyes were exchanged, and Ted was soon easing the Blazer out of the parking lot and into the busy traffic. He tuned the radio to an easy-listening station and soft, dreamy music filled the air.

A lovely sense of well-being floated over Hannah, causing a smile to form on her lips. With all the turmoil she'd endured in her life over the past months, she was acutely aware of how serene she felt, as though all was right with the world.

"Did you enjoy the evening?" Ted said.

"Oh, my, yes," she said. "It was lovely, absolutely perfect."

He nodded. "Good."

"I'm expressing my official thank-you, Ted, for tonight. I'll only say it once because you said I went nuts with all the thank-yous when you gave me Daisy. So...thank you."

"You're very welcome, Ms. Doodle. I had a great time myself and *I* thank *you* for that. I'm sure you could tell that Deedee and Ryan were more than pleased to meet and get to know you."

"They're marvelous." She paused. "No, the word you used was 'terrific,' and you were right. I'm so eager to see Teddy." She laughed. "And Scooter, the famous bouncing beagle."

"Okay, we'll make plans to go visit as soon as possible. We need to get shopping for baby furniture on the calendar, too."

"Yes."

We, we, we, Hannah's mind echoed. Ted said it so easily, so naturally, as though it was a given that they were a "we." It had a nice sound to it, made her feel warm inside.

There were times when the reality of her being alone caused a chill to sweep through her. It would sneak up on her when she least expected it, making the "alone" become "lonely."

We.

Such a small word, two letters, but it possessed remarkable powers for its size.

Tonight, just for tonight, she mused, she was going to keep and savor the soothing comfort of Ted's "we." The whole evening had been splendid, and she'd top it off with the warm fuzzy feeling his "we" evoked. There was no harm in indulging herself like this for a short time. It would be like having a snifter of rich brandy after a delicious meal.

With the dawn of tomorrow, she'd accept with a smile that her world comprised herself, the baby and Daisy. That was fine, the way it was. It would be a sunny daffodils-and-daisies day.

But tonight? Tonight, she was part of a "we."

At the apartment complex, Ted parked in his designated spot, then came around to assist Hannah from the vehicle. He encircled her shoulders with one arm, and she moved close to his side as they went into the building, then entered the elevator.

At her door, Ted extended his hand for her keys, which she placed in his palm.

"Coffee?" she said.

"Yes."

Daisy greeted them as Ted closed and locked the door behind them.

"Hi, Daisy," Hannah said, smiling. "Did you have a nice evening? Mine was marvelous."

"Yours," Ted said, "isn't quite over."

Hannah looked up at him and her breath caught as she saw the raw passion radiating from his blue eyes.

Oh, dear heaven, she thought frantically. There was no doubt whatsoever that Ted Sharpe wanted her, wanted to make love with her now, right now.

She had to move, run or shake his hand and say good-night. She had to do *something* to break the spell he was weaving over her with those mesmerizing eyes.

Ted lifted his hands and framed her face.

"We have to end this evening properly," he said, his voice low and husky. "We really do, Hannah."

We, her heart sang.

Ted lowered his head and captured her mouth.

And Hannah was lost in a sea of raging desire.

She parted her lips and met his tongue eagerly as her lashes drifted slowly down and her hands entwined his neck.

The kiss was ecstasy, heated and hungry, sensuous.

Sharpe, stop, Ted's mind hammered. He was losing control. He ached with the want of Hannah, was slipping past the point of reason, going right over the edge.

He tore his mouth from hers, forming the words *good night, Hannah* in his head, pulling them forward from the depths of the passion-laden haze that consumed him.

Say it, he mentally ordered himself. *Say, 'Good night, Hannah.'* "I want you, Hannah," he heard instead. "I want you so damn much."

Hannah opened her eyes slowly, and a soft, womanly smile formed on her moist lips.

"Yes," she whispered, "I know. I want you, too, Ted. We want each other, and it's right, it truly is, because...because it's *we.*"

Chapter Seven

A groan rumbled deep in Ted's chest as his mouth melted over Hannah's once again. He drank of her sweet taste, savoring it.

When he finally broke the kiss, she kept him close to her side as she led him down the hall to her bedroom. Hannah snapped on the small lamp on the nightstand, casting a rosy glow over the room, then brushed back the blankets on the bed. She straightened and looked at Ted.

Neither spoke, but words weren't needed.

It was as though they'd been transported to a magical world where thoughts were known, sent and received, understood.

There was an interwoven aura in the room of crackling sensuality, combined with the peaceful calmness of realizing that what they were about to share was so very right and real.

Ted drew Hannah into his arms and kissed her; gently, reverently, communicating the message that she was special, cherished.

She trembled.

He took a step backward and began to remove his clothes, dropping them unheeded to the floor. Hannah started to undress, placing the garments neatly on a chair by the nightstand.

Her back to Ted, Hannah suddenly stilled, her eyes skimming over her own naked body, seeing the heavy breasts, the protruding stomach where the baby was nestled. How would he view her swollen body? She reached out with a visibly shaking hand to retrieve her dress, to cover herself from Ted's scrutiny.

But Ted knew her thoughts as though she'd spoken aloud and he moved behind her and rested his hands on her shoulders. He dipped his head to bury his face in the silky cascade of her dark hair. Shifting his hands, he turned her toward him, slowly, so slowly, then looked directly into her eyes.

"Hannah," he said, "*we,* just like you said, *we* are the only ones in this world we're creating at this moment. Just the two of us."

"Yes," she whispered.

He smiled as he traced the shape of her lips with one fingertip, then dropped his gaze to her body, his smile changing to an expression of awe and wonder.

"Ah, Hannah," he said, his voice raspy. "You're so beautiful, so beautiful."

So beautiful, his mind echoed. She was woman personified. Femininity in its purest form. Within her was a miracle, a new life. She possessed the ability to nurture that baby, carry it safely until it was ready to meet the world. It was breathtaking. Wondrous.

Ted lifted one hand, then tentatively splayed it across her rounded stomach.

He met her gaze again and Hannah smiled at him warmly, her flicker of fear now forgotten.

She felt...beautiful, she realized, so incredibly feminine. She was woman. And Ted was the epitome of man. It was so simplistic, yet held the complexity of a wonderful mystery never to be solved.

Her eyes roamed boldly over his naked body, savoring the sight of his broad shoulders and chest, his flat belly and powerful legs, his arousal that announced his want of her, the blatant desire that *she* had evoked.

She inched her fingertips into the moist curls on his chest, relishing the feel of them and the taut muscles beneath.

Ted leaned toward her to kiss her and she parted her lips to receive his questing tongue. Moments later, he ended the kiss, lifted her into his arms, then laid her gently in the center of the bed. He stretched out next to her, resting on one forearm.

"You're exquisite," he said, his voice rough with passion. "I want you, Hannah, but it's more than that. This..." His gaze swept over her, then back to her eyes. "This is a miracle you're sharing with me, and I'm honored, I truly am."

"Oh, Ted," she said, unexpected tears misting her eyes. "What a lovely thing to say. Thank you."

"No, *I'm* thanking *you.*"

They touched, caressed, explored. Lips followed where hands had gone, glorying in each new discovery. Passions soared until their breathing was labored and hearts beat wildly.

Finally, *finally,* Ted moved over her, keeping his weight from her on straightened arms as he entered her. He watched her face for any sign that he was hurting her, but saw only want and need as raw and earthy as his own.

"Yes," Hannah whispered. "Oh, Ted, yes."

He started to move, slowly at first, then with increasing tempo. She matched him, meeting him, welcoming him, as she clutched his shoulders.

Tension began to build within them tighter, hotter, coiling in spiraling currents. Lifting them up and away from reality.

Higher.

Soaring.

"Ted!"

Hannah was flung far, far beyond anything she had ever known before to a wondrous place of sparkling colors and intense physical sensations that defied description.

Ted joined her there a heartbeat later. Throwing back his head, a groan of pure male pleasure rumbled from his throat as he found his release.

They stilled, hovering for a second, for eternity. Memorizing the moment, etching it indelibly in their hearts and minds; their very souls.

Then Ted shifted off of Hannah and collapsed next to her, spent, sated, staying close to her side.

And neither spoke, because no words were needed.

Ted reached for the blankets and covered them as their bodies cooled. He kissed Hannah on the temple, then snapped off the lamp.

"Go to sleep, Ms. Doodle," he said quietly.

"Yes," she said, snuggling closer to him.

As Hannah drifted into blissful slumber, Ted placed one hand on her stomach in a protective gesture. He looked at Hannah's peaceful face again, then back at his hand.

A strange tightness gripped his throat and his eyes burned with what he realized were unshed tears. Emotions tumbled through him in a maze, too many and too foreign to decipher.

He closed his eyes, took a deep, ragged breath, then gave way to the somnolence that claimed him.

Ted was pulled from the depths of a deep, peaceful and dreamless sleep by a strange, irritating sensation. Even in his foggy state, he realized there was something moist stroking his chin in a steady rhythm.

He opened one eye and saw Daisy curled next to him on the pillow, her full attention devoted to giving his chin a morning bath.

Ted frowned in confusion, wondering how Daisy had gotten into his apartment. In the next instant, reality struck and he snapped his head around to look at the pillow next to him. The jerking motion caused Daisy to tumble away in a fluffy ball, complete with an indignant squeak of protest.

Hannah, Ted thought, staring at her. Beautiful Ms. Doodle. She slept pretty. Yeah, she really did. Her hair was spread out on the pillow like a dark, silky fan, her features were relaxed and lovely, her lips...those sensational, kissable, sweet-as-honey lips, were slightly parted. A cameo.

The events of the previous night floated into Ted's mental vision, vivid and sensuously detailed. Heat came to life in his body, causing the now-familiar ache of wanting Hannah to build steadily. He tore his gaze from her face to look beyond her to the clock on the nightstand.

It read 7:12 a.m.

It was a new day, Sunday morning, he mused. What would Hannah do, say? How would she feel about having made love with him? Would this be, to her, a daffodils-and-daisies morning? Or would she be filled with regret, remorse? Demand that he leave her bed, her home, her life?

Lord, what if she said he was never to darken her doorway again? Tossed him out and slammed the door, locking it firmly behind him?

Well, there was no way to know what her frame of mind, her mood or attitude was until she woke up. He'd just stay put and wait patiently for her to open her big, gorgeous dark eyes.

Ted stared at the ceiling for two seconds, three, then four.

"Hell, forget it," he mumbled.

He raised his head to see Daisy sitting by his knee, busily grooming her tail. He scooped up the kitten and placed her gently on the pillow next to Hannah's face.

"Go for it, Daisy," he whispered.

Rolling onto his side, he propped himself up on one forearm, then nudged Daisy on the bottom. The kitten inched forward, leaned toward Hannah, studied the sleeping human, then began to wash Hannah's nose.

Ted smothered a chuckle before it could erupt.

Hannah frowned in her sleep, then brushed a hand in the direction of the annoying whatever-it-was on her nose, missing Daisy entirely. The busy little pink tongue continued its chore.

"Mmm," Hannah said, opening her eyes, which immediately crossed as she focused on Daisy. "Oh, good grief, would you go away?"

"Good morning," Ted said quietly.

Hannah's eyes flew to his, then widened for a moment at the shock of seeing him there.

Ted's heart thudded wildly as he met her gaze. He willed her to speak, to give him some clue as to what she was feeling, before he had a nervous breakdown.

He did *not* want Hannah to regret what they'd shared. Why that was so very important to him, he had no idea, but it was. And if she didn't say something in the next second, he was going to go right out of his ever-lovin' mind.

"Hannah," he said, hearing the unsteady tone of his voice, "it's a daffodils-and-daisies morning." He paused and lifted Daisy off the pillow, putting her farther down the bed between him and Hannah. "Right?"

Hannah continued to stare at him, no readable expression on her face. A trickle of sweat ran down Ted's chest as he waited, hardly breathing.

Then slowly, so slowly, a smile began to form on Hannah's lips.

"Yes, Ted," she said softly. "It *is* a daffodils-and-daisies morning."

Ted flopped back onto his pillow. "Oh, thank God." He dragged both hands down his face, then turned his head to look at her again. "I was so afraid that you'd... Never mind."

"That I'd be sorry about what happened last night? Be filled with guilt or regret?"

"Well, yeah. I mean, I know that you wouldn't treat something like this lightly. Believe me, Hannah, I *do* know that. I'd hate it, really hate it, if you were upset, angry, sorry it took place, whatever. But... you're not?"

"No."

"Why not?"

"Isn't just saying no enough?" she said, frowning slightly.

"Humor me. I'm a wreck here, Hannah. I've been waiting hours for you to wake up so I'd know how you felt about this. Well, that's stretching it a bit. It wasn't hours, but it sure seemed like it was. I'm shook up here, Ms. Doodle, so take pity and tell me why this is a daffodils-and-daisies day."

"Well, because we made exquisite love together, Ted," she said, her smile returning. "It was glorious, like nothing I've ever experienced before. You made me feel special, cherished, and... and beautiful. Even though I'm shaped like a volleyball, I felt beautiful."

Heat rocketed through Ted's body as he listened to

Hannah's softly spoken words and saw the gentle, womanly smile on her face.

Ah, Hannah, his mind thundered. *I want you again. Now. Right now.*

"And," she went on, "I'm a woman who is free to make her own decisions as long as I realize I have to take responsibility for them. I wanted to make love with you, Ted. So I made the choice to do so, and I'm not sorry that I did. There. That's it. Last night was last night. Today is a new day. End of story."

Ted frowned. "Wait a minute. That doesn't sound quite right to me."

"What's wrong with it?"

"Last night isn't erased, forgotten or wrapped up in a package and shoved onto a back shelf somewhere. It has a bearing on this morning. It came with us into the new day. You can't separate the two like cutting a pizza."

"Yes, I can, and I have." She paused. "Would you like some breakfast? I make a delicious omelet, if I do say so myself."

"Hold it," he said, slicing one hand through the air. He sat up, shoved the pillow against the headboard, then moved backward to lean against it. The sheet and blanket dropped, then draped low across his hips. "We haven't finished this discussion yet."

Hannah clutched the sheet over her bare breasts with one hand, then wiggled into a position matching Ted's.

Daisy yowled her disapproval at being disturbed and jumped off the bed, rolling head over tail when she landed on the floor. She shook herself, then ran from the room.

Hannah tucked the sheet beneath her arms, then folded her hands on her stomach. She looked at Ted and raised her eyebrows.

"What?" he said, obviously confused.

"You called this meeting to order," she said. "Go ahead and speak your mind. Do be aware, however, that I'm eating for two, and this duo is hungry. Well? Carry on, Mr. Sharpe."

"I most certainly will. You, Ms. Doodle, have a wacky attitude, do you know that? You put things into slots, compartments, or something, then close the door, lock it and ignore them."

Hannah nodded thoughtfully. "You're right...sort of. I mean, you're basically correct, but the way you describe it makes it sound as though I do it on a whim, like I'm just shrugging and saying, 'Oh, well, what the hell.'"

"Mmm," he said, crossing his arms firmly over his chest. "Mmm."

"You're starting to get angry, and that's not fair, Ted. I don't have an 'attitude' in the negative way you said it. I have a philosophy for living my life, one that has made it possible for me to survive some rough blows. If I get mired in the past, it would be impossible to be in the now, then move forward into the future."

"That's fine, dandy, really great. I can see where that philosophy helped you deal with the reality of your husband being a total jerk. But Hannah, we made love last night. A handful of hours ago. I think it's lousy that you've put it away somewhere like yesterday's newspaper. Damn it, what we shared was important!''

"Don't yell! I know it was important, and special and... But, darn it, don't you see that if I bring it into today, I'm giving it the power to dictate to my emotions, my state of mind?

"What do you want me to do? Go around with a silly grin on my face, staring dreamily into space and sighing as I say 'Ted, oh, Ted. Oh, Ted, Ted, Ted,' like a besotted teenager?''

Ted narrowed his eyes. "That has possibilities. It's a helluva lot better than my feeling like old news, like I'm Mr. 'What's-his-name.'"

"Ah-ha," she said, pointing one finger in the air. "Oops," she said as the sheet began to slip down. She tucked it back into place.

"Ah-ha? That indicates you've drawn some sort of conclusion. Do enlighten me, Hannah. I'd hate to miss this."

"It's as clear as a bell. Your male ego is bruised, Mr. Sharpe." She nodded decisively. "You're accustomed to women being all dewy-eyed and breathless the morning after. Despite the fact that you're a confirmed bachelor who wants no part of commitment or entanglements, you don't know what to do with a woman who cherishes having made love with you last night, but greets the morning thinking of omelets."

"Oh, man," he said, squeezing his temples with one hand. "You're scrambling my brain. I've never met anyone like you before, anyone who thinks like you do. You are definitely driving me crazy."

"I don't know why, because it's very simple. Well, maybe it's complicated to you, but it's simple in its complexity." She laughed. "That didn't make one bit of sense."

"No joke. I need some time to sort through this puzzle. That means I'm not yet in a position to convince you to allow last night to be part of today.

"However, since I feel so strongly that our love-making should be in the here and now, I'll have to make adjustments to the situation until I have a clearer picture of this maze."

"What sort of adjustments?"

"Elementary, my dear Doodle. It's called compromise. We'll leave what we shared in last night's slot, where you feel it belongs, even though I adamantly disagree.

"So, in order to keep our making love in today, where I believe it deserves to be, we'll take care of today's slot, which you decree to be empty. Get it?"

"Oh. Well, yes, I do understand what you're saying, but…"

"Lord, I'm brilliant." He slid one hand to the back of her neck and leaned toward her. "I amaze myself at times with my genius-level thinking."

"But…"

He brushed his lips over hers. "Don't you agree, Hannah—" he traced her lips with the tip of his tongue "—that I'm extremely intelligent?"

"I…um…"

Ted slipped the sheet free of her arms and swept it away, his hand returning to tenderly cradle one of her breasts.

"Yes?" he said, close to her lips.

"Yes," she said breathlessly. "Oh, yes."

It was all, and it was more, than the exquisite love-making of the night before. It was slow, teasing, tantalizing. Hands and lips were never still; roaming, caressing with feather-like gentleness, discovering more of the mysteries freely revealed.

"Ah, Hannah," Ted said, his voice hoarse with building passion.

He kissed her stomach, then his breath caught as he felt the baby move. He splayed one hand on the rounded flesh, awe evident on his face and in his eyes as the miracle beneath shifted again.

"Incredible," he whispered. "My God, Hannah, do you realize what you're sharing with me? What you're allowing me to be a part of? Thank you. Oh, Hannah, thank you. I sincerely mean that."

He captured her mouth and kissed her deeply, foreign emotions intertwining with his raging desire.

Ted, Ted, Ted, Hannah's mind sang. Besotted teenager? Oh, who cared? It didn't matter, not now. She'd think later...later. She just wanted Ted, needed Ted, before she went up in flames and disappeared into oblivion.

He entered her slowly, his arms trembling from forced restraint. She met his smoldering gaze, knowing desire showed in her eyes, as well.

"Please," she said, pressing her hands more firmly on his back. "Come to me, Ted. I want you so much, so very much."

He thrust deeper, and a sigh of pleasure escaped from Hannah's lips.

"Oh, Ted," she said dreamily.

He stilled within her, savoring the moist heat that had received all he'd brought to her, welcoming him into the dark, feminine haven of her body.

"This is today, Hannah," he said, the raspy quality of his voice sounding strange to his own ears. "We're making love *today*."

"A daffodils-and-daisies day."

"Yes."

He kissed her again, then began a rocking rhythm. Hannah moved with him in perfect synchronization. He increased the tempo and they began to soar, each anticipating the summit; wishing to postpone it, yet wanting, needing it, now.

They reached the pinnacle seconds apart, each calling the name of the other, holding on tightly.

They were there...and it was glorious.

It was a celebration of man being man, woman being woman, counterparts meant to mesh into one entity that was creating an ecstasy far beyond definition in its splendor.

They drifted among the spectacle of vibrant, sparkling colors, delaying the return, staying in a world that belonged only to them.

Reality tapped gently on hazy minds, and Ted reluctantly moved from Hannah to settle close to her side.

"Oh, Ted," she said. "Oh, my goodness."

"Ditto, kiddo," he said, then drew a deep, steadying breath. "Unreal. I'll move in a week. Just dust around me."

Hannah smiled. "Okay. However, as unromantic as

this statement is about to be, my human cargo just plunked himself, or herself, on my bladder. As the saying goes, 'I'm outta here.'" She kissed Ted quickly on the lips, then left the bed, hurrying to the bathroom.

Ted closed his eyes, savoring the sated contentment consuming him.

Hannah, his mind hummed.

He opened his eyes, laced his fingers beneath his head and stared up at the ceiling. A frown crept over his features.

Hannah was so different from any woman he'd ever known. She was evoking emotions within him that he couldn't clearly identify.

Was he headed for trouble?

Was he being drawn deeper and deeper into a situation where he didn't belong?

Should he exit stage left immediately?

No!

Damn it, no.

He was okay, doing fine. Of course he felt a protectiveness toward Hannah, any decent man would, considering her circumstances. As for the foreign emotions, he'd ignore them. What he didn't address couldn't affect him. That made sense.

He was still determined to convince Hannah that her resolve to never love again was wrong. There was no reason for her to sentence herself to a life alone, just her and the baby.

The baby. Lord, when he'd felt the baby move, he thought his heart was going to jump right out of his chest. Beneath his lips, his hand, a miracle had made its presence known. Incredible. Awesome. Humbling.

"Really something," he said aloud.

So, Sharpe? he asked himself. *Have you got your act together?* Yeah, he did. Making love with Hannah didn't mean he'd *fall in love* with Ms. Doodle. No way.

But he'd stick close to her, help her fix up the nursery, show her, prove to her over time that he was exactly who he said he was. Not *all* men changed their stripes after gaining a woman's trust.

Once she realized that *he* was real, she'd have to admit that there must be other guys out there who were, too. Then she'd...

Ted sat bolt upward.

Then she'd what? Fall in love with one of *them?* Make love with one of *them?* Pick one of *them* to have the privilege of helping her raise her child?

Well, yeah, that was the ultimate goal of his campaign.

So why did he suddenly have a cold knot in his gut?

"Because you're hungry, fool," he said, flipping back the blankets.

He needed some protein, some brain food, then he'd be right as rain. Everything would be fine, under his control.

Chapter Eight

That evening, Ted dropped a sponge into a plastic pail filled with soapy water, then stepped back and planted his hands on his hips.

"There you go, Ms. Doodle," he said. "Crib, high chair, playpen and changing table are assembled and washed with soap and disinfectant. I'd say we've done a good day's work."

"*You* did all the work," Hannah said, smiling. "I just stood around watching."

"Every job needs a supervisor. This stuff is in excellent condition, considering it's used. I think it looks great."

"Oh, it does." Hannah swept her gaze over the room. "It's a nursery. This morning it was an empty room, and now it's an honest-to-goodness nursery."

"Yup."

"It makes the baby seem even more real. I guess that sounds dumb, but I look at that crib and I can visualize a little one sleeping there." She laughed. "I'm going to have a baby."

Ted chuckled. "Yes, ma'am. You certainly are, ma'am." He paused and frowned. "The drawers in the changing table sure are empty. I guess next up is to start getting those sleeper gizmos, diapers, blankets, bibs, the whole nine yards."

"Yes. There's a place called Grandma's House that sells used baby and children's clothes. I'm going to see what they have."

Ted picked up the pail and started toward the bedroom door.

"Ted?"

He stopped, then half turned to look back at her. "Hmm?"

"Thank you so much for all you did today. I can't begin to tell you how much I appreciate it."

"You just told me. Come on, I'm a starving man. I've got a couple of pizzas in the freezer. Let's go to my place and stick them in the oven."

"You can't feed me dinner on top of everything else you've done for me today."

"Sure I can. I'm in the mood for some cheap, cardboard pizza. I'll dump this water, then we're on our way."

In Ted's apartment, Hannah made a quick scrutiny of the living room.

"Your apartment is the reverse of mine. Everything

goes in the opposite direction." She smiled. "I'd better stay alert or I'm liable to walk into a wall."

"Another big difference is that your place is neat as a pin. I'm a slob, pure and simple."

"What do you use your second bedroom for? A guest room? Office? Nothing?"

"Take a look if you want to," he said, "I'll go put the pizzas in the oven."

When Ted entered the spare bedroom ten minutes later, he found Hannah peering into the glass-fronted cabinet. She turned to face him, her dark eyes sparkling.

"Oh, Ted, these miniatures are beautiful. I had no idea you were so talented."

"Well, that's stretching it a bit. They come in kits. I have to carve away the excess, but it's not as if I start from scratch with a hunk of wood. I enjoy it, though. It's very relaxing."

"That tiny cradle you're doing now is exquisite. The details are incredible for something so small. I'm standing firm on my statement that you're very talented."

"Whatever. Next I'm going to build a dollhouse to hold all this stuff. I bought a book at Deedee's store and I have to decide which one to make."

"Could I see the book?"

"Sure. Bring it out to the table. I need to check on the pizzas. Cardboard doesn't take long to cook."

"I'll help with dinner," she said. "Do you want me to set the table, or pour the drinks?"

"Nope. You've been on your feet a lot today. It's time you put your bottom on a chair."

Hannah laughed. "Says the expert on such things?"

"Hey, I hang out with the MacAllister clan, remember? I've heard, 'Put your feet up, drink your milk, here's a pillow for behind your back,' and a long list of other things during the pregnancies I've witnessed. I'm very good at the waiting-room-at-the-hospital bit, too."

He handed her the book on making dollhouses and they left the room.

"However," he said, circling Hannah's shoulders with his arm, "if you want to know if you're having a girl or a boy, you'll have to ask Forrest MacAllister. He's The Baby Bet champion. The guy never misses. It's really getting creepy."

"Forrest *always* wins The Baby Bet?"

"Yup, and some of them have been very high-tech bets. When Forrest said Jillian was going to have triplets and they'd all be girls, I figured he was cooked. But I'll be damned if Jillian didn't have three baby girls. When you meet Forrest, just ignore the gleam he'll get in his eyes. He'll look at your volleyball and start mentally counting twenty-dollar bills."

"Oh, I doubt that I'd have occasion to meet Forrest MacAllister."

Ted stopped, forcing Hannah to do the same. He dropped his arm and moved to stand in front of her, placing both hands on her shoulders.

"Of course you'll be meeting Forrest…and Jillian, the kids, Jenny and Michael and…well, the whole gang." He frowned. "You want to, don't you?

They're all as nice as Ryan and Deedee, and you liked *them*."

"Yes, I did like them very much, but—"

"Listen, the MacAllisters get together all the time and I'm included in whatever they do. There's no reason why you can't go with me to birthday parties, potlucks, that kind of thing. It'll be fun, and you can talk about babies with the other moms to your heart's content."

"But what about the...the women you date? I mean, won't someone, or someones, get upset if you take *me* to where you've always taken them?"

"No, Ms. Doodle, because I've never taken a woman to a MacAllister gathering. The women I date aren't the type who would enjoy those sorts of outings. *You* will enjoy them, so you'll go with me. Okay?"

"But—"

"Hey, would you deprive Forrest of the opportunity to anticipate The Baby Bet being put into operation down the line? That would *not* be nice. The guy gets a major rush from The Baby Bet, along with a big stack of twenty-dollar bills."

"I—"

"Oh, hell, my cardboard pizzas are burning!"

The pizzas were very well done around the edges, but eatable. Ted placed a glass of soda by Hannah's plate, then produced a glass of milk, which he set next to the soft drink.

"Soda with a milk chaser?" she said, raising her eyebrows.

"Mothers-to-be need their milk," he said, sitting down opposite her. "I know about this jazz, remember?"

"If I drink two full glasses like those, I'll float away."

"Okay, then skip the soda and go for the milk."

"Pizza and milk? Yuck."

"Tough. There's a cow somewhere who donated that to your cause. The least you can do is drink it to show your gratitude for its contribution."

Hannah laughed.

"Hey, wait." Ted got to his feet, went into the kitchen and returned with a bowl of green grapes. "There you go." He plunked the bowl in front of Hannah.

"Pizza, milk and grapes?" she said. "This combination is getting worse by the minute."

"Fresh fruit is good for you. We may be starting a whole new eating fad with that menu you have there. We'll sell the idea to a fast-food chain and make a bundle." He leaned toward her. "Eat."

"Mmm," she said, glaring at him.

To Hannah's surprise, having pizza, milk and grapes together wasn't all that bad, a fact she decided not to share with the smug Mr. Sharpe.

"Ted," she said a few minutes later, "why are you so determined that I mix and mingle with the MacAllister family? I *do* have friends, you know. I'm not some pathetic orphaned waif who's all alone in the big, cruel world."

Ted frowned. "I realize that, but you did mention that your teacher friends don't have kids. People with babies like to hang out with people with babies.'' He shrugged. "Makes sense to me.''

"With you being the exception to the rule. You don't have children, but you spend a great deal of time with a group who do. How do you explain that?''

Ted leaned back in his chair, crossed his arms over his chest and narrowed his eyes.

"Is there some reason,'' he said, "that you're attempting to pick a fight with me?''

Hannah opened her mouth to retort, closed it again, then sighed.

"I'm sorry,'' she said. "It's just that you're being so *nice* to me. You said yourself that I'm not your type, not the sort of woman you'd usually see socially. So what am I? Your cause or do-gooder thing? You're going to be certain that I make new friends I can relate to and that my libido doesn't get neglected? I'm not a charity case.''

"No, you're not. At the moment, you're a very crabby woman. Eat your grapes.''

"Would you stop that!''

"Whew,'' he said, shaking his head. He took another bite of pizza.

"Look,'' Hannah said, "keeping our lovemaking separate and apart from anything else—''

"Which I think is nuts, but go ahead with what you want to say,'' Ted interjected.

"Thank you,'' she said coolly. "I repeat, keeping our making love an entity unto itself, why did you spend your entire Sunday shopping for, toting, assembling, and scrubbing baby furniture for my nursery?

Why are you suggesting—no, insisting that I accompany you to MacAllister outings? Why are you being so...so nice?''

Ted glowered at her. ''I'm after your money.''

''Would you get serious?''

''Hannah, as unbelievable as this will sound to you, I *am* a nice guy. I don't have a hidden agenda behind a phony facade. I enjoy your company, we get along great with each other. Well, we usually do, but right now you're being a real pain in the butt. Maybe your pregnant hormones went into overdrive. Could green grapes do that to a woman in your condition?''

''Sharpe, you're pushing me.''

''Okay, okay,'' he said, raising both hands.

He dropped his hands and captured one of her's on the top of the table.

''Hannah,'' he said quietly, ''there's nothing fishy going on, I swear it. You're set on automatic 'don't trust your own judgment' in regard to men, but I'm exactly who I present myself to be. I like you, respect you, enjoy being with you. Hell, I even think your cat is cute.

''We're lovers, which you insist on keeping in its own compartment. Fine. Weird, but fine, if that's the way you want it. I think you'll have fun with the MacAllisters, so we'll join in on MacAllister doings. I spent today helping set up your nursery because I chose to do so. Okay? There's no sinister plot that you're afraid you're not recognizing.''

He released her hand and popped a grape into his mouth.

''Lighten up, Ms. Doodle.'' He splayed one hand

on his chest. "This is me, Theodore Sharpe. What you see is what you get, upfront and honest. If I'm being nice to you, it's because you're a nice person who deserves to be treated nicely. That's an overdose of the word *nice,* but that's how it is. Pure and simple."

"Oh," Hannah said, nodding. "Oh-h-h," she wailed in the next instant as tears filled her eyes. "I can't handle this."

"Jeez." Ted pulled the bowl of grapes toward him. "Quit eating these things."

Hannah sniffled. "I'm sorry. I just... But I... So sorry..." She threw up her hands in a gesture of frustration. "Oh-h-h."

Ted got to his feet. "You're exhausted, that's what you are. We did a lot today, too much, obviously. Come on, sweet Hannah, I'll walk you home so you can go to bed. Get some sleep and...bingo... tomorrow will be a daffodils-and-daisies day. Guaranteed."

Hannah nodded, sniffled again, then got to her feet. She welcomed the feel of Ted's powerful body as he slid one arm across her shoulders and tucked her close to his side.

She was suddenly so tired that it was an effort to place one foot in front of the other, and she was most definitely too exhausted to think. She would allow herself the luxury of being taken care of for now; escorted to her door, told to go to bed. So be it.

At Hannah's apartment, Ted unlocked the door, pushed it open and gave her the keys. Then he cradled her face in his hands and kissed her deeply.

"Sleep well, Ms. Doodle," he said when he finally raised his head.

"Thank you, Ted," she said, tears still echoing in her voice, "for everything."

Ted chuckled. "Especially that gourmet dinner I fixed you." He brushed his lips over hers. "Go."

Ted waited until he heard the lock snap into place and the jingle of the safety chain. He stared at the closed door for a long moment, then turned and walked slowly back to his own place.

In his living room, he stopped and gazed at his surroundings, seeing Hannah in his mind's eye, hearing her voice, her laughter, inhaling the lingering fragrance of flowers.

He crossed the room to the cluttered table and picked up the glasses, smiling as he looked at the bowl of green grapes.

He should be ticked, he supposed, at the way Hannah had switched moods and geared up for battle. But he couldn't be angry because she'd been so endearing, so befuddled by his actions. And he understood that she'd verbally attacked him because she'd been so badly hurt in the past.

And then she'd lost it, burst into tears and looked so tired and forlorn. He wanted to scoop her up and hold her, comfort her, tell her there was nothing to be afraid of when she was with him.

Ted took the glasses to the kitchen, then returned to the table to retrieve more of the debris. A frown settled over his features as he continued his cleaning chore.

Hannah's theory of how she was handling the issue of their lovemaking was unusual, to say the least. She placed it in its ever-famous slot and left it there.

Weird.

Well, maybe not. The women he slept with did the same thing, in their own way. They didn't expect anything of him the next day, just said, "see ya," and were receptive when he contacted them for another date.

So why did it bother him so much that Hannah insisted on leaving in the bedroom the intimacy they shared, refusing to allow it to have any influence whatsoever on the other hours they spent together?

Her attitude wasn't all that different from what he was accustomed to, what he actually preferred. So why had he been on her case, insisting her outlook was completely nuts? he wondered.

Hell, he didn't know.

He'd felt a knot tighten in his gut when Hannah had cut loose with her tirade, demanding to know why he wanted to take her to MacAllister events. That knot had been fear that she'd refuse to go. He wanted to have her with him when he took part in things with the MacAllister clan, he really did.

Sharpe, he told himself, *you'd better watch your step.* Hannah Johnson was getting to him, inch by emotional inch. He had to stay very alert, be certain he didn't get caught up by Hannah's bleak circumstances, continually see himself as the dashing hero to the rescue, her knight in shining armor arriving to save the damsel in distress.

What he'd told her was the truth. He enjoyed her

company, and sincerely believed she'd reap great rewards from associating with the MacAllisters, from having them as friends.

And what she would learn over time was that there really were nice men around, the real goods. She'd see that a few mistakes in judgment in the past shouldn't sentence her to a life alone.

Yup, he thought, sticking the bowl of grapes into the refrigerator, everything would be just fine.

Ted wandered back into the living room. Then why was he so hell-bent on changing Hannah's attitude about keeping their lovemaking separate. Why did the idea of having Hannah by his side at the next MacAllister gathering hold so much appeal?

And why did it suddenly seem so damn quiet and empty in his living room?

"Forget it," he said aloud. "Go carve a cradle."

On his way to the spare bedroom, Ted changed directions and went to the table to retrieve the book on making dollhouses.

As he started back across the room, he flipped through the pages.

He'd pick the model that struck his fancy, he thought, and send for the kit. It would be a challenging and complicated project, but he'd enjoy it. Besides, he needed a house for his growing collection of furniture.

After turning on the light in the bedroom-workshop, Ted leaned one shoulder against the door frame and his gaze roamed over the room.

This was not, he supposed, remotely close to what people would expect to find in a so-called swinging bachelor's apartment. Fast-lane guys were not known for having a collection of handmade miniatures in residence, or for being in the process of deciding which dollhouse to build for the tiny furniture.

He frowned and shook his head.

It was actually borderline dumb, now that he really thought about it. A single man was intending to eventually have a completely furnished dollhouse in the spare bedroom of his apartment? *Definitely* dumb.

So, yeah, the MacAllister kids could visit it and play with it, but still.... A dollhouse belonged in a little girl's room where she could give free rein to her imagination whenever the mood struck. A dollhouse was something a daddy could share with her, too. They'd sit on the floor together, rearrange the furniture, make up stories about the people who lived in the house. Very special memories could be created by the hours a man spent with his daughter and a dollhouse.

Ted sighed.

A daughter. A miracle. A living, breathing human being, who existed because two people had joined their bodies in the most intimate and beautiful act ever.

A daughter or a son, neither of which he would ever have.

A chill coursed through Ted and he pushed himself away from the door frame and went to the chair by the worktable. He sank onto it heavily, placing the dollhouse book in front of him.

His mind was yanked back in time, haunting ghosts of the past giving no quarter. Over the years, he'd not allowed the truth the space to tear him apart, he'd refused to address what he knew was true.

But tonight? He was suddenly powerless against the memories that assaulted him....

He was sixteen years old and had just recovered from a severe case of the mumps. The doctor had run a test to see if any permanent damage had been done, and he and his parents were waiting for the results.

It was raining, and had been a gloomy day, ominously dark when it should have been sunny. He'd approached the kitchen door, then stopped in the hallway as he heard his parents talking.

"That was the doctor on the phone, Maggie," his father said. "Ted's test results show that he... Oh, God."

"Dean?" his mother said. "Dear heaven, what did the doctor say?"

"Ted...Ted is sterile because of his having had the mumps. He'll never father a child. Dear Lord, do you realize what he's been robbed of, what this means?"

Ted had turned, run down the hall, and barreled out the front door into the cold rain. He'd run as fast and far as he could before sinking to his knees in an empty field, his lungs burning.

He knew what his father had been about to say and hadn't been able to bear hearing it.

He'd been robbed of his manhood.

He was not, nor would he ever be, a whole man.

Ted had sprawled facedown on the wet grass, sobbing, his tears mingling with the driving rain that pelted him, his father's words echoing over and over in his mind, tormenting him.

From that day forward, there had been something missing from his relationship with his father, a breach that had never been repaired. He knew that in his father's eyes he now fell short of what a son should be.

Robbed of his manhood.

Not a whole man.

Ted had listened when his parents told him gently about the test results. He'd shrugged, said it was no big deal, and it had never been discussed again.

His folks never knew about the tears he'd shed, the pain he'd buried deep within himself.

The years had passed, he'd become a police officer, and lived the life of a swinging single. For weeks, months at a stretch, he was actually convinced that his existence was exactly the way he wanted it.

Then the ghosts would rear their ugly heads in the dark hours and he'd struggle against them. Push them away, winning each battle before they could grip his heart and soul.

Always winning...until tonight.

A shudder ripped through him and Ted dragged his hands down his face, his fingers trembling as he realized they were wet with tears.

"Oh, damn," he said, staring up at the ceiling.

He leaned forward, propped his elbows heavily on the table and sank his head into his hands. Time lost meaning as he sat there, alone and cold, empty, wrapped in a cocoon of misery.

Hannah lay in bed, willing sleep to come and carry her off into blissful oblivion. The baby was especially active tonight, probably objecting to the dinner menu of pizza and green grapes.

She turned her head toward the other pillow she couldn't see in the dark, envisioning how magnificent Ted had looked there, close, his attention centered on her and the world they'd created together.

Daisy crawled up the bedspread, then settled by Hannah's waist and went to sleep. Hannah stroked the kitten absently, deep in thought.

Her ridiculous performance at Ted's had been just that...ridiculous. She'd been smiling one moment, picking a fight in the next breath, then had trekked right into being a weepy mess. How mortifying. How patient and sweet Ted had been.

Maybe she should blame the whole episode on pregnancy hormones and green grapes, and forget it.

Hannah sighed.

She'd never get away with a cop-out like that, because she knew it wasn't true. Ted was throwing her off-kilter, confusing her, making her nervous.

Because he was being just so darn nice.

She'd fallen prey to his damnable *niceness* through-out the day, had relaxed and enjoyed their shopping spree for the baby furniture.

Ted's enthusiasm had been infectious, and she'd felt happy and carefree. She'd laughed in pure delight when he whipped out his tape measure to check the crib slats, as Ryan had instructed. He'd been so serious about it, insisting on measuring every one, refusing to assume that if the first few met code, the rest would.

As she'd watched him, she made no attempt to hide

the smile that remained on her face, and had been aware of a lovely warmth filling her, stroking her like a comforting blanket she could gather around herself.

Ted obviously objected to her plan to keep their lovemaking in its proper place. Why? He should be pleased and relieved that she didn't view their intimacy as a right to demand some sort of commitment from him.

Oh, he was a complicated man, so difficult to understand at times, so honest and open at others. He was weaving his way into her life, her day-to-day existence, and that was very dangerous.

Should she refuse to see him again?

Decline invitations to accompany him to MacAllister outings?

Not allow herself to share in exquisitely beautiful lovemaking with him ever again?

"Oh, dear," she whispered into the darkness.

That all sounded so bleak, so lonely. Ted made her smile, laugh right out loud. And Ted made her feel beautiful.

She didn't want to force him out of her life, not now, not yet.

Hannah frowned as a new thought struck her.

She wouldn't have to send Ted on his way later. He'd leave on his own, hightail it out of her life in the very near future.

Why?

Because she was pregnant. He might think her volleyball stomach was intriguing, but she was going to be much bigger than a *volleyball* before this baby was born.

She'd be fat, pure and simple. She'd waddle like a duck, forget what her feet looked like, be as attractive as a blimp. She might even grow to life-raft size, as Jillian had.

Hannah told herself she wouldn't have to work at not becoming too emotionally involved with Ted Sharpe because he wouldn't be around that long. Nature would take care of the job for her as the baby grew. She'd prepare herself for his inevitable exit stage left, and enjoy his company in the meantime.

After all, Ted was a confirmed bachelor who existed in the fast lane of the singles' scene because that was the life-style he preferred and intended to keep.

When she began to impersonate a whale, he'd be gone by *his* choice, *his* decision.

The only thing *she* had to do was make certain when Ted left, he didn't take her heart with him.

Chapter Nine

The following weeks passed quickly, one flowing into the next. Hannah and Ted were together at some point each day, depending on his shift. They shopped for baby clothes, attended MacAllister clan events, and spent a great many quiet and lovely evenings at home.

"Ted?" Hannah said.

"Hmm?"

"Would you put the VCR on stop, please? I need to talk to you about something."

Ted snapped his head around to look at Hannah where she sat next to him on the sofa in his living room.

"Sure," he said.

He pressed a button on the remote control and the

movie they had been watching halted just as the sheriff reached for his gun to shoot the outlaw.

"You're frowning," he said, matching her expression. "What's wrong?"

"Nothing. I mean, well, it's not nothing exactly, it's…" She took a steadying breath. "I went to the doctor today for my routine checkup."

Ted shifted on the sofa to fully face her. "And? What did he say? Why are you frowning? You were very quiet during dinner, preoccupied. Hannah? Talk to me," he said anxiously.

"I *am* talking to you, but you're taking up the air space."

"Oh. Sorry. Go ahead. You went to the doctor today. And?" He leaned toward her.

"This is November first, the beginning of my eighth month."

"And?"

"Well, he said that…um…"

"Hannah, please," Ted said, taking her hands in his. "Is the baby all right?"

"Oh, yes, he's fine. She's fine. Maybe I should have had an ultrasound. This 'he' or 'she' gets to be a nuisance sometimes."

"Forrest is gearing up to let you know what it is. We're getting closer to The Baby Bet extravaganza. Hannah, please, take pity on me. You're driving me crazy. What did the doctor say?"

"Ican'thavesexanymore," she said in a rush of words.

Ted's frown deepened. "I didn't catch any of that. Could you go a little slower?"

"Oh, dear. Okay. Ted, I can't have sex anymore. I'm no longer allowed to make love from now until about six weeks after the baby is born."

He nodded. "And?"

Hannah blinked. "And what? That's it. The bad news, the gruesome bulletin, the it's-been-great-but-goodbye announcement."

"Man, you've really lost me here, Ms. Doodle. Did I miss something? Goodbye? Who's leaving for where?"

"*You're* leaving," she said, nearly shrieking.

Ted's eyes widened. "*I* am? Why? Where am I going?"

"Out of my life," she said, pulling her hands free. She flapped one hand in the air. "You're gone. Poof. You're outta here."

"You're sending me away?"

"No, no, no, but why would you stay? My gosh, Ted, look at me. I'm as big as an inner tube and heading toward life raft. My feet are swollen by the end of the day, I waddle worse than Donald Duck, I wear tents instead of clothes and now I can't even make love." She sniffled. "I understand, I really do. So goodbye. I can't talk about this anymore or I'll cry."

Ted lunged to his feet to tower over her, his hands planted on his hips.

"We damn well *are* going to talk about this. I've never been so insulted in my life. You're really ticking me off, Hannah Johnson."

"I am?" she said, shock evident on her face. "I am *not*. I'm being realistic and mature. If I don't burst into tears, I will have accepted the facts with dignity and class.''

''Facts? Facts! You don't have facts, you have a bunch of bull!''

''Don't yell at me!''

''Well, hell, what do you expect me to do?''

''Leave!''

Ted groaned and shoved both hands through his hair. He stared at the ceiling and counted aloud to ten.

''Okay, I'm calm.'' He sat back down. ''Cool. Collected. In control. I won't yell. I won't tell you you're nuttier than a fruitcake, even though you are. Have you been binging on green grapes again? You're really wacko.''

''You're babbling.''

''And you're crazy!'' He shook his head. ''No, I won't raise my voice.'' He took her hands again. ''Hannah, listen to me, and please hear every word I'm saying. Are you paying attention?''

''Yes, but...''

''Please just listen, and don't interrupt.'' When she nodded, he continued, ''Ah, Hannah, what you said really hurt. Do you think I'm a sex maniac, or something? We can't make love anymore. Okay, I can live with that. I can still hold you in bed, rub your back when its aching, tell you how cute your toes look because you can't see them.''

He shifted his hands to frame her face.

''Hannah, the only way I'd leave you is if you sent me away, which would tear me apart. You surely realize I haven't seen anyone but you all these months, because I've obviously spent every spare minute with you. I don't want anyone but you."

"It has been wonderful," she said, struggling against threatening tears. "I've been so happy with you, and I've enjoyed every minute of the time we've spent together and with all the MacAllisters. They've made me feel like one of the family. And you've made me feel special, cherished and beautiful."

"Because you *are* special and beautiful. You *should* be cherished, and I do. And I love you and—" Ted stopped speaking and stiffened. "What?" he said.

"What?" Hannah echoed.

"I...well, I'll be damned." A grin broke across his face. "I do. I love you, Hannah Johnson. I, Theodore Sharpe, am in love with you."

Hannah's eyes widened. "You are not." She leaned back a bit, forcing him to drop his hands from her face. "Don't you dare say such a thing."

"I have to say it, because it's true. I wonder when it happened? This love stuff is sneaky. Man, oh, man, I'm in love. Hannah, you look like I just told you that Daisy had fourteen kittens in the middle of your bed. You're as pale as a ghost."

"I...I don't want you to be in love with me," she said, her voice trembling. "We were doing fine as we were. Everything was in its proper slot. Don't be in love with me, Ted. Please? Erase it, ignore it, make it go away."

His smile faded and was replaced by a frown. "I don't think I can do that." He shook his head. "No, that's impossible. Love is a heavy-duty emotion, Hannah. When it gets you, it gets you, a done deal. A person can't take two aspirin for it and feel better in the morning. I've never been in love before, but I can tell I don't have any control over it.''

''Oh, dear me,'' she said, shaking her head. ''This is terrible, just awful.''

''Thanks a lot, Ms. Doodle.''

''Oh, I'm so sorry, Ted. That sounded as though having you in love with me is a grim truth to be endured. That's not what I'm saying at all. It isn't personal. I just don't want *anyone* to be in love with me. Because it's you, and because I'm with you all the time, I'll have to figure out how I feel about *you*, and I don't want to do that.''

''Why not?''

''Because everything was perfect the way it was, don't you see?''

''What I see by the clock is that I have to get to work. I hate to put this discussion on hold, Hannah, but duty calls. I'll change into my uniform, then walk you home on the way to the elevator.'' He picked up the remote control and handed it to her. ''Watch the movie and find out if the good guy wins.''

He got to his feet, then leaned down and brushed his lips over hers.

''Until we can talk again after I wake up tomorrow,'' he said, close to her lips, ''don't think. Have you got that? You'll get yourself smack-dab in the middle of a major stress attack if you dwell on this. Okay? Promise me you'll at least try not to think?''

Hannah nodded, unable to speak due to the ache of

unshed tears in her throat. She watched Ted leave the room, then took a shuddering breath.

Don't think, she told herself. *Oh, please, Hannah, don't think.*

Ted stood under the spray of hot water in the shower, mentally repeating his own directive like a mantra.

Don't think, Sharpe.

Don't think.

He could not, would not, dwell on the discovery that he was in love with Hannah Johnson, not now, not when he was about to go on duty.

Oh, Lord, he was in love.

How in the hell had that happened? He kept in touch with himself, knew how he felt about things, what his reactions to events meant. How could a man suddenly find that he was deeply in love with a woman and not have been aware of his changing and growing feelings?

He sure hadn't been kidding when he'd told Hannah that love was sneaky. It was powerful, potent and…sneaky.

His first reaction had been shock that had shifted almost instantly to pure joy. An incredible warmth had suffused him, and he'd had the urge to shout his declaration of love from the rooftops.

But now?

It was really sinking in, and felt like a rough punch in the gut. He'd betrayed himself, broken his own vow made years before to never become seriously involved with a woman, never fall in love and definitely never entertain the idea of marriage.

Damn, what a mess.

He was in love with Hannah.

Mumbling several earthy expletives, he turned off the water, left the shower and began to dry himself with an oversize towel.

Don't think.

But how could he shut down his mind? The realization that he loved Hannah was beating against his brain.

Ted left the bathroom and began to dress, a frown knitting his eyebrows.

If he looked at the situation in the short term, it was great, fantastic. His beautiful Ms. Doodle was everything and more that a man could ever hope to have in a wife. The past months spent with her were the happiest of his entire life.

And the baby? The baby had captured his heart. He could hardly wait to see it, hold it. To be a father to that child, that miracle, would be one of the greatest gifts and honors he'd ever received.

The baby would be Hannah's and his. *His.* He would love it as his own, watch it grow and blossom like a wondrous flower that *he* was helping to nurture. Hannah would be his wife, he would be her husband, and the child now within her would be theirs.

But later? A few years down the road? The ugly truth would rise to the surface and destroy everything. It would be time for another baby, a sister or brother for the one they had.

But he couldn't give Hannah that child.

Because he wasn't a whole man.

"Damn it, Sharpe," he said aloud, "don't think. Not now."

Several hours later, Ryan drove the patrol car slowly down a residential street, automatically scanning the area for anything that appeared out of order.

"You're awfully quiet tonight, Ted," he said.

"What? Oh, I guess I don't have anything brilliant to say."

Ryan chuckled. "You rarely do, but that doesn't keep you from talking."

"Yeah, well…" Ted paused. "Ryan, are you and Deedee going to have another baby?"

"Where did that come from?"

"Just answer the question."

"Yes, we're planning on having two kids. Teddy is still a baby, so there's no rush. We'll probably talk about it in a year or so."

"What about Jenny and Michael? Their Bobby is getting to be a big boy."

Ryan nodded. "They're trying for another one. It just hasn't happened yet." He laughed. "Jillian says she and Forrest are finished producing little Mac-Allisters. They got three at once and that's it, thank you very much.

"Andrea hasn't said anything, but I have a feeling she'll get pregnant again, in spite of having twins already. She'd probably be thrilled out of her socks to have another set of twins. She's a natural-born mother."

"So is Hannah," Ted said. "I mean, granted, she

hasn't even had her baby yet, but all you have to do is watch her with the MacAllister brood to know the mothering instincts are there.''

''There's no doubt in my mind that she'll be a good mother,'' Ryan said. ''She could probably handle a houseful.''

''Yeah.'' Ted sighed. ''Yeah, I know.''

Ryan glanced over at him quickly, then redirected his attention to his driving.

''What's on your mind, Ted? Why the subject of who's having how many babies? And why are you so bummed-out? Are you and Hannah having problems?''

''No, we're doing fine,'' he said quietly.

''You sure seem happy together. At times, I actually forget that you're not the father of her baby. You hover over her, tell her to put up her feet, talk about the baby clothes you two bought, the whole nine yards. Don't slug me, but I think you're in love with Hannah. I also believe you consider that baby yours.''

Ted looked out the side window for several long seconds, then shifted his gaze to Ryan.

''You're right,'' he said. ''I *am* in love with Hannah. I didn't intend to be, but I am. And the baby? Hell, it's mine. I didn't have anything to do with its conception, but it's mine and Hannah's.''

''So what's the problem here?'' Ryan said. ''Marry the woman and give the kid your name from day one. Hannah's ex-husband relinquished his claim on that baby, so go for it, man.''

''It's not that simple, Ryan.''

"It sure sounds simple to me. Unless…" Ryan's voice trailed off.

"Unless what?"

"Hannah doesn't love *you*. No, that's nuts. The whole family has seen you two together. She's in love with you. That's a given. Has she told you she loves you?"

"No."

"Well, be patient. You know she's been badly hurt in the past, and her idea was to never trust her judgment about a man again. You're the real goods, Ted. I bet she realizes that but is wary, afraid to say it out loud. Is *that* why you're bummed? Because Hannah hasn't said she's in love with you?"

"No. Let's change the subject."

"But—"

"This discussion is over and out, MacAllister."

"Well, hell."

Early the next afternoon, Hannah said goodbye to one of her piano students, then began to close the door.

"Hold it," Ted called from down the hall.

He sprinted to her door, stopped, then stepped into the living room. Hannah closed and locked the door behind him. As she turned to look at him, their eyes met and neither moved, nor spoke.

He was in love with this woman, Ted thought.

He wanted to spend the rest of his life with her, sharing, caring, protecting her.

He wanted to make love to her at night and know she'd be next to him each morning.

He wanted to be a father to her child, the baby she carried within her that he loved as his own.

He wanted to ask her now, right now, to be his wife until death parted them.

Oh, how very much he wanted in regard to Hannah Johnson.

But none of it was his to have.

"So," he said, managing to smile, "how's life?"

Hannah blinked, bringing herself from the hazy place she'd floated to while being held immobile by Ted's mesmerizing blue eyes.

How's life? her mind echoed.

"How's life?" she said aloud, none too quietly. "As in, 'What's cookin', toots?' You announce that you love me, tell me not to think, which is like ordering a person not to breathe, then breeze in here as cocky as you please and say, 'How's life?' You have a lot of nerve, Ted Sharpe."

Ted nodded. "Got it. You're not in a daffodils-and-daisies mood."

"Not even close." She moved around him and crossed the room to lower herself onto the sofa in a not-very-graceful maneuver. "If I get any bigger," she muttered, "I'll need a crane to get up from here."

Now what? Ted wondered, turning slowly to look at her. He didn't know what to do or say, how to handle this. Damn, if only he hadn't told Hannah that he loved her. She was right; everything had been perfect until he'd blown it by opening his big mouth.

No, correct that. It wasn't perfect.

Perfect would be to hear Hannah declare her love for him, then accept his proposal of marriage.

Perfect would be raising the baby, then creating another one together in a few years.

Perfect wasn't going to happen.

Hannah smoothed her dress over her protruding stomach, averting her eyes from Ted's.

She had to quit screaming like a shrew, she told herself. It wasn't Ted's fault that his telling her he loved her had terrified her at the very same time that it filled her with the greatest joy she'd ever known.

It wasn't Ted's fault she was a befuddled, confused basket case.

It wasn't Ted's fault that she'd thought and thought, even though she'd tried so hard not to, had gotten in touch with herself and discovered...

Oh, dear heaven, discovered that she loved Theodore Sharpe with every breath in her blimp-size body.

"I'm...I'm sorry I yelled," she said, then slowly raised her eyes to look at him.

"Don't apologize. You had every right to holler." He went to the opposite end of the sofa and slouched onto the cushion.

Was this it? Hannah thought. Was this where Ted said he wanted to marry her? It was the natural order of things—*I love you and want you to be my wife.*

But what about the baby? Ted seemed enchanted with the idea of the baby. He'd made it clear that he wished to be involved in every aspect of her pregnancy, and all the preparations necessary for the baby's arrival.

Loving her meant loving the baby, too, and she knew, just somehow knew, that Ted realized that.

She knew what Ted was thinking and feeling? She,

of the lousy track record, was presuming, assuming, deciding that this man was honest and real? She was out of her tiny mind.

And she loved Ted so very much.

Oh, what a mess. And, oh, mercy, what was she going to do and say if the next words out of Ted's mouth were a proposal of marriage?

"Well," Ted said, then sighed.

Get ready, Hannah, she told herself. Gear up. This was it.

"Well," he said again, "hell."

Hannah's eyes widened. "Hell? Oh." Was she disappointed? Relieved? Why didn't she know? Hell?

Ted shifted to face her, a frown on his face. "Hannah, do you love me?"

"Yes," she heard herself say.

That was great, just dandy, she fumed. He'd caught her off guard and she'd answered the question honestly, by reflex, as calmly as though he'd asked her if she wanted another slice of pizza. This situation was going from bad to worse, *very* quickly.

"I see," he said. "You love me."

Hallelujah! his mind sang. Hannah loved him! Hannah Johnson, his beautiful Ms. Doodle, was in love with him.

That was fantastic.

No, that was *not* good, not good at all.

She loved him and she knew he loved her. The next thing on the agenda should be to discuss getting married. But he couldn't marry Hannah; she deserved more than he was. She deserved a husband who was a whole man.

"Look," he said, "we love each other and we both love that baby. You *do* know how I feel about the baby, don't you?"

Hannah nodded, her gaze riveted on his face.

"We...um...have a nice routine worked out," he went on. "My duty shifts don't cause a problem with your giving piano lessons, because I have my own apartment where I can sleep at odd hours. We cook together, spend the evening together, sleep together, there, here, wherever the mood strikes. It seems to me that our loving each other..."

Damn it, he thought, he hated this. He couldn't leave her, not yet. He had to see her safely through the birth of the baby. Then he'd go, give her the opportunity to find a man who could give her everything she deserved to have. But what he really wanted was to marry her!

"Yes?" Hannah said, leaning slightly toward him. "Our loving each other...what?"

"Shouldn't change anything," he said, feeling a knot tighten in his gut. He shrugged. "We'll just keep on keeping on...exactly as we're doing."

"Oh, well..." Hannah waved one hand in the air. "Sure. You bet. That sounds just fine, Ted."

Yes, it was the best plan, she told herself. Now she didn't have to worry if loving Ted was another of her mistakes in judgment. It wasn't as though she was going to marry the man, for Pete's sake. If she was wrong about him, it would be much easier to deal with under the structure of their relationship as it now stood.

It was really a splendid idea, no doubt about it.

Then why did she feel as though her heart were splintering into a million pieces?

Chapter Ten

Thanksgiving, Ted thought, standing in front of the bathroom mirror to adjust his tie. It hardly seemed possible that the holiday season was already here.

Ted left the bathroom, then looked at his watch.

There was plenty of time before he and Hannah were due at the senior MacAllisters home for the traditional gathering of the clan for the Thanksgiving feast. This year, the event would also include celebrating Teddy's first birthday.

Thanksgiving, Ted mentally repeated as he wandered aimlessly around the living room.

He and Hannah had watched the parades on television that morning. No, that wasn't quite accurate. Hannah had watched the parades, while he'd watched Hannah watching the parades. He hadn't been able to take his eyes off her, nor curb his smile. She'd been like an enchanted little girl, her dark eyes sparkling, her continual "Oh, look, Ted, look" an absolute delight.

She was something, all right, his beautiful Ms. Doodle, and he loved her more with every passing day.

Ted's glance fell on the telephone and he replayed in his mind the conversation he'd had earlier with his parents. Thanksgiving greetings had been exchanged, along with the usual chitchat about his job, their leisure activities and the weather.

He had not said one word to his folks about the existence of Hannah Johnson in his life.

What was the point?

Why tell them he was in love for the first time?

Why tell them that Hannah had stolen his heart and there was no way possible he could ever get it back?

Why tell them that a baby, a miracle, was to be born with the coming of the New Year, a baby that in his heart, mind and soul was his?

What was the point, when he knew that after Hannah gave birth, he would be moving to another apartment, away from the building, out of her life?

Why explain that, because he loved her so deeply, he had to leave?

"Oh, man," Ted said aloud, dragging his hands down his face. Too restless to sit down, he went into the spare bedroom to stand in front of the worktable.

The dollhouse was just about finished. He had a few more touches of paint and stain to apply, then he'd assemble it and place the furniture in the rooms.

He enjoyed the project, but the closer he came to completing it, the more he wondered why he bothered to spend countless hours laboring over it. It would sit there gathering dust between rare visits from one or more of the MacAllister little girls.

Ted picked up one of the pieces—the framework and the front door of the house. He'd carved an intricate pattern on the door, then stained it dark and glossy.

He opened and shut the door several times, nodding in satisfaction that it moved smoothly back and forth.

A dollhouse, he mused, putting the piece back on the table. A doll *home?* No, it was a house, because there were no people. There would be walls, rooms, a roof and furniture, but as yet there wasn't a toy family to take up residence, to make it a home.

He had to decide if he'd make the figures, or buy them. He also had to decide when he would add the family, thus changing the house to a home.

A family. A mother, father and two babies. Two. Not one child, but two.

Ted closed his eyes for a moment, shook his head, then opened his eyes again and left the room.

He sat down on the sofa, leaned his head back and stared at the ceiling.

For years, he thought, he'd buried and ignored the truth of his inability to father a child. Now? The harsh reality was with him every day, tormenting him, haunting him, forcing him to accept his inadequacy and the ultimate price he was to pay for it.

He was going to lose Hannah and the baby.

One night when he'd been unable to sleep, he'd

gently rested one hand on Hannah's stomach as she slept peacefully beside him. He'd savored each precious time he'd felt the baby move.

He'd fantasized about telling Hannah the truth, mentally supplied her with a smile, a shrug and the words, "Oh, well, no problem, Ted. We'll have one baby and Daisy the cat. You can't give me another child? Don't stress. It's no big deal."

He had jerked his hand away from Hannah's body, from the baby, and left the bed, trying to escape from the pain of knowing it *was* a problem, it *was* a big deal.

But there was nowhere to run or hide from the crushing truth, from reality.

Thanksgiving, he thought, with Christmas close behind, then the New Year, the birth of the baby, then...

Nothing.

Just emptiness.

Loneliness, cold and dark.

Ted shifted forward to rest his elbows on his knees, sinking his head into his hands.

"Ah, Hannah," he said, his voice raspy with emotion, "I love you so damn much."

He was jolted from his misery by the sound of the piano being played at full volume. He jerked his head up and listened.

"'Yankee Doodle,'" he said, recognizing the song. He looked at his watch. "Yes, ma'am, Ms. Doodle, I read you loud and clear, very loud. It's time to get going."

He grabbed his sport coat from the back of a chair and left the apartment, anticipating the moment when

Hannah would open the door and greet him with a smile on her face and love shining in her incredible, big dark eyes.

And she did, along with the addition of her laughter, which made Ted's smile grow even bigger.

"You got my message," she said, stepping back so he could enter. "I wondered if playing 'Yankee Doodle' would accomplish the job of bringing you over here."

"It certainly did." He encircled her with his arms and drew her as close to him as the baby allowed. "You look beautiful, Ms. Doodle."

"Thank you. I thought burnt orange was an appropriate shade to wear for Thanksgiving. It's an autumn color."

"Mmm," he said, then captured her lips with his.

Hannah welcomed the kiss, parting her lips so Ted's tongue could slip between to seek and find her tongue, stroking it in a sensuous duel.

She filled her senses with his aroma of woodsy after-shave, soap and man, savored the feel of his powerful body, and the taste of his mouth molded so perfectly to hers. She could hear the rapid tempo of her heart echoing in her ears.

Ted reluctantly raised his head and had to draw a deep breath before he could speak.

"Ready for some turkey and all the trimmings?" he said finally.

Hannah nodded. "I'm really hungry. I'll probably make a piggy of myself." She paused. "Ted, we still have a few minutes before we have to go. I'd like to talk to you. All right?"

"Sure." He released her, then grasped one of her hands. "Come with me to the sofa, my dear."

Hannah laughed. "No, I'll sit in the straight chair so we don't have to use up an extra ten minutes prying me out of those puffy cushions."

"Oh, okay," he said, chuckling.

He sat down on the sofa and Hannah settled onto the chair. Daisy jumped up next to Ted.

"Hey, big stuff," he said, scratching her under the chin. Daisy purred and closed her eyes. "You make it up here in a single bound now." He patted her on the head, then looked at Hannah. "You have the floor, Ms. Doodle. You can have the ceiling and walls, too, if you want them."

Hannah smiled, then became serious.

"Ted," she said, meeting his gaze, "my gran and I had traditions on Thanksgiving. We watched the parades on television, then cooked dinner together. Before we ate, we would talk about what we were thankful for. Gran said it wasn't just a day for parades and lots of fancy food, it was a time to stop, take inventory and give thanks for our blessings."

Ted nodded. "That's nice. It sounds exactly like something your gran would say."

"Well, I did that today, stopped and took inventory. I want you to know..." She took a steadying breath and lifted her chin. "I want you to know that I not only love you, but I believe in you, trust you and have no shadows of doubt about whether or not you really are who you present yourself to be."

A chill swept through Ted and a painful knot twisted in his gut.

"For the first time in my life," she went on, "I've chosen well. I haven't made a mistake about the man I love, the one who holds my heart in his hands for safekeeping. For that, I'm very grateful and felt that today, Thanksgiving, was an appropriate time to tell you."

Oh, dear Lord, Ted thought, what had he done? Hannah's words were beautiful, a precious gift to be treasured. She'd moved past her fears and was now prepared to go forward with her life.

She loved him. Believed in him. Trusted him.

And she was making a terrible mistake.

He had a dark secret that he had knowingly kept from her. And because of that, he was going to hurt her, just as the men in her past had done, the ones she'd chosen to love and trust.

He couldn't bear the thought of Hannah's disillusionment because of him. She'd feel betrayed yet again, because of him. She'd blame herself, restore power to her fears, and resurrect her ghosts, because of him.

Oh, God. He had to tell her the truth about himself now, *right now,* Ted declared to himself. He had to tell her that he couldn't give her a baby, and because he loved her so very much, he had to leave her so she could find a man to love who could give her more children. He was lying to her with his silence.

But what if… The thought came to Ted suddenly. Could it be possible that Hannah would still love him, agree to marry him and spend the rest of her life with him if she knew the truth? Would the child she now carried be enough to fulfill her maternal needs, her nurturing nature?

Or…would she consider adopting a child? Maybe two or three… Hell, a houseful of little ones who needed love, and a home, and parents who would consider them their own? Oh, man, Ted thought, that would be fantastic. They'd buy a big house and it would ring with the joyous sound of children's laughter.

"Ted?" Hannah said, bringing him from his racing thoughts.

"What? Oh, I'm sorry, Hannah. I was digesting what you said."

Hannah frowned. "You don't look too pleased about it. I thought…well, I thought you'd be happy to hear that I love you totally, with absolutely no reservations or doubts. I also believe that you love me and the baby in the same way."

"I do," he said quickly. "Oh, yes, Hannah, I do love you and the baby."

Tell her the truth! his mind hammered. *Lay it all out there and pray.*

"I'm honored that you believe in me," he said, "and trust in me. I really am." *Damn it, Sharpe, tell her.* "Thank you, Hannah."

She smiled at him warmly. "You're welcome."

I want to marry you, Ted Sharpe, her mind sang, *spend my life with you, raise this baby together, as well as the babies we'll have in the future. Ask me to be your wife, Ted. Ask me so I can say yes, yes, yes.*

"Hannah, I…" Ted's voice trailed off. A trickle of sweat ran down his back. No, he couldn't do it, not yet. It was too risky. What if he lost his Hannah? What if he saw disappointment on her face, then disgust, then the warm love in her eyes turn cold as she sent him away forever? No! "I think we'd better hit the road. If we don't get going, we'll be late."

He got to his feet and glanced around.

"Where's our birthday present for Teddy?" he said. "I swear, that stuffed toy beagle we got him looks exactly like nutso Scooter. Ryan is picking up my share of the wine for dinner when he gets his. Oh, you're taking fruit salad. Right? Come on, Hannah, we've got to be on our way."

Hannah looked at him intently, wishing she could peer into his brain.

She nodded, got to her feet, then headed toward the kitchen to retrieve the salad from the refrigerator.

Ted was acting strangely, she thought. He was talking too fast, wasn't looking directly at her and appeared suddenly nervous and edgy.

Should she have kept silent about believing in him, trusting him? She thought he'd be pleased to know she'd dealt with her ghosts and her fears; she had put them to rest at long last.

She was the one who had panicked when he'd first told her he loved her. She'd begged him not to love her, just erase those emotions like chalk from a blackboard. *Things were perfect as they were,* she declared at the time. *So couldn't they just continue on status quo?*

Ted had agreed, but she'd felt as though she'd let him down, hadn't been able to give to him what he wanted, needed and deserved to have.

But now?

Now they could have it all—a future, family, forever love—that would withstand the rigors of time.

When Ted had agreed to leave the structure of their relationship as it was, she'd thought he was compromising, settling for less than he'd hoped to have. Had he since realized that the way things were suited him just fine? Did he intend to assume his Professional Uncle role in regard to her baby?

What was Ted thinking? Feeling?

They had to sit down and have a long talk, communicate, have questions asked and answers given, she decided. But there wasn't time for that today.

"Yo, Ms. Doodle," Ted said. "We're going to be unfashionably late."

"I'm coming. Teddy's gift is in the linen closet. Would you get it, please?"

"Sure. Hey, Daisy, want us to bring you a big ole drumstick?"

Several hours later, the scrumptious meal had been consumed, the kitchen cleaned, and to everyone's amazement, all the little ones were taking naps at the same time. The family would celebrate Teddy's birthday after the children had rested and were once again bundles of energy.

"Football-game time," Michael said. "I'm heading for the family room."

"Whoa," Forrest said. "There's important business to tend to first."

"Uh-oh," Andrea said. "I'm getting vibes about The Baby Bet."

"Oh, dear," Hannah said, laughing. "Don't you think there's too much other betting going on today, Forrest?"

"As the champion of The Baby Bet, I can put it into action when I so decree." He pressed one fingertip to the middle of his forehead. "Ah, yes, it's time to make my unbeatable prediction." He whipped a pen and a small notebook out of his shirt pocket. "Get your money ready, people. Crisp twenty-dollar bills. I don't take credit cards."

"Margaret," Robert MacAllister said, "your son is extremely obnoxious about The Baby Bet."

"*Your* son," she said, "has a head about the size of Toledo because he has never lost The Baby Bet. So *please* give very serious consideration to your prediction."

"Get as serious as you want to, Dad," Forrest said, "but I'll still win. What can I say? I'm an ace at this."

"Honey," Jillian said, smiling, "you're going to have a lot of crow to eat one of these days."

"Never happen, my sweet," Forrest said. "Okay, here's my bet. Hannah will have a boy on New Year's Day."

"Nope, nope, nope," Andrea said. "Hannah's baby is a smart cookie. He'll arrange to be a tax deduction for all of this year. I'm betting it's a boy on New Year's Eve. He'll be born on December thirty-first."

"Got it," Forrest said, recording his sister's bet on the pad of paper.

"No," Robert said, "a boy on my birthday, January fifth."

"A girl on New Year's Day," Michael said.

"No way," Ryan said. "He won't want to share the limelight with a holiday. He's going to be his own man. Twenty bucks on a boy on January second."

"Check," Forrest said, scribbling away. He glanced around the room. "Anyone else?"

No one spoke.

"All right," Forrest said, "all bets are recorded and—"

"A baby girl," Ted said quietly. "She'll be born on…on Christmas."

Hannah turned to look at Ted, her eyes widening. "Christmas?"

Ted nodded. "Yes. She'll arrive on Christmas. It's a girl with dark, silky hair like yours. We'd better have a present for her under the tree. It would be very tacky not to have a gift for someone you know is coming for Christmas. Did you write that down, Forrest?"

"Yup. Kiss your twenty goodbye, Sharpe."

Ted looked directly into Hannah's eyes. "Not this time. I know what I know."

"You really believe that you're right," Hannah said, an incredulous tone to her voice.

"Ms. Doodle…" Ted leaned forward and brushed his lips over hers. "It's guaranteed."

"Goodness," Deedee said, "you've convinced me, Ted. Ryan, withdraw your bet. You just threw away twenty dollars."

"All bets are final," Forrest said, flipping the notebook closed. "Ted, my boy, it will be a pleasure taking your money. I had the market cornered on being cocky about The Baby Bet, but you're outshining me here, you arrogant bum."

Ted just grinned at him.

"Cut it out," Forrest said. "You're making me nervous."

"*You're* nervous?" Hannah said, laughing. "I adore Christmas. I love opening presents and eating all the goodies, singing carols, everything that goes with the day. I wasn't planning on having a baby instead."

"Sorry, ma'am," Ted said, "but that's how it is. We'll celebrate Christmas a day late. No problem."

"Enough, enough," Andrea said, flapping her hands in the air. "You're giving me goose bumps, Ted. Hannah, have you chosen names for the baby yet?"

"If it's a girl, I want to name her after my gran, Patricia Elizabeth, and call her Patty. I haven't decided on a boy's name yet."

"You won't need one," Ted said. "Patty." He nodded. "Patricia Elizabeth. Patty. Nice, very nice."

Patty Sharpe, Hannah thought wistfully. Patricia Elizabeth Sharpe. It sounded absolutely perfect.

"Football," Michael said, getting to his feet.

Patty Sharpe, Ted thought. Patricia Elizabeth Sharpe. Mr. and Mrs. Theodore Sharpe and their daughter, Patricia Elizabeth, cordially invite... *Sharpe, shut up.*

"Football," Ted echoed.

"Bye," Hannah said, waggling her fingers at him.

"Don't you want to watch the game?" Ted said.

"Well, it's tempting. There are some very nice tushes displayed by those tight pants the players wear. But then they totally gross me out by spitting all the time. Spit, spit, spit. Their poor mothers must be mortified when they see that."

Ted hooted with laughter and joined the male exodus from the room. Hannah watched him go, a soft smile on her lips. When she turned her head again, her gaze collided with Deedee's.

"Patricia Elizabeth...Sharpe?" Deedee said.

"No, Deedee," Hannah said quietly, "I don't believe so." She splayed one hand on her stomach. "I think this is Patricia Elizabeth Johnson."

"Time will tell, dear," Margaret said. "Men, bless their silly hearts, are very unpredictable."

"Amen to that," Jillian said.

"You'd better have a boy's name ready, Hannah," Andrea said. "Forrest has never lost The Baby Bet, you know, and he says you're having a boy."

"Then it's a boy," Jenny said. "Forrest just doesn't lose The Baby Bet. You'll have a boy on New Year's Day, just as he predicted."

"Time will tell," Margaret repeated. "Babies are just as unpredictable as men."

"Uh-oh," Jillian said. "I hear little voices from down the hall. I think the troops are waking up. I'm going to convince the triplets that they want to watch football with their daddy."

"Good idea, Jillian," Deedee said. "I'll plunk Teddy in Ryan's lap, too. We'll let the daddies chase them around the family room for a while."

As Deedee, Jillian, Andrea and Jenny left the room to collect the children, a wave of chilling loneliness swept over Hannah.

A daddy, she thought, resting her hands on her stomach in a protective gesture. She'd hoped, more than she'd even realized at the time, that telling Ted she trusted and believed in him, knew she had finally chosen the right man to love, would bring a smile to his face, then a change in the structure of their relationship.

She wanted to marry Ted Sharpe.

She wanted the baby to have Ted as her daddy.

But he had acted so strangely when she made her grand announcement that she'd counted her blessings, per the Thanksgiving tradition her gran had taught her. He'd seemed uncomfortable and suddenly nervous as she told him she now knew he was exactly who he presented himself to be.

Then she'd decided they needed to sit down and talk things through, communicate, share their thoughts and feelings.

But now? During the hours since that scene in her apartment, she was having second thoughts about the idea of a serious discussion with Ted. He knew how she felt, where she was emotionally. What more could she say that he didn't already know? Nothing.

The ball, as the cliché went, was in Ted's court. Her future, the baby's future, were in his hands. Did he want to be a husband and father? Or would he be satisfied with the roles of lover and Professional Uncle?

She didn't know. She just didn't know what Ted really wanted.

"Hannah," Margaret said gently, bringing her out of her reverie, "I feel I need to say this again. Time will tell."

Hannah managed to produce a weak smile as she nodded her agreement, unable to speak as unshed tears closed her throat.

Late that night, Deedee wiggled close to Ryan in their bed.

"Ryan," she said, poking him on the arm, "are you awake?"

"I am now," he mumbled.

"This is important. Has Ted given you any indication, even the slightest hint, that he intends to ask Hannah to marry him?"

"No."

"Have you asked him about it?"

"No."

"Why not?"

"If he had something to tell me, he'd tell me. Good night, Deedee."

"Men. Good grief, if a woman wants to know what another woman is thinking, she asks her. Couldn't you sort of nudge Ted toward the subject of his marrying Hannah and see what he says?"

"No. Good night, Deedee."

"But, Ryan, he's obviously in love with Hannah, and he's thrilled to pieces about that baby. Why doesn't he make them all a family, marry Hannah, give the baby his name? What on earth is that man's problem?''

"Deedee?"

"Yes?"

"Good night!"

"Well, darn. Good night, Ryan."

Chapter Eleven

Immediately after Thanksgiving, merchants rushed to transform their stores into Christmassy fairylands, hoping to entice holiday shoppers.

Everyone took deep, fortifying breaths and began to make endless lists of what needed to be accomplished to assure wonderful celebrations, and then rolled their eyes heavenward as they envisioned the balances due on credit cards in January.

Ted, Ryan and police officers across the country geared up for hectic work shifts, knowing the crime rate would increase in the frenzy, as it did each year.

The MacAllisters, like many large families, drew names for gift giving among the adults, while agreeing that presents should be bought for all the children.

At a bring-a-dessert-to-share gathering at Jillian and Forrest's two weeks after Thanksgiving, Robert

Mac-Allister announced that he had put the names on slips of paper into a bowl, per the tradition, and the drawing would commence after the vast array of desserts were consumed.

Hannah frowned and leaned close to Ted, hoping the chatter taking place around the large table would muffle what she was about to say for Ted's ears only.

"Ted," she whispered, "you didn't tell me this get-together was for the purpose of drawing names for Christmas gifts. I shouldn't be here."

"Why not?" he said, matching her whisper.

"Because I'm not one of the family."

"Either am I, but I'm in the draw each year. You're considered part of the group, just as I am. I meant to tell you what we were going to do here tonight, but it slipped my mind."

"But—"

"Hey, you belong here, just as I do." He brushed a kiss over her lips. "Trust me."

"Mmm," she said, glowering at him.

Ted laughed, then directed his attention to Michael, who had just asked him a question.

Well, Hannah thought, so be it. She couldn't very well refuse to draw a name, nor ask that hers be removed from the bowl. She'd just sit back and savor being part of this marvelous family.

She took a bite of carrot cake and inwardly sighed.

What would be happening in her life a year from now? Would she and Ted still be together, as they now were; Ted living in his apartment, she in hers? Would Ted be interacting with the baby in his favored role of Professional Uncle? Would her child be just another little one he lavished with attention before merrily going on his bachelor way?

There had been no serious discussion after Thanksgiving regarding her heartfelt announcement to Ted that she believed in him and trusted him. Ted had continued to be attentive, thoughtful and loving. She couldn't find fault with anything he'd said or done, but...

There was, Hannah knew, a seed of sadness within her that she hoped wouldn't grow bigger, all-consuming. She was trying, she really was, to view each dawn as a daffodils-and-daisies day, not dwell on her yearning to be Ted's wife.

She'd mentally scolded herself on more than one occasion, telling herself that she should count her blessings for what she had, not even be thinking about what was missing.

To have a wonderful man in her life who loved her and who loved a baby who had been fathered by someone else, was a rare gift to be cherished. She'd fully expected to be alone during and after her pregnancy. But Ted was there for her, as was the whole MacAllister family.

She *was* grateful, she truly was, but she was also human, with natural desires. She wanted to marry the man she loved. The man she loved with an intensity she never would have dreamed possible.

But it wasn't going to happen.

Nothing had changed since her declaration on Thanksgiving. Well, that wasn't entirely true. Ted seemed to like saying, 'Trust me,' when it fit the circumstances, because now he knew she did. But that was it—the only difference in their relationship between before and after Thanksgiving.

Time will tell, Margaret MacAllister had said. Time was telling, all right, Hannah thought. Ted Sharpe had no intention of marrying Hannah Johnson, nor being a real father to the baby. And the truth was making her sad, so very, very sad.

"So, Hannah," Forrest said, bringing her from her gloomy thoughts, "how's the New Year's Day baby doing? Been to the doctor lately?"

Hannah smiled. "Yes, I have, as a matter of fact. Said boy is turning and dropping right on schedule. Gosh, Forrest, when he's born on New Year's Day, do you suppose he'll be tossing confetti around the delivery room?"

"Now, there's a thought," Forrest said. "It wouldn't surprise me at all."

"You're cooked, MacAllister," Ted said. "It's a girl, remember? Born on Christmas, remember? The Baby Bet championship title is changing hands, remember? I have to decide what I'm going to buy with those pretty twenty-dollar bills."

"Never happen, Sharpe," Forrest said, a *very* smug expression on his face. "Facts are facts when it comes to The Baby Bet. I can't be beat." He leaned forward and peered at Hannah's stomach. "Yo, Baby Doodle, this is Uncle Forrest speaking. Don't let me down, kiddo. I have my reputation, as well as my wallet, to protect."

"Your sanity could use some scrutiny," Jillian said, laughing. "Baby Doodle has a mind of his own."

"Her," Ted said. "Girls are referred to as 'her,' Jillian."

"Attention, attention," Robert MacAllister said suddenly. "It's time to do the deed. The rules are the same as every year. If you draw your own name, or your husband's, wife's—" he smiled at Hannah and Ted "—or significant other, put it back in the bowl and pull out another slip of paper."

"We should change that rule," Andrea said. "I'd love to buy myself a super Christmas present."

"You *do,*" said her husband, John. "You even wrap it and put a tag on it that says, To Andrea from Santa Claus."

"I know," she said, laughing. "But if I picked my own name, I could do it legally."

"Nope," Robert said, "the rules stand. You can't have your important person's name, either, because it goes without saying that you'd better buy them a gift if you want to live long enough to see Hannah's son born on January fifth."

"Oh," Jillian said with a moan. "Please don't bring up the subject of The Baby Bet again. Forrest is getting hard to live with."

"You're just figuring that out?" Michael said. "You're a tad slow on the uptake, Jillian. Forrest has been a pain in the tush since the day he was born."

"Children," Margaret said, smiling at their nonsense, "your father is speaking. Behave yourselves."

"Thank you, Margaret," Robert said. "This is serious business. There are only three weeks until Christmas. Prepare to shop, people." He picked up the bowl. "Let the ceremony begin."

Robert moved around the table, bowing as he presented the bowl to each participant. Everyone was soon laughing, talking and making grand performances of hiding the name on their slip of paper.

Hannah drew Andrea's name, then turned to Ted.

"Who did you get?" she asked him.

"My lips are sealed."

"You won't even tell *me?* We're going Christmas shopping together."

"Only to a point, Ms. Doodle," he said, grinning. "You won't be around when I buy a gift for the person on this slip of paper, *or* when I shop for you."

"Phooey on you," Hannah said, poking her nose in the air.

"Well said," Deedee said.

"I'm macho and tough," Ted said. "I can handle 'phooey on you.'"

Just then, the telephone rang and Forrest went to answer it. A few moments later, he yelled from the kitchen. "Hey, Ryan, Ted, one of you guys come take this call."

"Uh-oh," Ryan said, getting to his feet.

"Oh, boy," Ted said, shaking his head.

Hannah looked at him. "Do you think you're being told to come back on duty?"

"Guaranteed. We're all on standby until after New Year's. We have to leave a number where we can be reached twenty-four hours a day. It's not just the season to be jolly."

Ryan strode back into the room. "Let's roll, partner. We've got a dozen cars or more in a pileup. They need traffic and crowd control, and reports written."

"Oh, joy and rapture," Ted said. He gave Hannah a quick kiss, then swept his eyes over the group. "Someone take Hannah home, okay? All the way home. Don't just drop her off at the complex. See her safely inside her apartment, and listen for the lock to snap into place."

"Yes, sir," Forrest said, saluting. "I understand, sir."

Ryan kissed Deedee, then Ryan and Ted hurried from the room.

"Ah, the perks of being a police officer's wife," Deedee said. "Guess what, Hannah? You *don't* get used to this, or the worry that goes with the title, either. You just deal with it the best you can."

Hannah nodded absently, then conversation resumed around the table.

Oh, she *was* learning to 'deal with it,' Hannah thought. But the glaring difference between herself and Deedee, was that Hannah Johnson was *not* a police officer's *wife*.

Late the next afternoon, an exhausted Ted entered his apartment. He and Ryan had been kept busy through the night, then had stayed on duty for their assigned day shift. He'd telephoned Hannah before leaving the station, saying he was dead tired but fine, and would see her late that evening after he'd slept for an hour or two.

He'd no sooner crawled naked between the cool sheets on his bed and lowered his head to the inviting pillow, when the telephone rang.

"Hell," he muttered.

He snatched up the receiver from the telephone on the nightstand.

"What!" he said, his head still burrowed deep in the pillow.

"Oh, dear," a woman said, "I woke you. I'm terribly sorry. Shall I call later?"

"Mom?" Ted said, jerking upward to a sitting position.

"Yes, it's your mother," Susan Sharpe said, laughing softly, "who knows from experience that a wise person never wakes a sleeping baby. Tell me what time I should call you back."

"No, no, I'm awake. I just got off a double shift and hit the sheets, but I wasn't asleep yet. What's doin'?"

"I'll make this quick so you can get your rest. Your father and I have decided to come over there in the motor home after Christmas.

"We'd love to spend the actual holiday with you, but your aunt and uncle are joining us here on Christmas Day. We'll celebrate with you a couple of days late."

Holy hell, Ted thought, his mind racing. His parents couldn't come for a visit. Hannah was here!

"We'll stay at that nice park that we discovered last time we visited you," Susan went on. "We can hook up the motor home to electricity, they have lovely shower facilities, shuffleboard, all kinds of goodies. We'll entertain ourselves and connect with you when you're off duty. How does all this sound to you, Ted?"

"It sounds...um," he started. Terrible. It was a disaster in the making. Oh, man, what a mess. "Great, just great."

Susan laughed. "I'll chalk up your lack of enthusiasm to the fact that you're tired. Well, get some sleep, my darling. I'll give you more details about when we're arriving after we've figured everything out. Your father and I are looking forward to seeing you."

"Oh, I'm...I'm eager to see you both, too. Yup. You bet, Mom."

"Goodbye for now, dear."

"Yeah. Bye."

Ted replaced the receiver, then sank back onto the pillow with a groan.

"Oh, man," he said, dragging his hands down his face. He dropped his arms to the bed with a thud.

"Mom, Dad," he said aloud, "this is Hannah, also known as Ms. Doodle. That cute lump is her baby. I love this woman and child, but don't get excited about it, because I'm walking out of Hannah's life right after the baby has arrived safely.

"Why? Because I can't give her *another* baby in the future. That's not fair to her. Get it? So, say hello, Hannah, then goodbye, Hannah, and be done with it."

Ted closed his eyes and moaned again.

"I don't believe this. What in the hell am I going to do?"

The next day, as Ted and Ryan were cruising in the patrol car through the parking lot of a large shopping mall, Ted sighed.

"Okay, Sharpe," Ryan said, "that's ten."

Ted looked over at Ryan, obviously confused. "Ten what?"

"Ten sighs, moans, whatever you want to call them. What's on your mind?"

Ted sighed.

"Eleven."

"Yeah, okay, okay. My folks are coming to visit right after Christmas."

"Oh? That's nice. They're good people, fun to be with. All the MacAllisters like them a lot. So far, I'm missing the problem here."

"Damn it, Ryan, how am I going to keep them from seeing and meeting Hannah?"

Ryan frowned. "Why would you want to?"

"Because... Oh, hell, forget it."

"Is there some reason that you think they wouldn't like or accept Hannah? And the baby?"

"No, they'd love her on sight. And the baby? My mom would be ecstatic. She'd run, not walk, to the nearest store for yarn so she could knit the baby something. It wouldn't matter to them if I was the father of that child or not. They'd be thrilled out of their socks that I was involved with Hannah. In fact, they'd know that I wasn't the..." His voice trailed off.

"Wasn't the what?"

"Nothing."

"The father of the baby?" Ryan said. "Come on, Ted, I know your folks. They're very together. They don't think for one minute that you're living like a monk. They might wonder why you haven't married Hannah, but.... Okay, I'm going for it. Ted, everyone in the family can't figure out why you haven't married Hannah.''

''Yeah, well, I go around with a twenty-four-hour-a-day knot in my gut because I have a feeling that Hannah is wondering the same thing. She's just too classy to come right out and ask me what the holdup is.''

''*I'm* not that classy. Sharpe, why haven't you married Hannah?''

Ted shifted his gaze out the side window of the vehicle.

''I can't,'' he said quietly.

Ryan glanced over at him quickly, then redirected his attention to his driving. He left the parking lot and drove into a residential area. The heavy silence in the car was broken only by an occasional exchange over the radio.

''Want to talk about it?'' Ryan said finally.

''No.'' Ted paused, then looked at Ryan. ''Yeah, I think maybe I *would* like to talk about it. It's been bottled up inside of me for so damn long, buried where I didn't have to deal with it. Now, because of Hannah, I have to face it head-on and it's ripping me up.

''The thing is, Ryan, I realize that you and Deedee share everything. I couldn't handle her knowing about this. It's going to be tough enough telling *you*.''

''I give you my word that whatever you say is just between the two of us. Deedee would understand and respect that. You're hurtin', buddy. I can hear it in your voice. You've seen me through some really bad times, Lord knows. I'm here, I'll listen, if you want to talk.''

Ted drew a shuddering breath.

''Ryan, I love Hannah so much. And that baby? I love her like she was my own. She *is* mine, in my heart, my mind. I can hardly wait to see her, hold her. She's a miracle. I feel her move, dance a jig inside Hannah, and I choke up. I'm awed by the wonder of her.''

Ryan nodded but didn't speak.

''Sometimes,'' Ted went on, his voice raspy, ''I allow myself to fantasize about marrying Hannah, the two of us raising the baby together in a nice house filled with love, laughter, daffodils and daisies. Man, what a beautiful picture that scenario is in my mind. Perfect. Absolutely perfect. Until...'' He shook his head.

Ryan waited silently.

''Until,'' Ted continued, ''it's time to consider having another baby. Then the dream vanishes, destroyed by the truth. Ryan, I'm...I'm sterile. I had the mumps when I was sixteen and it left me... I'm not a whole man. I can't give Hannah a baby, not ever. Now do you understand why I haven't asked her to marry me? Why I won't ever ask her?''

Ryan released a pent-up breath. ''No.''

''Hell. You can't possibly relate to how I feel. You fathered Teddy. You'll click off another kid when you decide you want one. Forget it. There's no sense in talking to you about this.''

''Hold it, buddy. I listened and now I have the right to speak. Where is this 'I'm not a whole man' stuff coming from? Ted, a guy isn't measured by his sperm count!

"So, okay, you had the mumps and you're sterile because you did. It happens. That doesn't make you less of a man, not in the things that matter. I can't believe you have the attitude you do. What...or maybe it's who...made you come to this conclusion?"

"My father!"

"Dean Sharpe?" Ryan said, shock evident on his face and in his voice. "Your dad? I've known him for years and I can't... He said to your face that you weren't a whole man because you can't father a child?"

"No. No, I overheard him talking to my mom after the doctor called with the test results," Ted said, suddenly weary, totally exhausted. "I ran out of the house, ran as fast and as far as I could. My folks didn't know I was there when they were discussing it. Later, when they told me, I blew it off, said it was no big deal.

"My dad put his arm around me, said there were babies all over the world who needed homes, people to love them. I could get married and adopt kids. But I knew how he really felt about me. His precious son wasn't a whole man, never would be."

"You were sixteen years old. You could have misinterpreted what your father said to your mother. Didn't you ever sit down with your dad and clear the air?"

"No. There was nothing more to say. Ever since then, there's been something missing between me and my father. Things were never quite the same after that.''

''Oh, man,'' Ryan said, shaking his head.

''Time passed, I became a cop, a swinging-single bachelor to the max, then a Professional Uncle to the MacAllister kids. But then...''

''Hannah.''

Ted nodded. ''Hannah, my beautiful Ms. Doodle, and Patricia Elizabeth, the baby girl I'd sell my soul to hear call me Daddy.''

''Ted, don't you think Hannah has the right to make her own decision about this? You're deciding that you're not good enough for her. She has a mind, you know. Even more, she has a heart. She loves you, Ted.

''Tell her the truth. See how she feels about adopting, or just raising the one baby that's on the way. She's the other half of this scenario. She has the right to have a voice in this.''

''No. I can't tell her. I've left it too late. She's come to believe in me and trust in me. But I've lied to her with my silence. I'm no better than the other jerks who hurt her in the past.

''After the baby is born, I'm leaving. I'm getting out of her life so she can have what she deserves in a man. She'll find someone who can give her another baby.''

''Damn it, Ted, don't do this. You're making a terrible mistake. Go to Hannah, talk to her, tell her the truth.''

''No!''

''Why in the hell not?'' Ryan yelled.

"Because she loves me!"

Ryan opened his mouth, shut it again, then gave his head a sharp shake as though attempting to clear a sudden fog that had dropped over his brain.

"Did that make sense?" Ryan said. "No, it definitely did *not*. Want to run that by me again, Sharpe?"

"Not really, but I will. Look, Ryan, suppose, just suppose, that Hannah forgave me for withholding the truth from her. I doubt that she would, but let's pretend she did. The issue at the moment is truth, trust, not the subject matter of what I was withholding."

"Check."

"Then suppose she forgave me for not telling her when I should have. I never told her I wasn't a whole man, normal, capable of fathering children. But we'll suppose for now that she forgave me for my false front."

"The 'not a whole man' bit is still a crock, but for the sake of whatever point you're trying to make here…check."

"Okay. Now. Hannah loves me and because she does, she'd probably say that it was all right that I can't make babies. She'd agree to marry me and off we'd ride into the sunset with Patricia Elizabeth."

"Check."

"No, damn it, that's the glitch, not a check. Later, Ryan, down the road, when Patty is a little girl, no longer a baby, Hannah would feel robbed, unfulfilled, because she'd yearn for another baby. She'd smile, laugh, be sunny Ms. Doodle embracing daffodils-and-daisies days, but inside she'd be crying. She'd be crying, MacAllister, and I'd be the cause of that pain.''

''No matter what she said to you,'' Ryan said, ''you'd be certain that she was miserable.''

''Yes.''

''Check.''

''There's no way for me to win here, Ryan, no matter what I do. I'm selfish enough to want to wait until the baby is born, to see her and hold her, then I know I'll have to leave. I don't have any other choice.''

''You're right.''

Ted blinked. ''I am?''

''Oh, yeah, no doubt about it. Want to know why? Don't answer that, because I'm going to tell you whether you want to know or not.

''Hannah Johnson loves you. You love Hannah Johnson. The big difference is, she *knows* how to love. She trusts you, believes in you, all that good jazz.

''But you, Ted? You love Hannah, but you really don't know how to go about it. If you did, you'd tell her straight up that you're sterile, then discuss whether to raise Patty as an only child, or adopt.

''Yeah, Hannah trusts and believes in you. But guess what? *You* don't trust *her* to tell you what's really in her heart about this situation.

''So, I agree with you that you should leave her. Not because you can't father a child, but because you don't deserve the kind of love she's offering you. You, Sharpe, aren't giving her that same kind of love, that depth, in return.''

"But—"

"So, yes, you're right, buddy," Ryan said, nodding. "As soon as that baby is born, you should hit the road."

Chapter Twelve

Ted lay stretched out on his back on Hannah's living-room floor, his hands beneath his head, eyes closed.

Daisy was curled on his chest, lulled into blissful sleep by the steady rise and fall of Ted's breathing.

Hannah was playing Christmas carols on the piano in the glow of the multicolored lights of the tree they'd decorated that evening.

This was, Ted mused, one of the most peaceful moments he'd had since his disturbing conversation with Ryan a week ago. The only reason he was completely relaxed and thoroughly enjoying the music was that he'd actually managed to shut down his mind and not think.

And he was *not* going to think for the remainder of the evening.

Got that, Sharpe? he asked himself. He'd been over the facts concerning his relationship with Hannah a thousand times, accomplishing nothing more than becoming extremely proficient at chasing around his own thoughts in a maddening circle.

Why he kept dwelling on the dilemma, he didn't know. It wasn't as though he was seeking an answer to the question of what he should do.

He knew what he had to do.

He was going to walk away from Hannah.

It was the proper course of action, the most loving and fair.

You're right, buddy, as soon as that baby is born, you should hit the road.

Ryan's words echoed in Ted's mind, and he opened his eyes and glowered at the ceiling.

Man, he'd hated hearing Ryan say that. The harsh reality of that statement had seemed to slice through him like a knife, causing him to flinch from the pain.

Ryan had done nothing more than agree with Ted's own theory and the conclusion he'd come to, but Ted's first reaction had been to want to angrily deny the accuracy of what Ryan had said, tell his partner he was nuts and should take a long walk off a short pier.

Leave Hannah? Never.

Oh, Lord, leave Hannah. He had to.

Damn it, Sharpe, don't think.

Hannah played "White Christmas" from memory, leaving her free to gaze at Ted where he was lying on the floor with Daisy.

Ted, Ted, Ted, she thought dreamily. She loved him. Oh, how very much she loved that magnificent man.

He'd shown up at her door early that evening with a Christmas tree and a shopping bag full of ornaments and lights.

When he'd inquired the week before about her plans for a tree, she'd told him that her ex-husband had taken the boxes of decorations, and her budget didn't allow for purchasing new ones. Next year, she'd have a small, pretty tree for the baby's first Christmas.

Then up popped Ted with a tree and all the trimmings, telling her that *this* was Patty's first Christmas. She was definitely here, he'd decided, giving Hannah's stomach a friendly pat. And besides, Patricia Elizabeth was going to be born on Christmas Day.

Such fun it had been decorating the tree with Ted. Such special memories she'd tucked carefully away in a cozy corner of her heart.

A wave of sadness suddenly swept through Hannah and she attempted to push it away, not allow it to linger.

She finished playing "White Christmas" and went on to "Silent Night," again knowing it from memory. It was her favorite Christmas carol, so hauntingly lovely. She felt threatening tears burning at the back of her eyes.

Oh, Hannah, she admonished herself. *Don't be sad.* No one got *everything* they wanted in life. Her desire to be Ted's wife, stay by his side in that role until death parted them, was a wish and prayer that was not hers to realize.

She could still be happy, she told herself, if she worked very hard on her outlook and attitude, approached the tomorrows as daffodils-and-daisies days. Ted would be there for her and the baby, just as he now was. That he wouldn't have the titles of husband and father were facts she had to handle and make all right as they stood.

I'll do it, Gran, she thought. *Somehow.*

Hannah played the last chords of "Silent Night," then lifted her hands from the keys. She leveled her bulky body upward and moved away from the piano.

"That was really nice," Ted said, still in his prone position.

"Thank you," she said, easing onto the straight-backed chair. "I would have played more, but my back hurts. I have to lean forward at a weird angle to reach the keys and I don't last long." She swept her gaze over the tree. "Oh, it's so pretty. Thank you, Ted."

He chuckled, causing Daisy to bounce on his chest. The kitten woke and began to wash one paw.

"You've thanked me forty-two times," Ted said. "Enough already."

"Okay. Then I'll thank you for buying gifts for the MacAllister kids for both of us to give them."

"You covered that one, too," he said, smiling. "You discovered that shopping in the crowds wipes you out, and your budget wasn't prepared to include a herd of munchkins. Elementary, my dear. I took care of it. Besides, I'm ready for any excuse to hang out in toy departments. That is really a kick. They've got dynamite stuff for sale this year.''

Ted lifted Daisy from his chest and placed her gently on the floor. He rolled to his feet, then sat down on the sofa. Looking over at the tree, he nodded in approval, then directed his attention to Hannah.

''How did your final childbirth class go last night?'' he said.

''Fine, I guess. I can pant and puff with the best of them.''

Ted grinned. ''I hope your friend Laurie won't mind having her Christmas interrupted. As your coach, she'll have to be there on the twenty-fifth when Patricia Elizabeth arrives.''

''I told her about The Baby Bet.'' Hannah laughed. ''She's cheering for Forrest. She said her husband is a couch potato on New Year's Day, watching football, and it would be a perfect time for her to be with me at the hospital.''

''Well, too bad for Laurie, because *I'm* winning The Baby Bet this go-round. Hear that, Patty?'' he said in a louder voice. ''Christmas Day, kid. Don't let me down.''

''You're so crazy.''

Ted smiled, shrugged, then became serious.

''Hannah,'' he said, ''my folks are coming over between Christmas and New Year's. They'll park their motor home at a camp near here and pop in and out of my place when I'm off duty.''

''Oh, how nice. You must be looking forward to seeing them.''

''Yeah, sure I am, but... Well, I thought I should

prepare you because they'll be, you know, curious about what you and I... What I mean is, they'll wonder if we're... Damn.''

Hannah cocked her head slightly to one side.

"Ted," she said, frowning, "are you saying you haven't told your parents that you're involved with a woman who's about to give birth to a baby?''

"No, I...um...I haven't mentioned it.''

Hannah's eyes widened. "Good grief, what if they take one look at me and assume the baby is yours?''

It is! his mind yelled. In all the ways that mattered, the baby was his.

"Patty will already be born by the time they arrive, remember?'' Ted's attempt at a smile failed.

"Born, not born, that isn't the point. Ted, why haven't you told them about me?''

Damn, he thought, what should he say? The lie he was *living* now was ripping him apart. He could not, would not, tell Hannah an out-and-out *spoken* lie.

"Look," he said, "my folks are great people, they really are. I'm not as close to my dad as I am to my mom, but...'' He shrugged. "That's not unusual, I guess. The thing is, I'm their only child, so they...my mom especially...want to know the nitty-gritty of what's going on in my life. You know what I mean?

"Not that they pry, or get pushy about it, but one question leads to another, then another, so I just sort of keep my mouth shut about a lot of things. Get the drift? Anyway—''

"You're babbling.''

"I am? Oh.'' He cleared his throat. "Well, I'll stop talking, then.''

"You *do* intend to introduce me to them?"

"Yeah, sure. That's why I was warning you that they were coming."

"That's dandy," she said, throwing up her hands in frustration. "Let's see, how's this? It's a pleasure to meet you, Mr. and Mrs. Sharpe. You have a wonderful son, but this isn't his baby. Ted and I are lovers, but I was already pregnant when I met him by waking him playing 'Yankee Doodle' on the piano.

"I wanted to clear up the baby business right away so you wouldn't think your Theodore hadn't done the honorable thing after getting me pregnant. Okey-dokey, folks? Great. No problem."

Ted nodded. "That about covers it. I don't think you need to throw in the bit about us being lovers, though. My parents aren't stupid or prudish, but there's no reason to hit them over the head with it."

"Aaak!" Hannah yelled.

Ted jerked in surprise at her outburst.

"What!" he said, matching her volume.

"I was being sarcastic, you dope. I was attempting to make it clear that you can't produce a very pregnant woman out of the blue and expect your parents to just calmly sit down and have a chat about the weather."

"Oh."

"That's not fair to them, or to me, Ted. It's your responsibility to tell them about me *before* I meet them. If you don't, I'm going to be very uncomfortable and I'm certain they will be, too."

"Oh." He sighed. "All right, I'll take care of it."

"Well, I'm sorry it's such a burden on you." She

folded her hands on her large stomach and lifted her chin, glaring at Ted for good measure.

"You're angry," he said.

"No. My feelings are hurt. You're treating me like this was the Victorian age, when they stuck the disgraceful pregnant female in the broom closet when guests came."

Ted got to his feet and crossed the room. He hunkered down next to Hannah's chair and covered her hands where they rested on her stomach with one of his own.

"You wouldn't fit in a broom closet," he said, producing his best hundred-watt smile.

"You," she said, turning her head to look at him, "are a dead man."

His smile instantly disappeared.

"Just a little humor there," he said. "Sorry. Hannah, I wouldn't hurt your feelings for the world. I was taking the easy road with my folks, that's all. My mom will want details, details, details, but I'll tell them about you before you meet them. I promise. Okay?"

Hannah nodded.

Ted stood, then shifted to stand in front of the chair. He braced his hands on the arms, then leaned over to claim Hannah's mouth in a searing kiss.

Hannah's lashes drifted down as she parted her lips to receive his tongue, savoring his taste as well as the heated sensations of desire that instantly swirled within her.

Oh, Ted, her mind hummed. She was so tired of being pregnant; fat and clumsy and unattractive. She wanted to be slender again, womanly. She wanted to make love through the night with the man she loved, with Ted.

Ted reluctantly broke the kiss and straightened.

"Whew," he said, taking a ragged breath. "You're potent stuff, Ms. Doodle."

"I'm fat stuff," she said miserably. "I've had enough of toting this load around and looking like a blimp, a life raft, a whale. I want to tie my own shoes, for crying out loud."

Ted chuckled. "I've heard MacAllister ladies sing that song. Isn't it nice to know you're normal? Hey, Christmas is only two weeks away. You're in the home stretch, my sweet."

"I know, but... Ted, do you realize you've never seen me *not* pregnant?"

"I hadn't thought about it, but you're right. So?"

"So, could we make a date now to go out to dinner after the baby is born and I get my figure back? I hope it doesn't take too long to have a flat tummy again. I'll wear a pretty dress, a slinky number, that announces 'I am woman,' and we'll do up the town. That would be so nice to look forward to."

"Ah, Hannah, the way you are right now declares you to be a woman to the maximum. You're so beautiful. I'm going to remember what you looked like pregnant, memorize every precious detail."

"Heaven forbid."

"I'm serious, I really am. But, yes, after the baby comes, I promise I'll take you to the fanciest restaurant in town and you can wear your slinky dress."

Hannah pointed one finger in the air. "Not until I

lose whatever weight doesn't evaporate when Patty is born.''

"How...how long will that take?"

She shrugged. "I don't know. I've had friends who fit into their old jeans the day they came home from the hospital. Others had to exercise and diet for weeks.''

Weeks? Ted thought. How many weeks? He'd promised, fool that he was, to take her out to dinner. Promises made, were promises to be kept.

But, oh, hell, the agony of it all. Each day he was with Hannah and the baby, impersonating a family, sharing Patricia Elizabeth while knowing he had to leave them, was going to be torture.

Oh, Lord, what he wouldn't give for things to be different, for the truth *not* to be the truth. If only he was whole, the man that Hannah deserved to have. If only—

"Ted!"

"Huh?" he said, snapping back to attention.

"Daisy is crawling up the Christmas tree!"

"Oh, Lord. Hey, you," he said, hurrying across the room. "We have an angel on the top of that tree, thank you very much. The job has been filled.''

And her heart had been filled, Hannah mused, with Ted. Forever.

A week later, Ted sat on the sofa in his living room, the telephone receiver propped between his head and shoulder.

"So, there you have it, Mom," he said. "Hannah is my pregnant neighbor, and we've been seeing a lot of each other. She made me promise to tell you about the baby before you met her so you wouldn't be caught off guard, not knowing what to say, or whatever.''

"I see," Susan Sharpe said. "Yes, it's better that we know so it won't create an awkward moment. That poor girl. Imagine having such a heartless husband. She's well rid of him."

"No joke."

"But Hannah certainly has a lot to deal with. Tending to a new baby is difficult enough, even if you have help at first, but Hannah has no family."

"Well, the MacAllisters treat her as one of the clan. Hannah's teacher friends don't have any kids, but the MacAllisters make up for it. Deedee, Andrea, Jenny, Jillian, the whole gang will pitch in, I'm sure."

"And you, Ted?"

"Me? Oh, well, I can run errands for Hannah when I'm off duty. You know, go to the store for diapers and stuff like that. Besides, I had a long talk with Patricia Elizabeth about being a good baby, sleeping through the night early on, not hollering unless she has a real red-alert situation. Patty and I understand each other."

"You sound as though you're… Oh, what words shall I use?…attached, emotionally involved, with Hannah and her baby."

Ted grabbed the receiver and got to his feet, pacing as far the telephone cord would allow.

"Ted?"

"Well, sure, I'm emotionally involved, as you put it. Look how quickly *you* had an emotional reaction to Hannah's situation. Hey, the Sharpes are nice people, you know.''

"Somehow, dear, I don't think my feelings are coming from the same place as yours are. Well, we won't get into that.''

"Good idea,'' he said, frowning.

"I'm looking forward to meeting Hannah, and I want to knit something for the baby. I assume that Hannah had an ultrasound since you referred to the little one as Patricia Elizabeth. That's such a lovely name. I'll make her a pink sweater, cap and booties.''

"No, Hannah didn't have that test.''

Susan laughed. "Then Forrest MacAllister must have declared The Baby Bet to be officially in operation and predicted that Hannah will have a girl.''

"No, he said she'd have a boy on New Year's Day. That's where he put his twenty bucks. *I* announced that Patty will be born on Christmas. Forrest is going to lose The Baby Bet for the first time.''

"You're that positive, are you?''

"Yup.''

"Very interesting. Yes, that is *very* interesting.''

Ted stopped his trek back and forth in front of the sofa.

"It is?'' he said. "Why is it so interesting?''

"It's just motherly wisdom rising to the fore, Theodore.''

"I hate it when you call me Theodore. It usually means trouble for me one way or another.''

"Tsk, tsk, that's your suspicious police-officer mind clicking into gear. So, what did you buy Hannah for Christmas?''

"I've been shopping three times for her gift, but I can't find anything that rings my chimes."

"For heaven's sake, Ted, there's only a week left before Christmas."

"Plenty of time, plenty of time. I got Patty a cute stuffed kitten that looks just like Daisy. Oh, Daisy is the kitten I bought for Hannah so her apartment would seem more like a home. It worked, too. Daisy is nuts. She's into climbing up the Christmas tree."

"You've never fussed with a tree before."

"It's not in my place. I bought the tree and decorations, and Hannah and I put it up in her living room. Looks great. I got Daisy a little ball with a plastic mouse inside for Christmas."

"Interesting."

"Would you quit saying that?"

"I'm sorry, dear."

"Hey, listen, Mom. Hannah thinks she's fat and unattractive. You know what I mean? When you meet her, could you say something cool like being a new mom becomes her, or you're sure she was a very pretty pregnant person, or whatever?

"I think she looks beautiful and I've told her that a dozen times, but maybe if a new voice said it... No, forget it. By the time you get here, it won't matter anymore. Okay, that covers that."

Susan laughed softly.

"What?" Ted said. "I heard that funny little chuckle thing of yours. Dad always says that when you laugh like that, he and I might as well give up, because you're in your 'I know more than you know' mode."

"Do tell."

"No, *you* tell. What's going on in your nonstop brain?"

"Oh, this and that. Well, we're producing a huge telephone bill for you to pay. We'll get all caught up when we're together. Have a wonderful Christmas, Ted, and the same wish is extended to Hannah. Your father and I will see you a day or two after the holiday."

"Okay. Merry Christmas to you and Dad. Bye for now."

"Goodbye, dear."

Ted replaced the receiver, then stared at it with narrowed eyes.

His mother was a mother, *but* she was also a woman, which meant he didn't stand a chance of understanding her. What had Mrs. Susan Sharpe meant with her weird "interesting" and her all-knowing laugh?

There was no way his mom could have figured out he was in love with Hannah. He'd handled the conversation with genius-level expertise. Hannah was his neighbor. He'd befriended her during a rough time in her life because he was a nice guy. End of story.

Interesting.

"Hell," he said, "I'm going shopping for Hannah's Christmas present."

And this time, damn it, he was going to find the perfect gift for his beautiful Ms. Doodle.

And he did.

Ted stopped so abruptly in the crowded antique

store that three people bumped into him. He maneuvered his way to the counter and waited impatiently for a clerk to assist him. A matronly woman finally arrived.

"May I help you, sir?"

"There," he said, pointing at the glass case. "That's what I want."

"It's an excellent choice. Would you like it gift wrapped?"

"Yes, please. Make it really pretty. The gift, paper, bow, everything has to be absolutely perfect."

"All right," the woman said, smiling. "You must love her very much."

"Yes," he said quietly. "Yes, ma'am, I love her very, *very* much."

Chapter Thirteen

On Christmas Eve, Hannah shared a hymnal with Deedee as the congregation sang "Oh, Come All Ye Faithful." The entire pew was filled with MacAllisters, and the church was aglow with candles.

The junior members of the family were in the nursery in the lower level. A large crowd was attending the early-evening service, and the building rang with joyous voices.

Ted and Ryan were the only ones not present, as they were on duty until midnight.

The organist finished the song with a flourish, then everyone sat down, eager to hear the reciting of the traditional Christmas story.

Hannah eased herself onto the hard, wooden pew, stifling a moan as her aching back sent the message to her brain that a soft pillow would be a welcome addition.

"Are you all right?" Deedee whispered to Hannah.

Hannah nodded. "I'll live. I think."

"We can scoot out of here if you want," Deedee said quietly. "These pews aren't very comfortable under the best of circumstances, let alone your condition. Trust me, I understand. You ache from head to toe."

Hannah crossed her eyes to emphasize her total agreement with Deedee's evaluation, causing Deedee to smother a burst of laughter.

"Shh," Forrest said.

Deedee poked him in the ribs with her elbow.

Hannah directed her attention to the minister who was reading the Christmas story with a deep, rich voice that held everyone spellbound.

Just listen, she told herself. She would *not* dwell on her aching back, nor the fact that she had to go to the bathroom. She'd ignore the continual kicks and pokes as the baby did a gymnastics routine.

"Oh," she gasped as a pain shot across her stomach.

"Hannah?" Deedee said, her voice hushed.

Hannah shook her head and patted Deedee's leg to assure her that all was well.

Oh, please, Hannah silently begged the minister, talk faster. There was a very large, extremely pregnant and uncomfortable woman here who wanted to go home and sink onto her marshmallow sofa.

As another sharp pain radiated through her abdomen, Hannah shifted on the pew, settled, then wiggled again. She took a deep breath, exhaled and told herself to relax. Her eyes widened as the baby delivered a swift kick, then another.

"You're out of here, Hannah," Deedee whispered. She leaned toward Forrest. "Hannah is miserable sitting on these pews, and I'm taking her home. Pass the word."

Forrest nodded and turned to whisper in Jillian's ear. The message was sent along the pew, MacAllisters nodding in understanding one by one.

Deedee reached under the pew to retrieve their purses, then flapped her hands at Hannah. Attempting to rise, Hannah failed, then gripped the back of the pew in front of her and leveled herself to her feet.

In Deedee's car, Hannah sighed.

"Thank you, Deedee," she said. "I'm sorry you're missing the Christmas Eve service, but I appreciate this so much. I shouldn't have come, but I really wanted to, and—"

"Don't apologize," Deedee said. "You gave it your best shot." She maneuvered expertly through the surging traffic. "I'll stay with you until Ted gets off duty. When I don't show up back at the church, someone from the family will take Teddy home and wait for Ryan to get there."

"No, please don't even think of staying with me. I just want to get into a caftan and stretch out on the bed. I'll be fine, Deedee."

"Are you sure?"

"Yes, I'm positive. The pew was just too uncomfortable. I should have known better. Oh, my goodness, I'll be so glad when this baby is tucked in her crib, instead of in *me*."

Deedee laughed. "I know the feeling. The last few weeks are beauts. Since Forrest always wins The Baby Bet, you can at least count down the hours until New Year's Day."

"I said I didn't want to have a baby on Christmas, but the way I'm feeling now, I just might start hoping that Ted wins The Baby Bet."

"Ted certainly was adamant about Patricia Elizabeth being born on Christmas Day." Deedee stopped at a red light and looked over at Hannah. "Tell me to shut up if you want to, but I can't for the life of me understand why Ted hasn't asked you to marry him."

Join the club, Hannah thought dryly. It was a question that hammered at her peace of mind relentlessly. She was trying so hard to accept things as they were, but it was difficult, so very, *very* difficult.

"Ted obviously is in love with you," Deedee went on, accelerating as the light turned green. "Everyone in the family is aware of how he feels about you, and you love him in return. And the baby? Gracious, Ted Sharpe is ten times worse than Ryan was as far as fussing over you, hovering around like a frantic father-to-be."

"Ted has been wonderful," Hannah said quietly, "and, yes, I love him more than I can even begin to tell you."

"Then why, why, why aren't you two married?"

"That's not...not what Ted wants, I guess."

"You guess?" Deedee said. "Haven't you sat down and discussed it?"

Hannah shook her head. "There's no point in doing that. Ted knows how I feel about him. He loves me, too, Deedee, and he loves Patty. It's all in place, just as it should be."

"But?"

"But Ted obviously doesn't want any part of being a husband and father, a married man. The structure of our relationship as it now stands is apparently what he prefers for the future, as well."

"He's a dolt. I could wring his neck. Darn it, Hannah, I just don't understand him."

"I don't, either. All I can do is accept things the way they are."

"Well, drat. I swear, when men got their supply of muscles, they were shortchanged on brains."

Deedee saw Hannah safely into the apartment, hugged her while wishing her a Merry Christmas, and parted with the reminder that everyone was due at the senior MacAllisters at two o'clock the next afternoon for Christmas dinner and the exchanging of gifts.

Hannah took a quick shower, hoping the warm water would ease some of her aches and pains. It didn't. She put on her favorite faded blue terry-cloth robe and looped the sash loosely over her stomach.

With a weary sigh, she plugged in the Christmas tree, then fed Daisy. Deciding a mug of hot chocolate sounded appealing, she headed to the kitchen, only to stop halfway there as another hot pain radiated across her lower abdomen. Catching her breath, she continued on her way.

As she waited for the chocolate drink to warm in the microwave, she pressed her fists against her lower back.

"Oh, my back, my back," she said aloud, then looked at Daisy who was polishing off her dinner. "I have a roaring toothache in my back, Daisy."

The kitten looked at her with what Hannah labeled a bored expression, then began to wash her paws.

"Thanks for the sympathy," Hannah muttered, patting her stomach. "How are things in there, kiddo? It's nap time, so knock off the rock and roll. Please, Patty?"

A few minutes later, Hannah was settled in the straight chair which she'd turned to face the tree, taking small sips of the hot drink she'd poured into a festive ceramic Christmas mug.

"Oh-h-h," she moaned as another pain hit.

She rolled her eyes heavenward.

At this rate, she knew, she'd never be able to sleep, and she was thoroughly exhausted. She'd drag through Christmas Day in a fog, probably only half-aware of what was going on. Grim. Very grim.

She wasn't concerned about the pains she was having, as it had been explained in her childbirth classes that this sort of thing was very common in the last stages of pregnancy. Unless the pains were coming in steady intervals with increasing intensity, they were to be ignored.

"Easy for them to say," Hannah said, frowning. "Ignored? Oh, right." She paused. "Ow! There's another one. Ignored? Ha! No way. Hannah, shut up and quit feeling sorry for yourself.''

She wiggled further into the chair to give her aching back as much support as possible, and gazed at the pretty tree while she drank the hot chocolate.

Several hours later, Ted and Ryan got into the patrol car and closed the doors.

''You're a soft touch,'' Ted said, chuckling. ''The guy was speeding, MacAllister, and you let him off with a warning.''

''Yeah, well, I looked at my watch and saw that it was two minutes after midnight. I can't ticket a guy on Christmas, for Pete's sake.''

''Soft touch,'' Ted said decisively. ''Let's head on in. Our shift is over.''

''Yup,'' Ryan said, turning the key in the ignition.

He waited for an opening in the traffic, then eased onto the road. Cars traveling in both directions immediately reduced their speed at the sight of the patrol car.

''Well, hell,'' Ryan said, ''it's Christmas.''

Ted looked over at him. ''What's your problem, Mr. Scrooge? You like Christmas as much as a kid does.''

''Yeah, I know. It's a great day, very special, which is why I can't go through it with a guilty conscience. I have a confession to make.''

''Oh, yeah?''

''Yeah. Ted, remember when you told me you were going to leave Hannah because you can't have kids?''

"Of course I remember. What did you do? Break your word and tell Deedee that I'm sterile?"

"No, no, I haven't said a word to her about that conversation. She has no idea why you haven't asked Hannah to marry you. I think she's coming to the conclusion that you're certifiably insane."

"Then what's the big confession about?"

"I said I agreed with you, that you were absolutely right about leaving Hannah, and you should hit the road after the baby was born."

"MacAllister, I really don't feel like going over this territory again. Things are tough enough for me without—"

"I was lying through my teeth," Ryan interrupted. "Blowing smoke."

"What?"

"Oh, hell, I was trying reverse psychology on you. It's worked before. I've done it to you, you've done it to me. I was hoping you'd get really ticked at me for saying what I did, think about it, argue it in your mind and come to the conclusion that you were wrong and I was full of bull for agreeing with you."

"You're a great buddy," Ted said with a snort of disgust. "Thanks a lot."

"Damn it, Ted, you wouldn't listen to reason, and I knew it. I tried another approach, that's all. But now it's officially Christmas and I have to clear the air.

"Sharpe, you're a fool if you walk away from Hannah without giving her a chance to hear the truth and make her own decision regarding it."

"Look, MacAllister—"

"No, you look. Look at what you have with a sensational woman who loves you. How many times do you think love like that comes into a person's life? I almost lost Deedee because I wouldn't listen, and was a stubborn jerk.

"Well, you're the jerk on this trip, Ted. You're going to destroy something beautiful, rare, special. And Hannah won't even understand why you did it. It stinks, it really does. Damn it, you owe it to her to tell her the truth. You have no right to make her decisions for her."

"Are you finished yet?" Ted said, narrowing his eyes. "You're really pushing me."

"Somebody has to. You can deck me when we get to the station if you want to, but all that will do is give you a busted hand. You're running, Ted, like a coward. *A coward.* It'll take guts to go to Hannah and tell her the truth. You, apparently, are fresh out of courage."

Ted opened his mouth to deliver an angry retort, then snapped it closed again in the next instant. He drew a shuddering breath, then dragged both hands down his face.

"You're right," he said, his voice gritty with emotion. "Oh, damn, you're right. I should have done it weeks ago. Then I copped out by convincing myself it would be best to wait until after the baby was born, because Hannah has enough on her plate now. That was pure selfishness, because I want to see, to hold Patty so very much.

"But what you said about having a guilty conscience on Christmas really hits home. I don't want

Hannah to remember this holiday as the one she spent with Ted Sharpe while he was living a lie.

"I have to tell Hannah why I'm leaving her. I'll do it before we go to your folks for Christmas dinner. We may not show up there once I've told Hannah that I'm walking out of her life in a few weeks."

"Ted," Ryan said quietly, "you just may not be going anywhere in the next few weeks except to buy a marriage license. Women, bless their weird minds, have earned a reputation for coming through in the crunch."

Ted shook his head, then stared out the side window.

"You'll tell her?" Ryan said.

"Yeah."

"Good. Merry Christmas, buddy."

"Mmm."

Several minutes passed in total silence, then Ted suddenly stiffened.

"'Yankee Doodle,'" he said.

"What?"

"Have you ever had a song pop into your head and bug the hell out of you?"

"Sure."

"I'm hearing 'Yankee Doodle' over and over."

Ryan shrugged. "So sing 'Jingle Bells' or something, and block out 'Yankee Doodle.'"

"No, you don't understand. It's a message from Hannah."

"It's a what?"

"It's a signal from Hannah, I know it is. Step on it, Ryan. Hannah's in trouble. She needs me."

"You've got it," Ryan said, pressing harder on the gas pedal. "'Yankee Doodle'?"

"'Yankee Doodle,'" Ted said, nodding. "Hit the siren and take me to the apartment complex. I have to get to my Hannah. Now. *Right now.*"

Chapter Fourteen

A sob of fear escaped Hannah's throat as she pulled a caftan over her head with trembling hands. The terry-cloth robe she'd been wearing was in a sodden heap on the bathroom floor.

Dear God, she thought frantically, her water had broken and the excruciating pains were coming in rolling waves, one after the next.

She needed help.

She needed Ted.

Ted, she mentally begged. Please. Hurry. Ted, hear me, hear ''Yankee Doodle.'' It's our secret message, remember? ''Yankee Doodle.'' ''Yankee Doodle.''

She looked at the clock, knowing Ted was off duty and should be on his way home. But there was always the chance that he'd been delayed out in the field. She couldn't wait any longer. She'd have to deal with this herself, alone. *Alone.*

Dial 911, she thought. Yes, that was what she must do. No, first she'd unlock the door for the paramedics while she could still get that far, *then* make the call. Okay, good plan. *Move, Hannah.*

With her arms hugging her stomach, she stumbled from the bedroom, down the hall, and into the living room. Halfway to the door, another pain sliced through her, causing her to grip the edge of a chair, then sink to her knees, tears of panic streaming down her face.

"Ted," she whispered. "Please…"

When Ryan slammed on the brakes in the parking lot of the apartment complex, Ted bolted from the patrol car.

"Do you want me to radio for an ambulance?" Ryan yelled after him.

Ted stopped. "No. It may not be that serious. You go on into the station. No sense in both of us getting into trouble."

"Are you sure?" Ryan asked.

"Yes! Go! And I'll talk to you later," Ted yelled as he rushed across the parking lot toward the stairs.

Ted barrelled from the stairway, raced to Hannah's apartment and pounded on the door.

"Hannah! It's Ted. Open up. Hannah? I'm here. I heard 'Yankee Doodle' and I'm here. Hannah!"

Ted, Hannah's mind whispered. Oh, thank God, he'd come. He'd heard her, heard "Yankee Doodle."

She had to get to the door and unlock it, so that Ted could help her.

"Ted," she yelled. "I'm coming. Wait for me. I need you, Ted. Wait...for...me."

Every muscle in Ted's body tensed as he heard Hannah's plea. He curled his hands into tight fists at his sides, ordering himself not to kick in the door.

Wait for me.

Ah, Hannah. He'd waited a lifetime to find her. He was going to tell her the truth about himself, lay it all on the line and pray. It was time, long overdue.

But now? Right now? Dear heaven, Hannah, open the door!

He heard the clink of the chain, then the snap of the lock and grabbed the doorknob.

"Move back out of the way," he shouted. "I'm coming in, Hannah."

He opened the door just enough to slide through the opening and slammed it closed behind him. In the next instant, Hannah moaned and once again began to sink to the floor.

"Oh, Lord," he said, his heart racing.

He scooped her into his arms and hurried down the hall to place her on the bed. Bracing his hands on the pillow on either side of her head, he leaned over her.

"Hannah? What's going on, sweetheart?"

"Oh, Ted," she said, a sob catching in her throat, "you heard me, you heard 'Yankee Doodle.'"

"You bet I did. Talk to me. What's wrong?"

"The baby...Patty...I can feel...my water broke and the pains...I have to push, Ted...I... *Oh-h-h,*" she moaned, clutching her stomach.

Think, Sharpe, he told himself as sweat trickled down his chest and back. He'd taken a course in delivering a baby at the academy, but that was a century ago.

He couldn't do this.

He couldn't!

What if he made a mistake?

What if something happened to Hannah or Patty because of him, because he did something wrong?

No!

"I'll call for the paramedics." He snatched up the telephone receiver on the nightstand and punched in 911.

"Oh, oh, oh," Hannah said, panting. She raised herself to rest on her elbows. "Oh, God, the baby's coming right now, Ted."

"Not yet!" he yelled.

He rattled off the information to the person who had answered the telephone, then slammed the receiver back into place just as the woman told him to stay on the line.

"Ted!"

"Yes. Okay. Yes. I'll...I'll wash my hands. Yes, I need to do that."

He ran into the bathroom, emerged moments later, then dashed to the linen closet in the hall. He returned to the bed and dumped a stack of towels on the other side of Hannah. She sank back onto the pillow with a whimper.

Ted framed her face in his hands. "Hannah, I love you. You're going to be fine. Patty is going to be fine. I swear it. Trust me."

"I do trust you," she whispered. "I love you so much, Ted." She paused, then her eyes widened. "Oh, dear heaven."

Ted straightened and eased Hannah's caftan up over her large stomach.

Stay cool, Sharpe, he ordered himself. Get a grip. This is the most important thing you've ever done in your life. This is Hannah. This is Patty. These two are your world, your reason for being.

From a source unknown, a sudden calmness came over him, accompanied by a sense of determination and confidence. He moved to the foot of the bed as Hannah once again raised onto her elbows, gasping.

Ted's heartbeat roared in his ears.

"I can see her head, Hannah," he said. "Bend your knees. That's right. You're doing great."

"Push," she said, panting. "Push."

"Okay, go for it. I'm here with you, Hannah. Patty is definitely ready to say Merry Christmas."

"Oh-h-h. Oh, God. No. No more. Stop it, Ted, make it stop. The pain is... *No-o-o*."

"Push, Hannah."

"Yes, yes, yes. Push, push... Gran. Gran!"

Ted extended his large hands and...

She was there.

Patricia Elizabeth was born.

Ted caught her tiny head in the palm of one hand, her little bottom in the other, then laid her on the bed. After swiping a finger through her mouth to clear it, he reached for a towel.

"Ted?" Hannah said. "Ted?"

He wiped Patty's face gently. She opened her eyes, raised her fists, pulled up her knees...and wailed.

"Oh, my God," Ted said, his voice ringing with awe and wonder. "A miracle. She's a miracle. Oh, Patty, you're so beautiful, so perfect. You're my daughter. The only one I'll ever have. You're mine."

"Ted!"

He snapped his head up to look at Hannah, tears brimming in his eyes. Lifting Patty, he placed her on Hannah's stomach.

"Oh, my, look at her," Hannah said, laughing and crying at the same time. "And listen to her. Hello and Merry Christmas, Patricia Elizabeth. Welcome to the world. Oh, Ted, I..."

The sudden sound of someone knocking loudly at the door of the apartment broke the magical spell that had woven around the trio in the bedroom. Ted ran to the door and flung it open.

"Paramedics, Officer," a man said, acknowledging Ted's uniform. "You've got a baby on the way here?"

"In the bedroom," Ted said, stepping back.

"Uh-oh, by golly," the second man who entered said. "What I'm hearing says that we're arriving a tad late." He smiled at Ted. "Score one for the cops, huh? How'd you get the call?"

"I belong here," Ted said. "They're mine. Hannah and Patty are... I helped deliver Patricia Elizabeth." He grinned. "Yeah, son-of-a-gun, I did."

"Good for you, Daddy," the man said, hurrying after his partner. "Congratulations."

Daddy.

"Whew," Ted said aloud as tears once again filled his eyes. He looked heavenward. "Thank you." He nodded. "Thank you."

Daisy lifted her head from where she'd been sleeping beneath the Christmas tree, meowed, yawned, then went back to sleep.

"Not enough excitement for you, Daisy?" Ted said, smiling.

One of the paramedics came into the living room.

"Everything is fine," he said to Ted. "We've tied and cut the baby's cord, and checked her over. She's A-OK and mad as blue blazes for being disturbed. Your wife is fine, too. We've called for an ambulance to take them to the hospital. You can follow us over. Your little girl was sure in a hurry to get here, wasn't she?"

"Yeah, she was. She actually sort of delivered herself but, man, I'll never forget witnessing that event. It was really something. Awesome. Humbling. You know what I mean?"

"You bet I do."

"I knew Patty was going to be born on Christmas," Ted said. "I just…knew."

"Well, she got the message, all right. I'm going down and wait for the ambulance."

"Yo," Ted whispered a few minutes later as the ambulance driver stepped into the bedroom where Hannah and Patty slept quietly.

"Santa Claus bring a baby here?" the driver asked with a smile.

Ted grinned. "He sure did, and she's the most

beautiful baby girl in the world. She's fantastic, unbelievable. She looks just like her mother.''

"Hey," the man said, laughing, "you're not a cop, you're a proud new father."

"You've got that straight," Ted said. "Hustle up, you guys, my ladies are waiting."

When Ted reached the hospital, he was told by a nurse that both Hannah and Patty were being examined, and that then mother and daughter would be put to bed.

"Can't I see them for five seconds?" he said.

The nurse smiled. "Not tonight."

"But I only waved at Hannah when they put her and the baby into the ambulance."

"Go home, get some sleep and come back in the morning. You've had quite an experience. I—" The telephone at the nurses' station rang, and the woman answered it. "Maternity…Yes…Wonderful…I'll tell him." She replaced the receiver.

"Tell who him?" Ted said. "Me?"

"Your daughter weighs six pounds nine ounces, and is perfect. Your wife is fine, and is being tucked into bed for a very well-earned rest. Please stop at the admissions desk and give them the information they need for their forms, then off you go."

"But—"

"Shoo, Daddy, and Merry Christmas to you. This is certainly one you won't ever forget."

"No," Ted said quietly, "I certainly won't. Thank you and Merry Christmas. Good night."

* * *

By the time Ted returned to Hannah's apartment, the rush of adrenaline that had been coursing through him had ebbed and was replaced by total exhaustion.

He changed the sheets on the bed, gathered the towels and the soggy bathrobe, and set the bundle by the door to be washed and dried. After feeding Daisy, he checked the apartment once more to be certain everything was shipshape, then headed down the hall to his own place with the load of laundry.

Once in bed, he willed himself to shut down his mind and get at least a few hours' sleep. At a decent hour, he'd call the MacAllister clan to inform them of Patricia Elizabeth's arrival.

"Hey," he said aloud, "I won The Baby Bet. Eat your heart out, Forrest. You've finally been unchampioned, hotshot."

Ted took a deep breath, let it out slowly, then mentally ordered sleep to numb his senses. But echoing in his mind was an amalgam of voices, snatches of words spoken by various people who had taken part in the miraculous events of the night.

Good for you, Daddy. Congratulations...You're not a cop, you're a proud new father...Your daughter weighs...Your wife is fine...Your wife...Your daughter...Wife...Daughter...Wife...

"Oh, God," Ted said, dragging his hands down his face.

If only it was true. If only Hannah *was* his wife. If they were married, then Patty's birth certificate could read: Patricia Elizabeth Sharpe; Mother...Hannah Sharpe; Father...Theodore Sharpe. They would be a family, the three of them, together.

Maybe it could still happen that way. If the hospital would hold up the birth certificate long enough for Hannah and him to be married, then…

But first he had to talk to Hannah. He had to tell her the truth about his being unable to give her more babies. After his conversation with Ryan, he'd decided to tell her in the morning.

Well, he still would. He'd go to the hospital, sit down by Hannah's bed, take her hand and pour out his heart and soul.

"Hannah, please," he said, his voice gritty with emotion. "Please, my beautiful Ms. Doodle, please agree to marry me, be my wife, allow me to be Patty's father. Please, Hannah?"

With a weary sigh, Ted drifted off into a restless slumber, tossing and turning through the remaining hours of the night.

Early in the morning, Hannah stirred and opened her eyes. Her heart quickened as she realized she had no idea where she was. In the next instant, she smiled, placing her hands on her relatively flat stomach.

Patty. Patricia Elizabeth had been born, she thought. Let it not be said that her daughter was among the ordinary. No, not Patty. She'd been in such a rush to grant the world the honor of her presence, she'd arrived on the bed in the apartment. And on Christmas, no less.

Ted had been wonderful. He'd actually heard, somehow heard, her cry for help as she'd mentally sent him the "Yankee Doodle" signal. She's been so frightened, *so alone,* but then Ted had come with his quiet authority, calm demeanor and his strength.

And Patty was born.

Hannah sighed in contentment as she envisioned the beautiful baby and the magnificent man who were filling her heart to overflowing. Patty and Ted.

She frowned slightly as she came fully awake.

Something niggled at her, disturbing her blissful state of mind, hovering in a shadowy corner just beyond her comprehension.

What was it? What could possibly be wrong on this glorious Christmas Day?

Concentrating even harder, she narrowed her eyes, then slowly they came, the haunting words that Ted had spoken to Patty immediately after the baby was born.

Oh, Patty, you're so beautiful, so perfect. You're my daughter. The only one I'll ever have. You're mine.

"Dear heaven," Hannah whispered. She hadn't really comprehended at the time what Ted was saying.

You're my daughter. The only one I'll ever have. You're mine.

A chill swept through her and she shivered as she pulled the blanket up to her chin.

What had Ted meant? A part of her mind was insisting that she should be thrilled that Ted considered Patty his daughter, that he loved her that much.

But another part of her felt threatened somehow, very frightened. Why was Patty the only daughter Ted would ever have? And there was something so ominous about the words, *You're mine.*

Oh, stop it, Hannah, she admonished herself. She was overreacting. Ted's emotional outburst had occurred at a highly charged moment. The man has just taken part in delivering a baby, for heaven's sake.

But still...

No, she wouldn't think about it anymore. She'd tuck it away, then discuss it with Ted when he came to see her. Yes, that was exactly what she would do. Fine.

You're my daughter. The only one I'll ever have. You're mine.

Hannah pressed trembling fingertips to her lips and fought against threatening tears.

"Merry Christmas," a nurse said, bustling through the doorway.

"What? Oh, yes, Merry Christmas to you, too."

"You certainly received a special gift, didn't you? Your baby is just a doll, and such a good girl. Fill her tummy, and she's right back to sleep."

"When can I see her?" Hannah said.

"It's breakfast for you first, then a wash. By then, it will be time for the little ones to come visit their moms. You can count her fingers and toes, hold her, sing her a lullaby, whatever suits your fancy. It will be an hour of bonding between you and your daughter."

You're my daughter. You're mine.

"Yes," Hannah said. "*My* daughter. Patty is *my* daughter."

"Is something wrong, dear?"

"I hope not. Oh, God, I hope not."

"Pardon me?"

"Nothing," Hannah said, managing a small smile. "I'm just so eager to hold Patty. So much of last night is a blur, and I need to see her, touch her."

"Of course you do, and you will. That will perk you right up, and you'll realize what a marvelous Christmas Day this is."

"Yes," Hannah said quietly. "Marvelous."

Ted telephoned the hospital as soon as he awoke and was informed that he could visit Hannah at noon. He then called Ryan and related the amazing series of events of the previous night.

"Well, I'll be damned," Ryan said. "Hannah really *did* send you a message with that 'Yankee Doodle' bit. Is that weird?"

"No, it's communication in rare form, MacAllister." Ted paused. "Man, the whole thing was beyond belief, Ryan. Seeing Patty born was… Helping to deliver her was… Hannah was so brave and… man, oh, man."

Ryan chuckled. "You're very articulate this morning. Merry Christmas, Dad."

"Yeah."

"Ted, did you get a chance to tell Hannah that you… No, I suppose you didn't."

"No, but I'm going to the hospital at noon to see her and I'll tell her then. When I come to your folks later, I hope I'll be announcing that Hannah and I are getting married. Correct that. I hope and *pray* I'll be saying that."

"Right on, buddy."

"Listen, will you pass the word along to the family about the baby?"

"Sure thing, but don't you want to call Forrest yourself? The Baby Bet champion has been dethroned."

Ted laughed. "It's about time. I'll leave the pleasure of informing him of that fact to you."

"I'll enjoy every minute of it. Give Hannah a Christmas hug from us."

"I will. Thanks, Ryan."

"Good luck, Ted. I sure hope that... Well, go for it. Everything will work out great."

"It has to. God, Ryan, I don't know what I'll do if I lose Hannah and Patty, I really don't. Well, I'll see you later."

"Yeah. Bye."

Ted slowly replaced the receiver, then took a deep breath.

"I love you, Ms. Doodle," he whispered.

When Ted entered Hannah's room at the hospital, she was sitting up, flipping idly through a magazine.

"Merry Christmas, Hannah," he said quietly as he walked toward her.

"Merry Christmas, Ted," she said, meeting his gaze.

Neither smiled, nor hardly breathed, as Ted stopped next to the bed. He lifted one hand to gently cradle her cheek, then leaned over to claim her mouth with his.

The kiss was exquisite; tender, loving and filled with hope.

Ted reluctantly broke the kiss, then sat down in the chair next to the bed. Hannah placed the magazine on the side table, then clasped her hands in her lap.

"You look very festive," she said.

Ted glanced down at the bright red sweater he wore over dark slacks.

"My mom made this for me last Christmas. She's a whiz with a pair of knitting needles."

"It's, um, it's a very nice sweater."

Ted leaned back in the chair and stared up at the ceiling for a long moment before looking at Hannah again.

"I need to talk to you about something important, Hannah," he said. "I realize I'm tense right now, and I know why. The thing is, I get the feeling that *you're* uptight, too, and *that* I don't understand. Patty's all right, isn't she?"

"Oh, yes, she's wonderful," Hannah said, smiling for the first time. "They brought her to me and I burst into tears when they placed her in my arms. She's so beautiful, so tiny and perfect. I'll never be able to thank you enough for being there for me, for helping bring Patty safely into the world."

"I'll never forget it. It was an incredible honor to—" Ted stopped speaking and shook his head. "I can't find the right words. It's too big, too... I guess there's no way to describe being a part of a miracle like that." He paused. "Hannah, what's bothering you? What's on your mind?"

Hannah sighed. "I wish I could forget it, Ted, put it out of my mind and just concentrate on my blessings. I wish I could declare this a daffodils-and-daisies day, as well as the most fantastic Christmas I've ever had.''

"But?"

"But I can't. I have to ask you what you meant by what you said to Patty when she was born. I need to understand it.''

Ted frowned, then splayed one hand across his chest. "What *I* said to Patty?" He shook his head. "I don't remember speaking to her. I talked directly to her?"

"Yes.'' She drew a shuddering breath. "You said, 'Oh, Patty, you're so beautiful, so perfect. You're my daughter. The only one I'll ever have. You're mine.' Why, Ted? Why did you say that?"

Dear Lord, no! Ted thought frantically. He'd said all that aloud? He didn't remember doing it, saying it. He'd come to the hospital to explain things calmly and carefully to Hannah, but now he was in the position of having to defend himself. Damn it.

"Ted?''

"Hannah, look, this isn't going the way I planned it, not even close. I should have told you weeks, months ago, but...'' He leaned forward and took her hands in his, propping his elbows on the bed.

"There's something you should have told me, but didn't?" she said, the color draining from her face, followed by a stricken expression.

"Ah, Hannah, please don't look at me like that.''

"Are you saying there's something I don't know that will make you *someone* I don't know?"

"I came here to tell you today. Listen to me.

Please? I love you, Hannah. I love you, and I love Patty. You believe that, don't you?''

"Yes, I believe that. But why did you speak those words to Patty when she was born?''

Ted's grip on Hannah's hands tightened and his voice was raspy with emotion when he spoke again.

"Because...because I'm sterile. I had the mumps when I was a teenager and I can't father a child. Not ever.''

Hannah's eyes widened and her mind raced in a matching tempo with her thundering heart. She pulled her hands free and shifted slightly on the bed in an attempt to put distance between herself and Ted.

"Oh, dear God,'' she said, hardly above a whisper. "You want Patty. You see her as a way to be a father. You called her your daughter, said she was yours.''

"Yes, but—''

"You said you loved me, but you didn't ask me to marry you. I kept wondering why, and now I know. You're not interested in marriage, in *me,* in being a husband. You're focused on being a father. You want Patty, only Patty.''

"Hannah, no, it's not like that at all.''

She leaned her head back on the pillows and closed her eyes.

"No, no,'' she said, "not again, not again. I believed in you, fell in love with you. I'd vowed to never again trust my judgment about any man, but I was convinced that I'd finally made the right choice and...''

She lifted her head and looked at Ted, tears spilling onto her pale cheeks.

"I was wrong...again," she said, a sob catching in her throat. "You're not who I believed you to be. You don't want to marry me because you love me. You see me as a way to have a child, to be a father, to nurture, love, watch her grow up, be a part of her life. All you wanted from me is my daughter. *My* daughter."

Ted lunged to his feet. "No! I came here to tell you that I can't give you more children. I know I should have told you the truth sooner, but I was scared to death, Hannah, so afraid you'd send me away.

"I had made up my mind that I'd leave you after Patty was born, get out of your life, so you could find a man who was whole, a man who could give you more babies. But then—"

"But then?" she interrupted, her voice rising. "Then what, Ted? A better idea, a genius-level plan? You'd ask me to marry you? You'd be able to have a daughter, and for that you'd put up with the nuisance and commitment of a wife?"

"Damn it, no! I walked into this room hoping, praying, you'd accept me as I am, as not totally a man. We'd raise Patty together, love her, be a family. She'd be *our* daughter. We could adopt more kids, Hannah, if you'd be willing to. We could have it all, don't you see?"

"What I see," she said, sobbing openly, "is that I've been betrayed one more time, one *last* time. What I see is that you're scrambling, frantically searching for a way to keep Patty in your life. Your proposal of marriage is your last-ditch effort to accomplish that.''

She dashed the tears from her cheeks with trembling hands.

''No. No, I won't marry you. Not ever. Go away, Ted. Leave me alone. Don't come near me, or my daughter. Patty is mine. *Mine.* You can't have my baby. You can't.''

Hannah covered her face with her hands and wept, sobs wracking her body. Ted lifted one hand toward her, then dropped it back to his side. The pain consuming him took his breath away. It was excruciating in its intensity.

He'd lost. He'd lost Hannah, the only woman he had ever, or would ever, love. He'd lost Patty, the daughter of his heart. He was a beaten man, empty, cold and so alone.

Hannah, his mind screamed. *No. Please!*

But he didn't speak. There was nothing more to say.

With a shaking hand, he took a small box from the pocket of his slacks. It was wrapped in gold paper and topped by a tiny matching bow. He set it on the bed, then turned and walked from the room, the sound of Hannah's heartbroken crying beating against him like physical blows.

A few minutes later, Ted stood in front of the nursery window, gazing at a peacefully sleeping Patty, gazing at a miracle.

A moment later, he could no longer see Patricia Elizabeth, because his vision was blurred by tears.

* * *

An hour later, Hannah opened the pretty box Ted had left on the bed. Her tears started anew as she saw the exquisite gift nestled in the fluffy cotton.

On a gold chain, carved from the finest ivory, was a small and incredibly delicate daffodil.

Chapter Fifteen

Two days later, Ted paced his living room as he told his mother what had taken place and that he loved Hannah. His father was stretched out asleep on the sofa, enjoying an afternoon nap.

Susan and Dean Sharpe had arrived at Ted's apartment an hour before. With the special wisdom that mothers possess, Susan had waited until Ted brought up the subject of Hannah, rather than ask about her.

After Dean had dozed off, weary from the drive, Ted began his dismal tale, keeping his voice low so as not to awaken his father.

Ted stopped his trek and shoved a restless hand through his hair.

"There you have it," he said. "Great, huh? I blew it, Mom, big time. Hannah believes that I've stayed with her all these months because of Patty. I've lost

Hannah and I've lost Patty, too. I have no one to blame but myself. I knew, damn it, I knew, how important truth and honesty were to Hannah.''

He planted his hands on his hips and stared up at the ceiling, attempting to gain control of his emotions. Looking at his mother again, he shook his head.

"I'm such a jerk," he said. "Hannah was determined never to trust her judgment again in regard to her choice of a man. She had a major flaw, she said, of not being able to tell if a man was really who he presented himself to be, who she believed him to be. So what do I do? I withhold the truth from her and confirm her opinion of men as frauds.''

"Ted…''

"I was a fool to get involved with Hannah. I should have run like hell the minute I realized I was in love with her. I can't have a woman like Hannah in my life. I've known that for a very long time. Hannah is not mine to have.''

"Why on earth not?" Susan said. "You're a wonderful man. You're thoughtful, caring—''

"Mom, come on," he interrupted. "Reality check, okay? I'm not a *whole* man. I can't give Hannah more children. Look, I've never told you this because it would have served no purpose, but…''

He drew a shuddering breath, then said, "I heard you and Dad talking all those years ago after the doctor called to report that I was sterile. Oh, yeah, I heard Dad say, 'Do you realize what he has been robbed of, what this means?' In my own father's eyes, I wasn't totally a man, never would be. I never felt as close to him after that, because I knew I fell short, didn't measure up.

"Why do you think I went the swinging-bachelor route? Because I knew, Mom, that I couldn't ask any woman to marry me. I couldn't ask her to sacrifice her natural maternal instincts to want to have babies.

"What I did to Hannah was selfish and cruel. There's no excuse for my deception, for hurting her so terribly. I knew I couldn't have her. Hell, I've known how things stood ever since I was sixteen years old and heard Dad say—"

"You hold it right there," Dean Sharpe said, suddenly sitting up and swinging his feet to the floor.

"Well, that's dandy," Ted said, rolling his eyes heavenward. "I suppose you've been listening to this whole conversation."

"Indeed I have," his father said. "I kept silent because I realized you needed to get some things off your chest, and I didn't want to interrupt."

"So you eavesdropped, instead," Ted said with a snort of disgust. "You're cool, Dad, really terrific."

"Theodore, there's no call to be rude to your father," Susan said.

"That's all right, Susan," Dean said, "because I'm about to be rude to him. Ted, you're a dope."

"Thank you very much." Ted slouched onto a chair and glared at his father.

"Ted, listen to me," Dean said, his voice gentling. "I remember saying those words after the doctor called. They're as clear in my mind as though it were yesterday. You heard me. And?"

"And what?" Ted said.

"What did you do?"

"I ran. I bolted out the door and ran until I dropped. Then I cried. Okay, Dad? Is this what you want me to spill my guts about? I sobbed like a little kid because I would never be able to father a child, and because...because I was no longer the son for you that I'd been."

"Oh, my darling boy," Susan whispered. "No."

"Then when you two told me what the doctor had reported," Ted went on, his voice gritty, "I blew it off, said it was no big deal."

Dean shook his head. "So we didn't discuss it further. Dear Lord, I should have pushed you to talk about it. Ted, how can I ask you to forgive me? I'd sell my soul to turn back the clock to that day."

"Why?" Ted said. "Facts are facts."

"No, your facts are wrong," Dean said. "You ran out the door before you heard all of what your mother and I said."

Ted lifted one shoulder in a shrug.

"Ted, damn it, listen to me," Dean said, nearly shouting.

Ted blinked in surprise at his father's outburst and straightened in his chair.

"Okay, I'm listening," he said. "Calm down, will you? You'll get your blood pressure in an uproar, or something."

Dean leaned forward, rested his elbows on his knees and clasped his hands tightly.

"Son," he said quietly, "you listened that day with the mind of a sixteen-year-old boy, and you didn't even hear all that was said. It breaks my heart to realize you chose a life-style for yourself at that moment that was like an albatross around your neck all these years.

"Ted, when I said, 'Do you realize what he's been robbed of?' I wasn't referring to your manhood, nor did I for one second view you as less than a total man. My first reaction was pain for your loss, for never being able to witness the wondrous miracle of watching your wife grow big with your child, then seeing that baby born."

Ted stiffened, every muscle in his body tensing. "But I thought—"

"I now know what you thought," Dean said, "and my heart aches because of it."

"Do you realize that powers beyond our understanding," Susan said, "have set things to rights? You *have* witnessed the woman you love grow with a child you've come to love as though it were your own. You even had more than most other men, Ted. You were blessed by being given the opportunity to help deliver that baby, bring her into the world."

Ted nodded slowly, his mind racing.

"What you didn't hear that day you ran from the house," his mother said, "was my telling your father that you had so much love in your heart, even then at sixteen, that when you were grown, any child that you adopted would be, to you, truly yours, your very own. I said you needed only to find the right woman as your life's partner."

"And I agreed with your mother completely," Dean said. "I admitted that my first reaction that you'd been cheated out of something was wrong. Ted,

I swear to you, I have never felt you were less of a man because you can't father a child. Never.''

Ted dragged both hands down his face, then shook his head. ''I don't know what to say to you two, especially you, Dad. All these years, I believed... I misjudged you, I... Saying I'm sorry doesn't cut it, not even close.''

''I'm the one who is sorry, Ted,'' Dean said. ''I should have sat you down and talked the whole thing through, instead of accepting your laid-back attitude as being how you really felt.''

''Well, what's done is done,'' Susan said. ''The important thing now is the present and future.''

''Absolutely,'' Dean said. ''That means Hannah and Patricia Elizabeth. Theodore, you'd better mend fences with those special ladies, because I'll be very cross if I'm deprived of my daughter and granddaughter.''

''Mercy yes,'' Susan said. ''I want to see Patty in the outfit I knitted her. Well, actually, I knitted her two outfits. So, Ted? Don't you think it's time to quit moping and start putting together a plan to fix this disastrous muddle? I have a daughter to hug and a baby to spoil. You'd best get on the stick, young man.''

An achy sensation gripped Ted's throat as he look at his parents.

''I love you guys,'' he said softly. ''I hope you know how very much I love you.''

''And we love you, son,'' Dean said.

''Always, darling,'' Susan said.

Dean cleared his throat and blinked back tears.

"Now then, it seems to me that you've got a battle on your hands to convince Hannah that you love her as much as you love the baby. You're a Sharpe, and we don't give up. Not ever. Understood."

Ted smiled. "Yes, sir, I read you loud and clear." He frowned in the next instant. "Damned if I know what I'm going to do, though."

"Listen to your heart," Susan said. "Oh, and quit swearing so much. That's not the type of language to use around Patty. Well, I'm ready for a bite to eat. Let's go to a restaurant before you're due on duty."

Ted nodded and got to his feet. "Listen to my heart? I sure hope it has something brilliant to say."

Four hours into the duty shift, Ryan had had enough of Ted's total silence.

"How was your Christmas, Ryan?" Ryan said. "Great, really fun, and Teddy loved it. I covered for you after you called me at my folks, Ted, said you were bushed from impersonating the stork.

"Hannah? She came home from the hospital today. Her friend Laurie picked up her and Patty, saying she should be allowed to do at least that since her weeks of training to be Hannah's birth coach went down the tubes.

"Deedee took a hamper filled with food for a couple of lunches and dinners to Hannah this evening. She came home chatting like a magpie about that adorable little girl. I have a feeling I'm going to hear, 'Let's have another baby' pretty quick here.

"Deedee says Hannah is feeling fine, but is quiet and doesn't smile much. Deedee thinks there's trouble in romance-land, but has no clue as to what happened. She did mention that Hannah is wearing a knockout necklace that is a daffodil carved from ivory.

"Oh, yes, and Forrest is mad as hell at you for winning The Baby Bet. He's convinced you cheated, but can't figure out how in the world you did it.

"Well, it was nice talking to you, Sharpe."

"You're so cute," Ted said, shooting a glare in Ryan's direction. "It boggles my mind."

"Well, hell, man, it's been like driving around with a damn corpse."

"Don't swear like that around Patty. I don't want her hearing that stuff."

"Pardon me all to heck, *Dad*. What I want to know is, how are you going to fix this mess? How are you going to convince Hannah you love her and want to spend your life with her *and* Patty? Huh? Answer me that, Mr. Chatter Cheeks."

"I'm thinking," Ted said, none too quietly. "Okay, MacAllister? I'm thinking about it so damn much, I'm wearing out my brain. Hell, I've screwed this up so badly it's a sin."

"I can see it now. Patty's first and second words spoken will be *damn* and *hell*. Shame on you."

"Shut up."

Ryan chuckled. "Go back to silent thinking."

"Mmm."

Ted didn't speak for the remaining four hours of the shift.

During the following days, while being careful not to encounter Hannah in the hallway or elevator, Ted continued to turn his thoughts inward; sifting, sorting, going over a multitude of memories, recalling details of times spent with Hannah, reliving events and conversations.

The senior Sharpes informed him they were going to drive up the coast for several days. Ted absently told them to have a nice trip and he'd see them when they got back.

"Take care of yourself, dear," Susan said.

"Okay."

"Your sofa is on fire, dear."

"Okay."

Susan laughed. "Just keep thinking the way you are. You'll find your answers."

"Okay."

On New Year's Day, Ted slept until noon. He and Ryan had put in a hectic night shift dealing with holiday party goers, hauling half a dozen to jail to sleep off an overindulgence of alcohol. And now, having drawn duty on New Year's Eve, the pair had the next two days off.

Ted opened one eye, glanced at the clock and immediately decided he was hungry. As he started to get out of the bed, he stopped, sinking back onto the pillow.

"Wait a minute," he said aloud.

He didn't move, nor hardly breathe. Things finally began to fall into place, slowly, piece by piece, like a complicated puzzle coming together and making sense at long last.

"Yes!"

He flung back the blankets, then headed toward the shower.

A half hour later, Ted knocked on Hannah's door with the toe of his shoe, due to the fact that his hands were full.

Hannah tucked the blanket over a sleeping Patty, then hurried from the baby's room to answer the summons at the door. She peered through the peephole, but frowned in confusion as she realized she had no idea what she was seeing. Leaving the chain in place, she cautiously opened the door.

"Hello, Hannah," Ted said quietly. "May I come in? Please?"

"I... Yes." She closed the door, undid the chain, then reopened the door so Ted could enter. She looked at what he was holding. "That's the dollhouse you made."

Ted nodded, then crossed the room to set it on the coffee table. He took a box from the first floor of the dollhouse and set it next to it.

"This is the furniture." He straightened and turned to look at Hannah. "I'd like Patty to have this, if it's all right with you."

Ah, Hannah, he thought. His beautiful Ms. Doodle was exquisite. She looked sensational in jeans and a pretty yellow blouse, a daffodil-colored blouse. The necklace he'd given her was around her neck, falling to just above her breasts.

He wanted to take her into his arms, hold and kiss her, ask her to marry him and stay by his side for all time.

Oh, man, how he loved her.

"That's a lovely gift you're giving to Patty," Hannah said. "Thank you. I'm sure she'll treasure it when she's old enough to appreciate it."

Ted, Hannah's mind hummed. He looked so tired, just totally worn-out. She'd missed him so much, ached for his touch and kiss, and the feel of his strong arms encircling her in the wondrous and safe cocoon of his embrace.

Oh, she loved Ted Sharpe with all that she was as a woman.

No, that wasn't quite right. She loved the Ted Sharpe she'd *believed* him to be, not the Ted he actually was, not the Ted who wanted only Patty in his life.

"I see you're wearing the necklace," Ted said.

The fingertips of one of Hannah's hands fluttered to the delicate daffodil, then stilled, clutching the flower.

"It's so pretty," she said. "Thank you for giving it to me."

"Sure." He paused. "Hannah, I'd like to talk to you. Please? Would you sit down?"

"Well, I..." She sighed. "Yes, all right."

She sat in a straight-backed chair, clasped her hands tightly in her lap and stared up at him.

This is it, Sharpe, Ted told himself. The next few minutes were going to determine his entire future happiness. *Don't blow it.*

"Hannah," he said, too wired to sit down, "I've been doing a lot of thinking lately. In fact, all I've done is think. That day in the hospital, I felt I'd lost you forever, that it was over, everything that mattered to me was gone, beyond my reach.''

Hannah lifted her chin. ''You mean Patty.''

''No, damn it…excuse me. I'm not going to swear anymore because Patty's first words are *not* going to be *damn* and *hell*.''

He drew a deep, shuddering breath, then let it out slowly.

''Okay. Will you listen, really listen to me?''

''All right, Ted.''

''Months ago, you said you can't tell the good guys from the bad, and you shouldn't trust your own judgment about men.''

''Yes.''

''Well, *I* have a major flaw, too. I'm a coward. When things get tough, I run. I finally figured that out after nearly thinking myself to death the last few days.''

''A coward? Ted, you're a police officer, a very good one. You can't possibly be a coward.''

''Yeah, I'm a good cop. That's not what I'm referring to. I'm talking about my personal life. Hannah, when I was sixteen, I heard my dad telling my mom I was sterile from my having had the mumps. What did I do? I ran. I bolted out the door before I heard everything my parents had to say about the situation. I was a coward. I couldn't face what had happened, so I ran.

''That cowardice cost me the close relationship I'd had with my father. I was convinced he felt I was no longer a total man, a whole man, and I was no longer what he wanted in a son.''

He shook his head.

"It wasn't true. He didn't feel that way at all, and I would have known that if I'd had the courage to stand firm, talk it through with him.

"Hannah, I did the same thing that day in the hospital. You told me how you felt, and it hurt me so very much that I ran. I was such a coward, I couldn't handle the thought of hearing more of your accusations. The price tag this time? Your love, our future happiness, everything that is important to me."

He hunkered down in front of her and took her hands in his.

"Hannah, I've stopped running. I'm gathering my courage, stripping my soul bare, rendering myself totally vulnerable. Risky? Oh, yeah, it's risky, but you're worth it.

"Hannah Johnson, my beautiful Ms. Doodle, I love you more than life. I want to marry you and spend the rest of my life with you as your husband. I also want to be Patty's father. Ah, Hannah, can't we be a family, together? Have it all? That's what is in my heart, I swear it. I love you, Hannah. Oh, God, how I love you.

"If you can't marry me, be my wife, because I'm not capable of giving you more babies, then I'll have to deal with that...somehow. At least I'll know I wasn't a coward, not this time. I'm just a man, pure and simple, who loves you will all my heart. Total, whole and forever love, Hannah, that is what I have to offer you, from a total, whole and forever man.

"I can't give you more children, but I'm offering

you myself, all that I am. It's up to you if that's enough. It's up to you.''

Hannah flung her arms around Ted's neck with such force that he toppled backward, taking her with him. They ended up on the floor, Hannah stretched out on top of him.

''Yes, I'll marry you,'' she said, her eyes filling with tears. ''I listened, Ted, to what you said, and I *heard* you. I realize how difficult it was for you to run the risks you just did. I feel so loved, so cherished, so special.

''On behalf of myself and my daughter, *our daughter,* I accept your proposal of marriage. I'd be honored to be your wife. Patty will be a fortunate child to have you for a father. Oh, my darling Ted, I love you so much, so very, very much.''

Ted's tears mirrored those in Hannah's eyes, as he weaved his fingers through her silky hair and brought her lips to his to seal their commitment to forever.

Daisy strolled into the room, took one look at the nonsense taking place on the floor, and went in search of something to eat.

Epilogue

At the wedding of Hannah Johnson and Ted Sharpe, the bride carried a lovely bouquet of daffodils and daisies.

Patricia Elizabeth wore a yellow dress that had been knit by Susan Sharpe. During the ceremony, the baby was held in the arms of her loving grandfather, Dean.

At the reception, which was held at the senior MacAllisters' home, Jenny and Michael MacAllister announced they were expecting their second child.

"So, Forrest," Michael said, "are you going to be in charge of The Baby Bet when Jenny is due?"

"Not me," Forrest said, laughing and raising both hands. "I know when I'm licked. The new champion of The Baby Bet is Ted."

"Wrong," Ted said, encircling Hannah's shoulders

with one arm, "the new champion of The Baby Bet are Mr. *and* Mrs. Theordore Sharpe. Take a look at the wedding presents Hannah gave me. I set them up by the cake."

The group moved closer and everyone smiled.

Lined up in a row were tiny wooden figurines for the dollhouse. The miniatures included a man, woman and four children. The children were each of a different nationality from around the world.

"Perfect," Deedee said.

"Yup," Ryan said.

"Babies, babies, babies," Deedee said with a wistful sigh. "Ryan, don't you think it's time we..."

"Yup," he said, then kissed her on the nose. "If Ted intends to continue to be The Baby Bet champion, we'll make him really work to retain the title."

"No problem," Ted said. "I can handle it, right along with the other titles I have."

"Husband and father," Hannah said, smiling at him with love shining in her eyes.

"Forever, Mrs. Doodle," he said, matching her smile. "Forever."

Every day is

A Mother's Day

in this heartwarming anthology
celebrating motherhood and romance!

Featuring the classic story "Nobody's Child" by Emilie Richards
He had come to a child's rescue, and now Officer Farrell Riley was
suddenly sharing parenthood with beautiful Gemma Hancock.
But would their ready-made family last forever?

Plus two brand-new romances:

"Baby on the Way" by Marie Ferrarella
Single and pregnant, Madeline Reed found the perfect husband in the
handsome cop who helped bring her infant son into the world. But did his
dutiful role in the surprise delivery make J. T. Walker a daddy?

"A Daddy for Her Daughters" by Elizabeth Bevarly
When confronted with spirited Naomi Carmichael and her brood of girls,
bachelor Sloan Sullivan realized he had a lot to learn about women!
Especially if he hoped to win this sexy single mom's heart…

Available this April from Silhouette Books!

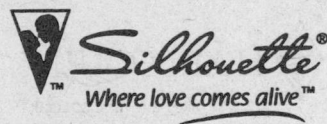

Where love comes alive™

The world's bestselling romance series.

HARLEQUIN®
Presents

Seduction and Passion Guaranteed!

Michelle Reid's
fantastic new trilogy

Hassan
Ethan
Rafiq
are

Hot-Blooded Husbands

Let them keep you warm tonight!

THE SHEIKH'S CHOSEN WIFE
#2254, on sale June

ETHAN'S TEMPTRESS BRIDE
#2272, on sale September

And look out for Rafiq's story,
on sale December

Pick up a Harlequin Presents® novel and you will
enter a world of spine-tingling passion and
provocative, tantalizing romance!

Available wherever Harlequin books are sold.

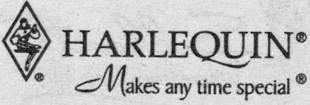

HARLEQUIN®
Makes any time special ®

These New York Times *bestselling authors* *have created stories to capture the hearts and minds of women everywhere.* *Here are three classic tales about the power of love—* *and the wonder of discovering the place where you belong....*

FINDING HOME

DUNCAN'S BRIDE
by
LINDA HOWARD

CHAIN LIGHTNING
by
ELIZABETH LOWELL

POPCORN AND KISSES
by
KASEY MICHAELS

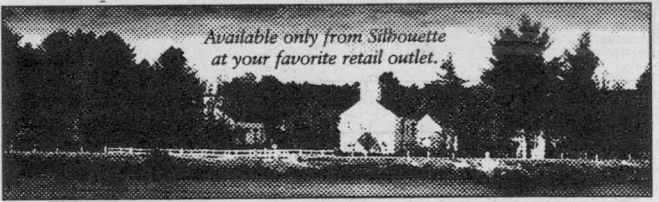

Available only from Silhouette at your favorite retail outlet.

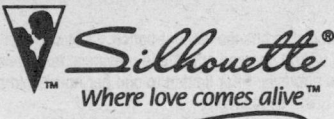

Where love comes alive™

MONTANA *Born*

From the bestselling series

MONTANA MAVERICKS

Wed in Whitehorn

Two tales that capture living and loving
beneath the Big Sky.

THE MARRIAGE MAKER by Christie Ridgway

Successful businessman Ethan Redford never proposed a deal he
couldn't close—and that included marriage to Cleo Kincaid Monroe!

AND THE WINNER...WEDS! by Robin Wells

Prim and proper Frannie Hannon yearned for Austin Parker, but
her pearls and sweater sets couldn't catch his boots and jeans—or
could they?

And don't miss

MONTANA *Bred*

Featuring

JUST PRETENDING by Myrna Mackenzie

&

STORMING WHITEHORN by Christine Scott

Available in May 2002
Available only from Silhouette at your favorite retail outlet.

Silhouette
where love comes alive™

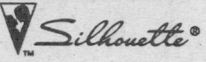

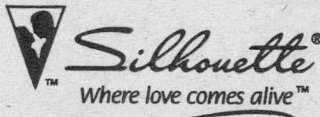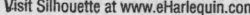